WINTER HOLIDAY

Also by Arthur Ransome

SWALLOWS AND AMAZONS
SWALLOWDALE
PETER DUCK
COOT CLUB
PIGEON POST
WE DIDN'T MEAN TO GO TO SEA
SECRET WATER
THE BIG SIX
MISSEE LEE
THE PICTS AND THE MARTYRS
GREAT NORTHERN?
RACUNDRA'S FIRST CRUISE
ROD AND LINE (FISHING ESSAYS)
OLD PETER'S RUSSIAN TALES
MAINLY ABOUT FISHING

SIGNAL STATION AND OBSERVATORY

WINTER HOLIDAY

by

ARTHUR RANSOME

ILLUSTRATED BY THE AUTHOR

"Dark at tea-time and sleeping indoors: nothing
ever happens in the winter holidays."

NANCY BLACKETT.

JONATHAN CAPE
THIRTY BEDFORD SQUARE
LONDON

FIRST PUBLISHED NOVEMBER 1933
SECOND IMPRESSION DECEMBER 1933
THIRD IMPRESSION JUNE 1935
FOURTH IMPRESSION DECEMBER 1936
FIFTH IMPRESSION MAY 1938
SIXTH IMPRESSION JUNE 1939
SEVENTH IMPRESSION JANUARY 1941
EIGHTH IMPRESSION OCTOBER 1941
NINTH IMPRESSION MAY 1942
TENTH IMPRESSION NOVEMBER 1942
ELEVENTH IMPRESSION MARCH 1943
TWELFTH IMPRESSION OCTOBER 1943
THIRTEENTH IMPRESSION MAY 1944
FOURTEENTH IMPRESSION NOVEMBER 1944
FIFTEENTH IMPRESSION NOVEMBER 1945
SIXTEENTH IMPRESSION DECEMBER 1946
SEVENTEENTH IMPRESSION APRIL 1948
EIGHTEENTH IMPRESSION APRIL 1949
NINETEENTH IMPRESSION DECEMBER 1949
TWENTIETH IMPRESSION JULY 1953
TWENTY-FIRST IMPRESSION 1955
TWENTY-SECOND IMPRESSION 1957
NEW EDITION, TYPE RESET, 1961
TWENTY-FOURTH IMPRESSION 1964
TWENTY-FIFTH IMPRESSION 1969

PRINTED AND BOUND IN GREAT BRITAIN BY
BUTLER AND TANNER LTD, FROME AND LONDON

CONTENTS

CONTENTS

LIST OF ILLUSTRATIONS

LIST OF ILLUSTRATIONS

AUTHOR'S NOTE

I have often been asked how I came to write *Swallows and Amazons*. The answer is that it had its beginning long, long ago when, as children, my brother, my sisters and I spent most of our holidays on a farm at the south end of Coniston. We played in or on the lake or on the hills above it, finding friends in the farmers and shepherds and charcoal-burners whose smoke rose from the coppice woods along the shore. We adored the place. Coming to it, we used to run down to the lake, dip our hands in and wish, as if we had just seen the new moon. Going away from it, we were half drowned in tears. While away from it, as children and as grown-ups, we dreamt about it. No matter where I was, wandering about the world, I used at night to look for the North Star and, in my mind's eye, could see the beloved skyline of great hills beneath it. *Swallows and Amazons* grew out of those old memories. I could not help writing it. It almost wrote itself.

A. R.

Haverthwaite
May 19th, 1958

WINTER HOLIDAY

CHAPTER I

STRANGERS

STEPS sounded on the wooden stairs, and counting, "Seven and eight and nine and ten and eleven and twelve and that's the dozen." Mrs Dixon was coming to tell the Callum children that it was time to get up. They had come to Dixon's Farm only the night before. Mrs Dixon had been their mother's nurse when she was a little girl, and Dorothea and Dick had come to stay at the farm for the last week of the winter holidays.

For some time already they had been lying half asleep, listening to the strange noises down in the yard, so very different from the roar of the traffic in the streets at home. They heard the grunting of the pigs, the clucking of hens, the anxious quacking of ducks, the hiss of an angry gander, the mooing of cows and the regular trilling of the milk spirting into a bucket. Now, waked properly by Mrs Dixon, they were out of bed and into each other's rooms, to find that the two windows looked out on exactly the same view, a corner of the farmyard, a low stone wall, a gate, and beyond it a frosty field sloping down to the lake, an island covered with trees, and away on the farther shore, the wooded side of the fells and farther still the snow-covered tops of the big hills sparkling in the first of the morning sun. "There'll be ice in the jugs this morning," Mrs Dixon had said, "and I've brought you up a can of hot water apiece. No need to start the day freezing."

A few minutes later they were hurrying downstairs. ("There *are* twelve steps," said Dick, "she was quite right.") They came down into the big farm kitchen, where Mrs Dixon had their breakfast ready for them, two bowls of hot porridge on the kitchen table, that was covered with a red-and-white chequered table-cloth, and some rashers of bacon sizzling in the frying-pan that she was holding over the fire. "I'm not going to make visitors of you," she said.

Mr Dixon, who had had his breakfast long ago, looked in at the door but, on seeing the children, said, "Good morning to you," and shyly slipped away. Mrs Dixon laughed. "He's not one for talking, isn't Dixon," she said, and then asked what they meant to do with themselves that day.

Dick, who had brought with him a telescope, a microscope and a book about astronomy, wiped away the mist that kept settling on his spectacles every time he took a drink from his big mug of tea. "I've got to find a good place for an observatory," he said.

"Eh?"

"For looking at stars."

"And there are a million other things we want to look at, too," said Dorothea. "We want to look at everything."

"That's your mother all over," said Mrs Dixon. "Well, look as much as you like, but dinner'll be ready at half-past twelve, and you'd best be here if you want any."

After breakfast they put on their coats and went out into the yard and made a round of it, visiting all the things they had listened to, lying in bed. Milking was over, but they met old Silas, the farm hand, crossing the yard with a great truss of red bracken for the cowshed. And Roy, the dog, rushed barking out at them, but stopped at once and wagged his tail.

"Just showing what he would do if we didn't belong," said Dorothea.

"It's a fine frosty morning," said Silas. "You'll be having some skating if it goes on."

Dick looked through the yard gate towards the lake.

"Nay, it'll be a while yet before the lake freezes. It's not often it does, but it's been a grand year for hollyberry, and that's a sign. But you'll be skating on the tarn up above yonder if we have another night or two like last."

"Where is it?" asked Dick. "We've got our skates packed."

Old Silas pointed up the fell behind the house.

"Let's go down to the lake first," said Dorothea.

From the yard gate a narrow footpath went down the sloping field to the edge of the lake. Dick and Dorothea went down it for the first time. They did not even know the name of the island that lay there, with its leafless winter trees, and the tall pine tree above the little cliff at the northern end of it. It had been dark when they arrived, and everything was new to them.

"I wish we'd thought of asking if they had a boat," said Dick.

"They probably have," said Dorothea. "What's that, down by the water?"

Dick stopped. His telescope was meant for stars, but it was good practice to use it for other things.

"Upside down," he said.

"It's a boat, anyhow," said Dorothea.

Down at the bottom of the field there were reeds, some on land and some growing in the water. There was a small landing-place. A narrow belt of dried bits of reed, sticks and other jetsam marked the point to which the lake had risen during the autumn floods. Half a dozen yards above this there was an old brown rowing boat, upside down, resting on trestles, a couple of feet clear of the ground.

"They must have put it like that for the winter," said Dick, walking round it, "to keep rain and snow out of it."

"What a pity," said Dorothea, who, as usual, was making up a story. She tried a sentence or two on Dick. "They launched their trusty vessel, put out their oars, and rowed towards the mysterious island. No human foot had ever trod ... "

"Well, look," said Dick. "There's somebody coming now."

A rowing boat was coming down the lake, the only thing moving on the water under the pale, winter fields, the dark woods, and the distant snow-topped hills. It was moving fast. There seemed to be four rowers, two to a thwart, each pulling on a single oar.

"Where's your telescope?" said Dorothea.

She watched the boat cutting its way through the reflections of the hills. The story she had begun to plan was gone. Instead, she was finding another to explain this solitary boat, with its four rowers, and the two passengers seated in the stern. Carrying a sick man to the doctor, perhaps. A matter of life and death. Or were they racing some other boat not yet in sight?

Dick pulled out his telescope again. He rested it on the keel of the overturned boat and with a little difficulty focussed it on that other boat that was coming so swiftly down the lake.

"Hullo," he said. "Dot! They aren't grown up."

"Let's see."

But she gave him back the telescope at once. "Bother the thing," she said. "I can see just as well without it."

"What's happening now?"

The four oars had stopped, as if at a word of command, and the two who had been sitting in the stern were changing places with two of the rowers. A moment later all four oars shot forward, and paused. The blades dipped, the four rowers pulled together and the boat, which had been gliding slowly on, gathered speed once more.

"Put your coat on, now you're not rowing."

The words sounded clearly over the water, as well as the reply.

"Aye, aye, sir."

Dick and Dorothea could see a small boy in the stern of the rowing boat, trying to put his coat on without really standing up, as the strong strokes of the rowers sent the boat shooting forward.

There were four girls in the boat and two boys. Two of the girls had red woolly caps like Dorothea's green one, and two of them had white. The larger of the boys and a girl in a red cap were rowing in the middle of the boat. Two girls were rowing in the bows, and a small girl with a white woolly cap was sitting in the stern with the small boy, who sat down suddenly just when it seemed he had got into his coat without an accident.

The boat came straight for the island. The watchers on the shore saw it pass under the little cliff, below the tall pine, and close along the island shore.

"Easy all!" they heard someone call.

The boat slid on with oars lifted from the water.

"Let's go to the old harbour," came another voice.

"Give way!" The first voice sounded again, a clear, confident, ringing voice, and the oars dipped once more.

"They've gone," said Dick, as the boat swung round the low southern end of the island and disappeared behind a shoulder of rock. For a long time he watched, so long that he had to put his hands in his pockets in turn to get them warm again after holding the telescope.

"Of course they may have rowed away behind the island," said Dorothea.

"I do wish this boat was in the water," said Dick.

"Even if it was, we can't row," said Dorothea.

"It looks easy," said Dick. "I'm sure we could manage."

"It's no good thinking about it," said Dorothea. "Look, there's one of them. They've landed ... "

Three or four of them could be seen hurrying about on the island beneath the leafless trees. Then, suddenly, at the northern end, the boat showed again. Only two were in it, the bigger of the two boys, and the smaller of the red-capped girls. They rowed out from the island towards the middle of the lake. On the island there was great activity, and presently a thin blue wisp of smoke climbed up among the trees, a flicker of flame showed low down, then more smoke and more flames as the sticks caught and the fire gathered strength. A girl with a kettle came down to the water's edge and dipped water from the lake.

"They must be making tea," said Dorothea, dancing first on one foot and then on another, because her toes were very cold.

"Scientific expedition," said Dick. "Landed to cook a meal. But ... Hullo! ... What *are* they doing now?"

Only one was left by the fire. The bigger red-capped girl, with the two children who had been sitting in the stern of the boat when they reached the island, came out on the cliff under the tall pine. She began waving a small flag on the end of a stick.

"Is it for us?" said Dorothea hopefully.

"No," said Dick. "Look!"

In the boat, far out on the lake, the boy was resting on his oars. The red-capped girl who was with him was standing up. She, too, had a flag and had begun to wave it.

A shout of laughter sounded on the island.

"Peggy, you donk. You've got that one all wrong. Try it again." That clear voice they had heard before rang out over the water.

There was more flag-waving in the boat, and more from the island. Then there was a pause, and a moment later the signalling began again, only this time the signallers had two flags apiece, and did not wave them but held the flags at arm's length, first in one position and then in another.

"It's awfully cold," said Dorothea at last. "Standing about like this." She had been very happy, waking up in this new place, but those children in the boat had somehow spoilt things. What fun they were having, six of them, all together. A new story began to shape itself in her mind, one that nobody would be able to read without tears ... *The Outcasts*. By Dorothea Callum. Chapter I.

"IS IT FOR US?"

"The two children, brother and sister, shared their last few crumbs and looked this way and that along the deserted shore. Was this to be the end?"

"Oh well," said Dick. "We can't help not having a boat. Let's go and find a really good place for an observatory."

★

Time had passed quicker than they thought, while they had been looking at pigs and cows and enviously watching the children on the island. Mrs Dixon called them in for dinner just when they were asking Mr Dixon whether it would be all right for them to go up the cart track that seemed to climb up the fell from the gate on the opposite side of the main road. Mrs Dixon was in a hurry to get dinner over, because she was baking pork pies for which she had a name throughout the district. Her mind was in the oven and they got only the vaguest answers when they asked her about the children they had seen. "Yes. Staying at the farm along the road. Six of them? That would be the Blackett lasses as well ... Dixon, *do* keep yon door shut, with pies in the oven and a cold wind enough to ruin all." And then, after dinner, looking over her shoulder with her hand on the knob of the oven door wrapped in a fold of her apron, she told them, "Come you in at four o'clock for a cup of hot tea. You'll be wanting dark for your star-gazing, and I'll give you your supper later."

The main road, along which they had come from the station the night before, after their railway journey with Mrs Dixon, ran close past the front of the house, where there was a strip of garden and a front door that was hardly ever used, for the Dixons and all their friends went through the farmyard to the door that opened into the big farm kitchen. Dick and Dorothea came round the house and out into the road between the garden and a huge barn. They looked both ways along the road, but they could not see far because, to the right, it bent sharply round towards the lake and, to the left, it disappeared in a wood. They crossed the road, went through a gate exactly opposite the farmyard, and followed a cart track up a steep little pasture, through another gate, and then to the left, up the fell, between patches of dead bracken and grey lumps of rock that thrust up here and there out of the short-cropped grass. "Not limestone," said Dick, picking up a bit and putting it in his pocket. Dorothea smiled to see him do it. The stone would wear a hole in his pocket, of course, but it was no use saying so when Dick was thinking about geology.

They climbed up and up, and with every step they could see more of the lake beyond the woods, while, on the farther side, the snow-topped mountains seemed to rise higher and higher. Suddenly, as the track came over a shoulder of the hill, they saw on the open fell ahead of them an old grey barn.

"It's the very place for an observatory," said Dick. Geology was forgotten in a moment and he ran on up the track.

Dorothea followed, not so fast. She was looking at the barn and thinking what sort of story she could make to fit it. It was built of rough grey stones, and she could see a big dark doorway and stone steps outside the wall going up to a smaller doorway above. The doors seemed to have gone. The place must at one time have been used for something or other, but now it was falling into ruin.

The barn stood on the top of a ridge of hill coming down from the fells towards the lake. There was a shout from Dick. He beckoned to her with his telescope and stood there, beside the barn, looking down at the country on the other side of the ridge. In a few moments Dorothea stood beside him. Now for the first time they saw the great ring of hills above the head of the lake. There was the lake, like a wide river. There were a group of islands, and a cloud of smoke above the village. Then, nearer to them, just below the barn, was a little frozen tarn, cupped in a shallow hollow in the side of the hill. Beyond it to the right, woods climbed the hill-side. Below them they could see woods going down to the lake, and beyond the woods they caught glimpses of the main road between the fields. And down there, between the road and the lake, was a white farm-house and some out-buildings, not far above what seemed to be a narrow bay.

"Dot," said Dick. "I bet that's the farm-house where those children are staying, the ones Mrs Dixon knew about."

"Bother them," said Dorothea. She had been meaning to think of something else. But if Dick remembered them, when his mind was full of stones and stars, how could she possibly forget them?

"Bother them," she said again. "What about your observatory?"

"You can see any amount of sky from up here," said Dick. "And we can have a light in the barn for looking at the maps of the stars by."

"It'll be pretty cold," said Dorothea.

But in the angle between the solid stone steps and the wall they found the remains of a fire, charred sticks, and a few stones to keep the fire in place. Someone had felt cold up there before them.

"What about that?" said Dick.

The barn itself was quite empty, and they decided that they could keep their firewood inside it. They climbed the stone steps. Nothing but the rusty hinges was left of the door that had been at the top of them. Gingerly, pressing with each foot before properly stepping on it, they went in. There were holes in the floor and the old planking creaked beneath them. They picked their way towards a big square opening in the end wall, through which, as it came right down to the level of the floor, they supposed bracken or hay had been pitched from a cart standing below.

"What a place to look out from," said Dick. "And for all the northern stars ... I say, you can see that farm even better from up here."

"Perhaps we wouldn't like them if we knew them," said Dorothea.

"Let's go and get wood ready for the evening," said Dick, "and see if the ice is bearing."

They went down the steep slope to the tarn. Dick stepped with one foot on the ice at the edge of it. It sank beneath his foot, and water oozed up at the side of it. He threw a stone towards the middle, and it crashed through the ice into the water.

"No good yet," he said. "But it soon will be."

They walked round the tarn, gathered two big bundles of fallen sticks in the outskirts of the wood beyond it, carried them up to the barn and spent a long time breaking them up into short handy lengths and piling them neatly just inside.

"Everything's ready now," said Dick. "Let's go down and get tea over." They were on the point of starting down the track to Dixon's Farm when they were reminded of those six strangers yet again.

"There's that boat," said Dick, taking a last look down at the lake with his telescope. "There, turning into that bay."

For some minutes they watched, but most of the bay below the white farm-house was hidden by the pine trees on a little rocky headland. Then, suddenly, Dick spoke again. "Coming up the field," he half whispered. "Just below the house. Waving at something ... There's the boat going away out of the bay. Only two in it. Both red caps ... "

Dorothea put a hand on the telescope for a moment and then remembered that she could never see through it.

"Where are they now?"

"Disappeared behind the house. Let's go up into the observatory. Just for one minute."

They ran up the steps and into the loft. Dick crouched on the floor by the big opening at the end of it and steadied his telescope against the wall.

"Dot," he cried suddenly. "They do come from that house. Look at this end, two windows one above another. Two of them are hanging out of that top window."

"What's the good of thinking about them?" said Dorothea. "They might as well be in some different world."

Dick started so sharply that he almost dropped his telescope.

"Why not? Why not?" he said. "All the better. Just wait till dark and we can try signalling to Mars."

"To Mars?" said Dorothea.

"Why not?" said Dick. "Of course they may not see it. And even if they do see it they may not understand. A different world. That makes it all the more like signalling to Mars."

"We're going to be late for Mrs Dixon's tea," said Dorothea, and a moment later they were down those steep stone steps and hurrying home. As she ran down the cart track beside him, Dorothea was thinking. You never knew with Dick. He always seemed to be bothering about birds, or stars, or engines, or fossils and things like that. He never was able to make up stories like those that came so easily to her, and yet, sometimes, in some queer way of his own, he seemed to hit on things that made stories and real life come closer together than usual.

"It's worth trying," she panted, just as they were coming to the gate into the main road.

"What is?" said Dick, who was already thinking of quite other stars. What constellations could they look for? He wished he could keep the star map in his head. But anyway, they would take the book with them, and have a lantern to read it by, in case the fire-light was too flickery.

"Signalling to Mars," said Dorothea.

CHAPTER II

SIGNALLING TO MARS

An hour later they were climbing the cart track again. Dick had the star-book with him, and the telescope. Dorothea was carrying the lantern.

Mrs Dixon had made no fuss at all about letting them have a lantern when they asked for it, though what they could want with going up to the old barn after sunset was more than she could tell. Stars? Couldn't they see stars as well and better from the farmyard, or from the scullery window for that, and keep warm into the bargain?

"You must have an observatory on the top of a hill," Dick had explained, "so as to get a larger horizon."

"Get along with you, you and your horizons," Mrs Dixon had laughed, shaking the kitchen table-cloth into the fire. Old Silas had got a spare lantern for them and put a drop of oil it it. And Dick and Dorothea, astronomer and novelist, had hurried out into the winter evening.

They lit the lantern almost at once. It seemed a pity not to carry a lighted lantern when they could and, though there was still a little light in the sky, the lantern made things much darker. The stars were already showing.

"There's Cassiopeia," said Dick. "It's supposed to be her chair, but it's no good trying to see it like a chair. None of the constellations are like what they're supposed to be. Even the Plough does just as well for a wagon or a bear."

But Dorothea did not feel like talking while they were going up the hill at such a pace.

They came to the barn and stood outside it high on the hillside. Dick was searching the skies while Dorothea peered down into the darkness of the valley.

"What about Mars?" she reminded him at last. "Have they had their tea?"

"Oh, them?" said Dick, and for a moment left the constellations to revolve unwatched. "Look there. Those'll be the lights of that farm-house. Hide the lantern in the barn and we'll be able to see better."

Dorothea put the lantern well inside the doorway and hurried out again into the dark. Dick had already got his telescope trained on those lights away below them.

"It's all right," he said. "One of those lights is the downstairs window at this end of the house. I can just see the end wall, all white. There must be some other light quite near it. There you are. There it is. Someone moving about with a lantern."

"Well, they won't be going to bed yet. If it's them. But that youngest one probably goes to bed pretty early."

It felt very queer to be up there, high above everything, guessing at those strange lives so far away.

"Anyhow," said Dick, "it's no good thinking about them till there's a light upstairs in that room they were putting their heads out of. Let's look at the real stars. We've got to get that fire going. It'll be all right in that corner round the steps. Then you can stay by the fire and see what the book says, and I can come round this side so as not to be bothered by the light."

They were not very good at lighting a fire, and instead of doing it in the proper way with a handful of dry grass or the tiniest twigs Dick, after a last regretful look by lantern-light at the picture of the rings of Saturn, took the paper wrapper off the star-book and gave it to Dorothea.

"It doesn't really matter," he said, "because the same picture is inside the book as well."

"It's not like lighting a fire in a proper grate," said Dorothea. "But the paper'll make it much easier."

It did, and in a few minutes they had a fire burning in the corner behind the steps. Smoke poured into their eyes, and reading seemed impossible. But presently the fire burnt clearer, and Dorothea crouched beside it to keep warm, and looked at the star-book in the light of the fire and the lantern.

"Get the chapter on the January sky," said the astronomer, who was keeping the stone steps between himself and the glare.

Dorothea turned rapidly over the pages. "Got it," she said.

Dick was staring up into the crowded sky.

"Now then," he said. "I've got the Plough all right. Almost over that farm. And I've got the Pole Star, and Cassiopeia on the other side of it, almost opposite the Plough. What are the other ones it tells us to look out for? Skip the poetry."

"Taurus," said Dorothea, running her finger along the lines of print, difficult to read with smoke-filled eyes. "The Bull. Major stars: Aldebaran. First magnitude. The eye of the Bull."

"Bother the Bull," said Dick, hurrying round the corner and crouching over the book beside her. "It isn't like one a bit. Let's have a look at the picture ... It's a wedge with Aldebaran at the thin end, and then three other small triangles, and the Pleiades away by themselves."

He took a last look at the picture and hurried back into the darkness.

"Got it," he said. "Just over the top of the hill. Come and see it."

Dorothea joined him. He pointed out the bright Aldebaran and the other stars of Taurus, and offered her the telescope.

"I can see a lot better without," said Dorothea.

"How many of the Pleiades can you see?"

"Six," said Dorothea.

"There are lots more than that," said Dick. "But it's awfully hard to see them when the telescope won't keep still. How far away does it say the Pleiades are?"

Dorothea went back to the fire and found the place in the book.

"The light from the group known as the Pleiades (referred to by Tennyson in *Locksley Hall*) ... "

"Oh, hang Tennyson!"

"The light from the group known as the Pleiades reaches our planet in rather more than three hundred years after it leaves them."

"Light goes at one hundred and eighty-six thousand miles a second," said the voice of the astronomer out in the darkness.

But Dorothea was also doing some calculations.

"Shakespeare died 1616."

"What?"

"Well, if the light takes more than three hundred years to get here, it may have started while Shakespeare was alive, in the reign of Queen Elizabeth, perhaps. Sir Walter Raleigh may have seen it start ... "

"But of course he didn't," said the astronomer indignantly. "The light of the stars he saw had started three hundred years before that ... "

"Battle of Bannockburn, 1314. Bows and arrows." Dorothea was off again.

But Dick was no longer listening. One hundred and eighty-six thousand miles a second. Sixty times as far as that in a minute. Sixty times sixty times as far as that in an hour. Twenty-four hours in a day. Three hundred and sixty-five days in a year. Not counting leap years. And then three hundred years of it. Those little stars that seemed to speckle a not too dreadfully distant blue ceiling were farther away than he could make himself think, try as he might. Those little stars must be enormous. The whole earth must be a tiny pebble in comparison. A spinning pebble, and he, on it, the astronomer, looking at flaming gigantic worlds so far away that they seemed no more than sparkling grains of dust. He felt for a moment less than nothing, and then, suddenly, size did not seem to matter. Distant and huge the stars might be, but he, standing here with chattering teeth on the dark hill-side, could see them and name them and even foretell what next they were going to do. "The January Sky." And there they were, Taurus, Aldebaran, the Pleiades, obedient as slaves ... He felt an odd wish to shout at them in triumph, but remembered in time that this would not be scientific.

He had not heard Dorothea come round the corner of the barn. For some time she had been looking at the star pictures in the book, and had been quietly busy with the fire. At last, hearing nothing from the astronomer, she had come to see what he was doing. There he was, close by, dark in the darkness. But she saw something else.

"Dick! Look! The Martians are going to bed."

Dick started.

"What? What? Oh, it's you, Dot. You did give me a jump."

"Well, you ought to hang out a notice when you're not there. Aren't we waiting for them to go upstairs? Look! There's a light in the upstairs window now."

Dick was wide awake in a moment. Yes. Where there had been one steady light in the end of the white farm-house there were now two, and one was exactly above the other.

"We'll begin signalling at once," said Dick. "They can't have been upstairs very long."

"But will they be looking out?"

"Why not? They may be looking out just like us, and wanting to signal to Earth. We always take a last look out before going to bed. Anyway, not knowing makes it more like the real thing. Have you got your torch?'

"Yes."

B

"We may want it, but we'll try the lantern. I wonder if they can see any light from the fire. Shouldn't think so. We'll go upstairs to signal. Come on, Dot."

Dorothea darted back for the lantern that she had put just inside the barn.

"Don't go and fall off the steps in the dark," she called.

"I'm keeping close to the wall. Come on."

She hurried after him. The steps going up outside the barn were broad enough in daylight, but in the dark, even with a lantern, she wished there had been some sort of a railing. Still, if Dick had done it, so could she, and presently they were both standing in the dark upper floor of the barn, looking out of the great square opening at the end of it.

"Don't go too near the edge."

"I'm not going to," said Dick.

"What are you doing?"

"Finding out where they won't be able to see the lantern. This corner is all right. Now. Hold the lantern well in the middle of the window. That'll do. Now shove it into this corner. Now show it again. That's enough. Into the corner. Three times."

Dorothea obediently showed the lantern in the middle of the big opening at the end of the barn, then hid it close against the wall in the corner where no smallest ray of it could be seen from Mars away down there in the valley. Three times she showed it. Three times she hid it. Dick carefully focussed the telescope on the lights of the farm, and watched for a sign that the Martians had noticed that someone on earth was trying to get into touch with them.

Nothing happened.

"Do it again."

Dorothea did it again. In matters like this, though she was the elder of the two, she always felt that Dick knew best. He could not make up stories about people, but he could think out things like this better than anybody.

"Again nothing happened.

"You try," said Dorothea.

"Well, you take the telescope and watch the planet. The Martians may answer at any minute."

But nothing happened.

"Perhaps it isn't their room," said Dorothea. "Perhaps the light in there now has nothing to do with them. It's the farm woman who's taken it up to see how much dirt they carried up on their shoes because they came in without using the doormat. So she's down on her hands and knees scrubbing and very cross indeed with them, and naturally she isn't looking this way at all."

"I say, Dot," said Dick. "You can't see all that through the telescope."

"Of course I can't," said Dorothea. "I never can see anything through the telescope."

"I'm going on signalling, anyhow. It may be two or three nights before they notice it."

Again and again he held the lantern in the middle of the big empty window. Again and again he hid it. Anybody looking at the old barn high on the hill-side might have thought it was a lighthouse. Flash ... flash ... flash ... and then dark for a long time, and after that another three flashes, and so on.

"It's most awfully cold," said Dorothea at last. "And we've got to get back to Mrs Dixon's."

"Once more," said Dick, and then, just as he hid the lantern at the end of the third flash, Dorothea said, "That top light's gone out. Perhaps it is their room after all. Somebody's told that youngest one to go to sleep."

"Oh well," said Dick. "We'll try again to-morrow. Hullo! Look! There it is again. Dot! Dot! Something's happening!"

There was the light in that upper window once more, one

spark on the top of another, far away below them. It went out. They watched the patch of darkness where it had been above that other light that went on steadily burning. And as they watched, the upper light shone out again.

"If it goes this time ... " said Dick, hardly able to speak. "It's gone. Dot! They've answered ... "

"What are you going to do?" asked Dorothea.

"Give them our signal again. That'll settle it."

Quickly the lantern was shown in the middle of the window, hidden, shown, hidden, shown, and then put finally away in the corner. This would settle it. The two watched, hardly daring to believe.

There it was, that answering light, flashing out in the farm far away below them in the valley. It was gone. There it was again. One, two, three flashes, and then darkness.

"We've done it! We've done it!"

"Don't go and tumble out. What are they thinking? Do they know it's us?"

"Where's your torch? Try them with another signal. Set it going and swing it in big circles like a wheel."

Dorothea stood in the opening, a few feet back from the edge, lit her pocket torch, and whirled it round and round.

"Fine."

"Shall I stop now?"

"Yes." Dick was already watching through the telescope, finding the place to look at by the light in the lower window. "Of course, they may not guess ... "

"They've done it, anyway," cried Dorothea.

Away down there, unmistakably, a small and feeble spark was spinning in a circle.

"Their battery is worn out," said Dick. "They ought to get a new one."

The Martians perhaps felt that the battery of their torch was not to be trusted. Almost at once the spark stopped spinning and, instead, there were a series of quick, short flashes at the window, and then a number of flashes, some long, some short, with intervals of darkness.

"They're trying to say something," said Dorothea.

"It's Morse code they're using, and we don't know it," said Dick with deep melancholy. But he cheered up. "Of course, it's all right," he said. "Morse. Morsian. Marsian. Naturally we don't know their language."

He interrupted the dot and dash flashing from Mars by a repetition of the first signal.

The Martians did the same.

"We can't do any more to-night," said Dick. "But we've got in touch with Mars."

"They'll come to see what it was in the morning," said Dorothea. "I know they will. We've simply got to be up here early. Come on."

They went down the stone steps with most uncertain feet. While Dorothea trod out the embers of their fire in the lower barn, Dick hid the lantern in the barn and kept an eye on Mars.

For some time nothing happened. Then, just as Dorothea came round from behind the steps, there were two long, separate flashes.

"Saying good night," said Dorothea.

Dick made two long flashes with the lantern by carrying it into the open and then hiding it again. That was the end.

A minute later they had made sure that nothing had been left behind. Dick had the book and the telescope, Dorothea the torch and lantern. They left the observatory behind them, and, picking their way along the cart track as fast as they could by lantern light, hurried home to supper.

"We won't tell her about the signalling until we know for certain it was them," said Dorothea.

"It's no good talking to her about astronomy," said Dick, who remembered how she had laughed at his need for wide horizons.

Mrs Dixon met them at the kitchen door as they came in.

"You must be fair perished with cold," she said. "And what stars did you see?"

"Oh, Taurus and the Pleiades," said Dick.

Nobody said anything about Mars.

CHAPTER III

STRANGERS NO MORE

Dorothea and Dick had rushed through breakfast and had climbed up the hill to the old barn as fast as they could, half afraid lest the Martians should be there before them. But everything was as they had left it. Dorothea dumped a bundle of newspapers she had brought with her for firelighting on the pile of sticks left over from last night. They went up the stone steps into the loft to get a better view. There was no sign of life in Mars. The white farm-house down there between the lake and the main road might have been uninhabited. No one could have believed that dwellers in so desolate a planet had caught and answered signals from the Earth.

And then Dick, who had been looking through the telescope, caught sight of a boat pulling into the little bay from which, yesterday afternoon, they had seen the red-caps row out. The boat was almost instantly hidden by the pinewoods on the nearer side of the bay.

Some minutes later they caught a glimpse of moving figures just below the house. Perhaps the others had gone down to meet the red-caps and they were all coming up from the lake together.

Suddenly that upper window from which the answering flashes had come in the darkness seemed to be crowded with heads.

"There's a red-cap," cried Dick. "Both of them. And somebody pointing."

"But where are they now?" said Dorothea, for the window was empty.

"There they are," cried Dick. "They're coming. All six of them."

"Where?" cried Dorothea.

"Up the field above the house ... Over the wall ... I wonder why they didn't go through the gate ... They've crossed the road ... Over the other wall ... coming up the next field ... They're still coming ... They'll be over that wall in a minute ... "

"Dick, Dick!" said Dorothea, forgetting how long they had been waiting. "They're coming straight here. Isn't it a good thing we got here in time."

"Gone," said Dick.

"The hill's in the way," said Dorothea.

Minute after minute passed. Almost the watchers began to fear that the Martians had turned aside up into the woods. And then first one and then another showed again coming over the ridge on the farther side of the little tarn and trampling through the bracken down to the edge of the ice. Dick trained his telescope on them. "The one in front isn't looking where he's going. He's looking at something in his hand. Probably a compass. I say, they can't be going to come straight across the ice. It won't bear. At least it wouldn't yesterday."

The next moment Dorothea and Dick exclaimed together: "She's in! They're both in!"

The bigger of the two red-capped girls had waved towards the barn and, leaping through the dead bracken, had charged down past the boy who had been leading the way. The other red-cap was close behind her. Almost at the same moment they were on the ice. There was a tinkling crash, a splash of water, and the two of them were floundering ankle-deep back out of the shallows.

"Oh! Oh!" said Dorothea. "And now they've got wet feet and they'll have to turn back and go home."

But they showed no signs of turning back. They took off their shoes and emptied the water out and put them on again. The others waited for them, and then turned to the right along the edge of the tarn, crossed the little beck that trickled out of it, and began to climb the steep slope towards the observatory.

"Look here," said Dorothea. "We signalled to them first. We ought to go and meet them."

"You do the talking," said Dick.

It was one thing to signal to Mars at night and to get into touch with distant Martians by the flashing of a lantern. It was quite another to meet them face to face in broad daylight. What ought to be said to strangers from another planet? Dorothea would probably know. Dick shut his telescope and followed her down the steps.

The leader of the Martians looked back, then up at the barn, then at the thing he held in his hand. He put it in his pocket, said a word to his followers and led them on. Dorothea and Dick had come down from the loft and were on their way to meet them.

Suddenly the smallest of the female Martians waved a white handkerchief she had fastened to a stick.

"That's to show it's peace," said Dorothea. "We ought to have thought of it, too. Can't you tie a handkerchief to your telescope?"

"Just wave yours," said Dick. "That'll show them we understand."

Dorothea pulled out her handkerchief and waved it.

The Martians came gravely on.

This was much more difficult than Dorothea had expected. If only the Martians would say something, or even smile.

They met about a third of the way down the slope.

There was a moment's dreadful silence.

It was broken by the smallest of the Martian girls.

"I don't believe they're in distress at all," she said.

"Don't they want to be rescued from anything?" said the smaller of the boys in a very disappointed voice.

"We were just signalling to Mars," said Dick, who found that, after all, it was for him to explain.

"To Mars?" said the bigger boy.

"Not to us?" said the smallest girl. "Was it all a mistake?"

"No, no," said Dorothea. "We wanted you to answer. It was Dick's idea to be signalling to Mars. You see, we didn't know you."

"Giminy," broke in the larger red-cap. "It was a jolly good idea."

"And of course," Dick went on, "when you started answering in Martian we couldn't understand."

"Morse code," said the elder of the boys. "We asked what was the matter and who you were. And then when you didn't answer we guessed you didn't know how. So I took a bearing by compass."

"Was that a compass you had in your hand just now?" said Dick.

"Yes."

"We saw you on the island yesterday," said Dorothea.

"*We* saw *you*," said the smaller boy.

The elder of the red-caps, who had been standing there, rising and falling on her toes, making her wet shoes squelch every time she did it, broke in impatiently:

"Here we are, anyway," she said, "but what are you?"

"Our name is Callum. He is Dick and I am Dorothea."

"Oh yes, yes," said the red-cap. "Dick and Dorothea, but *what* are you? In real life, I mean. We're explorers and sailors."

"Dick's an astronomer," said Dorothea promptly.

"Dorothea writes stories," said Dick.

"Well, I'm Nancy Blackett, Captain of the *Amazon*. This is Peggy, Mate of the *Amazon*." She waved her hand towards the others. "This is Captain John Walker, of the *Swallow*. This is Susan Walker, Mate of the *Swallow*. Titty is their able-seaman, and Roger is their ship's boy."

THE MARTIANS IN SIGHT

"Is that boat the *Amazon*?" asked Dick. "The one we saw you in?"

"That," said Captain Nancy with scorn. "That's a rowing boat. It belongs to our mother at Beckfoot. We use it just to row across every day to Holly Howe or Rio."

"Rio?" said Dorothea.

"That's what we always call the village. It's got another name."

"I know," said Dorothea.

"Only for natives," said Nancy.

"Do you live here?" asked Titty, the smallest of the girls.

"We're staying at Mrs Dixon's, just till the end of the holidays," said Dorothea. "Father and mother have gone to Egypt, to dig up remains."

The four Swallows looked at each other.

"Why, that's just like us," said Titty.

And then Susan explained that their mother had gone away only yesterday morning, to go to Malta, where their father's ship was stationed for a time, and that she had taken Bridget, their youngest sister, with her. "Father's never really seen Bridget since she was a person," Titty interrupted, not wishing it to be thought that their mother would leave them without good reason. Susan went on to tell them that they had been staying at Holly Howe ever since Christmas and that they, too, would be going back to school when the holidays came to an end.

"I suppose you've come to the Arctic to watch an eclipse?" said Captain Nancy.

"But there isn't going to be an eclipse," said Dick.

"Oh well," said Nancy, "don't be so particular. Come to that, Holly Howe isn't Mars."

"It isn't really," said Dick. "But why Arctic?"

Nancy looked round at the others. Titty looked at Dorothea. Roger laughed.

"We may as well tell them," said John.

"Everybody agree?" said Nancy. "They deserve to be told. That Mars idea was really pretty good."

"Tell them," said Titty.

"Well," said Nancy. "You know what it's like. Dark at tea-time and sleeping indoors: nothing ever happens in the winter holidays. And we had to think of something that we could do without our ships. *Swallow* and *Amazon* are both out of the water for the winter. And it had to be something that would make it all right for us to sleep in the houses of the natives instead of in our tents. So we started a Polar expedition. We sleep in the Eskimo settlements at night, the same as you, and we've been building an igloo of our own to use as a base. You'll see it."

"The idea was that as soon as we could we'd go to the North Pole over the ice," said Peggy, the other red-cap. "We've got a splendid North Pole."

"Only, the beastly Arctic won't freeze," said Nancy "and the holidays'll be over in no time. And it never will freeze unless we get another fall of snow. The lake's so jolly deep."

"There's another week yet," said Peggy.

And then the others joined in, all talking at once, and Dick and Dorothea heard how the four Swallows were living in the Eskimo settlement at Holly Howe, while the two Amazons were sleeping in the Eskimo settlement at Beckfoot at the mouth of the Amazon river and rowing across every day. They heard how yesterday they had rowed down to Wild Cat Island for signalling, because on the day Mrs Walker and Bridget had gone away no one felt quite like settling down to ordinary work on the igloo or hut they were building. They heard how the explorers had been waiting, day after day, for the little tarn to freeze so that they could begin skating practice. There was little hope now that the great lake would freeze all over so that they could go the whole way to the Pole over the ice. But there might yet be snow and they were putting off the dash to the Pole to the very last day of the holidays, to give the Arctic a chance of living up to its name.

"Now you know all about it," said Nancy. "Let's just have a look at your signal station."

"Observatory," said Dick.

"All right," said Nancy. "Ow, my feet are cold. What about yours, Peggy?"

"Icicles."

"We were a pair of mutton-headed galoots to go through the ice like that," said Nancy, hopping up and down.

"Oughtn't you to get your things off and dried at once?" said Susan.

"We must just see the place they did their signalling from."

They all went up to the old barn, climbed the steps outside it and looked out from the loft. Dick showed them just how Dorothea and he had managed with the lantern, and Titty told Dorothea how she had first seen the flashes up on the hill-side.

"It's a f-f-f-fine p-p-p-lace to signal from one settlement t-t-t-to another," said Nancy, whose teeth were beginning to chatter.

"Shall we light the fire?" said Dorothea. "I've got some sticks and lots of newspaper."

"Newspaper?" Susan and Peggy were staring at her. "Newspaper! For lighting a fire!"

They hurried down the steps and looked at the charred wood and ashes left from last night, and at the pile of sticks and at Dorothea's bundle of newspaper.

"You'd better come along with us at once," said Nancy, "and see how to make a fire and how to light it with one match and no paper at all. Ow! My feet are going to fall off."

"We'd love to come," said Dorothea.

"Doesn't Mrs Dixon expect you back for dinner?" said Susan.

"She does rather," said Dorothea.

"Well, you'd better tell her you're going to be out. It's no way down there. We'll all come. March, Roger, or you'll be getting cold, too."

"C-come on," said Nancy. "The P-p-p-polar exp-p-pedition v-v-visits the f-i-friendly Eskimos."

"You wouldn't like to go straight to the igloo and start the fire?" said Susan, looking at her.

"It'll be all right as long as we k-k-k-keep moving," said Captain Nancy and, followed by Peggy, she set off at full gallop down the cart track to Dixon's Farm.

CHAPTER IV

THE IGLOO

Mrs Dixon did not seem in the least surprised when Dick and Dorothea, who had set out alone, came back to the farm in a party of eight.

"You've not lost much time about it," she said. 'I was thinking you'd be running into each other somewhere. Well, Miss Ruth and Miss Peggy, and how's your mother keeping, and what's the news from your Uncle Jim? It seems no time since I was cooking toffees in the summer for you others when you came up to fetch the milk in the mornings. Time does flit on, to be sure."

"Can we be out to dinner?" asked Dorothea.

"Glad to see the backs of you," said Mrs Dixon. "I've washing to do to-day. You've come just at the right time, Miss Ruth, or Nancy is it? I'm forgetting. I've been meaning to send one of my pork pies to Mrs Blackett, and you can take it for me, and then you two can take another to make do for your dinner. And there's a bag of toffees for the lot of you. Eh! come in, Dixon, none but old friends here."

Mr Dixon was standing in the doorway.

"How do you do, Mr Dixon?" said Titty.

"How do you do?" said all the others.

"Champion, thank ye," said Mr Dixon, and went off again out of the kitchen.

"And now then," said Mrs Dixon, as she came back from the larder with two of the new pork pies, "what have you two lasses been doing with your shoes?"

Nancy and Peggy were holding first one foot and then the

48

other towards the kitchen fire, and the steam was pouring up.

"The tarn," said Peggy.

"I was sure it would be bearing all right," said Nancy, "and it very nearly is, but I never thought about not going on both together. We were a bit galootish. At least I was."

"Fair couple of gummocks, I'd call you," said Mrs Dixon. "You'd best be having them shoes off and let me be drying the stockings."

But the red-caps were in a hurry to get on.

"Yon's the way to catch a death of cold," said Mrs Dixon.

"We'll be drying them in a few minutes," said Nancy. "Come on, you others. Have you got knapsacks, you two?"

"They're in our school trunks," said Dorothea. "I'll go and get them."

"Never mind for now," said Nancy. "I can put mother's pork pie into my knapsack, and Peggy can put your one into hers."

"What are you going to drink?" asked Mrs Dixon.

"Tea," said Susan. "We've got milk to spare for them."

"They'll want a couple of mugs," said Mrs Dixon.

"One between them," said Nancy firmly. "Let them travel light."

"And if one's broken they'll have none," said Mrs Dixon, and she gave them two mugs, one of which was packed in Peggy's knapsack and one in Nancy's.

And with that the whole lot of them poured out of the hot farm kitchen into the cold air, out of the yard, across the road, through the gate, and away up the cart track to the barn.

Dorothea felt a little as if she had tumbled into a river and was being swept away in a strong current. Yesterday she and Dick had been alone as usual, just looking at things and planning stories, and now here they were in a crowd of eight, hurrying up the hill-side in the winter sunshine, with a pork pie for dinner in the knapsack of a girl they had only known about half an hour, going they did not know where, to do they did not know what. Eight of them! In all her stories there were usually not more than two, or at most four, and then perhaps a villain. She looked from face to face. But no, not one of these six strangers looked in the least like a villain. She found Titty walking beside her, and smiling at her in a very friendly way.

Dick was walking close in front of them, being questioned by Roger.

"Do you really know all about the stars?"

"I only know a few of them," said Dick.

"I know the saucepan and the Pole star," said Roger.

"The saucepan?"

"The one you find the Pole by."

"It's much more like a saucepan than some of the things they call it," said Dick. "I've got a book that has them all in, all the constellations, at least. We're going to watch them every night. Till we have to go."

"Where's your school?"

Close behind her came the four whom Dorothea put down in her mind as the elders, though she did not think that Peggy could be very much older than she was herself. She could not help hearing what they were talking about.

"Shiver my timbers, but why not?"

"An astronomer might be quite useful."

"But what's *she* going to do?"

"We'll soon know if they're any good."

This was dreadful, and Dorothea hurried out of earshot along the frozen track, sweeping Titty with her, in pursuit of Dick and Roger, who had just broken into a run, to have another look at the observatory, even if the others should not mean to stop there.

"It's a pretty good place," said Nancy, when the elders came up to the barn, and Susan was calling to Roger to hurry up and come down from the upper storey, where he was looking at Holly Howe through Dick's telescope. "It's a pretty good place, but just wait till you've seen ours."

They hurried on round the shore of the frozen tarn. "We don't want anybody else going through the ice," Susan said, "and John said that there would be skating to-morrow, and that there was no point in spoiling the ice to-day."

Beyond the tarn Titty and Roger ran on ahead, taking Dorothea and Dick with them. Presently they turned up the side of the hill through the remains of an old wood. There were a lot of fallen larches, that had not been able to stand against the wind. There were short, bushy hazels and willows that had been cut many times, for kindling or for charcoal-burning. There were little stunted oaks, rowans, and birch trees, bare, excepting that a few of the oaks still carried some of the dried leaves of last year, which made a noise almost like water when the wind stirred them. There was no cart track here, but they were walking along what Dorothea thought must be an ancient pathway through the wood. And this pathway suddenly ended in a sort of platform on the hillside, among the little trees, and, at the back of this platform, nestling against the hill, was a low hut with no windows, looking almost like a heap of stones.

"That's the igloo," said Titty.

Dorothea had never seen anything like it before, but Dick, who remembered looking at ancient remains with his father, said at once, "It's very old. You can tell by the big stones and the round corners."

"Part of it's old," said Roger.

"We've been working at it for ages," said Titty. "Every day until yesterday."

The walls of the building were low and rough. There were very big stones near the ground, and it was easy to see where the new builders had begun by the smaller stones they had used. All the stones had been fitted one on another without mortar. Then, across from one side of the building to the other, larch poles had been laid on the top of the walls. They stuck out on either side, thick ends and thin ends alternately. On the top of the larch poles there seemed to be a sheet of metal. The corners of it showed, but some big stones had been put on the top of it to hold it down, and earth had been heaped over all. But the strangest thing of all was that at the back of the hut a rusty iron chimney-pipe sprouted up out of the rude stone wall.

"The chimney was the hardest to do," said Titty, who was watching Dorothea to see what she thought of it all. "What was left of the old chimney was far too big and when we tried to build on it the stones kept falling down inside. And then John thought of crossing long flat stones at the corners so that the hole in the middle got smaller and smaller and we could jam that pipe in. It's been drawing better and better since we got the worst leaks stuffed up with earth."

"Why do you call it an igloo?" asked Dick.

"An igloo is an Eskimo hut," said Titty.

"Oughtn't it to be all snow?" said Dick.

"Well, you should have seen this one last week," said Titty, "before the snow melted. When there was that big fall of snow it got covered altogether, and looked just right."

"Only then we hadn't such a good roof," said Roger, "so we all got wet inside it."

"We had only the larch poles then," said Peggy, who had just come up with the other three. "Only poles and a bit of tarpaulin, and when we lit the fire and got all snug, the snow melted on the top of us and came pouring through."

"Then when the snow was gone," Titty went on, "John found a bit of old iron roofing in the shed at Holly Howe, and we harnessed a team of dogs to it."

"Titty and I weren't the only dogs," said Roger. "Even John

THE IGLOO

and Susan and Captain Nancy harnessed themselves and pulled like anything."

"The chimney was the worst," said Susan. "Masses of snow fell through and put the fire out."

"Some of the snow fell bang into Susan's saucepan," said Roger.

"It won't do it again," said Nancy, "not now we've got a proper stovepipe. Jib-booms and bobstays! Everybody's got to learn. Come on. Let's get ahead with the caulking. The snow may come again to-morrow, and you can still see daylight through in lots of places."

"We must get your things dry first," said Susan.

"All right, Mister Mate," said Nancy. "Now then. Visitors first." She pulled aside a piece of sacking that hung down and covered the doorway. "Yes. All fours. I know it's a bit low. But it ought to be. Real igloos have tunnels."

Just for one moment Dorothea hesitated, crouching down and looking out of the daylight into that pitch black hole. " 'In you go,' said the gaoler, and, as the unsuspecting maiden crept into the darkness, the gate clanged behind her, and she heard the rusty key grate in the lock. She was a prisoner. *Iron Bars. A Tale of the Past.*" But, after all, a bit of sacking was not much of a prison door. And nothing could really happen. Everybody was friendly.

"Shall I wriggle in first?" Dick was waiting, eager to see the igloo from the inside.

"No," said Dorothea.

It was a moment or two before either of them could see very much by the light that filtered into the igloo through holes between the stones and down the chimney. And behind them the others were crowding in.

"Half a minute, and we'll have a lantern lit," said John.

"Keep to the left," said Nancy, "and you won't have to stoop. It's a bit low on the other side."

"Hurry up, Peggy. Let's have some of the small twigs. In that pile. Just by your hand."

Dorothea and Dick felt themselves being pushed out of the way first by one and then by another in the bustle of getting the fire lit and the lantern hung up in its place under the roof.

"What a splendid fireplace!" said Dick, as Susan blew a handful of twigs into a blaze.

The fireplace was, indeed, the chief beauty of the igloo. The old ruin on the foundations of which it had been built had had a big open fireplace, built of rough stones. The arch over the fireplace and part of a chimney had been left standing, and John and Nancy and the others had begun their building above it. But they had managed to wedge an iron bar in among the stones and across from one side to the other, and a black kettle was hanging from it by a double hook of wire. No igloo in Greenland ever had a fireplace as good.

"I got a pocket-knife with a file in it at Christmas," said Captain Nancy, sitting down close by the fireplace on one of several short, stumpy logs, which were clearly meant for stools. "Jolly lucky. But we pretty nearly wore it out filing through an old railing to get that cross-bar. It took us ages, turn and turn about, working in shifts, you know. Go on, sit down anywhere. It'll be as warm as anything in two secs."

The lantern was burning now, and on each side of the little hut they could see rough benches, made of planks nailed to short billets for legs. Dick noticed the saw that had been used to cut them hanging from a wooden peg driven in between the stones of the wall. A saucepan was hanging on the wall beside it. In one corner there was a pile of cut wood reaching from the floor almost to the roof.

"That's in case we get snowed up," said Titty.

"I only w-w-wish we were," said Nancy.

"Snowed up or not, now is the time to use it," said Susan.

"Come on. Your teeth are chattering again. Another few sticks and it'll do. No, Roger! No toffee till after dinner."

Peggy was passing sticks from the pile to Susan, who was building a cage of them over the twigs that were now blazing in the fireplace.

"Skip along, somebody, and fill the kettle," said Susan, and Roger grabbed it and went crawling out, with Titty after him.

"Let's go with them," said Dick to Dorothea.

"Can we?" said Dorothea.

"Why not?" said Nancy.

"Is there anything else that'll hold water?" said Dick.

"Good man," said John.

"Let him take the saucepan," said Susan.

The four of them crawled out of the igloo, stood up outside and, led by Roger, went off among the thin, straggly underwood and over the frozen leaves of last year's foxgloves to a little trickling beck that was finding its way down from the high fells to the lake. It was small enough to step across, and its tiny pools had edgings of ice, as if the stream had shrunk and left the ice outside itself. Branches that hung across splashed by its little waterfalls had turned to thick glass bars, inside which could be seen, like cores, the twigs on which the splashes had frozen. Dick dipped the saucepan.

"Wait a minute," said Roger, who was busy breaking off bits of ice. He put them one by into into the saucepan till they floated level with the brim like small icebergs. "Better than nothing," he said. "Captain Nancy'll be jolly pleased."

Titty filled the kettle from under one of the little waterfalls.

"Let me carry it," said Dorothea, who badly wanted to be of some use.

"Better not," said Titty. "You left your gloves in the igloo. Your hands would freeze to the handle."

On their way back, they met John, who was gathering moss to pack the holes between the stones of the igloo.

"Why not earth?" asked Dick.

"Frozen too hard," said John. "We have to melt even the moss before it's really any good."

He picked up the box in which he had been putting it, and came back with them.

"Any amount of leaks to caulk," he said, and they saw that the smoke which was pouring in a most homely manner from the stovepipe chimney was also finding its way out through all sorts of small holes in the stonework.

"It is a lovely place," said Dorothea, looking at the rough little hut with the smoke climbing from it.

"Not half bad," said John, "if only there was some snow."

They crawled in. There was a grand fire now blazing in the fireplace, and in spite of all the leakages in the walls and the cold outside, the igloo was very warm. Nancy and Peggy were sitting on two of the log stools, wriggling bare toes before the flames. Their stockings were hung just above the fireplace on a string stretched between two pegs. Their shoes were being dried, turned every minute like pieces of toast. The lantern hanging from the roof and the leaping flames on the hearth filled the little hut with cheerful light. John emptied his box of moss on a pile that was already thawing. Peggy spread it so that as much of it as possible should be warming at once. Susan had been waiting for the kettle, and hung it from the cross-bar in the chimney so that it dangled in the hottest of the fire.

"We've got some real ice in the saucepan," said Roger, and Dick, half blinded by the mist that settled on his cold spectacles in the warm hut, held out the saucepan to Nancy.

"In the kettle, too?" she asked eagerly.

"No."

"It'll boil a lot quicker without," said Susan.

"All right," said Nancy, "it can't be helped."

"But why did you want it in the kettle?" asked Dick.

Titty answered him. "Well, if we had to melt ice to make our tea," she said, "anybody could see it would be much more like the real thing."

To Dick and Dorothea, as they sat on a bench sharing their pork pie with the explorers, and being given slabs of Holly Howe cake in return, things seemed very well, even as they were. The Arctic might be in a poor way for ice, but inside the igloo, with the lantern and the fire, what did it matter whether the world outside was as they had left it or fathoms deep in snow? Eagerly, when dinner was over, they helped in the washing up (the icebergs by that time had melted in the saucepan). Eagerly, during the short winter afternoon, they helped in the gathering of firewood. Eagerly, when they were allowed, they crammed warm moss between the stones of the walls until someone inside the igloo sang out that in that place at least he or she could see daylight no more. Eagerly they worked the moss into chinks in the stones round the chimney where wisps of smoke found their way through. Nothing was said about asking them actually to join the Polar expedition. But last thing, when it was time to go home, and Dorothea picked up the mugs they had been lent by Mrs Dixon, Nancy stopped her.

"They may as well leave these with ours, mayn't they, Susan? We'll all be up here to-morrow."

That was enough for Dorothea. As she and Dick walked down the cart track to the farm, they were not talking. Dick was already thinking of the evening's stars and his observatory. Dorothea, for once, was inventing no stories. She was living in one. Those two mugs, left in the igloo, were as good as a promise that there was more of the story to come.

*

The council among the explorers began the moment Dick and
Dorothea were out of sight.

"Of course, they aren't sailors," said John, "but that idea about
Mars was really pretty good."

"They'll have to sweat up signals," said Nancy. "Think of
having an idea like that and then not being able to say two words
when the other side answered."

"She wears pigtails," said Peggy.

"There's nothing absolutely *wrong* with pigtails," said Nancy.

"Sailors used to wear them once," said Titty.

"But not one at each side," said Roger.

Nothing was definitely settled, but that night, when it had
been dark a couple of hours, and Susan was talking of bedtime for
Roger, Titty said, "We may as well give them a flash or two."

The astronomer and his assistant must have had at least half an
eye on Mars, for the flashing of a lamp in that upper window was
instantly answered by other flashes high on the hill-side.

"They're watching," said Titty.

"It would be rather beastly to leave them out of things," said
Susan.

CHAPTER V

SKATING AND THE ALPHABET

MR DIXON had been up the fell before breakfast, and brought down the news that the ice on the tarn was bearing properly at last. Mrs Dixon had passed the news on. "Well," she said, "you'll be coming to no harm, if you follow Miss Susan." School trunks had been opened, and skates and boots and knapsacks taken out. Mrs Dixon had made them two packets of sandwiches, given them a couple of oranges apiece, and put a big bottle of milk in Dorothea's knapsack. "They'll be bringing milk from Jackson's, I've no doubt, but there's no call for any to go short." They rolled up their skates in newspaper and stowed them in the knapsacks for easy carrying.

It was a fine, crisp day after a night of hard frost. There was a clear sky overhead, and as Dick and Dorothea climbed the cart track they could see above the trees every cleft and gully of the distant mountains. The climb to the old barn seemed only half as long as it had been when they had gone up there for the first time. Dorothea felt more like dancing than walking. Every now and then Dick seemed to be on the very point of breaking into a run on the cropped pale grass at the side of the track, and these sudden jerkinesses in his walking showed Dorothea that he, too, was as eager as herself.

"I wonder if they're at the igloo already," she said.

"They can't be," said Dick. "Not with the red-caps having to row across the lake."

But as they came up to the barn and caught the first glimpse of Holly Howe they saw that the business of the day had already

60

begun. There was the end of the old whitewashed farm-house showing between the trees. There was that upper window that had once been Mars. But there was something new.

"What's that they've got on the wall?" said Dorothea. "Above the window."

Dick pulled out his telescope.

"A big black square," he said. "Up on end. Like a diamond."

"It's a signal," said Dorothea.

"But how are we to know what it means?" said Dick.

There was a hail in the distance, and they saw John, alone, scrambling through the dead bracken on the ridge beyond the tarn. Anybody could see that he was in a hurry as he came to the ice, stamped on it once or twice and then came quickly across, walking and sliding. He had a knapsack on his back and was carrying a big, awkward white parcel. Dick and Dorothea went to meet him as he came racing up the slope.

"How does our signal look from the barn?" he panted. "Can you see what it is?"

He turned and looked back to Holly Howe.

"Not half bad," he said.

"But what does it mean?" asked Dick.

"We haven't decided yet," said John. "Let's try how it works from this end. I stuck some whitewash on these to make them show against the dark stone. Can I go up?"

"Of course," said Dorothea.

"Let's," said Dick.

They went up the steps and into the loft where Dorothea and Dick had shivered two nights before while sending out their flashes to catch the attention of the Martians. John propped his parcel against the wall, where Dick examined it carefully. It was simply two big flat pieces of wood, one of them a triangle and the other a square.

"Look out!" said John. "The whitewash is only just drying!"

"Have you lost something?" said Dorothea, seeing John looking this way and that about the loft.

"I just want something for a hammer," said John. He ran down the steps again, and came back with a biggish stone.

"This'll do," he said, trying it in his hand, and went to the big window. He stood there on the sill, holding to the wall with his right hand and reaching round it and as high up it as he could with his left. He found a crack between the stones, pushed into it a big nail that he fished out of his pocket, battered it firmly in with his stone hammer, and gave it a last knock from below to make it turn upwards.

"But I won't be able to reach as high as that," said Dick, who guessed what he was doing.

"Half a minute," said John. "You won't have to."

Out of his pocket he brought a ball of string, another large nail, some double hooks of thick fencing wire, and a big brass curtain ring.

Dick and Dorothea watched, open-mouthed.

John threaded the string through the curtain ring, reached round the wall to hang it on the nail he had just fixed, pulled the string through until it was long enough to reach the ground outside, dropped the ball after it, picked up the other nail, the hooks and the wooden shapes, and hurried out and down the steps. The other two ran down after him.

He cut off the ball of string and put it in his pocket. Then he fastened one of his hooks to the string, tying the two ends of the string together so that neither end should slip through the ring high up on the end of the barn.

"If it ever comes down," he said, "don't either of you try reaching out of that window to put it right again. Wait for Nancy or me."

He hung the triangle on the hook by a hole in one of its corners. Then, hand over hand, he hoisted it up until it reached the nail on the wall, where it hung staring white against the dark weather-beaten stones.

"It'll hang either way," he said, "pointing up or down. There's a hole in one of its sides on purpose. And you can make the other one hang either like a square or like a diamond. And the double hooks are so that you can hang one above another. Well, we'll soon know if it works. Watch Holly Howe."

"There's someone at the window," said Dick, whose telescope was already pointing at Mars. "Red-caps."

"Nancy and Peggy."

"The black square's going!" cried Dorothea.

"They're hauling it down," said John. "They've seen all right. Yes. I thought so. There comes the triangle!"

A black triangle was climbing slowly up the white wall above the upper window at the end of the farm.

"Now we'll try the other way." He hauled his own white triangle down, unhooked it, and hooked it on again by a hole in the middle of one of its sides, so that it hung point downwards.

"South cone," he said. "When they hoist that in harbour it means a storm from the south."

"May I pull it up?" said Dick.

"Go ahead!" said John. "Your signal station."

"Observatory," said Dick, but he hoisted away all the same, and the triangle had no sooner reached the nail than that other triangle on the wall of Holly Howe shot downwards. A moment later it was climbing again, and this time, it too, was upside down.

"Good work!" said John. "Hullo! Theirs is going down again. They want to start skating. Anyway we've done enough for today. All we've got to do now is to make a code. Half a minute! I'll whack another nail in down here, so that you can belay the halyards and leave a signal hoisted, without having to stand by and hang on."

"Halyards?" said Dick.

"String," said Dorothea.

A good place was found for a nail, within easy reach of the ground. John drove it in and showed Dick and Dorothea how to fasten their halyards. Two or three times, just for practice, they hoisted square and triangle, and both together. There were no answering signals from Holly Howe, but that, they knew, was because the others were already climbing the hillside.

John explained how the idea had come during the flashings of the night before. "You see, this way, we'll be able to signal what the plans are for the day even before you know Morse. Nancy said last night you'd got to learn."

"But what are the signals going to mean?" asked Dick.

"Look here," said John, "we've got four single ones. North cone, with the triangle right way up; south cone, the other way; square, and diamond. And then by hanging two together, one above another, we can make a whole lot more. The main thing is to be able to say what the plans for the day are. We want to be able to hang up something meaning 'Come to the igloo' or 'Come to Holly Howe.'"

"Or 'Come to Mrs Dixon's,'" said Dorothea.

But very little had been done towards making a code when they saw two red-capped explorers leaping through the dead bracken on the other side of the tarn.

"Here they are," cried Dorothea.

Hurriedly the halyards were belayed, the wooden triangle and square stowed with the hooks in the loft. Hurriedly they picked up their knapsacks and ran down the steps. Already Susan, Titty, and Roger were in sight. There was a distant cheer and the sun glinted on Roger's skates as he held them high above his head.

"You see," John was saying as they crossed the ice together, "the whole point of these signals is that once they're hoisted there's no need to hang about for an answer. We can start for wherever we're going, and you'll know where to come. We can hoist the signals the moment Nancy comes over in the morning, and we can leave them up till we come back. No one will be able to read them except us."

It certainly sounded as if Dorothea and Dick were considered members of the party. But it was the skating that settled it.

"Jib-booms and bobstays!" shouted Nancy Blackett, violently wrestling with a screw in one of her skates. "Nobody could beat those signals. We could see them as clear as anything, even without the telescope."

"What about fixing the code?" said John.

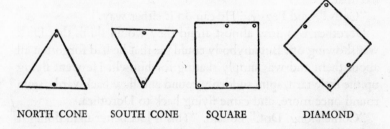

NORTH CONE   SOUTH CONE   SQUARE   DIAMOND

"In the igloo," said Nancy, "when we're stewing with the dinner. Skating first, anyhow."

Dorothea had been a little shy of skating with these Arctic explorers who knew all about ships and could signal in half a dozen different ways. She thought they would probably be as much better than Dick and her at skating as they seemed to be at everything else.

She and Dick sat together on some heather at the side of the tarn, fixed their skates on their boots and fastened the straps. She looked round. Everybody else was still busy with the screws. She fumbled with her straps, not wishing to be the first to start. But Dick had never a thought of the others who might be watching. The moment his skates were on he pushed himself off from his clump of heather, rose to standing height as he slid away, and

C

was off. Every day of the holidays he had been with Dot on the indoor skating rink close by the University buildings at home, and this was a trick he had practised again and again, to start off from a sitting position instead of stepping awkwardly about before getting under way.

The Arctic explorers stared, open-mouthed.

"But he can skate," said Titty.

"Like anything," said Roger.

"Why didn't you tell us?" said Nancy. "Of course, you ought to be in the Polar expedition. Not one of us can skate like that."

"Golly!" said Peggy. "He can do it either way."

Dorothea was now almost afraid they would think that Dick was showing off. But anybody could see that he had forgotten all about them and was simply skating for himself. He went flying up the little tarn, spun suddenly round and flew backwards, spun round once more, and came flying back to Dorothea.

"Come along, Dot," he said. "This is lots better than doing it indoors."

Titty and Roger were skating for the first time. John and Susan had had a little skating at school the winter before. But the Walkers lived mostly in the south, and year after year had gone by with never a patch of ice for them to skate on.

Nancy and Peggy were sturdy, straightforward skaters. Living in the north, at the foot of the great hills, they had had skating every year since they could remember anything, even though the big lake had frozen only once or twice. The smaller lakes and tarns were frozen every year. And at school, too, they had always had a few days when skating took the place of duller games. They could skate, but they knew enough about skating to know that skating was to Dick as natural and easy a thing as sailing their little *Amazon* was to them.

"You too?" said Nancy to Dorothea. But Dorothea did not

hear her. She was already gliding off to join Dick, who had held out his hands to her. They crossed hands and went off together. Left, Right, Left, Right. Dick, in his methodical way, was keeping time aloud as he always did.

"They're letting us be part of it," said Dorothea, "because of your skating. Nancy's just said so."

"Part of what?" said Dick.

But they were turning now at the end of the tarn where a beck trickled in and warned them to keep their distance in case the ice might be weak near the running water. Nancy was coming to meet them. She was coming at a good pace, with a balancing jerk now and again, for this was her first day on the ice since last year, but anybody could see that she was putting her strength into it. She did not come swooping over the ice like a bird flying. And she knew it very well.

"Hi!" she called out. "You teach me how to twiddle round and go backwards and I'll teach you signalling. You've got to learn anyhow."

"You just put your weight on one foot and swing yourself round with the other," said Dick. "At least that's what it feels like."

"Like this," said Nancy, and swung herself round in the bravest manner while going at full speed, coming down with such a bump that if the ice had been a little less thick she must have gone through. But she picked herself up with a laugh. "Not quite like that," she said. "Let's have a shot at doing it slowly."

John and Susan were on the ice now, moving with the earnest care of those who know how easy it is to fall. Roger, who had tried to copy Dick's start, had sat down three times, quicker than it is possible to say so. He had pushed himself off, sat down, struggled up, sat down, struggled half up once more and come definitely to rest. Titty was standing on her skates but moving just an arm now and again when something happened to make her feel that even standing still was a fairly dangerous adventure.

"What did I do wrong?" Roger asked, sitting where he was. "I bet Susan's put my skates on crooked."

"Can I help?" Dorothea asked Titty.

"No. No. No. Don't touch me," said Titty. "I'm going to do it by myself."

And a little later, John and Susan, skating solemnly by, met Titty almost half-way up the tarn, moving on one foot and kicking herself slowly along with the other. Roger was being pulled along by Dick. Peggy and Dorothea were skating together at the far end, while Captain Nancy, glancing rather nervously over her shoulder, was moving jerkily backwards with a fixed smile on her face.

But before long everybody, except Dick and Dorothea, who were already in practice, was more than ready for a rest. Skating uses muscles that seem to be mostly on holiday. There were aches in ankles and shin bones and hurried struggles towards the sides of the tarn where it was possible to ease the pain by sitting down for a minute or two on a clump of heather.

No time was wasted even while they were sitting about. Dick and Dorothea, who had been teaching Arctic explorers how to skate, became pupils once more. Some little flags on sticks had been brought up from Holly Howe and messages were flapped from one side of the tarn to the other, until when it was Roger's turn he signalled "W-H-A-T-A-B-O-U-T-D-I-N-N-E-R" and Susan said it was high time to go and start the fire in the igloo. Nancy gave Dick and Dorothea their first lesson in flag-flapping and showed them how to make a short flap for a dot and a long sweep from side to side for a dash.

"But it's no use until you know Morse," she said. "You've simply got to learn it at once."

"We will," said Dorothea.

They took off their skates and went up the wood to the

igloo for dinner, and while Susan and Peggy were dealing with the fire and boiling water for tea, Nancy wrote out the Morse alphabet for them twice over, once on the last page of one of the

Private Code

▲ = Yes
▼ = No
◆ = Come to Igloo
■ = " " " Tarn
⬥ = " " " Holly Howe
⬦ = " " " Beckfoot
⬘ = " " " North Pole
⬙ = " " " Island
⬚ = " " " Dixon's Farm

PRIVATE CODE. FROM DICK'S POCKET-BOOK

tiny note-books in which Dorothea was accustomed to write her romances, and once in Dick's private pocket-book of scientific notes. Meanwhile, John was working away on the back of an envelope and had found that the two shapes, the square and the triangle, each of which could be hung up in two positions and either separately or together, made it possible to send twelve different messages. "We shan't want more," he said, "but if we do we can easily make another shape."

It was agreed that the most likely signals were "Come to the igloo" and "Come to the tarn." These were to be the diamond and the square. Then somebody suggested that there ought to be a "Yes" and a "No," and it was decided that these had better be the north cone or cheerful triangle, looking up, and the south cone or melancholy triangle, looking down. Then diamond over north cone was to mean "Holly Howe." Diamond over south cone was to mean "Beckfoot."

"Same thing as Holly Howe really," said Nancy, "because we'd be rowing over to Holly Howe to fetch you."

"But it might mean bringing different luggage," said Susan.

"Gear," said Titty.

Everybody agreed at once that a north cone on the top of a diamond was the best signal to mean "North Pole."

"But how are we to know where it is?" asked Dick.

"We don't," said John, "except that it's at the head of the lake. Nancy and Peggy know, of course, but that can't be helped. But we've never been up there at all. We've got to find it."

South cone over diamond and south cone over square were clearly the right signals for the island and for Dixon's Farm, because both of these were towards the southern end of the lake.

"The signal for the day goes up first thing in the morning," said John, "and whoever sees it hoists the same one, so that there can be no mistake."

"That leaves three signals not settled," said Dick, who had also been working out the possible combinations of squares and diamonds and north and south cones.

"Something's sure to turn up for them," said Nancy. "Anyhow, these'll be jolly useful, because you can read them right away."

"Before we've done any of our homework," said Dorothea,

looking doubtfully at all the dots and dashes of the Morse code and wondering how long it would take her to learn them.

After dinner they went to the tarn and skated again, and then,

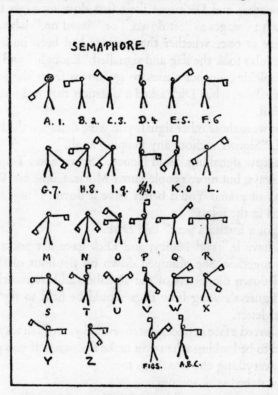

SEMAPHORE CODE DRAWN BY NANCY IN DICK'S
POCKET-BOOK

late in the afternoon, Nancy called another signal practice. Dick and Nancy went up to the observatory, while John and Dorothea climbed the bracken ridge on the farther side of the tarn. The others rested their shins and ankles but would not leave the ice.

With much looking up of the alphabet and prompting from their teachers, who now and then had to take the flags themselves and explain the muddle by some hurried, skilful flapping of their own, Dorothea and Dick sent their first slow messages to each other, such messages as "Sit down," or "Stand up," when it was easy to see at once whether the message had been understood.

At last John took the flag and signalled "Enough," and Nancy was just picking up her skates to go down from the loft and back to the tarn, when Dick asked a question that had long been in his mind.

"What were those other signals you were doing on the island?" he asked. "Signals without any flapping at all."

"Scarecrow signalling," said Nancy. "Semaphore. Tons better in some ways, but more people know Morse. Come on. Where's that book of yours? You'd better have it down. Hang, I've left my pencil in the igloo."

"I've got a fountain pen," said Dick.

"Let's have it," said Nancy, and Dick gave her pocket-book and pen together. She plumped down on the floor of the loft, scribbled down the letters of the alphabet, and over each letter drew a figure showing how flags should be held to signal that particular letter.

"I've shoved a face in once, just to remind you which way you're supposed to be looking when you make the signal. If you get that wrong, everything else is wrong, too."

Dick watched with interest.

"Which matters most?" he said. "This or Morse?"

"You ought to know both," she said. "You can't mix them up because one is dots and dashes and moving about all the time, and in the other each letter stays still while you make it, or at least you stay still while you're making a letter."

"We'll do it," said Dick, "but it'll take some time. That's two whole codes and the signals between here and Holly Howe."

"Those don't count," said Nancy. "They just hang and you can be as slow as you like about looking them up."

"What about signalling to you?"

Water = H_2O

Sulphuric acid = H_2SO_4

Speed of Light = 186,000 miles per second

Mother's Birthday = March 17th

Jupiter is the one with moons

Mars is the red one

Flag on Beckfoot = Start for Pole

ANOTHER PAGE FROM DICK'S POCKET-BOOK

Nancy looked out from the loft, across the lake, beyond the islands.

"It's too far," she said, "except with lights. You could do it with a lantern. We will some time or other, when you've learnt Morse. Anyway, there's not much point in it because we come to

Holly Howe every day and we'll be signalling from there. But I'll tell you what," she went on. "The day we're all going to the North Pole, I'll yank a flag up on the Beckfoot promontory so that everybody can see it ... Over there, beyond the islands, running out into the lake on the far side ... No ... farther along ... Woods behind, at the back of it, then just heather and rock. You can see our old flagstaff near the point."

Dick was looking through his telescope.

"Not a very big one," he said.

"Big enough to hang a flag on," said Nancy. "Yes. I'll hang one up to mean 'Starting for the Pole.' They can see it from just above Holly Howe and you can see it from here."

"I'd better write that down," said Dick, and at the bottom of a page of notes, mostly scientific, he scribbled, "Flag at Beckfoot = Start for Pole."

"If only the snow would come," said Nancy, "and give the Arctic half a chance. If it comes quick there might still be a bit of ice round the edges. And anyway, with snow, we can use the sledge. Beastly going to the North Pole over plain grass. Hullo, what's that brat trying to signal?"

Everybody else was back on the tarn, looking up towards the observatory and beckoning to Nancy and Dick to come down and join them. Roger had got hold of one of the flags, and, standing on the ice, was busily flapping a message. Nancy read the letters out as they came. "L-A-Z-Y-B-O-N-E-S." "Shiver my timbers," she said. "What cheek. He means us. Well. Come on. Let's have one more good go of skating before going home."

She went racing down the stone steps and away to the tarn to put on her skates, while Roger, his arms whirling like the sails of a windmill by way of helping his legs, was getting himself as far out of reach as the ice would allow. Dick followed her. But there was no more talk of signals that day. Susan thought Titty and Roger had done about enough skating. It was time to go home. And that night there were no lantern signals from Holly Howe or the observatory. The sky was clouded over and the astronomer and his assistant sat in the farm kitchen, trying to learn the Morse code by writing letters to each other in dots and dashes. Softly, at first, as if it hardly meant it, the snow began to fall.

CHAPTER VI

SNOW

DOROTHEA woke with a dreadful fear that she had overslept. The room was full of light. The ceiling gleamed white. The blue flowers that made a pattern on the wall-paper (in slanting lines, in straight lines up and down, and in straight lines from side to side, whichever way she chose to count them) were somehow brighter than they had been on any other morning. Had the sun been up a long time? And then, looking at the window, Dorothea saw the white snow deep across the sill. She leapt out of bed and ran to the window. There was a new world. Everything was white, and somehow still. Everything was holding its breath. The field stretching down to the lake was like a brilliant white counterpane without a crinkle in it. The yew trees close by the farm-house were laden with snow. The lower branches of the old fir were pressed right down to the ground by the weight of snow they were carrying. The island was a white island, except where the rocks rose straight up out of the still water. The snow seemed to have spread downwards from the tops of the hills until everything was covered. It lay like a slab of icing on a slice of cake along the stone wall of the garden. The grey outhouses had thick white roofs. And then there was this magical brightness in the air. At home, in the town, Dorothea had seen snow more than once, where it lay for a few hours in the streets, growing grimier from the smoke, until it was swept into dirty heaps along the gutters. She had never seen anything like this.

She listened. It could not be late, or Mrs Dixon would have waked her, even if Dick had not. Ah! There was the clink of the hot-water can, and Mrs Dixon's counting, "Eight and nine and ten and eleven and twelve and that's the dozen," as she reached the landing.

"Well, and what do you think of this?" said Mrs Dixon. "It's been snowing half the night."

Dorothea could hardly say what she thought. She was thinking of people looking out of windows at Holly Howe, and of Nancy and Peggy rowing across the lake, from one white shore to another. This was just what they had wanted.

Dick came thundering at her door. "It'll be a real igloo to-day," he said. "I wonder if it'll be cold enough for the snow not to melt when they've got the fire going inside. I say, there are tracks in the snow. I can see a bird's, thrush, I think, and Roy's across the yard, and two rabbit tracks in the field."

"Pity you're going so soon," said Mrs Dixon. "With a fall of snow like this, and no wind, we'll be having ice on the lake if the frost holds."

"If only we could," said Dorothea.

"Where's Mr Dixon?" she asked a little later, coming downstairs and finding nobody but Mrs Dixon about.

"Up on the fell," said Mrs Dixon. "Him and Silas, looking for outlaying sheep. Snow's good for the land, right enough, but it's a peck of trouble when you've sheep on the fells, and we've more'n a few."

After breakfast, Dorothea and Dick packed their knapsacks (with skates, milk bottle, cake and sandwiches) and set off for the observatory. The snow came up to the top of their boots as they crossed the road, and there was little of the cart track to be seen, but Silas and Mr Dixon had gone that way, looking after their sheep, and Dorothea and Dick stepped carefully in those footprints, so very much larger than their own. Close to the barn the big, deep prints turned away to the right, straight up towards the high fells.

"I thought so," cried Dick, looking down at the gabled end of Holly Howe, white and today hard to see against the snow-laden trees and the white fields above and below it. "I thought so. It's a diamond all by itself. It'll be something like an igloo today. Come on, Dot." He climbed the steps to the loft, leaving sharp footprints on each step, and came down again with the whitewashed wooden square John had left.

"I've got to hoist one too, to show we've got the message, but they've probably started already."

He hooked the square on the halyard by a hole in one of its corners and hoisted it up the wall of the barn. It hung there on the dark grey wall like a big white diamond.

"Come along," he said, anxious to see what it looked like from a little distance.

But Dorothea could not make herself hurry. The snow had changed everything. Almost she felt like walking on tiptoe through this new sparkling world. A whole jumble of things was in her mind, Good King Wenceslaus, the Ice Queen, Ib and Little Christina, and the little girl who sat on her wedding chest in the winter forest, waiting for the coming of Frost. It was not much good talking about these things to Dick, whose mind worked differently. Why, the first thing he had done that morning when they had run out into the glittering snow had been to put a scrap of snow on a bit of glass, so that he could look at the crystals under his microscope. And then he had stuck a bit of stick upright in the snow and made a notch on it, and taken it indoors to borrow Mrs Dixon's measuring tape to see exactly what depth of snowfall there had been. And now, she knew, he was eager to get to the igloo, to see how the snow covering would stand the heat of the fire inside. Dorothea was thinking more of Captain Nancy. Well, here was the snow she had hoped for. Already, long before they were anywhere near the igloo, Dorothea could almost feel Nancy stirring things up and filling the air with adventure.

"It won't be very good skating with all this snow," said Dick, as they stepped out on the smooth white blanket that covered the tarn.

"But it looks a good deal more like the Arctic," said Dorothea. The ice was slippery under the snow, but it was easier going on the other side. They waded through the snow-covered bracken, and turned at last into the path up the wood.

"They've got a sledge," cried Dick. "Just look at the tracks." Presently they heard a noise as if someone were beating the ground with a cricket bat. People were talking, too, and they heard Nancy's cheerful, ringing voice. "Go it, skipper! Flatten it in good and hard."

"It really is like coming to an Eskimo settlement," said Dorothea.

"I say, just look at it!" cried Dick.

It was worth looking at. The rough stone hut with the roof of old corrugated iron held down by a few big stones, had vanished under the magic of snow that had changed all the rest of the world. Instead, there was a great white mound of snow, a real igloo in which any Eskimo would be very pleased to live. The old stovepipe stuck up through the snow and a steady stream of smoke was pouring from it. Even the rough doorway looked now like the entrance to a snow tunnel. A long sledge with high, trestled runners was standing close by with the last of a load of snow. And there were John and Nancy hard at work with spades, piling more snow on the mound and beating it firmly together.

"Come on, you two," shouted Nancy as soon as she saw them. "This is what it ought to be like. I told you it only needed a little snow."

"What's it like inside?" said Dick.

"Good and stuffy," said Nancy. "They always are."

They crawled in, Dorothea first, to find the lantern lit, Susan and Peggy busy with a big iron pot, and a basket full of carrots and potatoes, and Roger and Titty sitting by the fire, putting their boots on.

"Have you gone through the ice?" said Dorothea.

"Only snow," said Roger, "tobogganing. Dry enough now."

"You wouldn't have been wet at all if you'd dusted the snow off before letting it melt into your stockings," said Susan.

Dick took off his spectacles and blinked while he wiped the steam that had settled on them as he crawled in out of the cold air. He put them on again and looked round. It was much better even than he had thought. He had forgotten that sheet of iron that lay across the roof. He had been thinking that the roof would be dribbling all over with melted snow working through the larch poles. But the middle of the igloo was perfectly dry. Of course, nobody could help the steady sizzling in the fireplace as the snow melted round the chimney pipe and found its way down into the fire. Now and again the smoke seemed to think twice about going up the chimney. But the wood smoke had a fine smell and Dick felt sure that in an igloo in Greenland his eyes would have smarted just the same.

"We're going to sweep the tarn," said Titty. "Captain Nancy says it's no good having skating practice till we've swept away some of the snow."

"We're taking the sledge," said Roger. "It won't be only sweeping."

"What are you going to sweep with?" asked Susan. "Who's going down to Holly Howe for brooms?"

"Not me," said Roger. "Nobody is. We're going to have brooms like the one you and John made in Swallowdale."

The four younger ones poured out of the igloo into the snow, leaving Peggy and Susan to their cooking.

"We're ready for those brooms," said Roger, and John and Nancy left their spades and went off with Roger and Titty, breaking twigs from the bare trees, shaking the snow off, and

THE IGLOO IN SNOW

splicing them firmly in bundles to the ends of stout sticks. Meanwhile Dick and Dorothea took the spades and did a little work in shovelling up snow and adding it to the thickness of those massive walls.

"Shiver my timbers," said Nancy, when she came back to the clearing and saw the igloo gleaming under the trees, a great shining mound of white snow. "Shiver my timbers, but isn't it beastly to be going away so soon and leaving it to the sheep."

"It's pretty good," said John, who had been helping to tie the new brooms on the top of the sledge.

"But it's all coming just too late," said Nancy. She took her spade from Dorothea, went to the side of the clearing, dug it savagely into the snow, lifted an enormous spadeful, came back and battered it down on the top of the igloo. "It doesn't bear thinking about," she said. "The lake was only waiting for this snow to begin to freeze. Everybody says it's going to freeze all over, and instead of being at the North Pole we're going to be back at school messing about with Magna Carta ... "

John said nothing, but took up his spade and went on with his work.

"Come on," said Roger, "there's a rope for each dog, and we can all jump on when it's going downhill."

Dorothea grabbed her rope. They were off, the four of them, towing the sledge, jostling each other as they squeezed between the bushes with the sledge at their heels, plumping sideways on the top of it as it threatened to run away from them down a slope, hauling with the ropes over their shoulders as they climbed a rise.

"It's a very good sledge," said Dick, "built just like a bridge."

"It's a Beckfoot sledge," said Titty. "We haven't got one of our own. Nancy and Peggy brought it across when that first lot of snow came."

"They hunted for another one for us, but they couldn't find it," panted Roger.

They charged down through the bracken, and out on the smooth, snow-covered ice. Sweeping began, but did not go on for very long. There was too good a slope between the observatory and the shore of the tarn. It was soon found that if the sledge were started close under the observatory wall it flew down the slope, shot out on the ice, and across it, very nearly to the other side. The sweepers stuck their brooms upright in clumps of heather so as not to lose them. Again and again four dogs with lolling tongues dragged the sledge up to the old barn. Again and again four human beings, astraddle on the sledge, flew down again.

"It's all good practice," said Roger.

"You see, there isn't time for the lake to freeze," said Titty, "but if the snow lasts we'll be able to toboggan a good bit of the way."

They were standing by the barn, resting after the hundredth climb. Time had gone at the terrible pace at which it always goes during the last few days of the holidays, and everybody was startled when Peggy's red cap showed on the ridge. She had brought a flag with her, and began to signal.

Dorothea and Dick, trying to remember what they had learnt the night before, stared hard.

"Long and two shorts. D. I know that one," said Dick.

"Two shorts," said Dorothea.

"I," said Titty.

"D-I," said Roger. "I know the message before she's flapped it. It's dinner."

"But it can't be dinner already!" said Dorothea.

"Why not?" said Roger.

And dinner it was.

Peggy waited for no answer, but was gone. The four of them had a last wild rush down the slope and over the ice, picked up their brooms, tied them on the sledge, and went back to the igloo at the gallop. There they found the four elders cooling down after work indoors and out. John and Nancy could do no more to the igloo, which was now a perfect dome, with a trodden path leading to the door. Susan and Peggy had been making a hot-pot, with potatoes, onions, and carrots, and a whole tin of bully beef (known by the Swallows and Amazons as pemmican). The pot itself was cooling down outside the igloo, because it was too hot for anybody to eat, and Susan was prodding at the potatoes with a fork through clouds of steam, though she had really made sure everything was ready before taking the pot off the fire.

"It's sure to be all right, Susan," said Nancy. "Let's get at it."

It was taken back into the igloo to be eaten. The explorers sat round it on benches and logs under the light of the lantern that was hanging from one of the poles of the roof. They had not enough spoons and forks for everybody, but fingers, as Roger said, came in useful once somebody with a fork had helped by getting something out. Dick and Dorothea were, of course, invited to share the hot-pot with the others. "After all," said Peggy, "a hot-pot's a hot-pot, and sandwiches are just ... " She stopped, but Roger helped her out. "Sandwiches," he suggested, and, catching Susan's eye, added, "Why not? They are." The sandwiches came in very useful for everybody, as plates that could be eaten up after the juice had soaked into them and they had served their first purpose.

And then, when they had just got well started with dinner, they heard steps outside the door.

"Polar bear," said Roger. "Smelt the food."

But if it was a bear it was too much out of breath to be a fierce one.

"It's mother!" cried Nancy, looking out. "Come on in. We've got room for one Eskimo, and you're the one."

"Thank you for that," said a voice, and through the low doorway Mrs Blackett came crawling into the igloo. She was a very little woman, and rather plump, and she had a cheerful, clear voice very like Nancy's. "Well," she said, "I must say you've made a very good hut for yourselves. But, pouf, isn't it hot? Open-air life indeed! It's like an oven. And what a pull up from Holly Howe. Easy enough to find you with all those tracks in the snow. But if I'd remembered how far it was I'd ... I'd have sent you a message to come down and pull me up on the sledge."

"We'd have run you up in style," said Nancy. "Team of six dogs, eight with Dorothea and Dick ... Here's a place for you on this bench ... it won't let you down unless you joggle it ... and there's lots of dinner."

"It's Dorothea and Dick I came up to see," said Mrs Blackett, looking round under the lantern. "Staying with the Eskimos at Dixon's farm, aren't you? ... By the way, Nancy, *do* remind me to thank Mrs Dixon for that pork pie ... Well, I wonder if you'd care to come across the fiord to an Eskimo settlement on the other side. You could join the others at Holly Howe after break-fast tomorrow, and Nancy and Peggy can pull over with the boat and bring you all across."

"We'd like to come very much," said Dorothea, and managed to catch Dick's eye, so that he said "Thank you" before it was too late.

"The days are so short now," Mrs Blackett went on, "you'd have to come first thing in the morning, because of getting back before dark. You might take a run up the Matterhorn — Kanchen-junga, I mean — or something like that."

"It'll be quite all right," said Nancy. "We won't be going to the Pole till the very last day."

"Good," said Mrs Blackett. "So that's settled. Meet at Holly Howe first thing, and don't bring any food. Better tell Mrs Dixon tonight, or she'll be filling your knapsacks before you start. Oh, thank you, Peggy. What is it? Hot-pot? It smells very good. You're not taking it out on the tarn ... ?"

"On the tarn?" said Susan.

"I was thinking of another hot-pot," said Mrs Blackett. "It was once upon a time when I was young, and the lake was frozen all over."

"If only it would hurry up and do it now," said Nancy.

"And a whole lot of us spent the day on the ice. A big hot-pot and a basket of other things were sent down to us from the house, and brought out to where there was figure-skating going on in the middle of the lake. And the hot-pot was put down on the ice while the basket was being unpacked to get at the plates and knives and forks. And we all came skating along very, very hungry, and found no hot-pot. Just a little cloud of steam drifting away, a pleasant smell, and a neat round hole in the ice through which the hot-pot had that moment gone to the bottom of the lake."

"What did you do?" asked Roger.

"Went without," said Mrs Blackett. "What else could we do?"

"This one was so hot we cooled it in the snow," said Peggy.

"Lucky it's a long way to the tarn," said Roger, who thought that if the ice had been a little nearer this hot-pot might have gone the same way as the other.

After dinner, when Mrs Blackett had admired the outside of the igloo as well as the inside, she said that she must be going, and that Nancy and Peggy must come with her.

"Your dinner was a fairly late one, you know, and it'll be getting dark in an hour, so it doesn't make very much difference. I'm sorry to take them off, but I was given a lift round the head of the lake, and the boat's the only way to get back."

"We'll give you a full dog team now," said Nancy, and they put Mrs Blackett on the sledge, and the whole Polar expedition pulled on the ropes or pushed behind as they ran the sledge along the old path through the wood until they came out of the trees and the snow stretched clear before them down to the road, with only one stone wall across it and that with a wide gap in it. Dozens of tracks showed where there had been tobogganing early in the morning.

Peggy, Nancy, and John joined Mrs Blackett on the sledge. "Tomorrow won't be wasted," said Nancy to Dorothea. "Something always happens on Kanchenjunga. All right, mother? Tuck your feet in. John's coming to bring the sledge up for the others. Let go at the stern there. Shove her off!"

There was a faint squeak from Mrs Blackett, and the sledge shot away over the snow, faster and faster, straight as an arrow down the steep hill-side, through the gap in the wall, and on towards the road.

"Come along," said Susan, "we must tidy up in the igloo. Specially as we shan't be there tomorrow."

They raced back up the path through the trees, made everything what Susan and Titty called shipshape, and were back at the edge of the wood when John came toiling slowly uphill again with the sledge.

The six of them flew down the hill together.

"What about tomorrow's signals?" asked Dick, as they were saying good night in the road.

"No point in climbing up there tomorrow," said John. "Come straight to Holly Howe as early as you can."

"I do wish it hadn't all got to stop so soon," said Dorothea, as she and Dick walked home along the road under trees heavy with snow. "Only three more days."

Dick was thinking of something very different.

"Remember that first day, Dot?" he said. "Well, we're going in a boat after all."

CHAPTER VII

ARCTIC VOYAGE

It froze harder than ever that night, and in the morning Dick and Dorothea set out for Holly Howe with the joyful news that there was an edging of thin ice along the shore of the lake. Dorothea had asked Mrs Dixon if she thought they ought to put on their best clothes. "They won't be your best clothes if you spend a day in them with Mrs Blackett's two," Mrs Dixon had said. "If you ask me, you'd best go just as you are." "But it's a party." "It won't be that kind of party if those two have anything to do with it." So they set out, just as they were, in ordinary Arctic rig, with woollen gloves and mufflers as well as their coats, for anybody could see that it would be pretty cold rowing across.

They found that news of the ice had already reached Holly Howe. A local Eskimo (the postman) had said there would be skating before night by the town landings, and John had just come up from the boathouse to say that there was a good deal of ice in the Holly Howe bay.

"Thicker than cat ice," Roger told them. "John says it would bear a jolly big cat, a wild cat, or even a small puma."

"They'll have a job to bring their boat in," said John, coming out with a big coil of stout rope, for use on Kanchenjunga. "I wonder what it's like over on the other side."

Titty came running round the corner of the house. She had been watching at the top of the field. "The boat's just coming," she called out, "but there's only one of them in it." She was gone.

"Come on, Susan," John called in at the window, and they all hurried out by the garden gate. Titty was already running down the field to the boathouse. Roger was racing after her. Dorothea, in spite of what Mrs Dixon had said, could not help having a feeling that they were going to a party, though they saw that none of the others were tidier than usual. She did not run. Nor did Dick, but that was because he had pulled out his telescope, and was looking through it at the Beckfoot rowing boat, which was already in the bay.

"It's Peggy," he said.

"She's taken the point of the bay very wide," said John. "More ice out there, very likely."

A moment later they saw Peggy looking round over her shoulder, and changing the direction of the boat.

"Come on," said John. "Let's get down there. She may not be able to bring the boat to the jetty. There may be less ice under Darien, where it's deeper."

Susan had caught them up, and now, party or no party, they ran full tilt down through the snow, through the little gate at the bottom of the field, and out on the stone jetty beside the Holly Howe boathouse. Roger and Titty had cleared a good deal of the snow off the jetty the morning before when they had gone down to meet the Amazons, and now they were stamping their feet on the stones to get rid of the snow from their boots.

"Look! Look!" cried Roger. "She's met an iceberg." And indeed they saw Peggy lift an oar and bring it down with a splash through a thin piece of floating ice.

John went scouting along the shore towards that high rocky southern point that they called the Peak of Darien, where pine trees rose above a cliff, but it was clear that, ice or no ice, Peggy meant to come straight in at the usual place. Dorothea shivered at the thought that in a few minutes she and Dick would be themselves afloat in this ice-strewn sea, though she would have been willing to do almost anything rather than be left behind and miss the chance of such a voyage. Dick was eagerly watching for the boat to meet the edge of thin ice that stretched for a good many yards out from the jetty. Would the boat simply cut the ice or would it lift its nose over the ice and then break through it from above by its own weight?

"Hullo!" called Peggy, from out in the bay and then, heading directly for the jety, settled down to row as hard as she could.

"She's going to ram it," cried Titty.

"Now, now, now!" shouted Roger. "She's into it."

Dick, his eye to the telescope, watched the nose of the boat cutting through the water.

Everybody held their breath.

There was a queer, cracking sound, taken up all round the bay, as the boat drove on, forcing a sheet of thin ice aslant out of the water before it, then another, then another, until Peggy's oars were slipping and hitting ice on either side of her.

"She's going to get stuck," cried Roger.

"Go it, Peggy!" called Titty.

"It's easier under Darien," shouted John.

Peggy scarcely glanced towards them. She was standing up now, holding one of her oars the wrong way round, and, with its blade above her head, was bringing the solid end of it down again and again on the ice round the bows of her boat. She smashed the ice as far as she could reach and then paddled the boat nearer, using her oar as if she was in a canoe. Again she stuck. Again she stood up in the bows and used her oar like a pike.

"Don't fall in," shouted Titty.

"Teach your grandmother," came from the boat, but Peggy did not even look up as she said it.

She hurried to the stern and drove her oar downwards to find bottom. She found it, and pushed. The boat moved forward. She prodded downwards again, and found it not so deep. Again the boat moved forward in the tinkling ice. She was close in now.

PEGGY IN THE CAT ICE

"Let's have hold of an oar," called John, who had come running to the jetty on seeing that Peggy meant to land there and nowhere else.

Peggy looked up at last, came forward again, and reached as far as she could with her dripping oar. John caught the end of it, and in another moment she had her hands on the jetty.

"Nancy'll be jolly sorry she missed that," said Peggy, with a grin.

"Where is Nancy?" everybody asked.

"She's got a bit of a jaw-ache," said Peggy. "She was holding it to the fire when it was time to start, and she said there'd be more room without her and told me to get along at once. She didn't know what it was going to be like."

"I'm coming now," said John, throwing the coiled rope into the bottom of the boat, "and then you, Susan. We'll want as much weight in her as possible to keep her steady while the others come aboard. We can't get her alongside. Are you two accustomed to boats?"

"No," said Dorothea.

"Well, you come along after Susan. And as soon as you're in the boat, sit down. You can shift afterwards. But sit down right away. It's horribly easy to tip over, coming aboard by the bows."

"And a cold bath waiting," said Roger.

Dorothea managed better than she had expected, sitting on the edge of the jetty, sliding down into the boat and kneeling instantly while grabbing the gunwale on each side. Luckily she had nothing to carry. Dick, who had put his telescope back in his pocket, scrambled down after her, and then, when the visitors were safely aboard, Titty and Roger, the able-seaman and the ship's boy, did not say anything, but just showed how it ought to be done.

"Shall I shove off now, sir?" asked Roger.

"Peggy's the skipper," said John.

"Sorry," said Peggy, "I was forgetting Nancy isn't here. Shove her off forrard."

"Aye, aye, sir," said Roger, and the boat began to move stern-first out again through the broken ice.

"Heads out of the way," said Peggy, swinging an oar forward, getting the end of it against the jetty, and giving a final shove ... "I say, John, we can't row yet. Will you paddle over that side?"

"If it goes on freezing it'll be solid again by this evening, and you'll have to land us under Darien on the way home."

"Cook says it's going to freeze for a month on end," said Peggy. "If only the snow had come ten days ago we'd have been going to the North Pole over the ice."

"The snow's better than nothing," said John.

"Couldn't we go to the North Pole in the boat?" asked Dick, but all the others, except Dorothea, looked at him with astonishment.

"Not in a *rowing* boat," said Peggy.

"*Swallow* and *Amazon* are out of the water, or we might have sailed," said Titty. "Rowing boats don't count."

"Too easy," said John, "and too much like summer. Sledges are the proper thing. Sledges and skates. If only the ice had come a bit sooner."

As soon as John and Peggy had worked the boat out of the cat ice into the open water there was some careful changing of places. Four oars were put out. John and Susan on the middle thwart, and Titty and Roger in the bows, took an oar apiece. Peggy, captain for the moment, sat in the stern with Dorothea and Dick. She was glad of a chance to cool down after rowing the whole way from Beckfoot.

"Pull left, pull left," she shouted, and they saw why as they passed the point on the northern side of the bay, where the water was shallow and ice was showing for ten or a dozen yards off shore.

"I say," said Dick, "we never *have* rowed."

Dorothea found Peggy looking at her.

'We'd awfully like to try," she said.

"All right," said Peggy. "You can take an oar apiece as soon as we're through Rio Bay."

"Thank you very much indeed," said Dick, and settled down to watch the rowers to see exactly how it was done.

Pull. Blades out. Swing forward. Dip. Pull. Blades out. Swing forward. Dip. All four rowers working exactly together. It was like a piece of clockwork. No splashing either. Just a dribbling of water from the blades as they swept forward after each long pull. And the boat slipping along with a gentle noise under her bows. Would he ever be able to do it? It looked easy enough, and yet ...

A narrow ribbon of thin ice stretched round the promontory and all along by the boathouses and building sheds into Rio Bay. Looking across the channel towards Long Island, they could see that it too had a fringe of ice. By the steamer pier in the bay there were a crowd of people.

"They think it's going to bear," cried Peggy. "Look, there's Sammy, the policeman, trying the ice under the hotel. If it'll bear him it'll bear anybody. That's why he's prodding it with a pole and keeping safe on the landing stage."

"It must be a lot thicker in there," said John.

"It always freezes in Rio Bay first of anywhere," said Peggy. "Hi! Pull right. Pull right. I ought to have been watching. My fault. We were nearly into the Chicken."

"Chicken?" said Dorothea, looking about her for the drowning bird.

"That rock," said Peggy, as they swept past it, near enough to touch the ice round it with the blades of their oars. "There's the steamer buoy, and then the Chicken and then the Hen, and after that it's more or less clear, except for good-sized islands."

They swept on, past the Hen, across the Bay, and out beyond Long Island. There were two or three smaller islands to be seen, but not a single other boat on that great sheet of water that lay there as still as if it were already frozen between the snow-covered shores and the great hills rising above them, every gully and ravine shadowed blue in the sunlit snow.

"It wouldn't be much good even if *Swallow* and *Amazon* were afloat," said John. "There isn't wind enough to stir a candle-flame."

"That's why it's freezing so fast," said Peggy.

"Does the whole lake freeze?" asked Dorothea, looking far ahead to where the water seemed to disappear under the hills.

"It does sometimes," said Peggy, "and it will this year. Everybody says so, and it'll all be wasted on Eskimos, because we shall be going back to school."

"And the North Pole's right at the top of it?"

"As far as you can see ... Easy all!" she called out, and the oars rested and the rowers turned round to look towards the north, like many explorers before them.

"Well, the snow's come in time, anyway," said John. "It would have been pretty rotten going to the North Pole over dry land."

"Didn't you two say you wanted to row?" said Susan.

One by one, carefully instructed by experienced seamen, Dorothea and Dick changed places with John and Susan, and took each an oar.

"Now then," said Peggy. "The main thing is to keep time with each other."

"And don't you two in the bows go bunting them in the back," added John. "Remember, they've never done it before."

"Aye, aye, sir," came from the bow thwart, where Titty and Roger were waiting, their oars raised from the water.

"Give way," said Peggy.

"That means, row," said Titty, for the ears of the two beginners. They had guessed as much and, very nearly at the same moment, reached forward, dipped their oars, and pulled.

"Not so deep ... That's better. Keep together. Don't lift the oar so high on the way back ... It ought to go back in a straight line ... As far forward as you can. Don't bend your arms till the last moment. Pull with your back and your legs." The air seemed full of flying directions. And something seemed inclined to hit one in the back if one changed the time while trying to do what one was told. Dorothea did her best. So did Dick, who had already found some private method of his own. "One and two. And one and two." Dorothea heard him counting and carefully kept time with him. The voices from the stern came again. "You're not doing half badly for a first go." Gradually she became able to think of things calmly, watching the blade of her oar as it went forward. "They're doing jolly well." "Don't try to go too fast." "It's no good racing." "There ..." A heavy bump shook the boat. Dick had somehow disappeared from beside her. His feet were in the air. His oar had missed a stroke and splashed across the top of the water.

"How did it happen?" asked Dick.

There was a laugh from the experienced seamen. "It was a crab. Catching one. You didn't get hold of the water with your oar. We've all done it. Why, Roger ... '

"I didn't catch a single crab last year," said Roger indignantly.

"You were catching them all the time the year you learnt. Everybody does. You needn't mind."

Dick struggled to his place again, and the rowing went on, after an unfortunate attempt to begin at once, before the others were ready.

"Try again," said Peggy. "Now. Give way."

With less hurry and greater care Dick and Dorothea pulled on up the lake, while Roger and Titty, sitting behind them, watched their moving backs and rowed with even greater care, to prevent accidents of another kind.

"That's enough for now," said Peggy at last. "We'd better have John and Susan at the oars for getting into the river."

Again there was changing of places, and Dick and Dorothea, very hot and oddly trembly at the knees, moved back to the stern, and sat beside the skipper. They looked at each other across her, smiled faintly, but said never a word.

Now that they were sitting still once more, and being rowed by other people, it seemed as if they were looking at a new lake. Close ahead of them was that promontory of rock and heather that Captain Nancy had pointed out to Dick. It looked now as if it were made of white sugar. There was the flagstaff sticking up out of the snow. Dick turned round to look back down the lake. They ought to be able to see the observatory from here. Somewhere up on that hill-side, beyond the islands.

"Trim the boat," said the skipper sternly, but explained a moment later, "You see, if you don't keep her balanced it's beastly for the men at the oars."

They rounded the Beckfoot promontory, that glittered in the sunshine. Beyond it two great banks of brown and withered reeds marked the entrance to the river.

"Here we are," said Peggy to the visitors. "This is the Amazon River. Pull left. Pull left. Easy right. Pull left. Back water with your right. Pull left." The boat swept round and headed in towards the reed beds. Suddenly the reeds opened, and they could see the clear way into the river and up towards a grey house that stood a little way back from the banks.

"This is where Nancy and I hid in *Amazon* the night the Swallows made a raid on our boathouse. We were in among those reeds."

"And what happened?" said Roger gleefully from the bows.

"Somebody found an octopus," said Peggy.

D

"And after that?" said Roger. "Who lost their ship?"

But Peggy took no notice of these jeers.

"Pull right," she said. "Easy ... Left a little."

The boat was slipping up the river between the banks of reeds. There was a faint crackling as the wash from the boat stirred the reeds and broke the ice with which they were encrusted at the level of the water.

"That's our boathouse."

"What's that crest?" said Dorothea. "What is it? There's a skull and cross-bones."

"Oh, that," said Peggy. "All part of the same thing. It belongs to the Amazon Pirates. Summer, you know. Nothing to do with the Arctic ... Hullo! Where's Nancy? She promised she'd be down to help with the landing."

The rowers stopped pulling.

"Aren't you going to take her into the boathouse?" said John.

"Ice in there already," said Peggy. "It's out of the current, and not deep. I had a job to get her out this morning. We'll push her nose into the bank by those reeds. She'll be all right there for going back this afternoon. But where on earth is Nancy? Gently. Left. Left. Easy. Ship your oars. Ready, Roger? Roger always jumps out with the painter," she explained to Dorothea. "He always does it in their own boat."

Roger had shipped his oar and had the painter in his hand. The boat slid on through a yard or two of reeds. As it touched the bank Roger was ashore.

But of Captain Nancy there was nothing to be seen.

CHAPTER VIII

LOST LEADER

From the first moment of their landing, Dorothea knew that they were not wanted. Something had happened. The very house looked absent-minded, as if it were thinking of something else. This was not the sort of welcome they would have had if all had been as it was yesterday when Mrs Blackett had been so laughing and jolly, asking them to visit an Eskimo settlement on the other side of the fiord. And for Captain Nancy not to be at the boathouse to meet them ... It was queer enough for her to have let Peggy make that Arctic voyage without her, but this was queerer still.

"Nancy's probably lurking somewhere," said John doubtfully.

"She's probably still toasting her jaw," said Peggy. "She said it was very stiff and beastly. Anyway, we'll soon know."

She took the painter from Roger and tied it to a post in the bank. There was deep snow everywhere and, with Peggy at the head of them, they followed a trail of footprints across the lawn towards the little door that opened into the garden on that side of the house.

But, before they had come anywhere near it, that door opened and Mrs Blackett came out on the step.

"Oh, Peggy," she said, "I do wish you had waited a minute or two ..."

Anybody could see that Mrs Blackett was bothered about something. She went on at once, "Now then, you others, you mustn't think I'm not very glad to see you, but I'm not at all sure I ought to let you into the house ..."

99

"But you asked them," said Peggy.

"What is it poor Nancy calls you?" said Mrs Blackett. "Galoot, isn't it? Of course I asked them. And I'm very glad to see them. But I want you now, all of you, to slip along the road to the bridge and catch the doctor. You'll only just be in time. I telephoned just now, but they said he'd already gone this way, up the valley to Nook Farm, where somebody's broken an ankle. You'll catch him on his way back if you're quick. I won't let you into the house just now. Not that it makes much difference when you've been stewing with her in that igloo of yours all these days ... "

"Is it Nancy?" asked Peggy.

"Yes, of course it is," said Mrs Blackett. "Now then, if you want to help, you'll hurry along to the bridge and hold up the doctor, and ask him to come and have a look at her."

She gave them a cheerful, kindly smile, but they knew that it was only the front of a smile, because, behind it, she was thinking of something else.

"I wonder if Nancy's really ill," said Susan, as they came out of the Beckfoot gates into the road.

"She never is," said Peggy. "And anyhow, she must have been awfully quick about it. It was only a jaw-ache when I set out to fetch you."

"Mrs Blackett thinks she is," said Dorothea.

"Oh, that's just mother," said Peggy. "Well, anyway, we'll give a bit of a shock to the doctor."

"He's probably accustomed to illness," said Dorothea.

"Holding him up, I mean," said Peggy.

They hurried along the road at a good pace. The others were telling Dick and Dorothea about the Kanchenjunga expedition, and the trouble over the Great-aunt that had happened in the summer. "We camped out all night half-way up the mountain," Titty said. "And saw wild goats," added Roger, "and then I slept in a charcoal-burner's hut." These children, thought Dorothea, certainly did seem to have all the luck in the way of adventures. Why did things like that never happen to her or to Dick, but only in the books that she was always planning to write?

"You mean it really did happen?" she asked.

"Honest Pirate," said Peggy, forgetting that at the moment they were Arctic explorers. "That's the wood where John came and made the owl noise."

"You can just see the lagoon if you climb up on that gate," said Roger.

John had said nothing for some time. He was looking more and more serious. Something was on his mind. "I say," he said at last, "it'll be pretty rotten if Nancy isn't all right for going to the Pole."

A sudden gloom fell over everybody, though Peggy did say, "Of course she'll be all right. She planned the whole thing, and she isn't going to miss it now."

They came to the place where the road forked. To the right, it turned sharp over a bridge, crossing the river, on its way to the head of the lake and round to the little town that the Swallows and Amazons never called by any other name than that of Rio. To the left it turned up the valley between the fells. Nook Farm was up that road, and the doctor would have to cross the bridge on his way home.

"Perhaps he's gone already," said Titty.

"He hasn't," said Dick.

"How do you know?" said Dorothea, not that she did not believe him, but because she knew he must have some very good reason to be so very sure.

"There's a motor car gone up this road with chains on its wheels, and it's never come back," said Dick.

John, Susan, Peggy, Titty, and Roger examined the tracks with great care.

"Not half bad," said John at last. Dick blushed, and Dorothea felt a pleasant glow of pride. You never knew with Dick. Sometimes he would be thinking about nothing but geology or stars, and then, when nobody was expecting it, he would come out with something that even people like John and Nancy could not help admiring.

"About the holding up," said Peggy. "If Nancy were doing it, she'd hide in those trees at the other side of the bridge, with all of us, of course, and then we'd leap out with a terrific war whoop just as he came along."

But here, Susan put her foot down.

"All right in a wide road," she said, "and if it's just one or two. But he isn't expecting us, and he won't be able to pull up. Anyhow, Titty and Roger can't do it."

"And he'll be going too fast," said John. "He'll be past us before he knows what's happened. He'll drive right on and never know he was really wanted."

Peggy gave way at once.

"All right," she said. "We'll stop him gradually. We'll spread ourselves out all along the road, and by the time he's passed seven of us, all signalling to him and yelling like fury, he'll know something's up."

"Listen," said Dick.

They were standing on the bridge, and the noise of the little river, pouring over the stones higher upstream before settling down to glide quietly between its snow-covered banks, made it difficult to hear much else. But Dick had been carefully trying to make himself deaf to all noises except the one for which he was listening.

"He's coming," said Titty.

"Spread out. Spread out!" cried Peggy. "That way. Hare along as far as you can."

"Don't stand in the middle of the road, you two," Dorothea

heard the careful Susan say to Titty and Roger. She said the same herself to Dick.

In a few moments the whole seven of them were scattered at intervals along the road that led up the valley. The road was narrow and winding, and Dorothea, near the bridge, could see only Titty, standing in the nearest bend. She could hear a distant car. It stopped. Perhaps the doctor was talking to someone at the roadside. It came on again, a low hum with the rattle of snow-chains swinging against mudguards. Suddenly, far away up the road, she heard a most blood-curdling yell. Who would ever think that Peggy could made such a noise? Then another, a loud, urgent shout. John's probably. Then a shout from Dick. Then Roger's shrill, ear-piercing screech. Then a loud "Hallo," like someone trying to make themselves heard through a telephone in the middle of a thunderstorm. Susan, no doubt. Then she saw Titty waving frantically. She heard her screaming, "Stop! Stop!" and just then, already slowing up, the motor car came round the corner. It stopped. She could see Titty climbing on the running-board, and talking to the driver. The others came running up. Dorothea ran to meet them, wondering what would happen next. How would the doctor take this method of letting him know that somebody wanted to see him?

She came up in time to see a small, neat, pink-faced man, with a bowler hat and white chamois leather gloves, leaning over into the back of his car and opening both the side doors.

"What's that?" he was saying. "Toothache? Nancy? Ruth? Oh, all right, Peggy, I know the young woman you mean. How many of you are there? So these are the Swallows? I've heard of them from your Uncle Jim. Four of them, and then ... What? Dorothea and Dick? All right. Let them all come. The car's meant to hold four, so there ought to be room for a mere eight. Last come first served. Dorothea, did they say your name was? Hop in here. No, I won't have more than one in front. It's none too easy driving, even with chains. Make sure that door's shut."

They were off.

"We'll be having the lake frozen over if it goes on like this," said the doctor over his shoulder.

"What's the good?" said Peggy, from behind. "We're all going back to school in three days' time. Day after tomorrow's our last day."

"I'd forgotten that," said the doctor. "Hullo. Steady then." The car skidded a little in the snow as he turned a bend on a steep little dip in the road.

In a very few minutes the car was turning in at Beckfoot. The front door opened as it pulled up. Somebody must have been watching for it from a window. Again Dorothea had that queer, unpleasant feeling that somehow it would have been better if they had not been there.

"Will you come straight up, doctor?" said Mrs Blackett. "I'm so glad they were able to catch you. And you children can wait in the study a few minutes. No, Peggy, not in the dining-room. Nancy was in there a long time holding her head to the fire … "

Dorothea saw Susan and John look seriously at each other, but not even Peggy said anything. There was a general wiping of boots (Roger was caught and brought back for this purpose before he had taken much snow into the house). Then the seven went into a room in which a fire had only just been lighted. Dick at once noticed a microscope under a glass cover. Titty and Dorothea went straight to the bookshelves, but the books seemed to be mostly about geography, chemistry, mining and such things.

"Uncle Jim uses this room when he's at home," Peggy explained. "These are all the things he hasn't got room for in the houseboat."

"What houseboat?" asked Dick.

"On the lake," said Peggy, "between Holly Howe and our island."

Nobody sat down. They wandered about the room, looking at things, touching the queer paper weights on the desk, mostly lumps of dark stone with a glitter of metal in them, and staring up at a bundle of spears, a couple of spotted leopard-skin shields, and an assegai, a club with a large round knob at the end of it, and the jawbone of some big fish, dried and mounted on a wooden plaque. At any other time there would have been talk about these things, but just then even Dick was wondering what was happening upstairs, and whether Captain Nancy was going to be all right for the expedition to the Pole.

At last they heard a door open up on the landing, and the doctor's voice, "You'll just have to make the best of it, Nancy, and keep away from looking-glasses ... " Then they heard him coming downstairs with Mrs Blackett ... "Mumps, my dear madam, mumps. She'll have a face like a pumpkin tomorrow. Of course ... Yes, keep her in bed and keep her warm. The sooner the swelling comes up, the sooner it'll be down again ... Three to four weeks. Oh, no. She'll not be free from infection till at least a week after the swelling's gone down."

"And what about Peggy?"

"You'll have to isolate her, of course. Not that it really matters ... Some schools ... "

The drawing-room door closed, and they heard no more.

"If it's mumps," said Susan, "she won't be able to come to the North Pole."

"Well, we can't go then," said John.

"We'll have to put it off for another year," said Peggy.

"We shan't be here another year," said Titty. "Not in winter."

"What's that noise?" said Dick suddenly.

There was the slow creak of a door being stealthily opened upstairs, and then, very low, but still loud enough for everybody to hear it, a very bad imitation of an owl.

"Tu-whooooooo ... Whoooooooooo."

"It's Nancy," whispered Peggy.

"They simply can't do owls," said Roger. "She ought to have done a duck."

But nobody heard him. Peggy first, they had hurried out into the hall.

A queer figure was leaning over the banisters above them. In blue pyjamas, with a handkerchief round her face, and her red woolly outdoor cap pulled right down over the handkerchief, Nancy looked a good deal more piratical than usual.

She held one hand to her jaw, and spoke in a dreadful whisper: "Mumps!"

"We know," said Susan. "We're most awfully sorry."

"And the day after tomorrow's the last day," said Peggy.

"There's no point in going to the Pole without you," said John. "And it wouldn't be fair, anyhow."

Nancy began a laugh, but the expression of her face changed suddenly, and she put up the other hand, tenderly, as if she were going to put a broken jaw back into place.

"Galoots!" she whispered. "Galoots! Oh, donks, idiots, turnip-heads! Don't you see it's the very best thing that could have happened? It just puts everything right. It's saved the whole expedition. It means another whole month to the holidays. And the lake'll be frozen all over long before the end of a month. The expedition will go to the Pole in the proper way, over the Arctic ice."

"But you can't make much of an expedition with only one," said Peggy.

"We shall all be at school," said Roger dolefully.

"Will you?" whispered Nancy. "Will you? Ow! My jaw!

Galoots, the whole lot of you. Why, that was the very first thing
I asked him ... "

"Nancy, Nancy!" cried Mrs Blackett, coming out of the
drawing-room with the doctor, "go back to bed this minute."

"Ask him yourselves," said Nancy, and disappeared in a hurry.

"She means we can't get rid of you," said the doctor. "They
won't have you back at school until I can say that there's no
chance of your coming out with mumps after you get there and
giving it to everybody else."

"Mrs Jackson's got a spare room at Holly Howe, hasn't she?"
Mrs Blackett asked Susan.

"There's the one mother and Bridget were in."

"We'll have to get her to put Peggy in it. She'll go back with
you now. The doctor very kindly says he'll drive you round."

"Can't we go in the boat?" said Peggy.

"Who is to bring it back? And what about you Swallows?
Your mother told me she was leaving the health papers with one
of you for me to sign the day you go back."

"I've got them," said John.

"If they're the same as Nancy's and Peggy's you won't be
able to go back either. I don't know what your mother'll say.
I feel most dreadfully to blame. But really, where Nancy managed
to pick it up I don't know. There's no mumps in the valley."

"Not go back to school?" said Roger.

"For how long?" asked Titty.

"Oh, I don't know," said Mrs Blackett. "Pretty nearly a month,
I suppose, unless one of you comes out with it, and then it'll be
longer still."

"None of you feels like it now?" asked the doctor. "No stiff
jaws?"

And then, suddenly, Mrs Blackett turned to Dorothea. "And
what about you?" she asked, making a rueful face. "Have you
got certificates to sign, too?"

"Mother put them in an envelope and gave them to Mrs Dixon," said Dorothea.

"And money for the tickets," said Dick.

Mrs Blackett laughed. "Well, well," she said, "I'm coming round to see Mrs Jackson this afternoon to talk about Peggy, and I'll go on and talk to Mrs Dixon at the same time. Off you go now. You mustn't keep the doctor waiting."

"Oh, bother," said Peggy. "The boat's just tied to the bank, and there's ice in the boathouse. We ought to take it right out if we're not going to use it."

"I'll have it hauled out for you," said Mrs Blackett.

"I'm sure Nancy'd say we ought to do it now," said Peggy.

"I'll give them a hand," said the doctor.

"That's really very good of you," said Mrs Blackett. "I'll just scribble a note to Mrs Jackson."

The doctor, with seven helpers, made short work of hauling the rowing boat up the bank and turning it over on the top of a couple of low trestles that Peggy brought out of the boathouse. The alpine rope, now not to be used for Kanchenjunga, was stowed in the car. Mrs Blackett came out with her note.

"I suppose it's all right my going round there this afternoon," she said, "after being with Nancy?"

"Don't kiss her," said the doctor, smiling, "or Peggy either."

"I don't want to. Horrid little wretches, both of them," said Mrs Blackett, and made a face at Peggy, when she saw how surprised she looked.

"What about the party?" said Peggy.

"You'll just have to have it at Holly Howe," said Mrs Blackett. "I'm very sorry, Dorothea, but you see how it is."

"Of course," said Dorothea. She had known the moment they landed that something was wrong. Illness explained everything, and nobody could possibly mind.

"In you go," said the doctor. "Room for everybody."

Mrs Blackett waved from the step.

In another moment the car was moving out of the gate. The visit to Beckfoot was over, and they were on their way to Holly Howe, over the little bridge, and round by the head of the lake.

CHAPTER IX

QUARANTINE

"AND so Miss Nancy's got mumps," said Mrs Jackson at Holly
Howe, looking at the note Mrs Blackett had sent her. "And
Miss Peggy's to sleep here. And none of them had a bite to eat.
And you two from Dixon's and all. Eh, deary me, but it's a lucky
thing we've the cold roast beef to cut at."

"No one's ever gone short in your house yet, Mrs Jackson,"
said the doctor. "Well, good luck to you all. I'll be round to
see them every now and then. And better let me know at once
the moment any of them feels a bit stiff in the jaw."

He drove off out of the yard and up the field, taking Roger
with him to hop out, open the gate into the road, and shut it
after the car had gone through.

By the time Roger had come running down again, Mrs
Jackson had a cloth laid, and was dealing out platefuls of cold
roast beef and ham. John had bolted upstairs to fetch their school
health certificates. The doctor had just glanced at them and
nodded. Susan, Titty, and Peggy were reading them now, and
hungry as everybody was, they found the certificates so interest-
ing that Mrs Jackson asked them what had become of their
appetites.

Susan showed hers to Dorothea.

On the top of it, in large handsome letters, was the name of
a school, and then, under it, in ordinary type:—

"I hereby certify that during the last holidays...............
...............('That space is for our names,' said Susan) has

not suffered from any infectious disorder, and, to the best of my knowledge and belief, has not been where any infectious disorder existed ...

Signature..................................

Note. - If the above certificate cannot be signed, the pupil concerned must not return to the school without permission."

"There's no getting out of it," said Susan. "The things can't be signed."

"Who wants to get out of it?" said Peggy. "Nancy said herself it's the very best thing that could have happened."

"It's really as if the Christmas holidays began today instead of on the day they did begin," said Titty.

"It's lucky it's not the football term," said John. "A month might make just the difference about getting into the fifteen. But anyhow, it'll be pretty awful coming back to find everybody a whole month to windward and have all that leeway to make up."

"Mother'll be awfully bothered about it," said Susan. "She'll be wondering if she oughtn't to come home."

"Well, she jolly well mustn't," said John. "We've none of us got it yet anyway."

"I hadn't thought of that," said Titty.

Roger, like Peggy, thoroughly agreed with Nancy. For some minutes he had been busy and silent but he had been thinking things over like the rest of them.

"Of course it's too late now," he said at last, while his plate was being passed along for a second helping, "or we could have put an advertisement in the newspaper."

"What *do* you mean?" said Susan.

"Mumps for anyone who wants them," said Roger.

"Anybody'd be willing to pay quite a lot of his pocket-money to have mumps so that he'd get an extra month of holiday."

Everybody laughed, but Roger went on: "Why not? We've got an extra month just because we've seen Nancy. She could charge sixpence each to shake hands with people. Anybody'd be glad to pay. But it's too late now ... "

"How do you mean, too late?" said Peggy.

"By the time we got the advertisement printed everybody else will have gone back to school."

"Money-grubbing little brute," said John.

"Well, of course, she could shake hands free with anybody she really liked," said Roger.

Dorothea had been listening as if the whole question hardly concerned Dick and herself. It was these others who were going to be here a whole month longer than they had expected.

"Are your papers just the same?" Susan asked her.

"I don't know," said Dorothea. "Perhaps it isn't all schools that mind."

"I bet they do," said John. "No school wants to have a whole lot of people bursting out with spots all over, or faces like pumpkins, or turning red like lobsters or green and yellow with any kind of plague. Of course, they all do their best to keep clear."

"Roger's all wrong," said Titty. "Everybody'll want us to keep away. If it was summer, we'd have to hoist a yellow flag on *Swallow*."

"On *Amazon* too," said Peggy.

"But what for?" said Dick.

"Haven't you ever been to sea?" said Roger.

"Steady on, Roger," said John.

"Why yellow?" asked Dorothea.

"Quarantine," said John.

"To show that we've come from a plague port and can't go ashore till we've been passed by the doctor," said Peggy.

"Nancy wouldn't have a quarantine flag," said John. "She'd have the plague flag itself, squares of yellow and black."

"Let's make her one," said Titty.

And with that all doubts were gone. Good or bad, the mumps could not be helped. And here was something that could be done at once. The moment Mrs Jackson came in with a big cold apple tart, which she had luckily cooked the day before, Peggy and Susan and Titty, all together, asked her if she had some yellow stuff and some black that would do for the making of a flag.

"We must put a yellow flag on the envelope when we write to Malta," said Titty. "So as to break the news gently. I've got my paint-box."

"Let's get a plague flag done so that mother can take it back with her this afternoon," said Peggy.

"We must hoist a yellow one on the igloo," said Titty.

"And we'll take it with us to hoist at the North Pole," said John.

"The Polar bears won't be keen on getting mumps," said Roger. "It'll keep them off like anything."

Luckily some visitor or other had been making a yellow silk frock while staying at Holly Howe and had left a lot of bits. Mrs Jackson had been meaning to send them across the lake to old Mrs Swainson down at Low End, who always wanted scraps for her patchwork quilts. "But you know how it is," she said, "what with one thing and another, jobs don't get done by thinking of them," and so the yellow silk scraps were still at Holly Howe.

"Mrs Swainson won't mind," said Titty. "She's got baskets and baskets full of scraps already."

"And a quarantine flag's more important than a quilt," said Roger. "It doesn't matter what colour a quilt is, but a quarantine flag's simply got to be yellow."

So, later in the afternoon, when Mrs Blackett arrived at Holly

Howe in a hired car, bringing with her into the house a strong smell of carbolic soap, she found everybody busy. Mrs Jackson had torn up an old black petticoat, and Susan had cut out two yellow squares and two black ones and she and Dorothea had stitched them neatly together, folding the edges one over another so that there should be no fraying when the flag was flying in the wind. John, with Dick and Roger as eager pupils, had put a loop in one end of a short piece of thin rope, and at the other end had fixed a little wooden toggle carved out of a bit of firewood. Susan was now putting in the last stitches in fixing the little plague flag on its rope, while the three boys were busy with more ropes and toggles for the quarantine flags of plain yellow silk that were being hemmed by Peggy and Titty.

"What on earth are you all doing?" asked Mrs Blackett. "Is this a Dorcas party?"

Susan held up the black and yellow flag, finished and ready for hoisting.

"Plague flag," said Peggy. "For you and Nancy to hoist at Beckfoot. The plain yellow ones are for us, to show that we don't know yet whether we're plague-stricken or not."

"Poor old Nancy won't do much flag-hoisting just yet," said her mother. "She's got no end of a temperature this afternoon."

"She will when you show her the flag," said Peggy.

"Well, I'll take it," said Mrs Blackett, "but I don't promise to hand it over at once. And now I want to see those school papers. Oh, you've got them ready, have you? ... Yes. I thought so. You'll have to make up your minds to another month of holidays, and I dare say you're as pleased as Punch over it. I must just have a talk with Mrs Jackson and then I'll take you two on with me and we'll see what your schools have to say about it."

She went off and they heard her laughing in the kitchen with Mrs Jackson. Then they heard her going upstairs to look at Peggy's room. "Quarantine begins from today," they heard her saying as she was coming downstairs again. "Twenty-eight days, the doctor says, and if any of them gets mumps now, it'll be another twenty-eight days from then. No, I'll not be coming over again until Nancy's clear of infection. If it was only Peggy it wouldn't matter, but with the Walkers and these other children all with their parents out of England, I won't take any risk at all. Anybody who gets it will come across to Beckfoot to be nursed. Oh no, not the Callum children. I'm sure Mrs Dixon will want to look after them."

She put her head in at the door.

"It's all right," she said. "Mrs Jackson's got no one else coming, so she's going to keep the lot of you. I'm sure that's what Mrs Walker would like best. I'm going to write to her this evening."

"We all will," said John.

"Put a yellow flag on the back of your envelope," said Roger.

"I'll paint one at once," said Titty.

"Good," said Mrs Blackett. "I'll use it if you have it ready by the time I come back. Are you ready, you two?"

"Are you going to signal tomorrow?" said Dick as he went out.

"Signalling as usual," said John.

"Don't forget your quarantine flag," said Titty, and Dick put it in his pocket and took it with him.

*

Ten minutes later, Mrs Blackett, Dorothea and Dick were at Dixon's Farm, and Mrs Blackett was saying that really just then she would rather not have any elderberry wine, and how was Mr Dixon, and was Silas still bothered with his rheumatism, and what a hand Mrs Dixon had for pastry ... those pork pies ... and so to the question she had come about — of Nancy's mumps, and whether it would affect Dick's and Dorothea's going back to school. With Mrs Dixon and Mrs Blackett in the room together, the air was so full of talk that it left Dorothea feeling almost out of breath, although she herself had said nothing at all.

"Aye," said Mrs Dixon, at last, "I have them. Mrs Callum, poor lamb, she gave them to me just as we were catching that train, and you know what it is, Mrs Blackett, catching trains in towns, not like going up to the station here and having a word with old Bob, that's been porter and guard these thirty year. Yes, she gave me all their papers, but I've never looked into them to this day, though I had it in my mind to look tomorrow, with them going back to school so soon."

"But they won't be going back. At least I don't think so. Mumps. Didn't I explain? Nancy's gone down with it today, so I've sent Peggy over to stay with the Walker children at Holly Howe. They can none of them go back to school for a month, because they've been playing with Nancy right up to the last minute. The same with these. They may not be able to go back, either. And what's to be done about that? We'd better have a look at those papers, to make sure."

"What's to be done about it, Mrs Blackett? Why, what do you think, now? I nursed their mother through mumps thirty year ago, and if they get mumps here, why, they're welcome, and I'll nurse them, too. With Mrs Callum away with the Professor, digging up bones and rubbish heaps, poor lambs, they'll be better with me than in any school ... "

"I'm sure they will."

"And what is mumps, after all?" said Mrs Dixon. "Why, in my young days we thought nothing of it. But where's the good of them taking it back to school with them and having it there, lying in a draught likely, and Mrs Callum so far away ... Why," Mrs Dixon suddenly laughed, "I mind now, when she had mumps herself, she had two of her dolls have mumps at the same time, and the way she looked after them would have been a lesson to a doctor. She kept me fairly on the run, what with hot poultices for their poor cheeks, and tying handkerchiefs round their swollen jaws. And I mind now how angry she was if I said owt to make her laugh, not that she cared for herself, oh no, but her two dolls had mumps so bad they couldn't bear laughing, no, not so much as a smile."

"Mother's often told us about those two dolls," said Dorothea.

"And are you like Nancy and Peggy, not caring about dolls?" asked Mrs Blackett, when Mrs Dixon had hurried upstairs at last to find that envelope.

"I used to like them once," said Dorothea, "a long time ago."

Mrs Blackett was already thinking of something else. "There's this about it," she said. "You might have picked up mumps any-where – in the train or, oh, anywhere, even if you had never met Nancy at all."

Mrs Dixon came down with the certificates, and one glance was enough to show Mrs Blackett that it was the same with the Callums as it was with the Walkers. "There you are," she said, " 'suffered from … associated with any person suffering from any infectious disorder … not to return to school until expiration of the normal quarantine period for such disorder.' No. There's no going back to school for either of them."

Letters had to be written to explain that Dick and Dorothea would not be coming back on the usual day, and as Mrs Dixon said she was no hand at letter-writing and Dixon was no better, Mrs Blackett sat down to write the letters at once so that Mrs Dixon could sign them. After that she drove off again in a hurry to call at Holly Howe to make sure of Mrs Walker's address in Malta, and then to go back to Beckfoot to care for her exulting patient.

*

Nancy's face was beginning to swell and it hurt her very much to laugh. She suppressed her chuckles as much as she could be-cause of the pain in her jaw, but nothing could prevent her from

bouncing up and down in her bed at the thought that everything
was coming right after all, that the winter was not going to be
wasted, and that the Polar expedition would not be a tame affair
of mere pretence. She, herself, might not be able to take part in it,
but it would be the real thing, a march across the frozen sea.

CHAPTER X

DOING WITHOUT NANCY

"SIGNALLING as usual," John had said, and for the first three days they tried to do everything else as usual, too. Each morning the black diamond was hoisted at Holly Howe and the explorers met at the igloo, where they hoisted their yellow flags, made roaring fires, cooked their dinners, and talked of Eskimos instead of mere natives. They swept the snow from the ice on the tarn and had skating practice morning and afternoon. Titty was already giving both her feet an equal chance and Roger was getting through an hour of skating without sitting down, except when he tried to turn a corner too fast. John had let Dick use the saw, and as well as the woodpile in the corner of the igloo, a neat stack of sawn firewood was piling up outside. They might, John said, have nearly a month to wait before ice conditions were suitable and it was as well to be prepared. There were signal practices once or twice a day, and Dick and Dorothea, by going very slowly and looking up the code, could signal messages to each other in dot and dash. Dick was happy enough with his sawing wood, skating, and the stars at night, but Dorothea knew very well that, for all the others, things were somehow very different without Nancy.

Peggy was doing her best. She knew what had been in Nancy's mind when she had first planned the expedition to the Pole. None of the others had been born on the shores of the lake, and now, with Nancy ill, Peggy was trying to fill her place. She even tried to use Nancy's language, but, somehow, it was not the same thing as when Captain Nancy had been there herself, shivering timbers,

119

talking of jib-booms and bobstays, and keeping everybody busy.

People kept on saying, "If only Nancy was here," or "What would Nancy have said about that?" The expedition itself seemed to have lost its point, until they agreed in council that it was to be put off until she was done with the mumps and able to come too.

"But will she be done in time?" Roger had asked.

"If she hurries up, she will," said John. "And, of course, if one of us gets mumps there'll be another month."

People looked at one another by the light of the lantern in the igloo. Who was going to drop out into a sick-bed to make sure that the others would still be here to go with Nancy to the Pole?

"There may be no need for that," said John. "The doctor says she may be up and about in a fortnight and all clear in just over three weeks if the swelling doesn't hang about."

This sounded hopeful, but, at the end of only three days, Peggy was desperately wanting to ask Nancy what she thought they ought to do next.

And then on the fourth day, Mr Dixon, coming back from Rio with the milk cart, brought the news that folk had been skating clean across the lake by the islands, and after breakfast, when Dick and Dorothea went up the cart track to the observatory and looked down to Holly Howe, they did not see the usual diamond meaning "Come to the igloo," but a diamond over the north cone, meaning "Come to Holly Howe."

"Shall we go straight on?" said Dorothea.

"Quicker by the road," said Dick, and they ran back down the cart track to Dixon's Farm, and then, running and sliding, hurried along the road to Holly Howe, where they found the others waiting for them at the gate at the top of the field.

"You've got your skates?" called Peggy, as soon as she saw them. "That's all right. The lake's frozen right across."

"I know," said Dorothea. "Mr Dixon says people skated from one side to the other last night."

"We're going to now," said Roger.

"But where are we going?" asked Dick, as they set out, not down the field to Holly Howe but along the road to Rio.

"The ice is still weak in our bay," said John.

"We're going across from Rio," said Peggy. "We've simply got to see Nancy."

"But we can't, can we?" said Dorothea. "Isn't she in bed?"

"She can skip out just for a minute," said Peggy. "It'll be all right if we're in the garden and she just comes to the window. Even Susan says mumps can't be catching through glass."

"We'll be signalling to her," explained John.

"I've got my pocket-book," said Dick.

There was no argument about it. Nancy, mumps or no mumps, was the real leader of the expedition. The plans were hers, and every one of the explorers felt that a council was the thing most needed. Besides, with the lake frozen across, everybody wanted to do some skating on it as soon as possible. Skating on the tarn was just for practice. The lake was the real thing.

They nearly turned back when they first saw the crowds in Rio Bay. The news that the lake had begun to freeze had been sent far and wide, and already visitors, hoping that this would be one of the good years when the lake froze from end to end, had been booking their rooms. The hotels that had closed for the winter had hurriedly opened again. The little town was busier than in summer. The ice round the steamer pier and out beyond Long Island was black with skaters, though a row of red flags warned people that farther north the ice was not strong enough for skating. A little way beyond the flags, indeed, a man in a boat was rowing slowly along in open water. "Hoping somebody will fall in," said Roger. Close by the steamer pier a coffee stall had been set up on the shore where in summer rowing boats are drawn up for hire. People were going about selling roasted chestnuts.

Everywhere in the bay were skaters, flying along arm-in-arm, or singly, or turning in circles, figure-skating or dancing.

"Never mind," Dorothea heard Titty say, "we can count them seals."

It was the only thing to do. Unless they were to count all these hurrying, laughing, shouting, grown-up skaters as seals or walruses, or something like that, it would be impossible to make much of an Arctic out of the crowded ice.

"It'll be all right when more of it's frozen," said Peggy. "There'll be plenty of room then. The seals'll just hang about the Eskimo settlements. They always do. There'll be thousands in Rio Bay and hardly any out in the open, especially up near the Pole."

They went down to the shore and sat on one of the boat piers while they put on their skates.

"It's a good thing we had all that practice on the tarn," said Roger, looking round him at the skaters.

"Come on," said Peggy. "Make for the end of the island."

"Not too fast," said Titty.

"You skate with me," said Dorothea. "Let's have that other hand."

"Hullo," said Titty, striking out with Dorothea and finding she was doing better than she had expected. "Hullo, that must be a school!"

A crowd of about twenty little girls in green coats were slipping about on the ice, with two young women looking after them.

"Keep away from them," said Susan. "It wouldn't be fair to give it them."

"It wouldn't be any good to them now," said Roger.

"They don't know we're a sort of lepers," said Titty. "We ought to have brought our flags."

Keeping together, the expedition skated out from the pier, through the crowds, past the rocks they had seen from the rowing boat on their Arctic voyage, and close round the end of Long Island. Presently Rio was all but hidden behind Long Island's wintry trees.

"Make for that cottage," said Peggy. "Just there the road's only a few yards from the shore."

They skated on between two smaller islands, making for a small white cottage, with the blue smoke from its chimney climbing straight up in the still, frosty air, close under the dark woods on the side of the fell.

A strip of ice seemed to run along the shore towards the Beckfoot promontory and, for a moment, they were tempted to see how far it would take them. But Susan said there was no point in somebody getting wet so that they would all have to turn back. And Peggy said that if they came to Beckfoot round the promontory and up by the mouth of the Amazon they might easily be seen before they got near enough to the house to let Nancy know they were there. "It isn't as if we could possibly catch mumps, but you know what Eskimos are."

So they landed just below the cottage, scraped the snow off a fallen tree so that they could use it as a bench while they took their skates off, crossed a narrow field, went through a gate and set out northwards along the road. Above them, on the left, steep pine woods covered the side of the fell. On the other side of the road, along the shore, a few oaks, ashes, and chestnuts lifted their bare branches above the snow, and between these scattered trees the explorers could look out over the wintry lake. Far out in the middle of it they could see islands of thin, floating ice, smooth, dead patches on the water. There could be no doubt now that the Arctic was doing its best. But there was no loitering. They marched on at a good pace, and soon had turned away from the lake, up over the shoulder of the Beckfoot promontory. They were going downhill again when, on the right-hand side of the road, they came to a low stone wall and a wood.

"Here we are," said Peggy. "We nip over here, and there's a path just a few yards away. Then we creep along through the wood and right up to the house and come out on the lawn close under our windows."

"Do our tracks matter?" asked Titty.

"It looks as if a herd of buffaloes had gone this way," said John, looking back over the low wall at the trampled snow in the road. "Anybody could see how we've come."

"None of our Eskimos use this road," said Peggy, "anyhow, not in the winter. Single file now."

"Aye, aye, sir," said John, and Roger stared at him for a moment and then said "Aye, aye, sir" himself.

Dick and Dorothea were last in the line, except for Susan, who said she liked that place best so as to be sure that Roger did not get left behind. They walked on in the tracks of the leader.

"Anybody might think there was only one of us now," said Dick, "to look at our footprints."

"Sh," said Dorothea. If only she had a minute or two, what a story she could make out of this! But there never was a minute. Peggy, stooping low, was hurrying along at a tremendous pace, and there was no time to think of anything but putting feet in the right places and keeping out of the way of the snow-laden branches of the trees.

Suddenly Peggy stopped. John signalled back for the others to do the same.

She was off again now, working along through the edge of the wood, the others after her.

"Now," she said at last.

The grey stone house showed through the trees.

"All ready? Come on."

The expedition came out on the white lawn.

"Nancy's expecting us," said Titty.

It almost looked like it. Over a window on the second storey of the grey house a little flagstaff had been fixed, and from the end of it the plague flag, black and yellow in squares, dangled over the wintry garden.

"They've fixed it up awfully well," said Peggy.

What would happen next? How were they going to let her know they had arrived? Suppose they were seen by Eskimos first. Dorothea looked at John and Susan. They seemed today to be leaving everything to Peggy.

Peggy hesitated only for a moment. She picked up a handful of snow and squeezed it into a small snowball.

"If there's reading aloud going on, or dominoes, it just can't be helped," she said, and, taking careful aim, let fly. The snowball flattened itself in a white splash on the glass.

"Good shot," said John quietly.

In a moment Nancy appeared at the window.

But what a Nancy! "A face like a pumpkin," the doctor had said, but no one had really believed him. But now, "Pumpkin" seemed to say less than the truth. It said nothing about colour. Wrapped in a pink shawl, Nancy's face, unbelievably swollen, was a deep feverish red. She had on a red dressing-gown over her blue pyjamas.

Yet nobody felt like laughing.

The moment was too serious and Nancy had begun making her semaphore signals the instant she saw them.

"Get a bit of paper, somebody, quick," said John, "Peggy and I'll read out the letters." He signalled to Nancy to wait.

Not one of the Swallows had any paper. Nor had Peggy. Dorothea rather shyly pulled a pencil and tiny notebook from her pocket. On the first page of the notebook was written, "*Frost and Snow. A Romance. By Dorothea Callum.*" On the second page was written, "Chapter 1." But she had got no further and, hastily turning back these two pages, she made ready to write.

"Use the sundial for a desk," said Susan.

An old stone sundial stood up in the middle of the lawn. It was just the right height. Dorothea scraped the snow off it to make a dry place for her book, and was ready to scribble down the letters as the others called them out.

"Q-U-I. We've got those already," said John. "C-K. End of word. I. End of word. C-A-N-T. End of word. L-O-C-K. End of word. E-S-K-I-M-O-S. End of word. O-U-T. End of word. T-H-E-Y-L-L. End of word. B. End of word. H-E-R-E. End of word. A-N-Y. End of word. M-I-N-U-T-E. End of word. That's all. Go ahead, Peggy, you do the talking."

Peggy began now, throwing her arms into one signal after another, while that strange figure at the upstairs window nodded its huge head to show that it was getting the message letter by letter.

"What's Peggy saying?" Dorothea asked Dick, who had got his scientific pocket-book open at Nancy's page of semaphore signals and was trying to recognise each letter as it came, but was always finding himself two or three letters behind. "Look out! Nancy's talking again." She settled herself with her pencil to take down the letters as John called them out.

"s. End of word. M. End of word. T. End of word. What does she mean by that?"

"Shiver my timbers," said Titty, and for the first time the whole expedition burst into laughter.

Nancy shook her fist at them, and went on signalling at dreadful speed.

"G-A-L-O-O-T. End of word. She means that for Peggy. W-A-I-T. End of word. T-I-L-L. End of word. I-T-S. End of word. A-L-L. End of word. F-R-O-Z-E-N. End of word. Tell her we're going to wait for her."

But Nancy would not stop for an answer. John went on reading her signals.

"L-O-T-S. End of word. T-O. End of word. D-O. End of word.

IT
WOULD BE
UNFAIR TO
DRAW
NANCY'S
PUMPKIN
FACE

CAPTAIN NANCY GIVES INSTRUCTIONS

Y-E-A-R-S. End of word. O-F. End of word. T-R-A-I-N-I-N-G. End of word. F-O-R. End of word. A-R-C-T-I-C. End of word. J-O-U-R-N-E-Y-S. End of word. M-A-K-E. End of word. W-I-L-D-C-A-T. End of word. S-P-I-T-Z-B-E-R-G-E-N. End of word, and about time, too. Have you got it all? T-R-Y. End of word. A-L-A-S-K-A. End of word. C-R-O-S-S. End of word. G-R-E-E-N-L-A-N-D. End of word. P-E-G-G-Y. End of word. K-N-O-W-S. End of word. W-H ... "

But at that moment the signalling stopped short. The signaller spun round, the pink shawl slipping from her swollen head. She seemed somehow to be whisked from the window. Just for one moment the watchers in the garden saw Mrs Blackett not looking at all pleased.

"Oughtn't we to go away?" said Susan, as the expedition, cut short in the middle of a council, hesitated, almost as if Nancy might find some way of showing herself again.

Mrs Blackett answered that question.

A downstairs window opened, and there she was.

"Peggy, you little wretch," she said, "you must *not* do this sort of thing. Why did I send you over to the other side of the lake? No. Don't come any nearer. Be off with you at once. The sooner Nancy gets well the sooner she'll be out and about again, and here are you hauling her out of bed just when she ought to be keeping warm. No. It's all right. I know you didn't mean it. But off you go. If you want to send messages to Nancy, give them to the doctor. Much better leave her alone. Never mind, Susan. But don't let her do it again. Keep to your own side of the lake. Good-bye ... " And the window closed with a click.

"Come on," said Susan.

But they had not had time to leave the lawn before there was a bang on the window under the plague flag. Mrs Blackett had run upstairs again, and, now that they were going, was waving to them in the friendliest manner.

"Jolly decent of her," said John.

"She's a very good Eskimo," said Titty. "Mother would have done just the same."

"Of course we oughtn't to have come," said Susan.

"It was worth it," said Peggy.

They filed slowly back through the wood and out on the road. One thing was clear, that for the next few weeks they would have to do without Nancy. But she had sketched them a tremendous programme.

"Let's have a look at what she said," John asked Dorothea, when they were over the wall and back in the road again. Everybody crowded round as Dorothea, very glad to have been useful, showed the page in her book where the messages had been written down.

"We can't do Spitzbergen till we can get to Wild Cat Island over the ice," said John.

"What about Alaska?"

"Greenland's better," said Peggy. "I know what she means. It's the country up on the fells above the tarn. It's as wild as wild. Jib-booms and bobstays!" she cried, with as good a reflection of Nancy as she could manage. "We'll do a crossing of Greenland tomorrow."

They crossed over the ice to Rio, and, as it was already very late for dinner, ate their sandwiches on the way up to the igloo, where they made themselves hot tea, and planned an early start for the morning.

"It just can't be helped having only one sledge," said Peggy. "Captain Flint has a little one of his own, but nobody knows where he's gone and stowed it."

"They won't mind being dogs with Titty and me," said Roger.

"Not a bit," said Dick and Dorothea.

CHAPTER XI

CRAGFAST SHEEP

"Hi!" called Roger, "it's somebody else's turn."

"They've had it a good long time," said Susan, as John stopped to look back at the dog team – Dorothea, Dick, Titty, and Roger, each at the end of a short length of rope fastened to the sledge on which were some nearly empty knapsacks and the big coil of the Alpine rope.

"We'll take it again," said Peggy, and the three leaders waited till the panting dog team came up.

The Greenland crossing was in full swing. Dorothea and Dick had met the others at the igloo. They had climbed through the woods, all seven of them pulling on the ropes, dragging the sledge up the steep fell side. They had travelled far and fast on the top of the fells. They had had their dinner up in High Greenland sitting on the sledge and watching the blue shadows of little fine-weather clouds sweep across the shining slopes of snow. And now, with food inside them instead of in the knapsacks, they were swinging up and down along the fells towards the foot of the lake. Sometimes the four dogs would be pulling the sledge up out of a dip in the moorland. Sometimes, sitting on the sledge, they would go sliding down into another. In the hollows of the moorland they might have been in Greenland indeed. On the top of the ridges they could look about them and see the distant mountains, some of which Peggy knew by name, climbing, white, into the clear sky. Somewhere to the right of them they knew the fell must drop steeply into the valley, but where, they could not see. It was as if the fells on one side of the lake met those on the other in an

DOG TEAM IN HIGH GREENLAND

unbroken sheet of snow. On the left were grey crags, with snow-covered screes at the foot of them. Just here, where the three elders waited to take over the sledge, the crags were very near, and high rocky spurs with ravines between them ran down into the fell country.

The four dogs slipped out of their harness.

"It's hotter than it is in summer," said Titty.

"It won't be if you don't keep moving," said Susan.

"Well, we're jolly hot now," said Roger.

Dick, who had never before been in such country as this, was looking up towards the high crags, and listening. What was that queer, thin noise up there, like the mewing of a kitten? Two birds, far-away brown specks, were floating round the summits of the crags.

"Is it those birds making that noise?" he asked.

"Buzzards," said Peggy. "Just calling to each other. There are nearly always some of them up there round the crags."

"I've seen them in books," said Dick, speaking more to himself than to anyone else.

Roger was watching the harnessing of the elders.

"Good strong dogs," he said to Dorothea. "They'll be able to go a long way. Look here. I say, Titty, we'll have the rope now. We'll go in front with it, in case of accidents. The dogs are sure to follow." He pulled the Alpine rope off the sledge.

"Shiver my timbers!" said Peggy, in her best Nancy manner. "Sure to follow, indeed!"

And with that the sledge was off, John, Susan, and Peggy together, at a good round trot, up over the top of a ridge and down out of sight into the dip beyond it.

"Don't go so fast," shouted Titty, a few minutes later. But the others did not hear her. That first rush with which they had started had carried them out of hearing while Roger and Titty had been uncoiling the rope.

"I wish we had ice axes, too," said Roger.

"Hi, Dick," said Titty, "you've got to make a loop for yourself in the rope."

Dick woke up suddenly and turned round, looking at them with eyes that hardly saw them, dazzled after staring so long up into the bright sky where the buzzards, with hardly a flap of their great wings, wheeled round and round the crags.

"Do you think they've got a nest up there? Let's just try to see it. I've never seen them before except in books."

"Come on," said Roger, "it's our turn to explore. Lucky I thought of the rope."

"We could go just a bit nearer," said Titty, looking first towards the crags, and then at the deep tracks of the sledge and of those three sturdy dogs who had gone off at such a pace. "We can't possibly lose our way. We've only got to come back here and follow their trail."

"A very little bit nearer might be enough," said Dick, trying to bring his telescope to bear on those endlessly moving brown birds.

"Let's try," said Dorothea.

*

The four explorers, strung out along the rope, had left the sledge track and were working their way towards the crags. A steep-sided rocky ridge ran down to the right of them. They were in a narrowing gully between that ridge and another on their left. Titty led. After all, she and Roger were far more experienced explorers than the others, and she was the older of the two. Dorothea followed Titty. Next along the rope came Dick, with Roger some way behind him. And all the time from far up there in the sky came those strange shrill mewings of the buzzards, and Dick, with his eyes on the birds, hardly noticed where he put his feet, and was moving like a sleep-walker. Once Roger, out of mischief, or just out of Rogerishness, stopped suddenly, so that Dick was brought up sharp by the taut rope. But Dick never knew what had happened. He gave a bit of a pull, as if he thought the rope had somehow got stuck, and then walked on as before, with his eyes on the birds and on those high rocks, looking for any signs of their nest.

"Let's get up on the top of the ridge," said Titty, "and just see what the others are doing."

She turned up the steep slope and presently, reaching the top of it, caught a glimpse of the sledge, with Peggy, John, and Susan harnessed to it, small, dark figures moving on the snow.

"Good dogs!" cried Roger. "Good dogs!"

"We ought to go after them," said Titty. "They don't know we've gone another way."

And just then Dick, who for the moment was not interested in sledges and had forgotten Greenland, thought he saw what he was looking for.

As the ridge lifted towards the crags its sides became steeper. Not far beyond the place where they had climbed it an almost precipitous rock rose nearly to the top of it out of the gully they had left. Dick was looking at something high on the face of this rock.

"There's something there that might be a nest," he said. "Not up by the buzzards. There ... On that ledge."

"I think we ought to go back," said Dorothea, "the others are a tremendous way ahead."

"Just let me get my telescope on it," said Dick. And then, a second or two later, "It's not a nest. It's a sheep. It's a dead sheep."

"Where?" said Roger. "Let me see it."

"But it isn't dead," said Dorothea. They had all seen a grey head lift an inch or two and fall again.

A faint bleat floated down wind to them, very different from the shrill, sharp cries of the buzzards.

"It's ill," said Dorothea.

"Come on," said Titty.

All thoughts of catching up the elders were forgotten.

The sheep was lying on a narrow ledge, so that when they got down into the gully below it they might have thought it was sticking to the face of the rock. But the ledge ran back along the rock, widening at last at the point where the rock stuck up out of the fell.

"It must have started along the ledge where there was lots of room," said Dorothea, "and gone on and on, nibbling at bits of grass, with the ledge getting narrower and narrower until it couldn't turn round. And it couldn't go on either, because the ledge comes to an end. It's probably starving."

"That does happen to sheep on the fells," said Titty. "Specially when there's a bit of snow. They get on the sheltered side of a ridge and get stuck in all sorts of ways."

"How are we going to get it down?" said Roger.

Dorothea looked at Dick. This was one of the moments when she was sure he would come out of his dreams and be more practical than anybody else.

"Along the ledge," said Dick. "We can climb up here at the side of the rock. If the sheep could get along, I can, and there won't be any bother about turning back, because I've not got four legs."

"Let me come," said Roger.

"Rubbish," said Titty. "Who fell down when we were climbing Kanchenjunga?"

"But, Dick," said Dorothea, "what can you do when you get to the sheep? You can't carry it."

"I'm going to take the rope," said Dick. "Perfectly safe. You others will have to go along the top of the rock with the other end of the rope. You'll go along the top. I'll go along the ledge. Then I'll fasten the rope to the sheep and you'll be able to lower it down."

"But what'll you do without any rope at all?" said Titty.

"Sit on the ledge," said Dick. "It isn't really harder than sitting on a chair. Scientifically speaking. The only thing that matters is to keep your Centre of Gravity on the right side of the edge. And, of course, you mustn't look down. I won't. I'll look at the buzzards. It'll be perfectly easy."

Just then there was another faint bleat from high on the face of the rock, and again they saw the sheep move its head as if it were too weak even for that.

"Will he really be all right?" asked Titty. "I couldn't do it, and I know Roger couldn't."

"Yes, I can," said Roger.

"Well, you're not going to try," said Titty, remembering that for the moment she was in Susan's place.

"He'll be all right," said Dorothea stoutly, and then, "But *don't* go and forget where you are. You'd better not look at those buzzards."

Dick had already wriggled out of his loop in the Alpine rope and was busy undoing the knot.

"Undo yours, too," he said to to Dorothea. "It mustn't go and catch on a bit of heather or anything like that."

They went back a little way along the gully and climbed up the steep slope of the ridge close beside the rock. When they came to the place where the ledge started it was easy to see how the sheep had been tempted to go along it. Dick stopped there, and pushed his head and shoulders through the loop at one end of the rope. The others climbed on, paying out rope as they climbed.

"I wish John was here," said Titty, as they left him.

Dick hardly heard her. He was thinking now of nothing but the details of his plan.

"You mustn't come too near the edge of the cliff up on the top," he said, "just in case I slip. A sudden jerk might pull you over if you were right on the edge. Sure you've got enough rope?"

"Lots," said Titty. "But, Dick, it's awfully overhanging in places."

"Well, the rope won't have any weight on it till it's fastened to the sheep. We'll have to twitch it along. Like a skipping-rope," he added, to make sure that the others understood what he meant.

★

"Ready!"

The three on the slope above him moved out of sight along the top of the rock.

"Starting!"

He set foot on the ledge, left the steep snow-covered slope, and had a sheer drop below him to the rocky screes. But, at first, the ledge was broad enough for easy walking, and he stepped out confidently, every few yards taking hold of the rope and flicking it outwards so that it moved with him along the cliff. Here and there the snow had been blown from the ledge, or melted, and he could see tufts of grass. Scientifically speaking, of course, it was no harder than walking along a narrow path. But it somehow felt very different when he looked down past his feet to the grey rocks that showed through the snow so far below him.

And then, as the ledge narrowed, he realized that he was in continual danger of slipping. He had never done any climbing, even in summer, and this was much worse than summer climbing. There was a thin film of ice on the ledge, partly hidden by little drifts of snow. It was not safe to put a foot down without first clearing the snow to make sure that the foot had something firm on which to stand and that it was not going to slip sideways off the ledge into nothingness. And the ledge kept on getting narrower. Dick found it best to keep his back against the cliff and to move sideways, always with his right foot foremost, after using it to scrape away the snow.

"Are you all right?"

That was Dorothea's voice from above him. Odd to know she was there, talking to him, when the only living things he could see were those buzzards still circling round the higher crags. He had a stiff corner of rock to get round before he would be able again to see the sheep.

"Are you all right?"

"So far."

There was really nothing to worry about, with those three on the rope. But, at the same time, it would not do to slip, and have to be lowered to the bottom and go back and start again at the beginning of the ledge. He tried not to let his eyes wander off the ledge, but it was difficult to look down at it without seeing past it, to the screes far below. And he must not think of buzzards. Not yet. Sheep. He would think only of the sheep and of how best to tie the rope round it. These sailors seemed to know all sorts of knots. Look at the neat way in which they tied things on their sledge. Oh, well, he supposed he would manage. And just then he felt the rope catch. He gave it the usual light, outward flick, to shift it along the top of the cliff. It did not stir. He looked up to see what held it, and saw that the face of the rock leaned out above him far beyond the ledge.

"Half a minute," he shouted.

This needed thinking about. He could still stand upright under the overhang, but he could see that a few yards ahead of him the overhang sloped out from so near the ledge that, though it had been no obstacle for a sheep, it left very little room for a boy.

"Half a minute," he called again. "I've got to sit down. Let out some more rope."

"Is anything wrong?" That was Titty's voice.

"No. But the rock leans out, so you'll have to let the rope out a lot and then jerk it round. Don't start jerking just for a minute. I've got to get sitting down."

"Why?" called Dorothea. "You're not giddy?"

"No," said Dick. "Centre of Gravity. If I try to get past standing up, my Centre of Gravity will get pushed too far out by the cliff."

Overhead, on the top of the rock, Titty and Dorothea and Roger looked at each other.

"I suppose he's all right?" said Titty.

"Quite," said Dorothea, "so long as he talks like that."

They could see nothing of what was going on below them.

Dick carefully chose his place, where the ledge was a few inches wider than usual, and a crevice in the rock gave him something to hold by. Carefully, slowly, he lowered himself till he was sitting on the ledge, with his feet dangling.

He rested a moment. It was a good thing to get that over. Then he began working himself sideways. At the worst place the overhang was so low above the ledge that there was only just room for him to pass. He had to bend so low, sitting as he was, that it seemed as if he must overbalance, fall outwards, and go toppling down. But he did not, and presently the three, waiting above him with the rope, heard his voice coming now from a little to their right.

"Swing it round now ... Hi! Steady! That's enough. I'm going on."

The ledge was now so narrow that he dared not get to his feet again. Above him the cliff seemed everywhere to slope outwards. Below him there was a sheer drop to the screes. Well, it was no good thinking about that. Where that sheep could walk, he could sit. One more corner to get round and he would be close to it. He wriggled along, crabwise, at a steady pace, giving a jerk to the rope every now and then, when the others, invisible above him, flicked it forward along the top of the cliff.

Suddenly, just as he came to the corner, the sheep bleated on the other side of it, a sudden, startling noise. Dick was never nearer falling than then. But he pulled himself together and went on, as quietly as he could, fearing now that, if he had been frightened by the sheep, the sheep might be frightened by its rescuer, and, with a last effort, struggle off the ledge and go crashing down.

And then, as he worked himself round that last corner and saw the huddled mass of grey wool only a few yards beyond him, he saw that the sheep was too far gone to move. It lay there, flat to the ledge. It had somehow shrunk away inside its wool, so that it was as if some very little animal, with a big sheep's head, lay there, covered by a bit of soaked rug.

Dick worked himself close to it.

The sheep bleated and, if it had had the strength, would have flung itself down. But it was as if that small thing under the wet sheepskin shivered a little, no more. It could not stir an inch.

Dick touched the clammy, soaked body.

"It's probably a good thing it's so tired," he said to himself and then, noticing a dull reddish stain on the left fore shoulder of the sheep, he called out, "It's one of Mr Dixon's."

"Is it much farther?" Titty called down.

"I'm touching it. Let out a bit more rope."

Just for a moment, and against his will, Dick looked down. The drop was not really so very great, but more than enough to break the back of a sheep, or a boy. He felt suddenly a little sick. He looked up at the farther crags, where the buzzards were still wheeling and mewing in the winter sunshine. He considered the sheep once more. The thing had to be done, and he had not wriggled all that way to give up now and come back without doing it. He had to give his rope to the sheep and sit there without a rope at all while the sheep was lowered into the gully. He told himself firmly that the rope was hanging loose anyhow, so that being without it would make no difference. But it is one thing to sit on a narrow ledge when you have a rope round you and three sturdy helpers somewhere above, ready to stand fast and hold on, if by any chance you should slip. It is quite another to sit there knowing that if you slip nothing will stop you till you reach the bottom. The rope had been very slack indeed while he had worked round under the overhang, but it had been there. Now he was to be without it, and at the same time, just sitting on the ledge on the face of the rock, to make the end of it fast round the terrified sheep.

Nobody was there to see him, to say a heartening word. This was something to be settled between him and himself.

He slipped the loop over his head and sat still for a moment, holding it. Then he untied it. A doubled rope would make more difficult what he had to do. He gave himself a short lecture on Centres of Gravity. After all, he told himself yet again, while he sat there and did not look down he was as safe without the rope as with it. And suddenly his mind was made up, and the thing seemed almost easy. He worked himself right up against the sheep and leaned sideways over it, his right hand at the back of the ledge between sheep and rock, while with his left he worked the rope in from outside under that wet, grey wool, those sharp bones. He felt a feeble fluttering against his fingers, a quick, weak, terrified heart-beat. The sheep made a desperate effort to move. Were they going to the bottom together? But it had no strength left, and its head dropped flat on the ledge. Another six inches to go, another four. Horrible how this wet wool clung and grappled as he worked the rope under it. At last. His right hand in there, close against the wall of rock, felt the rope touch it. He spared a thumb to hold it. He worked his left hand out again. He was already far too near the edge. His hand was free. He gripped the ledge again, and pushed himself back into a safe position. That was better. Then, inch by inch, he worked the rope through under the sheep until he had enough to knot it round the body. What sort of knot ought it to be, and how should it be made? He envied those others who seemed to know all the knots there are. Well, never mind. The sheep would not have far to go. It did not matter what knot he used so long as it held. He did the best he could.

"Pull in a bit now," he called to the others who were up there breathlessly waiting for news of him. "Pull in a bit. Then I'll push the sheep off and you can lower it down."

He remembered then that, after the sheep was lowered, one of the others would have to go all the way back and down into the gully to untie it before they could let him have the rope for the return journey. All that time he would have to sit on the ledge there, with his back against the face of the rock, and wait, and wait, and not look down at his feet. Well, those buzzards were still there.

And then, suddenly, he was startled by a shout from Roger, out of sight above him.

"Here come the dogs!"

And away to the left, far below him, he saw the sledge party coming up the gully, and knew that they had seen him.

John would be there to undo the sheep. It was too late now to try again, but he did wish he had been able to manage a rather more seamanlike knot.

CHAPTER XII

AMBULANCE WORK

THE sledge party had travelled far before thinking again of those four tired dogs who had so gaily proposed to lead the way for them. Then, on the top of a rise, they had stopped to rest, and Susan had served out a ration of chocolate, putting aside four shares for the others to have as soon as they should come up. But there were no signs of them on the great rolling sheet of snow.

"They must be in one of the dips," said Peggy.

They waited more than long enough for the others to come up into sight again out of even the deepest of the dips, and then Susan began to be worried.

"Let's go back and look for them," she said. "Hiding somewhere. They never will remember how short the days are."

"Bother those brats," said Peggy.

"I'll go and hurry them up," said John.

"I'm coming too," said Susan.

"What about the sledge?" said Peggy.

They had all but decided to leave it where it was, but, at the last minute, Susan remembered how Roger had sprained his ankle on the moor above Swallowdale on the other side of the lake. If anything like that had happened, the sledge would be badly wanted for the wounded. John agreed. They brought the sledge back with them, following their own tracks in the snow until with great indignation they came to the place where they had left the others and saw their footprints going off towards the crags. Broken ankles seemed now more likely than ever. They pulled the sledge behind them, following the footprints up the gully until suddenly they caught sight of Titty, Roger, and Dorothea, high on the ridge, standing in the snow above a grey precipice of rock.

"They're not fit to be left alone for a minute," said Susan, relieved all the same to see Titty and Roger still clearly able to stand on two legs apiece.

"But there's only three of them," said John.

And then they saw that the others were holding a rope that hung down the cliff. They saw Dick high up there against the rock, and they guessed that something horrible had happened, and fairly raced up the gully.

"Don't shout," said John suddenly. "Don't startle him. I don't believe he's got hold of the rope. They're trying to give it him."

A moment later they had seen the sheep, and understood what was going on.

"Cragfast sheep," said Peggy eagerly. "Good for them! Whoever it belongs to'll be jolly pleased."

"Look here," said John, "they'll never manage the weight." But as he spoke the rope tautened.

"Pull in just a bit more," called Dick.

The three above hauled in, and the sheep lifted like a dead thing, a limp, sagging bundle. Dick pushed it outwards.

"Let it down now," he shouted.

"Lower away," said Titty, in command on the top of the cliff. With their feet well dug into the snow, they let the rope go slowly down, hand over hand. Roger and Titty had been busy for some time, showing Dorothea how to do it. They could see nothing of what was happening on the face of the rock below them. They never knew how nearly the swinging sheep, slipping down against Dick's legs, had come to dragging him feet fore-most from his perch. The sledge party, down below, had seen clearly enough. John had started at the run, meaning to come round and up to the top to help with the rope, but when he saw

"LOWER AWAY"

that the sheep was on its way down he turned back and hurried up the screes to be ready for it. The sheep weighed so little that they had no trouble in lowering it, and Dick, after that one desperate moment, had got his legs free and jerked himself safely back on the ledge as the sheep went down.

John said nothing about Dick's knot, but simply untied it, and, when Peggy had taken the sheep, made a new bowline loop at the end of the rope.

Peggy was sitting on the screes with the sheep in her arms. "It's still alive," she said.

"How is he going to get down?" said Susan, still looking up at Dick, who, sitting seemingly on nothing at all, was looking far away towards the top of the crags.

"I can wriggle back all right," said Dick, "but perhaps I'd better wait for the rope." He did not look down as he spoke. He had looked down and seen the sheep reach the ground, and felt himself giddy once more. Buzzards were the things for him to look at.

"You stay where you are," said John. "It'll take ages wriggling back. Just wait till I get up to the top, and we'll lower you down in two shakes." He raced off down the gully to look for the nearest place where he could climb up and join the others.

A very few minutes later they were ready. Susan had swung the rope till Dick could reach it. He had worked the loop over his feet, so that he was all but sitting in it. John had hauled up the slack.

"Are you all right?" called John.

"Yes," said Dick. "Shall I put my weight on it?"

"Half a minute." John took his coat off, crawled to the edge of the cliff, spread his coat on an overhanging clump of heather, and led the rope across it so that it should not fray. He went back to the others, and took a good grip.

"Ready now."

Dick took a gulp of air, because, no matter how sure you may be scientifically that your Centre of Gravity is in the right place and that the rope is strong, it is not easy to launch yourself down even a very little precipice. His hands were cold, too, and he was very wet from sitting on the icy ledge.

But there were Susan and Peggy watching below, and all the rest of the expedition waiting for him, and Dorothea ...

"Now," he called.

"Go ahead."

He was off the ledge and swinging, sitting in the loop, hanging on to the rope with both hands and bumping against the rock. This was horrible. Well, he must think of something else. Buzzards. And the others, waiting below, were astonished to see that, instead of looking down towards them, he still looked up towards the crags. And at this very moment he had his reward. Inch by inch, foot by foot, he was going down. There could be no wriggling back to safety on the ledge, or to get a better view. But he had seen it. Buzzards. How odd that they choose a rocky crag for their home, and yet use sticks for their building. But it was a nest. He was sure of it. First one and then the other bird had rested in that place, and how else could the sticks he saw up there have found their way to the top of the crag? Hullo. What was that catching at his foot?

"Well done," said Peggy. "Jolly good work. And the sheep's still alive. We may be in time to save it, but it's pretty bad."

"You'll have to change the moment you get home," said Susan. "You're wet through with sitting up there."

"What sort of nests do buzzards make?" he asked.

"Buzzards?" said Peggy. "Any old sticks."

"Good," said Dick, "I thought it was, but I couldn't be absolutely sure." He pulled out his pocket-book, blew on his frozen fingers, and, with a pencil that would hardly do what he wanted, scrawled "Saw buzzard's nest," and the date.

"Heads," called John from above, and the end of the rope came flying. The four on the top of the cliff hurried down into the gully by the way they had left it. In a few minutes the whole expedition was standing round the rescued sheep.

"It's starving," said Peggy. "It may have been stuck there for days."

"Let's give it something to eat," said Roger.

Titty scraped in the snow at the bottom of the gully and found a little short grass, but the sheep did not try to nibble it, and would not open its mouth even when Roger tried to tempt it with a bit of strengthening chocolate taken from his own share.

"The farmers would give it warm milk," said Peggy.

"We haven't got any," said Susan.

"Why did you say it belonged to Mr Dixon?" asked Dorothea.

Dick, now that the rescue was over, was thinking entirely about birds of prey: buzzards, vultures, eagles, and their choice of nests. But Dorothea's question woke him. "Because it is," he said. "It's got the red patch on its left shoulder, and that's Mr Dixon's mark. I asked him about it when I saw it on all the sheep down in the field."

"We'd better take it back to him as quick as we can," said John. "Lucky we've got that sledge."

"We'll bump it to death if we try taking it down the way we came up," said Susan.

"There's a much better way," said Peggy. "We'll get down to the road through that wood where you saw the charcoal-burners that first summer. It's not far from here. There's a good track down the wood, and once we're on the road by the lake we'll be at Dixon's in no time."

They shifted the knapsacks and, with the coiled Alpine rope for a mattress, made the sledge into a comfortable litter. Peggy, Susan, and John between them, with Roger actively helping, arranged the sheep on the top.

"Those brats had better get properly warm again," said Susan. "Let them pull for a bit."

John fixed the ends of the long coil of rope (which nobody wanted to cut), so that people would be able to hang on to them or pull if necessary. The four younger dogs were already getting into the harness. In a very few minutes they were off, down the gully, back to the place at which the four of them had begun exploring on their own, then along the tracks made by their elders, and at last cutting off from those tracks to the right. There, where the white of the fells was broken by the browns and greys of leafless trees, must be the wood they wanted.

"It's a queer sort of crossing of Greenland," said Peggy, who was keeping close by the sledge, "coming back with a sick sheep."

"Count it a Polar bear," said Titty.

"It's not half a bad one," said Roger, "but, of course, there isn't any blood."

"I did see that nest all right," said Dick to Dorothea, as they trotted side by side, once more a pair of hard-working dogs.

"I am glad," said Dorothea; "I really am." After all, it had been Dick who had gone out along the ledge and rescued the sheep, even before the elders had come to help. It had been quite like a bit out of a real story, and though Dick's mind would keep running on buzzards instead of on Polar bears, she could not help feeling he had done very well. He deserved his buzzards.

Long before they reached the top of the wood they saw that it was divided from the fell by a stone wall with a gate in it. They made straight for the gate, and found, as they had guessed, a cart track going through it and down among the trees. They ran at full speed down that winding track, with the elders hanging back on the spare ropes to keep the sledge from going too fast.

The track came out in a white clearing where there was a sort of hut or wigwam built of larch poles, all sloping up to a point at the top of it.

"I wonder where the Billies are now," said Titty.

"Who are they?" said Dorothea.

"Charcoal-burners," said Titty.

"It wouldn't make half a bad igloo," said John, looking at the hut the charcoal-burners had left.

"Not as good as our own," said Peggy. "But we might use it some time."

"We mustn't stop now," said Susan, seeing that some of the dogs were thinking of looking inside it. "Dick's awfully wet, and we may be too late with the sheep."

"Polar bear," said Roger.

So they hurried on, out of the clearing and down the steep track towards the lake.

"That's where we turned off last time," said Titty. "I made a blaze on a tree. It's probably still there."

But today there was no stopping to look, and no turning off. Slipping and stumbling, picking themselves up and stumbling again, holding back the runaway sledge, they hurried down the old track until it ended in a gap where once upon a time there had been a gate between the wood and the road.

"Now then," said John, as they turned northwards in the road.

"Come on," said Peggy.

They fairly raced along the road, a full dog team of six, the four smaller dogs, Dorothea, Dick, Titty, and Roger taking short turns to rest on the sledge one at a time, and to look after the Polar bear, which, for its part, had never travelled so fast in its life, but was not enough alive to know anything about it. After they left High Greenland it seemed almost no time before they were turning into the farmyard.

★

"It's a near thing," said old Silas, who had been crossing the yard with a barrow and, after calling for Mr Dixon to help, had taken charge of the Polar bear the moment he saw it on the sledge. "Another night, and she'd have been a goner."

He asked a few questions from Peggy, who explained just where the Polar bear had been found. "And how in ever did you get her down out of that?"

"Dick did it," said Titty, who, after all, had led the part of the expedition that had done the actual rescuing. "He crawled along the ledge and we went along the top."

"It's not the first sheep to come cragfast just there," said Silas, "but it's a bad spot that to get them out of without men and ropes."

"We had a rope," said Titty, "and Dick went right along the ledge and tied it to the sheep. And then we lowered it down."

"Well, I'm beholden to you all," said Mr Dixon at last. "There's not many lads would go along that ledge."

And then Mrs Dixon came bustling out into the yard, and in three-quarters of a minute Dick was flying upstairs to get out of his wet clothes. "Freezing on him," said Mrs Dixon. "Arctic, indeed. He'll have had more'n enough of Arctic if he stands about there in wet breeches watching you doctor a sick sheep. We'll be having doctor here for something more'n mumps. Nay now, Miss Peggy, you've no call to be stirring yet. You've done a good job to-day bringing that sheep home for Dixon, and the lad'll be into dry clothes and down by the fire in two jumps. I've a rare baking of cakes, and there'll be trouble if all the lot of you aren't sitting down to see what's inside them. It's nigh teatime, and kettle's boiling, and if you're a bit late to Jackson's, Silas'll set you along the road with a lantern. You've no call to stir now till dark."

At tea in the farm kitchen, with Mrs Dixon seeing to it that everybody was eating as hard as anybody could, while Mr Dixon and Silas drank their tea and said hardly a word between them, the whole story of the Greenland expedition was told, and of how they had taken turns in pulling the sledge because there was only one, as Dorothea and Dick had none of their own, and of how the four young ones had gone off by themselves to have a nearer look at the buzzards, and then of exactly how the sheep had been seen and rescued. Peggy told most of the story, and Titty the rest, though neither of them had seen the worst part, when Dick had had to work his way along, sitting on the ledge, under the over-hanging rock.

Mr Dixon sat by the fireside, drank his tea out of a huge mug, and listened. But when he had gone back across the yard to the shippen, to see that the sheep was doing nicely, he had a good look at the sledge that had carried it. He stood it up on end, to see how it was built underneath. He scraped the snow from its runners. Silas stood with him.

"We might do worse," said Mr Dixon at last.

"It's not sic a job as we can't tackle it," said Silas.

And that night, after the main expedition had gone back to Holly Howe, and Dorothea and Dick had had an early supper and been bustled off to bed with a tremendous supply of hot bricks wrapped in flannel ("Better sure than hoping for the best," said Mrs Dixon), they were for some time kept awake by the noise of sawing and hammering down in the woodshed.

At last Dorothea could bear it no longer.

She slipped out of bed and went to Dick's room.

"Dick," she said, "Dick. The sheep's died after all, and I can hear them making the coffin."

Dick went to the window. Down in the yard he could see the light in the shed. Silas crossed the yard. Dick called down:

"Is the sheep all right?"

A NOISE OF SAWING AND HAMMERING

"Doing fine," said Silas.

And then there were a couple of loud bumps on the floor beneath them; and Dorothea, knowing well what Mrs Dixon meant by them, fled back to her room.

CHAPTER XIII

TO SPITZBERGEN BY ICE

NEXT morning when Dorothea came down to breakfast, beating Dick by two minutes, she was a little shocked to find Mrs Dixon putting her little finger into the milk she was warming in a saucepan, to see if it was getting too hot.

Mrs Dixon looked up and caught the expression on her face. She laughed. "The very spit of your mother," she said. "I've seen her look just so if the thunder had turned the cream and she had a taste of it in her tea. Come you along with me now, and see where this milk's going ... " She took the saucepan and a small bottle that was lying on the table, and went out of the kitchen, followed by Dorothea, and across the yard to the shippen. In there was lying the rescued sheep, Dick's sheep, as Mrs Dixon called it. She filled the bottle with the warm milk and poured it into the sheep's mouth, tilting its head up as she poured.

"Scarce strength to swallow," she said, "but milk's getting down and staying down, and we'll have her well again inside of a week. Aye. Dixon thinks a lot of you for bringing her down," she went on, seeing Dick in the doorway of the shippen. "I thought he'd be up all night with making that sledge, him and Silas."

"Sledge," cried Dick. "Was he making a sledge?"

"I thought it was a coffin," said Dorothea.

"You should have been asleep," said Mrs Dixon. "I heard you gadding round. Well, it's all done now, and wanting nobbut a couple of iron rails, and that's blacksmith's work, he says, and .he'll be going in to the smithy when you've done breakfast."

"But where is it?" said Dick.

"Not so far," said Mrs Dixon.

They found it in the woodshed, a new, strongly built wooden sledge, not so high off the ground as the big sledge from Beckfoot, not so long either, but, as anybody could see, a good strong sledge, fit for a lot of hard work.

"What's he going to use it for?" asked Dick.

"It's what are you going to use it for," said Mrs Dixon. "He's made it for the two of you, to have a sledge of your own as well as the one they've got at Jacksons'."

And just then there was the clang of the gate. Mr Dixon was leading the old horse into the yard.

Mr Dixon simply would not be thanked.

"Nay," he said. "One good turn deserves another, and that was a right good one you did me."

And after breakfast Mr Dixon, for the first time since they had known him, spoke without being first spoken to.

"Happen you'd be liking to come with me to the smithy whiles we get runners fixed and all trig?"

Mrs Dixon looked at him in astonishment.

"I'd like to very much," said Dick, "but I've got to run up to the observatory first in case there's a signal to answer."

"I'll do that," said Dorothea.

And presently Mr Dixon and Dick drove off together in the milk cart, with the new sledge and some lengths of iron railing that Mr Dixon thought would happen be just the thing.

"I've never seen him take to anyone like that," said Mrs Dixon as she and Dorothea watched them move slowly off along the slippery road. "It's that sheep's done it."

Dorothea, too, as she trudged away up the hill to the barn, was very pleased about it. Sometimes, she felt, Dick wanted a lot of pushing in affairs of that kind. But he had driven off with Mr Dixon as if they had been a couple of old friends.

Indeed, this was the beginning of a queer kind of alliance between Dick and Mr Dixon. They were neither of them great talkers, but together they got along very well. Of all the Eskimos Mr Dixon came to know most of what was going on among the explorers and of what was being planned. Sometimes for days he would not talk at all, and then he would come out with something to Dick that showed he had been thinking all the time about conditions in the Arctic, and of the things that might be needed on a sledge journey to the North Pole. He seemed always to be thinking that there was a kind of competition between the two settlements of Eskimos, and he didn't see why the explorers settled at Jackson's should do any better than those who were lodging with himself. Dick several times tried to explain that there wasn't really any competition, but Mr Dixon knew better. "Jackson's lot mustn't think they're doing all," he said. "We mun pull our weight, lad, pull our weight."

In the smithy, while Dick worked the bellows and the blacksmith heated the rails in the little snoring fire, shaped them on the anvil, made holes in them, and fastened them in their places under the wooden runners, there was talk of the frost.

"Freezing grandly," said the smith. "Did you hear Bill Bowness got right down to Low End on the ice and a wetting in the river and all, for trying to go too far? But t' lake'll be froze all over yet, and that'll be good for trade?"

"Eh?" said Mr Dixon, who was busy poking the ends of a rope through two holes he had bored in the front of the sledge, and knotting them at the other side.

"Trade?" asked Dick.

"Yours won't be the only sledge wanting runners," said the blacksmith. "There'll be hundreds before the week's out. I had twenty in yesterday. And if the frost holds there'll be ice yachts out and more wanted, and that means work enough, and welcome these days with no horses left but on the farms."

"Ah!" said Mr Dixon.

Dick was interested in many other things. He wanted to know why the hot rail had to be dipped in water, and why dipping it in water tempered it, and what temper in iron really means. But the news that there was ice bearing all along the edge of the lake was good news indeed, and he was not surprised when on their way home from the smithy they met Dorothea, carrying his knapsack as well as her own, coming along the road and close to the gate into the field above Holly Howe.

"No igloo today," she called out. "Diamond over north cone. Holly Howe. So I brought our things along."

"They'll be going on the lake," said Dick.

Mr Dixon took the sledge out of the cart for them, and set its shining runners in the snow.

"It does look a beauty," said Dorothea.

"Better'n nowt," said Mr Dixon. "Happen it'll take you down the field."

There was a steepish slope from the road down the field to Holly Howe. The cart track to the farm wound to and fro across it to make it easy for horses but, with the field covered with snow, there was nothing against going straight across country with the sledge, and they could see the tracks of the Beckfoot sledge on which the other explorers, going home, always tobogganed down the field to the house.

Mr Dixon stood up in the milk-cart to watch the start. Dorothea sat in front with the knapsacks. Dick sat at the back, astride of the sledge, worked it forward over the brow, felt it suddenly moving by itself, and flung his legs forward so that he could steer with his feet in the snow that flew up like spray when he touched it with his heels. Holly Howe, the old whitewashed farm, with the big yew tree at one end and the hollies and yews in the garden, seemed almost to fly uphill to meet them. Down there, Peggy and the others had been impatiently watching for them, wondering why those D.'s were so late just when there was good reason to hurry. And now, here they were, coming full tilt, and with a sledge of their own.

"Stick your heels in," cried Dick. "Jam them in. I can't stop it!"

Dorothea did her best. The snow poured up over them, and, just in time, they brought the sledge to a standstill. Another four or five yards and they would have crashed into the wall.

"Was that why you were late?" said Titty. "I knew it wasn't just breakfast."

"It's a jolly good sledge," said John.

"They won't want to be our dogs any more," said Roger.

Everybody crowded round to admire it, and to hear how it had been made at Dixon's Farm in the night, and how this morning it had been finished at the smithy, where Dick had worked the bellows of the fire. But Peggy would not let them waste much time.

"Look here!" she said. "We were just going to start without you. There's ice all along this side of the lake. Holly Howe Bay's bearing everywhere. We're going right down to Wild Cat Island — Spitzbergen, I mean. What's the ice like by Dixon's Farm?"

"I don't know if it's bearing all the way to the island," said Dick. "I meant to try, but I had to go to the smithy."

"Worth it for a sledge like that," said Peggy. "But do let's get going."

"How's the Polar bear?" asked Roger.

"They're giving it milk out of a bottle, and it's going to be all right in a week," said Dorothea.

"Come on, my hearties," said Peggy. "Let's start."

It always sounded a little odd when Peggy shivered her timbers or talked about hearties, but everybody understood that she was trying to make up for Nancy's being away in bed.

Everybody knew that Peggy was worrying all the time in case something or other was not being done that Captain Nancy would have thought important.

On the field sloping down from Holly Howe to the boathouse, Dick and Dorothea tried the new sledge again and took Roger and Titty as passengers. The Beckfoot sledge with the three elders came rushing after them. They took the sledges down on the ice beside the jetty from which they had started on that Arctic voyage in the Beckfoot rowing boat. The ice was solid enough today. They sat on the sledges to put their skates on. Then, cautiously, towing the sledges, they moved out over the ice towards the Peak of Darien, with its pine-topped cliffs that shut in the southern side of the Holly Howe bay.

"It's much more of an expedition with two sledges," said Peggy.

"Are you sure the ice is thick enough?" said Susan.

"Someone's been past here," said John. "You can see the marks of the skates."

"But not a whole crowd like us," said Susan.

They stopped a moment to put the Alpine rope to a new purpose. One end of it was looped over John's shoulder. He went first. Then, ten yards behind him, came Peggy. Ten yards behind Peggy was Susan and the Beckfoot sledge, to which the rope was fastened, so that John and Peggy were pioneers, testing the ice, and dogs to pull the sledge at the same time. The loose end of the rope was coiled on the sledge.

"If John goes through," said Roger, "we've got the rope, and we just grab it and howk him out again."

Roger and Titty were not yet strong enough skaters to be much good as dogs on the ice, but the days of practice up on the tarn had taught them a lot, and they were able to keep on their feet so long as they did not try to get along too fast.

Dorothea and Dick, proud of the new sledge, were towing it

together, skating in time with each other, but not hurrying, and sometimes giving lifts to weaker dogs.

They passed close under the steep little cliffs of Darien, listening for the loud cracking of the ice, almost expecting to see it break and let John go through into the water. Beyond the point they turned in again along the shore, for out towards the middle of the lake there was something that looked like open water, and farther down they could actually see ripples where the water was stirred by a slight wind. Near the shore the ice was strong and beautifully clear.

"Look!" said Dick. "There's a fish in the ice."

It was a little perch, close to the surface, looking as if it were swimming in glass. The others turned back to see it and crowded round it, till a loud cracking of the ice gave them a warning.

"Spread out!" cried John.

"Don't get in a bunch," cried Peggy, "or you'll take us all to Davy Jones!"

"Good for you, Peggy," laughed John.

"Who is Davy Jones?" asked Dorothea.

"He hangs about on the bottom of the sea and puts drowned sailors in his locker," said Titty.

"Do stop just a minute," said Dick. "Can't we cut a hole in the ice and take the perch out?"

"It wouldn't do any good," said John, "and somebody skating in the dark might come an awful smash if he caught his skate in the hole."

"It probably was a sick fish anyway, swimming right at the top," said Dick, comforting himself, as the expedition moved on. "But I wish I knew what would happen if we melted it out."

"We can't stop," said Dorothea; "not when they're going to Spitzbergen."

F

They skated on, but not until Dick had pulled his pocket-book out and written in it, "Saw perch frozen in ice. Right way up," and the date, under his yesterday's entry about the buzzard's nest.

And then, as they left that bay and rounded a point into another, they saw something that made even Dick forget frozen perch altogether.

"Hullo!" cried John. "The houseboat's frozen in."

An old blue houseboat, with a raised cabin and a row of windows, and a high railing round the after-deck, lay there in the smooth ice, heading north as if still riding to the big buoy that could be seen frozen in close under the bows. Once upon a time it had been a steamer, a little passenger launch carrying visitors to and fro on the lake. Long ago it had been turned into a houseboat, with a little mast for a flagstaff and, in summer, an awning over the after-deck. Dick and Dorothea had never seen it before, for the woods that ran round the little bay hid the boat except from the lake or from the nearby shore.

"But what is it?" said Dick.

"Does anybody live there?" said Dorothea.

"It's the houseboat we told you about," said Roger. "It belongs to Captain Flint."

"Nancy's and Peggy's Uncle Jim," explained Susan.

"Retired pirate," said Titty.

"Is he there now?" asked Dorothea.

"Gone abroad for the whole winter," said Peggy. "If only he hadn't he might have been useful."

"I say, Susan, unhitch the Alpine rope," called John. "We won't take the sledges, but I think we might just have a look. Don't come in a bunch till we know the ice is all right."

But the ice seemed firm enough, and presently all the explorers had come to the side of the old boat. Curtains closed all the cabin windows, so that they could not see in; but Dick and Dorothea heard strange tales of the things that were there, brought from all

"THE HOUSEBOAT'S FROZEN IN"

over the world, and of the night when the houseboat had been burgled and how Captain Flint had given Titty a green parrot and Roger a monkey because they had found the box that had been stolen with the book that he had written.

"Where's the parrot?" asked Dick.

"At the zoo," said Titty. "I couldn't very well have him at school, and mother couldn't take him to Malta. So he's gone to the zoo."

"Gibber's there, too," said Roger.

"Is Gibber your monkey?" asked Dorothea.

"He's called Gibber because he gibbers," said Roger, "especially when anybody's giving him monkey-nuts and hasn't got any more."

"Oh, look here!" said Peggy. "It's no good hanging about the houseboat if we're going to get down to Spitzbergen for dinner. What's the good of bringing a kettle if we don't?"

"I wonder if anything ought to be done about the houseboat," said John. "Being frozen in, I mean."

"We'll put it in dispatches to Captain Nancy," said Peggy, "but do come on."

And the expedition went on out of Houseboat Bay, leaving the forlorn blue houseboat, stuck in the ice, with the white snow on its decks and on the roof of its long cabin.

Spitzbergen was now plain to see; that rocky island covered with trees, with a steep little cliff at the northern end of it, and a tall pine, the tallest tree on the island, standing on the top of the cliff.

"Lighthouse tree," said Titty.

"Lighthouse?" said Dorothea.

"Yes," said Roger. "We had a lantern and Titty hoisted it up the tree at night, and the Amazons came down in the dark, and we were all sailing when it was absolutely pitchy. I was quite small then. Very small indeed, I mean."

Dick and Dorothea heard the story, but Dorothea was thinking of a story much newer than that. She was remembering how she and Dick had come down to the shore from Dixon's Farm that first day and had found only an upturned boat they could not use; and had seen the Beckfoot rowing boat, with Nancy in command, rowing to the island. That had been a lonely morning. The island and those children in the boat had seemed a thousand miles away. And now, here they were, she and Dick, sharing an expedition with those very children, and with every minute the island was nearer and nearer.

And then she noticed that the others were skating much faster than they had been. Roger and Titty had left them and caught up the Beckfoot sledge; and, with nothing to pull, were doing their best to overhaul the pioneers strung out along the Alpine rope. And these too, were not talking, but skating much faster than when they had set out from the jetty at Holly Howe. It was as if the island was a magnet and the explorers were scraps of steel pulled harder and harder towards it. It was almost as if they were trying to leave the D.'s behind.

But, once they had reached the island, and the two sledges had been drawn up off the ice at the little landing place, side by side, like two boats, the feeling changed and the old discoverers of the place seemed to want to tell Dick and Dorothea everything about it and to show them round as if they were guests being welcomed to a house.

"It's Spitzbergen," said Titty, "just for now, but you can see what a splendid place it is when it's Wild Cat Island and we live here by ourselves without any natives at all."

"Like to come and look at the harbour?" said John.

"This is the camp," said Susan.

"Our tents were this side the first year," said Roger. "Hung from the trees. But the next year we had four tents. I had one and so had Titty, the sort you can put up anywhere."

They were taken through the bare trees and bushes along the old path to the southern end of the island and shown a little sheet of ice almost shut in by high rocks, and told that it was a harbour.

"Oh, bother it's being winter," said Titty.

They came back to the camp and found Susan clearing the snow from her old fireplace.

"All hands to get firewood," she said, as they stood round watching her. "Here we are on Spitzbergen, and we don't want to freeze to death."

"Dry branches," said John, "but in a frost like this almost anything'll burn."

In a very few minutes a column of smoke was rising from Spitzbergen into the Arctic sky.

"We ought to have filled the kettle before we started," said Susan.

"Nobody'll be trying to skate in the harbour," said John, and took the kettle and went off with Dick and Roger. They smashed a hole at the edge of the ice, with the help of a big stone. They got their hands wet and extremely cold, but they filled the kettle and brought it back to find Susan and Peggy showing Dorothea the proper way to feed a fire in the open.

Then they went down to the landing-place and pulled the sledges up into the camp and ate their dinner by the fire, using the sledges as benches.

It was far too cold to do much sitting about. The moment dinner was over and the mugs rinsed out at the hole in the ice of the old harbour (there was no other washing-up to do), they did a little skating practice. John skated round the island, keeping close to the shore, but he was against anybody else trying this because there was open water not very far away, and there was no point in taking risks for nothing. Then they did some signalling, between Spitzbergen and the mainland. But the long slope of clear snow that came down from Dixon's Farm to the shore was very tempting to owners of a new sledge, and before long the expedition left Spitzbergen and got extremely warm, pulling the sledges up that slope, and racing them down again from the farm to the shore and out on the lake, where they were soon brought to a standstill by the stiff frozen reeds that stuck up out of the ice.

Then they called on the Polar bear, and watched Mrs Dixon give it a bottle of milk. She asked them all to come in to tea, but Susan remembered that Mrs Jackson had told her to bring Dick and Dorothea back to tea at Holly Howe.

"Come in then and have a cake or two to set you on your way," said Mrs Dixon. "There's a lot still left to be eaten."

They were just going into the farm-house when Peggy, who had been silent for some time, said to Dorothea: "Considering it's winter it's not so bad. Greenland yesterday. Spitzbergen today. Or do you think Nancy will wonder why we haven't done something more?"

"How are you going to let her know?" asked Dorothea.

"Dispatches," said Peggy. "It's all right our sending a dispatch, isn't it, Susan?"

"Yes, I should think so," said Susan. "If the doctor'll take it. Mrs Blackett said we were to send messages by him, and he's going there every day."

"Well, let's jolly well cheer her up," said Peggy. She looked at the clock in the kitchen. "We'll get it to him tonight if we're quick, and he'll give it her in the morning."

"I've got some writing paper," said Dorothea.

And there, in the Eskimo settlement at Dixon's Farm, while they were eating cakes and having a glass of milk all round, Peggy sat with a sheet of paper in front of her on which in big letters she had written "NORTH POLAR EXPEDITION," and waited, looking at the point of her pencil.

"Say, 'To Captain Nancy, Amazon Pirate,'" suggested Titty.

"But she isn't being a pirate now," said Peggy.

"Wrong time of year," said Roger, taking another cake.

"Don't say anything about what she is," said John. "Just stick down where we've been. That's all she'll want to know."

Dorothea watched and listened. What a chance for Peggy, she thought. Words poured into her mind. "Trackless solitudes ... marching by the glow of the northern lights ... heroic work among the frozen peaks ..." and so on. But she said nothing. These experienced seamen and explorers would perhaps know better what to write. Dick had lost interest very quickly, and was busy with his pocket-knife, carving out some little wooden cleats, copied from those on the Beckfoot sledge, so that he, too, would be able to rope down baggage in the proper manner, as soon as the cleats were fastened in the right places.

John, Peggy, Titty and Roger made up the despatch between them. Here it is:—

"NORTH POLAR EXPEDITION

"Crossed Greenland. Reached Spitzbergen by ice.

"Captain Flint's houseboat is frozen in.

"Signed – North Polar Expedition.

"PS. – The D.'s have got a sledge. That makes 2.

Peggy.

"PS. – Mr Dixon made it because Dick (and us too) rescued a Polar bear which was starving.

Roger.

"It is getting better with hot milk."

Dorothea thought that this despatch missed a lot of things that might very well have been said. In her own story about the Arctic she would have one altogether different and more exciting. But she said nothing. After all, the despatch did say what had happened.

And then, as there was little time left, they went off at full
gallop to Holly Howe, going by road this time, instead of over
the ice. Luck was with them. At the gate at the top of the field
above Holly Howe, they met Fanny, the girl who had been
helping Mrs Jackson, going home earlier than usual. She took the
despatch for them and promised to leave it at the Doctor's. Two
minutes later and they would have missed her and lost a whole
day. After tea, Dick and Dorothea set off home, with the lantern
to light their way, Dick thinking how best to fasten his cleats to
the sledge, and Dorothea thinking about the despatch and wishing
it had been a little more eloquent. Mr Dixon settled the question
of the cleats with a screwdriver, before they went to bed, and he
went so far as to say "Champion," and "I'm right glad of that,"
when they told him what a success the sledge had been. But, of
course, nothing could be done about the despatch, and when
Dorothea woke in the morning she thought of Nancy reading it,
and was afraid she would be very disappointed.

*

But Dorothea was wrong.

The doctor, with the despatch in his pocket, forgot all about it
while he was seeing Nancy. He remembered it only after he had
said goodbye, and was just going off in his motor car. He hopped
out and ran up the steps with it. Nancy did not get it until after
he had gone. She lay in bed and read it and was very pleased. So
that galoot, Peggy, was trying to keep things going after all. She
really wasn't doing too badly. And then a bit of news in the
despatch made Nancy throw her counterpane off and jump half
out of bed. A new idea had caught her mind. "Hi! Mother!" she
shouted. "Stop him! Stop him!"

"He's coming again tomorrow," said Mrs Blackett.

"Oh well," said Nancy, "I'm not really ready for him yet."

But, if he had not been coming next day, she would almost

have dipped her thermometer in her breakfast tea, to work up such a temperature as would mean that he would be telephoned for in a hurry. She had an answer to send to that dispatch. And such an answer. And somehow or other she would have to get the doctor to take it.

CHAPTER XIV

NANCY TAKES A HAND

Two days later, a postcard from the doctor came to Holly Howe at breakfast-time. "Collect the gang. Inspection of jaws at 9 a.m." John had run upstairs again at once to hoist the diamond over the north cone to let Dick and Dorothea know that they were to come to Holly Howe. And then, when breakfast had hardly been cleared away, there was the doctor, stamping the snow off his shoes on the doorstep and complaining of the slipperiness of the roads. "Chains on both back wheels," he was saying as he was taking off his gloves, "and in spite of all I was skidding on the hill. But it's grand weather for all that. Well, and where are the exiles?"

"Hullo!" said Peggy. "What's the proper way to treat frost-bite?"

"What?" said the doctor. "Frostbite? I hope none of you have been such idiots ... "

"Oh no," said Peggy. "But Roger asked what we would do if we did get frozen, and nobody knew for certain."

"Rub the part affected," said the doctor. "If you think you're getting a nose or an ear frozen, put a handful of snow on it."

"Why, that's what Dick said."

"He's quite right," said the doctor. "In cold countries it's the commonest thing to be walking along and to see someone else touch his nose or his ear. That means he's noticed that your nose or ear is getting frozen. Then you pick up a handful of snow and rub the place with it."

"But how does the other man know before you do?"

"Because when a bit of you is frozen, you can't feel anything in it, and it turns white so that other people can see it."

"Ours mostly turn red," said Roger.

"So long as they're red you needn't worry," said the doctor. "Now then. Any aches and pains? Jawbones? Anybody feeling a little stiff in the jaw. Not a bad disease for some chatterboxes. It's worked wonders with Nancy."

"How is she?" three or four voices asked at once.

"It's pretty hard on her not being able to laugh," said the doctor, "but everything's going on just as it should," and with a slight blowing out of his cheeks and a gesture of both hands round his jaw, the doctor somehow managed to make everybody see poor Nancy with a face like an enormous pumpkin. There was a roar of laughter.

"That's what I wanted," said the doctor. "Nobody holding aching jaws? That's right. If you can laugh like that there's nothing amiss. No toothaches? No earaches? Good. Clean bill of health. Where are those other two, Dorothea her name was, wasn't it? On their way here? ... I'll meet them and save time ... "

"Didn't Nancy send us any message?" asked Peggy. "Thank you very much for taking our dispatch."

"I don't think it's a message exactly," said the doctor. "It doesn't sound like one. But I have got something here for you."

"What is it? What is it?" said Roger.

"She's a masterful young woman, that Nancy of yours," said the doctor. "I told her I could take nothing because Mrs Blackett is so anxious to make sure that none of you comes out with mumps after you do get back to school. And before I quite knew what had happened ... Well, here it is, anyway ... "

He opened the bag in which he carried stethoscope and bandages and all the other things he might be needing on his rounds, and brought out a small parcel wrapped in paper that seemed to have been somehow singed. On the outside of it was written in big capital letters, "DON'T OPEN TILL HE'S GONE. HE KNOWS WHY."

"She offered to show it me," the doctor went on, "but I've known Nancy for some time now, and I said I'd rather know nothing about it. Your Uncle Jim gave me that bit of advice a good many years ago. And Nancy doesn't grow safer with age."

He handed the little parcel to Peggy, who looked at it and shook it, when there was a noise of something heavy banging about in a tin box.

"I asked her if it would stand heat," said the doctor, "and she said that so long as I didn't melt it, it would take no harm. So there it is, and whatever is inside it, I can guarantee it free from mumps. Not that I think there was any danger anyway. It isn't as if she had scarlet fever."

"What is it?" said Roger.

"Don't open till he's gone," said the doctor. "And he's just going. Well, so long. Any messages for Beckfoot?"

They all sent their love to Nancy and to Mrs Blackett, and he told them to keep their jaws working and to let him know at once if they felt any stiffness in them. With that he went out of the room, and they heard him outside asking Mrs Jackson after her husband's wrist that had been sprained some time before.

"Oughtn't we to see him off?" said Susan.

"He's gone," said Peggy. "Where are those scissors?"

In another moment string was cut and paper torn off and they were looking at an old tobacco tin.

"Navy Cut," said John. "That's what father smokes."

"So does Uncle Jim," said Peggy struggling with the lid.

It fitted tightly and flew open with a jerk. A key fell out on the floor. It was a large brass key, old and tarnished. There was a luggage label tied to it and on the label, in capital letters, was written a single word:—

"FRAM."

"Fram?" said Susan. "Fram? What does she mean?"

"The *Fram* was Nansen's ship that was frozen in the ice," said John.

"Of course it was," said Peggy. "I remember Captain Flint reading about it, when they went into the ice on purpose, and were frozen there and drifted right across the Polar sea."

"But what's the key?" asked John.

"It's the key of the houseboat," said Peggy.

Everybody looked from face to face.

"So that we can get inside?" said Roger.

"Not while Captain Flint's away?" said Titty.

"Why not?" said Peggy. Just for one moment she had been taken aback, but now, already, she saw things with Nancy's eyes. The houseboat, frozen in the ice, was better than any igloo on the hillside. Why, Nansen's *Fram* had been in the ice for years. His expedition had lived in her. And here was a *Fram* ready and waiting for them.

"Why not?" she said. "I'd forgotten the keys were at Beckfoot. He leaves them there when he goes away in case he wants anything, and sometimes mother rows across with us, to open the windows and give the cabin an airing."

John looked up.

"It's very bad for a boat to be left shut up a long time and not properly aired."

"But are you sure Captain Flint would like us going into his cabin?" said Susan. "He might not mind us just on deck."

"He'd be jolly pleased," said Peggy.

It was at this point that Dorothea and Dick arrived at Holly Howe after meeting the doctor and having their jaws inspected on the high road. There was Susan, looking very doubtful. There was John, sitting on the edge of the table, looking anxiously at Susan. Roger and Titty were looking at the big key and its label. Peggy, square and determined, was just saying, "Come on. Where are those D.'s? We ought to start at once."

"What's happened?" asked Dorothea.

"Oh, here you are," said Peggy. "We're just going to the *Fram*, Nansen's *Fram*, and we've got the key of the cabin."

Titty held out the key.

They looked at it and read the label.

"But the *Fram* was a real ship," said Dick.

"So is this," said Peggy. "You've seen her, when we went to Spitzbergen. Captain Flint's houseboat."

"The boat we saw frozen in the ice?" said Dick eagerly.

"Of course," said Peggy. "And we're going aboard now. Jib-booms and bobstays," she said, turning to the others, "What's the key *for*?"

"Well, if you're sure he'd like to have the cabin aired," said Susan.

"Can we come, too?" said Dorothea, "not knowing him?"

"You know *us*," said Peggy. "Nancy's sent the key. She'd be jolly sick if the whole expedition didn't go. Come on."

A minute or two later the two sledges were flying down to the lake. The North Polar Expedition set off, round Darien, to the little bay where the old houseboat lay motionless and fast in Arctic ice.

Dick and Dorothea looked at her with new interest as they turned the corner into the little bay. But they were not alone in this. The others, too, felt differently about her now, as they skated towards her with the key of the cabin in Peggy's pocket. When they had first seen her frozen in the ice, they had wondered whether Captain Flint would be aboard her in the summer. Today, in a very few minutes, they would be aboard her themselves.

"It's awfully like burgling," said Titty.

"He's our uncle," said Peggy.

"And we let him into the alliance," Titty comforted herself. "It isn't as if we were enemies."

"I wonder if he knows she's been frozen in," said John.

The more they talked, the clearer it was that the Swallows, except perhaps Roger, were not at all sure that they ought to go aboard, and were glad to have the excuse that it would really be a good thing to open the windows and let a draught through to keep the inside from getting too damp. Peggy, on the other hand, was worried only lest the others should fail her. After all, even if it was burgling, it was not for the first time. She remembered the capturing of the green feathers that Captain Flint had put aside for pipe cleaners, and the firing of the Roman candle on the cabin roof that summer when her uncle had gone native and been too busy to share in the adventures of his nieces. Burgling? Well, why not? Anyhow, Nancy would never have gone to all the trouble of getting the key and making the doctor bring it to them if she had not meant them to use it. As for Dick and Dorothea, they were not worried at all, but wanted very much to see what the houseboat was like inside. The houseboat belonged to Peggy's uncle. Peggy had invited them aboard, and they asked nothing better.

"Skates off first," said John, as the sledges pulled up under the houseboat's steep blue sides.

"Give me a leg up," he said, presently. "Wasn't the accommodation ladder on the fore-deck?"

"That's where he bathes from in summer," said Peggy.

"Remember him walking the plank?" said Titty.

"Did he ever?" asked Dorothea.

"We made him," said Roger.

Peggy and Susan, being the biggest and strongest, gave John two legs up, and hoisted him up to the fore-deck. He scrambled

aboard, and found a little wooden ladder, with two hooks at the
top of it, and a rope loop fastened to the bottom step for a
swimmer to get a foothold under water against the side of the
boat. He hooked it over the side.

"Better have it slung from the after-deck," said Peggy.

"We can't have people skipping over the cabin roof," said
Susan, "with all that snow. Somebody'd be sure to come an
awful smash."

"We've got sledges to take home the bits," said Roger.

"Thank you," said John. "Half a minute while I come
down."

Between them they brought the ladder aft, and hooked it on
once more. John went up first. Peggy followed.

"Come along, Dorothea," she said, getting the key out of her
pocket.

"Now, you three," said Susan, who seemed to count Dick,
Roger, and Titty as all of an age.

When Roger was safely on deck, Susan climbed up herself.

Peggy was just fitting the big key in the door. It was a little
stiff.

"Are you sure it's the right key?" said Susan. "We mustn't
force the lock."

"Probably some rain or snow's got in the lock and frozen,"
suggested Dick, and Dorothea was very pleased to hear John say,
"I bet that's what's the matter."

Peggy shook the door handle, and then turned the key as hard
as she could. There was a sharp click, and the next moment they
were looking into the dim twilight of the cabin. There were no
skylights, and curtains had been pulled across all the windows. A
queer, musty smell drifted out to meet them.

"Well, it certainly does need airing," said Susan, "and we'd
better draw the curtains for a bit and let some sunlight in."

Dorothea and Dick were in the houseboat for the first time, and even the Swallows had never been there except as guests of Captain Flint. Voices, for no real reason, were hushed while Peggy and Susan pulled back the curtains from the windows nearest the door.

"Of course, he's away," said Titty, "but doesn't it feel as if someone was here?"

"What about opening the door into the fo'c'sle and trying to get a draught right through?" said Susan.

John worked his way past the long table that ran down the middle of the cabin, past a sturdy little iron stove, and opened a low door, through which Dick and Dorothea caught a glimpse of oilskin coats and cooking things in racks, and a Primus stove or two. But, for the moment, there was enough to look at in the cabin itself. There were the long settees on either side, wide enough for anybody to sleep on. There were the neatly folded red blankets. There were the strong chairs round the table. There were the cupboards that ran along the settees below the level of the windows. And then there were all the things that this strange uncle of Peggy's had brought back from his travels, a knobkerry, a boomerang, a model catamaran from Ceylon, a bamboo flute from Shanghai, bright-coloured leather cushions from Omdurman, a necklace of sharks' teeth. All these things, except, of course, the cushions, which were in the corners of the settees, were hung on the walls, out of the way, between the windows; for, though the place was a little like a museum, it had also the neatness of a ship's cabin. On one side of the door that John had just opened into the fo'c'sle was a barometer, and on the other was a clock.

John tapped the barometer gently, but Peggy, seeing the hands of the clock standing still at half-past three, though it was in the middle of the morning, marched straight up to it, opened it, and wound it up with the key that was hanging beside it. She asked John what the right time was, and when he told her, set the clock and closed its glass door with a sharp click. It was like taking possession.

"There's a lot of mildew on the cushions," Dorothea heard Susan saying.

Dorothea was a little disappointed in the books. She, Titty, and Dick began at once to search along the two shelves that held Captain Flint's houseboat library. All the books seemed to be books of travel. Dorothea had been looking for stories, but there were none except *The Riddle of the Sands*, and that, when she glanced at the charts in the beginning of it, did not seem her sort of book. But Dick had found almost at once the very book he wanted.

"Here it is," he said. "*Farthest North*. The Voyage and Exploration of the *Fram*, and the Fifteen-Months Sledge Expedition. This'll tell us everything we want to know."

"There's an enormous lot of coal in the fo'c'sle," said John, presently.

"Well, I'm going to light the stove," said Susan. "We're here, anyway, and we may as well do some good. His things'll be getting dreadfully damp."

"He's got a tremendous lot of good stores," said Roger. "Jams, and pemmican, and sardines and ... "

"Shut that cupboard door, Roger," said Susan.

The stove burned very well, after the first few unfortunate minutes, when the smoke poured out in their faces, before they discovered the chimney that needed to be fixed on outside the cabin roof. Once that was done, the houseboat soon warmed up and began to feel, indeed, a little like a greenhouse.

"What are you going to do about tea to have with our sandwiches?" said John. "Our kettle's up at the igloo."

"He's got a beauty," said Peggy.

"Perhaps, if we clean it properly afterwards," said Susan.

For water, after a sad experience with the snow on the roof, which, when melted, tasted smoky and very unpleasant, the leaders of the expedition sent Roger and Dick ashore. A cart track came down through the woods to the head of Houseboat Bay, and close by this track in summer a little beck poured into the lake. It was all but dry now, but a trickle still ran over its stones, and under the icicles of a tiny waterfall they found a pool just big enough to let them fill the kettle. The stove was burning so well that there was no need to touch the Primuses, and Susan boiled the kettle in the cabin.

Peggy explored the drawers and cupboards one after another.

"He's got every possible thing," she said, just as they were settling down to dinner. "This is the best tin-opener I've ever seen; and loganberry jam," she went on, "in a tin, with pictures of the loganberries on the outside."

Roger looked sideways down the table at Susan.

"Oh, look here, Peggy, we must leave his things alone."

"He wouldn't grudge a tin of jam to a North Polar expedition," said Peggy.

"But we can't take it," said Susan.

"Well, I've opened it now," said Peggy. "It'll only go bad if we don't."

"One tin," said Roger.

They were very good loganberries, not at all spoilt by being made into jam. The berries were still separate, not squashed.

When the cabin clock told them it was time to go, it seemed as if they had only just finished dinner. Dick was hard at work reading the story of the real *Fram*, and most unwilling to be disturbed. Titty was reading *The First Crossing of Greenland*. Dorothea and Roger were helping in the wiping, while Susan and Peggy were still busy with the washing up which somehow had been put off a little because there was so much to look at. John had found a tin of metal polish, and was polishing up the brass work with a rag. Locking the cabin door from the outside,

climbing down on the ice, unhooking the ladder and pushing it
up on deck, and setting out for Holly Howe and for Dixon's
Farm, felt very much like leaving home.

Even Susan admitted it in a way.

"The cabin could do with a bit more airing tomorrow," she
said.

CHAPTER XV

DAYS IN THE *FRAM*

THIS was only the beginning. The airing of the houseboat went on next day, and the day after that, and for many days. Captain Flint, Peggy assured the others, would be very pleased. Anyway, he ought to be. That first tin of loganberry jam was followed by another, and yet another, and it was thought that even in tins sardines would not keep for ever, and that it would be a pity if, when Captain Flint returned, he should have to throw them away. Then nobody could tell if the Primus stoves were in good working order without trying them. There was plenty of oil in the fo'c'sle, and a big bottle of methylated spirits; and though John and Susan did not trust Peggy's rather rough and ready way with such things they came to think that it would be rather good for the Primuses to be properly used. Before very long even Susan had all but forgotten that the houseboat really belonged to somebody else. It had become the *Fram*, and there was such a lot to do aboard that Susan began to grudge the time they spent anywhere else, because her housekeeping arrangements, cleaning of pots and pans, etc., kept getting in arrears.

Dick and Dorothea, or one of them, mostly Dick, used to run up to the old barn every morning, just to see what signal was hanging on the end of the house at Holly Howe. But it was always one of two. On days when the doctor had sent word that he was coming, there was a diamond on the top of a north cone, and the D.'s went straight by road to the Jacksons'. On all other days it was a square over a south cone. It had been decided that this signal was to mean "Come to the *Fram*," because, as John said, a square on the top of a south cone is very like the midship section of a houseboat. There it was, day after day, when Dick, with telescope to his eye, looked down to Holly Howe. Day after day, in reply, square over south cone was hoisted on the old barn, to show the others that their signal had been seen and understood. Meanwhile, Dorothea, down at the farm, would be busy stuffing their knapsacks and getting the sledge ready, and they would set out at once for the *Fram*, sometimes down the field and over the ice, sometimes by road, turning through a gate in the wood half-way between the two farms, and following the cart track down through the trees to the shore of Houseboat Bay, only a few score yards from the icebound ship.

Plans for the day were decided aboard the *Fram* each morning. The *Fram* became the main base of the expedition. The igloo was all but deserted except when they went up there for old sake's sake, to keep it in repair, or because they were tired of skating and wanted some climbing practice. Except that everybody slept in comfortable beds in comfortable farmhouses, and had good suppers and breakfasts cooked by Mrs Dixon and Mrs Jackson, they lived the life of Polar explorers. The *Fram* became their home, and Nansen himself never waited more anxiously for news of ice conditions in the Arctic than the seven in the houseboat watched the freezing of the lake.

Day by day there was less open water in the middle of the lake. Day by day the areas marked out as dangerous by little red flags grew less and less. More and more people were skating, and several times the explorers were bothered by inquisitive seals, walruses, or Eskimos, who came skating into the bay and peered in at the windows of the *Fram*, curious to know what was going on in that old boat with a trickle of smoke from the chimney on the cabin roof. And then, one day, the whole expedition, who had taken the sledges down to Spitzbergen, gathering firewood from the wooded shores below High Greenland, strung themselves out along the Alpine rope, and crossed the lake at its deepest, between Spitzbergen and the little rocky patch of Cormorant Island on the farther side. The cormorants had flown away to the sea coast when the ice had put an end to their fishing, but Dick and Dorothea heard a story of treasure-hunting, and were shown the place under the roots of the fallen tree where Captain Flint's box had been hidden by the thieves.

Once or twice, in the middle of the day, there seemed to be half a promise of a thaw; and the explorers, seeing drops of water on the tips of icicles, looked glumly at each other. But then, as the sun weakened, the frost came hard again, and sometimes for days on end it froze so hard that there was never a hint of melting snow even in the full glow of the sun at noon.

"It'll never be what it was," said Mrs Dixon, one night, when Dick and Dorothea had come in too tired from skating even to run up to the barn to look at stars. "Not what it was in '95, with coaches with four horses and horns blowing crossing the lake from side to side. But it's a rare frost for all that."

"How long will it last?" said Dick.

"No signs of its breaking yet," said Mr Dixon.

Day after day, at Holly Howe and at Dixon's Farm, the first words said by waking explorers were the question: "Is it still freezing?" and the sharp nip of the morning air was welcomed like warmth in June.

They had plenty to do. Out of doors they were steadily training themselves for long journeys over the ice on skates, towing sledges. In the evenings, sometimes the D.'s went to tea at Holly Howe, and sometimes the others came to tea with them. Once or twice they all went up to the observatory to look at stars with Dick and Dorothea, but there was so much else to be done that Dick felt he was neglecting his astronomy, and used to bring the star-book with him to the *Fram*, meaning to work at it there, but somehow never could. The others made Dorothea tell them stories, too,

AIRING THE *FRAM*

but they insisted that all the stories should be about the sea, and then, whenever she said anything about what happened to a ship or a boat, everybody would start talking at once. "But, look here, didn't you say the wind was against them?" "They couldn't have done that if they were on port tack." "But they wouldn't go aloft to reef that kind of sail." It seemed to her that she couldn't mention a ship without going wrong, and yet how could she tell sea stories with no ships in them. Sometimes it was almost more than she could bear, and then they would tell her to go on and say what happened next, and everybody would be quiet for half an hour or so, while something was happening on an island; and then, when she simply had to take her hero to sea, uproar would break out again. It really was easier to read aloud.

Even while stories were being told, nobody in the *Fram* was idle for a moment. For as time went on, they had much more to do than they could manage, work of a kind they had never thought of when first the expedition had been planned. The idea had really come from the silent Mr Dixon.

Ever since that night, when he and Silas had built a sledge for the D.'s, and Dick had driven with him to the blacksmith's to have the iron runners put on it, Mr Dixon had known something of what was planned. They were going to the North Pole. Mr Dixon knew that, and went on turning it over in his mind. One day, for example, he said to Dick, "You'll find nowt better than this for keeping wet out of your boots if there's deep snow about the Pole." He nodded towards the north, and gave Dick a big tin full of goose-grease. And after that, of course, there was no getting any polish on any of the explorers' boots, because of the goose-grease that had been rubbed into them. And then, a day or two later, Dorothea had heard him talking with Silas about the far north. Silas said, "Aye. It's colder up there than here, likely, but with the furs them folk wear they don't feel it."

"Furs?" said Mr Dixon.

"Bearskins and such," said Silas. "Fair wadded out with 'em."

Mr Dixon grunted, and said no more; but next day, after Dick had been watching him at the evening milking, he had taken him up into one of the lofts and shown him there a great store of sheepskins, roughly cured, with the wool left on them.

"You'll be wanting summat like this," he said, "if half's true they say about yon Pole."

"But can we really take some?" Dick had asked.

"And welcome," said Mr Dixon.

So there had been a day when Dick and Dorothea had come to the *Fram*, with their sledge piled high with sheepskins. Sheepskins had been spread on the bunks and on the floors of the cabin, with an excellent Arctic effect.

Mr Dixon thought of the sheepskins, but that set old Silas thinking too. He talked to Mrs Dixon, and she got out needle and thread and some scraps of stuff, and old Silas came in with a lot of rabbit skins and between them they made a cap of rabbits' fur, lined within, and with the fur outside.

Dick was a little shy about putting it on, but Dorothea had said it was the very thing he ought to have, and the moment he saw it, Roger wanted one like it, and if Roger, why not Titty, as Susan said, and it turned out that Silas had any number of rabbit skins, and that Mr Jackson had a good few too. This work, once begun, could not be stopped, and the cabin of the *Fram*, while Dorothea was telling her stories, was like a tailor's shop in Siberia, or some such place. There were skins all over the table and the settees, and even on the floor, and Susan was kept busy cutting out, and the whole expedition was hard at work with needle and thread making fur hats like Dick's. In the end, nobody wanted to be left without one. Nor did it stop at fur hats. Mittens were even more useful. Everybody had felt their hands grow cold, pulling on a sledge rope, or when the snow had melted on a woollen glove. Rabbit-skin mittens, made with the skin double, so that there was fur inside and out, were very easy to pull on and off, very warm, and looked so real that everybody wondered how ever they had thought of going to the North Pole without them.

"Let's make some for Nancy," said Dorothea.

"Jib-booms and bobstays, of course we must," said Peggy, half cross with herself for not having thought of this before.

A fur hat and a pair of mittens were made for Nancy at once, and were taken across to Beckfoot by the doctor after one of his jaw-inspections at Holly Howe. Nancy was allowed to see them from a distance. There was no point in letting her handle them. "The fewer things we have to disinfect the better," said Mrs Blackett, "but you see what's waiting for you as soon as you are all right."

A good many days had passed since the doctor had carried back to Nancy not a dispatch (which might too easily give secrets away), but a simple mathematical formula, invented by Dick, to let her know that the key had arrived and was being used.

$$\text{``Fram}: \text{Igloo} :: 10,000 : 1.\text{''}$$

This meant, of course, that the houseboat was ten thousand times better than the igloo; and Nancy had bounced in her bed and hugged herself at the thought of what must be going on there. She was bursting to join the others, and there never was a patient who was in such a hurry to be cured. Every time the doctor came to Holly Howe to look at jaws, he brought good news of her to the explorers, who were anxiously calculating how long the frost must last if Captain Nancy was to join them on the ice. They heard that her face was rather less like a pumpkin than it had been. Then they heard of her getting up in the mornings, and even being allowed to go downstairs. "She'll be out and about before we know where we are," said the doctor.

They made no more attempts to see her by coming to Beckfoot.

Mrs Blackett had told them to keep to their own side of the lake, and they only once came north of Rio Bay. That was when all the Eskimos were talking of the lake being frozen from end to end, and it was more than anybody could bear not to have a look at the northern part beyond the islands. All seven explorers, with both sledges, and a quarantine flag carried by Titty (the D.'s had left theirs at the farm), set out from the *Fram* one morning, and skated close along the shores of Long Island, across the mouth of Rio Bay, until they could see that tremendous sheet of ice stretching before them into the hills.

"There's no doubt about the Arctic now," said Peggy. "It's good enough for anybody."

"If only it doesn't thaw," said Roger.

"If only Nancy was ready," said John.

Both telescopes were trained on the Beckfoot promontory, as if some miracle might happen, and Captain Nancy come skating down the lake to meet them.

"Let's just go to the farthest island," said Titty.

"We might do that," said John.

It was not very far, and presently the yellow quarantine flag was waving on the top of a little pile of rocks and stones that stuck up out of the ice.

"We won't go another yard," said John, "until the day. Much better keep it as unexplored as possible."

"This is our farthest north," said Dick, "not counting when we went to Beckfoot."

"Let's make a cache," said Titty.

"We will," said John, looking about him. "Good. Some untidy Eskimo's left a ginger-beer bottle. We couldn't have anything better."

"Cork in it, too," said Roger.

Dorothea wondered what they wanted it for, but was soon tearing a leaf out of the note-book, in which her romance was

still stuck at the beginning of chapter one. John borrowed a pencil
as well.

"What about Cache Island?" he said, "or has it got a name
already?"

"We've never given it one," said Peggy.

John wrote:

"Cache Island.
"Reached this point of northern latitude, 28th January.
"S., A., & D. North Polar Expedition."

"Swallows, Amazons, and D.'s," Peggy explained, looking
over his shoulder.

Titty and Roger were already building a little cairn of small
stones. The scrap of paper was put in the bottle. The bottle was
walled up inside the cairn, and after one last look into the frozen
north, the expedition left Cache Island and set off southwards on
the return journey to the *Fram*.

CHAPTER XVI

SAILING SLEDGE

LIFE in the *Fram* had become as regular as clockwork, when one day, after a busy morning in the cabin, they were setting out on a sledge run down to Cormorant Island and back, "to keep the dogs in good condition," as Peggy said, and stopped a moment in the middle of the lake, because Roger, as so often, was having trouble with a skate. John was screwing it up properly, and getting the strap in the right place, when there was a faint, breathless cry from Titty, "A sail! A sail!" and they saw the first of the ice yachts swooping out from between Long Island and the Rio shore.

Dick and Dorothea had never sailed themselves. They could not know what the sight of that white wing gliding past the dark trees meant to the mate of the *Amazon* and the captain and crew of the *Swallow*.

"It's very pretty," said Dorothea.

She got no answer at all. All five of her new friends were as if stunned. For a minute or two not one of them spoke, and then, as the white sail swept nearer and nearer to the shore, Dorothea heard John say, quietly, as if to himself alone, "Going about. She'll be going about. But how can she?"

And at that moment the white sail fell suddenly aquiver, narrowed, widened again, and seemed almost to leap from under the dark woods as it swooped out once more towards the middle of the lake.

"She's gone about," Peggy, Susan, Titty, and Roger spoke all together.

"But how does it work?" said Dick.

"Tacking," said Roger.

"How?" said Dick.

"If only it was summer we'd show you," said Titty.

But the white sail was coming nearer, swooping from side to side of the lake, faster than any boat, beating against the southerly wind that was blowing from Spitzbergen. Presently the ice-yacht passed close by them, and they could hear the roar of the runners, and see the ice-dust flying from under them. Soon it was far away, and they watched it until it disappeared behind Spitzbergen before showing again, a tiny flash of white flying to and fro as it neared the foot of the lake.

"It was on three skates," said Dick.

"Can't we put a sail on the sledge?" said Titty. "The whole lake's frozen now."

"Nansen did it," said Roger.

There was again a silence.

During those working days in the *Fram* before they had got into the habit of making Dorothea tell stories, Titty and she had been made to read aloud, for the good of the expedition, from the books on Arctic exploration they that had found in Captain Flint's cabin bookshelves. Nansen had been their favourite author. In his *First Crossing of Greenland*, his whole expedition had been even smaller than their own, six explorers, counting the Lapps, instead of their own seven, or rather eight as soon as Captain Nancy should recover.

In both Nansen's books they had found pictures of his sledges under sail. As soon as they had seen them they had thought of trying what they could do in the way of hoisting sail on their own. But at that time the lake was not yet bearing all over, and Susan had been very sure that this was an idea that would not be approved by their parents. "One good puff, and you'll be off the ice and into the water."

"And then what?" Roger had said.

That had been the end of the idea. There had been another reason, too. All the sledges in the Nansen books were rigged with a square sail, and though John could handle a little fore-and-aft sail, like *Swallow*'s, he knew square sails worked altogether differently. Besides, he had not got one.

The ice-yacht, skimming to and fro against the wind, going about exactly like *Swallow* herself, and with a sail almost like hers, made the thing seem possible once more, and by now there were no spaces of open water waiting to engulf a sailing sledge.

"I wonder what's become of *Swallow*'s old mast?" said John suddenly. "The one that was broken in the shipwreck."

"We brought it back from Horseshoe Cove," said Titty.

"Come on," said John. "Let's get back fairly early, and have a look for it in the boathouse."

★

Next morning, when the signal was the same as usual, the wind was blowing from the north, and so cold that Dorothea and Dick went to Houseboat Bay by road and down through the wood to get the shelter of the trees. It was cold enough even so, and as they came down on the shore they were looking forward to warming up again in the *Fram*'s snug cabin. But they found the cabin door was locked, and nobody there. It was far too cold to stand about on the ice, waiting, so they put on their skates, left their sledge by the houseboat, and skated out of the bay to see if the others were in sight.

At first they could see no sign of them. There were the usual lot of seals skating about round the end of Long Island, and they saw the white sail of yesterday's ice yacht racing along against the background of the trees on the farther side of the lake.

"They may be coming by road, too," said Dorothea.

G

"Not with the wind behind them," said Dick. "They wouldn't even notice it was cold."

And at that moment a little brown sail showed under Darien.

"Hullo!" said Dick. "What's that? Another ice yacht. But what a little one!"

Something seemed to be wrong with the sail. Two or three times it was dropped altogether, and hoisted again. Half a dozen people seemed to be busy with it.

"I believe it's them," said Dorothea suddenly. "That very small one must be Roger."

"It can't be," said Dick.

"It's a sledge," said Dorothea. "It isn't spidery enough for an ice yacht."

"And I've gone and left my telescope in my knapsack," said Dick.

He was on the point of skating back to the *Fram* to fetch it when he saw that the brown sail was moving. It was nearer. That little crowd that had been round it on the ice had disappeared. It was coming faster and faster, straight down wind, rushing towards them. The freezing wind from the north bothered his eyes. He screwed them up behind his spectacles, and stared as hard as he could. It did almost look like the Beckfoot sledge. But with a queer brown sail and a mast and ... yes, it could be nothing else.

"Dot," he said, "it is them. They've got their yellow flag on the top of the mast."

In a few seconds the sledge was half-way towards them. Its passengers were half-hidden by the brown sail. A row of legs stuck out on one side.

Dick and Dorothea shouted at the tops of their voices.

There was a cheerful yell. Someone on the sledge had seen them.

"They'll be right into us in a minute," said Dorothea. "Look out. They're coming straight for us."

They could see John at the back of the sledge leaning out and hauling in a rope as hard as he could.

A loud word of command rang out.

"Shove your port legs down ... *hard*!"

Five boots met the ice. The sledge swerved violently to the left, came broadside on to the wind, skidded sideways with a sharp screech from the iron runners beneath it, and turned over with a loud crash as its mast slammed down on the ice. Skates, knapsacks, and explorers seemed to be almost everywhere.

"Quick, quick," cried Dorothea. "They must have hurt themselves most awfully."

But the explorers had been luckier than they deserved.

"No damage done," John was saying. He was sitting up on the ice, with the main sheet still in his hand, looking at the overturned sledge. "The mast isn't broken. And the sail isn't torn. Only old ropes gone. We can easily rig her again."

"Are you all right, Roger?" Susan was limping towards the ship's boy, who, like the captain, seemed to be in no hurry about getting up.

"Usual knees," said Roger, "but not bad."

Dorothea was trying to help Titty to her feet.

"It's quite all right," said Titty. "Only don't hurry ... I say, wasn't she just going it?"

"No need to suck it when it's bleeding like that," said Susan.

Peggy was hobbling along, licking a finger from which blood kept dripping on the ice.

"Anybody hurt?" she asked.

"Come along to the *Fram*, everybody," said Susan. "There's lots of lint and a bottle of iodine in the cupboard." Even if Susan had remembered that the *Fram* was not theirs with everything in it, she would have decided at once that no one would grudge a bandage and some iodine to a finger that left a crimson trail.

"Some beastly thing cut through my glove," said Peggy. "A skate, probably."

"Come on to the *Fram*," said Susan, who had herself come down pretty hard. And then, sharply, "Look out, Dorothea! Peggy's going to faint."

"I'm jolly well not," said Peggy.

It was true she did feel rather sick; but, as for fainting, when she was in Captain Nancy's place, not she! "Shiver my timbers!" she said, with rather less than the usual ring. "Shiver my timbers! It's nothing at all. Shove your hand into my pocket, D., and get hold of the key."

She held up the hand with the bleeding finger to keep it out of the way, while Dorothea rummaged in the pocket of her coat and brought out the key of the houseboat. The wounded climbed painfully aboard, and a minute or two later the cabin had become a dressing-station as well as a tailor's shop, and Captain Flint's iodine was being generously slopped on cuts and scrapes.

Dick, John, and Titty were the last to come in. They had waited to collect skates and knapsacks, and to tow the now dismasted sledge.

"But why did it turn over?" Dick was asking, as they came down into the cabin.

"Not enough beam," said John. "Too narrow. She was all right until we tried reaching, and then we were over at once. And the trouble is, you can't really steer her at all."

"The quarantine flag was just right," said Roger. "It means 'Look out! These are dangerous people!' and so we were. It's a jolly good thing that nobody got in the way."

"Anyway, we've sailed," said Titty.

★

After dinner in the *Fram*, John and Peggy (whose hand had been impressively bandaged), decided to have another try.

"SHOVE YOUR PORT LEGS DOWN . . . *HARD!*"

Captain Flint had a good supply of spare ropes in the fo'c'sle, so that they were able to repair the rigging. Dick watched what they were doing, and tried to copy John's knots with a bit of rope they had discarded.

"Turning sailor?" said John. "Why not?"

"I'd awfully like to know how it works," said Dick.

"We'll want a bit more weight," said John, "if Susan and the others aren't coming."

"Do take care," said Susan, looking down from the deck of the *Fram* when they were ready to start. "Ice isn't like water. It's no joke capsizing on it. Roger's knees are in an awful mess, and so is Titty's elbow."

Dorothea was on the point of saying that Dick had better not go, but she stopped herself in time. She knew Dick's face very well, and one glance at it showed that at that moment it would not be any use to try to keep him back.

They towed the sledge up against the wind, and sailed down with it as before; and, though there was less wind than in the morning, again they upset the moment they tried to swing round and sail into Houseboat Bay. The sledge fell over, the mast hitting the ice a fearful crack. John, Peggy, and Dick picked themselves up rather glumly. And just at that moment the ice yacht came flying by, beating up against the wind, swooping from side to side of the lake like a swallow, turning as it neared each shore by what seemed to Dick as near as might be to a miracle.

"It's no good," said John, when they had rolled up the sail, tidied up the sledge after its adventures, climbed back to the deck of the *Fram*, and were going down into the cabin, "it's no good. We can sail with the wind, but it's no good trying to sail any other way. It's as bad as trying to sail a narrow rowing boat."

"Any more wounds?" asked Susan.

"None to matter," said Peggy.

Dick and John went straight to the bookshelf, got out the

Nansen books, and looked once more at the pictures of the sailing sledges, and read again what Nansen said about them.

"He didn't try to sail except with the wind," said John.

"It's much better than towing both ways," said Dick.

And that night, as Dick and Dorothea went home together over the ice to Dixon's Farm, he could talk of nothing else.

"Why shouldn't we sail, too?" he asked her. "Think if there was the right wind when we go to the North Pole, and they hoist a sail and we have to crawl behind. They'll beat us by miles and miles. And their sail wasn't the same shape as Nansen's ... "

At supper he was still talking of sailing, and of why the sledge had upset when the wind had caught it broadside on.

Mrs Dixon thought he was talking of the ice-yacht.

"Bonny sight it was and all. There was three or four of them rushing about on the lake in '95, and racing for a silver cup."

Dick explained that they had been sailing the Beckfoot sledge, and that he wanted to sail their own.

Mrs Dixon did not think he meant it, and went on talking of the racing of the ice yachts all those years ago, when she had been a young girl, and herself had skated from one end of the lake to the other.

Mr Dixon, as usual, sat silent.

But next morning, as Dick was hurrying across the yard to run up to the observatory to see what signal there might be at Holly Howe, Mr Dixon stopped him by the woodshed.

"There's a bit of a larch pole in there that happen might do you for a mast."

Dick and Dorothea were very late that day in coming to the *Fram*. They did not explain what had kept them.

"It's no good saying anything about it," said Dick, "in case we can't do it after all."

There was no wind that day, and so no sailing, but he took the opportunity of making a careful drawing of one of the sailing

sledges in the Nansen books, and that night after supper he was
late to bed, sitting up with Mr Dixon by the kitchen fire, looking
at the drawing by the light of an oil lamp on the corner of the
kitchen table, and planning how the mast should be made and
what would be the best way to fix it upright on the sledge.

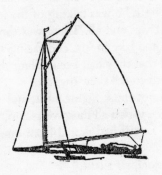

CHAPTER XVII

NANCY SENDS A PICTURE

"Diamond over north cone," said Dick, hurrying breathlessly into the kitchen. "We've got to go to Holly Howe. We'd better go at once and leave the mast till later."

"It can't be the doctor," said Dorothea. "We saw him only the day before yesterday."

"It's something urgent," said Dick, "or they'd have waited to tell us at the *Fram*."

It was a nuisance having to go to Holly Howe. If only it had been the *Fram* signal there would have been no hurry, and he would have been able to get on with that mast. Mr Dixon was about too, and would have been ready to help. But the Holly Howe signal meant that, whatever might be planned, the others would be waiting for them, and there was nothing for it but to start at once. In a very few minutes their provisions for the day were packed on the sledge and, pulling uphill and tobogganing down, they hurried along the road, ending up with a splendid run down the field and through the Holly Howe gate, which luckily happened to be open.

"At last," they heard Peggy's voice.

They got up from the sledge, stamped the snow off their boots, and went into the farm. There, in the big parlour, they found the others looking at something on the table.

"Is something the matter?" asked Dorothea, when she saw their serious faces.

"It's Nancy," said Peggy. "Look at this."

"The doctor met Mr Jackson and gave it him to give to us," said Roger.

The thing they were all looking at was a very small drawing, done on a sheet of writing-paper. Anybody could see the paper had been in the oven for disinfection, because it was faintly browned all over as if it had been scorched. Drawn in black ink upon it was a sledge, with four skating figures pulling it, two others sitting on the top of it, and another hanging on or pushing behind. On the shore (for the sledge was clearly going along on the ice) an excited crowd of people were talking to each other and waving their arms. A sign-post showed the way to the North Pole, and at the bottom corner of the picture was a compass sign also showing that the sledge party was on its way to the north.

"It must be meant for us," said Roger. "Seven of us, counting both of you."

"But why are all the people so excited?" asked Titty.

"Perhaps it's a race," said Dorothea.

"But there's only one sledge," said Peggy.

"She must be very tired of staying in bed," said Dorothea, "and she's been drawing pictures just for fun, and this is one of them."

"But she isn't in bed," said Peggy. "She's hopping about like anything. She only goes back to bed in the afternoons. The doctor said so last time he was here."

"And anyway, why does she send it to us?" said Titty. "She knows we can do pictures too."

"She wouldn't do it for nothing," said Peggy.

"Well," said John, "I still think it means that she wants us to start for the Pole, but I don't understand why."

"But how can she mean that, when she knows she'll be able to come herself if we wait and the frost goes on like it is?"

"I know," said John, "but there you are, seven of us, and

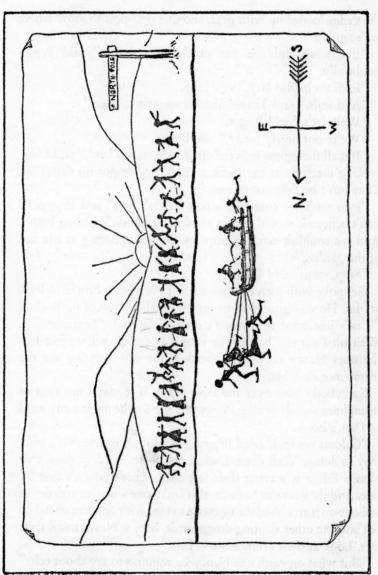

NANCY'S QUESTION

the sledge loaded up with gear, and that sign-post to show where we're going."

"But what did she put in the crowd for?" said Peggy doubtfully.

"Eskimos in Rio Bay," said John.

"And seals," said Titty. "She means start at once."

"Well, let's," said Roger.

"We're not nearly ready," said Susan.

"But all those people in the crowd are on dry land," said Dick, looking carefully at the picture, "and they've got no skates on. They can't be Eskimos or seals."

"I do wish we could go across and ask her," said Peggy. "I don't believe it would do her any harm now she's getting better. And we couldn't catch mumps by just semaphoring at her out of the garden."

"Stop, stop!" said Dick.

He spoke with such excitement that everybody turned to look at him. He was struggling to get his notebook out of his pocket. "That's just what the crowd's doing," he said. "Semaphoring. Wait till I get my book. The people in the crowd are just like the ones Nancy drew for me when she was showing me the semaphore alphabet."

Everybody bent over the table again. If it was a question of semaphore signals neither Peggy nor the Swallows had any need of Dick's book.

"Galoots we are!" cried Peggy. "Donks! Of course that's what they're doing. Well done, Dick. Look there. Look at those two plump Eskimos waving their left arms. That's two E's side by side. And the next one to them, that lanky one with one arm down and one up is an L. And the next one to him, with one arm stretched out and the other slanting downwards, is an S. Never mind their legs. Look at their arms. E-E-L-S. Eels."

"But what on earth can Nancy be wanting to say about eels?"

said Susan. "It must be just accident that those figures look like letters."

"Nancy'd jolly well shiver our timbers if she heard us say so. Anyway, let's get a bit of paper and see if it makes sense. Good for you, Titty. You write them down."

"The first one's an M," said Dick, who had been carefully hunting through the set of signals Nancy had drawn in his pocket-book. And the next's an A. I can't find the one like a washer-woman. Oh, yes, I have. It's an R."

But the others were already reading far ahead.

"M-A-R-F-E," said Peggy. "Stick them down, Titty. Ready? You can see they're all letters. This E is just like the others."

"Bigger and not so plump," said Roger.

"Never mind anything except their arms," said Peggy. "Go on. H-T-N. That's as far as the little she-Eskimo with her arms slanting down on each side. Then it goes on just the same. They're letters all right. She's made them all skipping about just to puzzle any native who might try to read it. That tall one's an I. Then there's a G and she's made it look like a governess. N-I."

"It isn't a bit like the other I," said Roger.

"Galoot," said Peggy. "Its arms are. P. Then the two E's. E-E-L-S-S-I-O-H-W."

"Steady," said John.

"Not quite so fast," said Titty. "S-S-I. What then?"

"O-H-W."

"Well, it doesn't make sense," said Susan.

Peggy looked at what Titty had written, and read it aloud with a rather puzzled expression.

"Marfeht nignip eels siohw?"

"It's like some Indian language," said Titty. "Have you and Nancy got one that we don't know anything about?"

"Not yet," said Peggy.

"What about the people pulling the sledge?" said Dick. "Are

they letters, too? That first one might be an A. Not very good though. All the four in front might be A's."

"But the ones sitting on the sledge aren't like any of the letters."

"Just being lazy," said Roger.

"And why has she put the compass in?" said John. "That means something."

"Shows they're going to the North Pole," said Roger. "And we are, too. I bet it all means 'Get ready to start.'"

"And a signboard as well," said John. "As if the compass wasn't enough."

"Remember that other letter of Nancy's up in Swallowdale," said Titty, "when we had to show the arrow to the parrot. Let's do just what she says. The sledge must be us, and it's going the way the signboard is pointing. Let's go that way. Right to left. Try from that end. W-H-O-I ... "

"You've got it," shouted Peggy. "Who? Who ISSLE ... ?"

"Wait a minute," said John. "Who is. Now then. S-L-E-E-P, sleeping. It's coming out now. I-N-T. In the F-R ... WHO IS SLEEPING IN THE 'FRAM'?"

"It's a jolly good thing Nancy doesn't know what an age we took to make it out," said Peggy.

"But what does it mean?" said Susan. "We've locked up every night before coming home. And we've never left the key in the cabin door. Peggy's put it in her pocket every time."

"Somebody may have got another key," said Roger.

"The only other one's still at home," said Peggy.

"It must be burglars again," said Titty.

"But how does Nancy know about it?"

"Somebody's seen a light there, and told them at Beckfoot, and she thinks we must have left the door open."

"We'd better go down there at once and look round," said Susan.

And the whole seven tobogganed down the field from Holly Howe to the boathouse, put on their skates at the edge of the ice, and then skated steadily away, round under the icicle-hung cliffs of Darien, and down the lake to Houseboat Bay.

But there seemed to be nothing suspicious about the houseboat when they skated up to it, and sat on their sledges to take their skates off before going aboard.

"Do you think the burglar may be still there?" Roger had asked.

"Not unless he's a fool," said John. "He must know we come every day."

All the same, John walked slowly all round the *Fram* on the ice, and had a look at her from all sides, just to see if there was any sign of the presence of an invader.

There was none.

John, Peggy, and Susan left the others on the ice and climbed aboard. When Peggy had unlocked the cabin door, John walked right through and into the fo'c'sle, rummaging about and making sure that no one could be hidden in the ship. Meanwhile the others had been watching, half expecting to see the fo'c'sle hatch lift suddenly up, and the burglar, whoever he was, some cheeky young seal or Eskimo, bolt from it like a startled rabbit. But nothing of the sort happened. The fo'c'sle hatch did lift, but only to let John put his head out and say, "All clear," after which the others climbed aboard and went down into the cabin in the ordinary way.

"Don't touch anything," said John. "Let's first make sure everything is exactly as we left it last night."

A careful search was made without anything being touched except one small piece of chocolate, which Roger found just where he had left it by mistake. He decided that as it had been given him yesterday, it had better be eaten at once lest Susan might count it as part of today's ration.

"Well," said Susan, looking over the piles of Arctic equipment scattered all over the cabin. "One thing's clear anyhow. If anybody slept in the *Fram* last night, he slept on the floor."

"And there isn't really very much room even there," said Dorothea. "At least, not to be comfortable."

In the end it was Peggy who guessed the truth. After all, she knew Nancy better than any of the others knew her. She knew the way in which Nancy's mind worked, planning adventure even when, with a pumpkin face, she was stretched upon a bed of sickness. At least, Peggy remembered, it wasn't a pumpkin any longer, and Nancy was getting up for more than half the days. But, no matter, she knew at last just what it was that her plague-stricken captain had wanted to say.

She came skating up to the others. After they had made sure that no one had slept in the houseboat, they had gone full tilt down to Spitzbergen and back, just to keep in training.

"It wasn't that someone else was sleeping in the *Fram*," she said. "Nancy wanted to know which of *us* was sleeping there."

"But we none of us are," said Susan.

"She thinks we ought to be. So we should be if she was all right."

"We'd be at school," said Susan.

"Oh yes," said Peggy. "But you know what I mean. Here we are with a *Fram* all waiting, much warmer than our own bedrooms. It really is warm, you know, with the stove going all day. And Nancy's always saying that the worst thing about winter is that you can't get away from a house at night. That's why she's thought of it."

They knew at once that Peggy was right. It was just like Nancy. But could it be done? John and Susan looked at each other. Old doubts as to whether they should be in the houseboat at all came flooding back into their minds.

"But we can't really," said Susan.

"Why not?" said Roger.

"Let's all sleep aboard tonight," said Titty.

"You won't anyway, either of you," said Susan very firmly.

"But you and John can," said Peggy.

John went skating off by himself to think things out.

"It would be a lovely thing to do," said Dorothea. She and Dick were somehow outside this altogether. Sleeping in the houseboat was something for the Swallows and Peggy. Dorothea felt that Nancy had never really thought of anyone else. But, like Nancy, she was aglow at the idea of the explorers sleeping in a real ship frozen in the ice; going to bed there, watching a red glimmer in a chink of the stove, and waking in the morning to clear a peephole in the frosted windows and look out over the frozen sea. It was not for her and Dick who were, after all, strangers, but just to think of the others doing it was next best to doing it herself.

Gradually, during the day, Susan weakened. John, too, who at first had remembered his old promise about night sailing, came round to think that you could hardly call it sailing to be in a boat that was frozen in and so not moving at all. And Peggy kept putting it to them more and more strongly. "We simply can't let Nancy down." Somehow it had never come into Peggy's mind to sleep in the *Fram*; and even now, not for anything, not even for Nancy's sake, would she sleep there alone in the dark, away from all the others. But if John and Susan were there too, everything would be all right, and Nancy, stuck at Beckfoot, would not have to feel that she could not trust her mate to do the things that were waiting to be done. Now that Nancy had suggested it, Peggy saw that they ought to have been sleeping there all along. What was the good of having a *Fram* if you went home to a farmhouse every night? "We've simply got to," she said.

Again and again the three elders went skating off with grave, serious faces.

John and Susan, even as they weakened, were still sure of one thing, and that was that neither Titty nor Roger was to sleep anywhere but in bed at Holly Howe. But, if the two young ones were going to bed at the proper time and in the proper place, they began to think that there was no very serious reason why they should not themselves do as Captain Nancy had planned. John felt as if Nancy had dared them to do it, and that, in itself, was enough to make him very unwilling to say "No."

No decision was announced, but at dusk, when they separated and went home, Peggy and the Swallows northwards to Darien, Dick and Dorothea southwards towards Spitzbergen, there was such a cheerful note in Peggy's "Goodnight!" that Dorothea could hardly believe that she had failed.

"I believe they're going to do it after all, the big ones," she said, as she and Dick hauled their sledge up the field to Dixon's Farm.

"I wish it was us," said Dick.

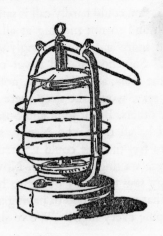

CHAPTER XVIII

THE *FRAM* AT NIGHT

At Holly Howe everything seemed to be in their favour. Mr and Mrs Jackson had gone off to the village to play whist with other Eskimos. Fanny, the girl who was lending Mrs Jackson a hand while the farmhouse was full of visitors, had given the explorers their supper, tidied up and gone home to her mother's. "There's no call for any of you to be sitting up," Mrs Jackson had said. "Fanny'll make up the fire, and you can just go to bed and leave the door on the latch." Nothing more had been said about sleeping on the *Fram*. It was not the sort of plan that could well be explained to Eskimos; and besides, if there had been any more talk about it, there would have been trouble with Titty and Roger. On that point Susan had put her foot down from the first. She was still very doubtful about herself and John, but as for those two, she knew very well that her mother would say that the houseboat was no place for them at night. After supper, she had been rather sterner than usual, and chivvied them both off to bed in good time, had gone up to see that they were properly tucked in and, finding them already asleep, had taken her chance and grabbed a blanket off John's bed and one off her own, and come down again to the farm kitchen, where she found John and Peggy talking like burglars, though there was not any need, and doing their best to cram Peggy's blanket into her knapsack.

"Good," whispered John, when he saw what Susan had brought down with her. "Good. Now we shan't have to go up again. These'll do. We shan't want any more with the red ones in the *Fram* and all those sheepskins."

211

They folded and rolled the blankets, knelt on them, made them into bundles as small as possible, and pulled the knapsacks over them, turning the knapsacks inside out first, as if they were pulling on stockings. The knapsacks were not big enough, and the blankets stuck out a bit at the top, but anything was better than having to carry them in their arms. They helped each other quietly on with their coats, wriggled their arms through the straps of the knapsacks, and were ready. On tiptoe they moved to the door. On tiptoe, Susan slipped back to turn down the lamp. A cinder startled them, falling in the grate; and they had never known before how loud was the slow, regular tick of the big grandfather clock in the corner.

"Those two are asleep all right?" whispered John.

"Sound," whispered Susan, who was closing the door by quarter inches. "But you know I don't believe we really ought to do it."

"We can't let Peggy go alone."

Peggy was already crossing the yard. They slipped after her. There was a little trouble with the gate, because the spring catch was stiff. A cow stirred in the shippen. Ringman, the dog, crossed the yard and snuffed at them. For a moment they were afraid he would bark, but John tickled him under the chin and whispered "'Sh!" to him, and he crouched down, sweeping the snow with his wagging tail; and, as soon as they were fairly outside the gate, went quietly back to the warm lair he had come from.

Out in the field, they listened for a moment. There was no sound from the house, and the dim light in the windows of the kitchen seemed almost a reproach, so little did it hint of what was afoot. Anybody, looking at it, might have thought they were sitting in the kitchen. There was no wind, and in the still air they could hear the noise of dance music. There was a bright glow in the sky from a bonfire on the shore by the steamer pier. Now and again a rocket soared into the night; and, though there was rising ground between themselves and Rio, they could almost see the crowds skating in Rio Bay. They were not going to skate themselves. That, they had decided, would be the same thing as sailing at night. Sleeping in the *Fram* was somehow different.

Peggy set off up the field track to get into the road. The others followed. The moon was shining, full and clear, over the top of the fells, and threw their shadows behind them on the snow. Peggy turned to make sure that they were close behind.

"Shiver my timbers!" she said. "A real smuggling night. Isn't it a pity Nancy isn't here. But she'd be making us slink in the shadow of the walls."

"No need," said John.

"We may meet Mrs Jackson," said Susan almost hopefully.

But Mrs Jackson was far away, trying to remember what were trumps; and everybody who was not indoors was down in Rio Bay, with the torches and the bonfires, listening to the music, skating or watching the skaters. The explorers met nobody at all. They came out in the road at the top of the field, turned right, and trudged along three abreast now, with their overstuffed knapsacks bulging on their backs.

"Nancy'll never believe we've done it," said Peggy.

"Those two never *do* wake," said Susan. "At least Titty never does. Does Roger?"

"He wakes early enough in the morning," said John.

Peggy comforted them. "We'll start back as soon as it's light," she said. "They'll be all right even if they do wake. And they won't. They were half asleep before they'd done their supper."

"We'll meet the Jacksons milking when we come in," said Susan.

"Who cares?" said Peggy. "Jib-booms and bobstays! Who cares? We'll have done it then. And anyhow, it isn't as if it was anything wrong."

The others said nothing in answer to this.

They came to the open gateway into the wood above Houseboat Bay. On the cart track between the trees they could no longer
walk abreast. Peggy went first. She was not content with herself.
Nancy, she felt sure, would be carrying the thing through in a
much more lively spirit. She began to sing:

"Oh, it's my delight of a shiny night
In the season of the year."

But she could remember only the chorus, and the others did not
join in. She walked faster and faster, beginning to be afraid that
they might even now draw back. But they hurried after her, and
in a few minutes left the criss-cross shadows of the bare trees and
came out on the open shore. There was the lake, and the moonlight
pouring down on the white hills on the farther side. And there,
out in the bay, lay the *Fram*, dark and motionless, frozen in the
Arctic ice.

All three of them cheered up wonderfully at the sight of her.
"Pretty gorgeous," said John. "Come on, Susan." He set out
over the ice, sliding his feet as if he were on skis. He came to the
houseboat, reached up on deck and got hold of the ladder. A
minute later all three of them had climbed up, and he and Susan
were waiting while Peggy fumbled with the key. Standing up
there in the moonlight on the deck of the *Fram*, with ice all round,
and the snow mountains in the distance (there was no need to
look at the wooded shores of the bay, and the glow above the
Rio bonfires and torches might well be Northern lights), it was
easy to believe that they were indeed in the Arctic, and a thousand
miles from any other human beings.

They went in, after a short struggle with the door, which had
frozen as usual and would not open at first even when it had been
unlocked. Peggy lit the lantern. Susan stirred up the stove. The
cabin was warm and the lantern made it cheerful at once. They
slipped off the knapsacks and dumped them on one of the settees.

"Look here," said John, "we simply can't go to bed right away. What can you do in the cooking line, Mister Mate?"

"What about cocoa?" said Peggy. "We've got half a tin left of that cocoa and milk."

"Well, it's easy enough to get ready," said Susan.

"And jolly good," said John.

There was plenty of water left aboard from the last water-carrying expedition to the beck. Susan filled the kettle and put it on the stove, while Peggy went to the store cupboard. (It was always Peggy's job to deal with Captain Flint's stores. After all, he was her uncle, not Susan's.) John sat by the stove, looking at the pictures in Dick's astronomy book which, by some accident, had been left behind on the cabin table. Anybody who had looked into the cabin at that moment would have said that everything was going well.

And then, suddenly, Peggy knew that everything was going very badly. She had been triumphant, thinking of the answer she would be able to send to Nancy in the morning. "Who was sleeping in the *Fram*?" "All the leaders of the expedition." And then she had caught sight of John's face, as he looked up from the astronomy book which, indeed, he hardly saw. John had imagined his mother sitting down with them in the cabin of the *Fram* to take a cup of cocoa in the Arctic; and instantly he had almost heard her words, "What have you done with those young ones?" John looked at Susan and knew that she, too, was unhappy. Susan looked at John. Peggy looked from one to the other of them. Cheerfulness was gone.

It might have been different if the kettle had boiled smartly, and they had been able to have their hot cocoa at once. But the kettle was in no sort of hurry. It was never as quick on the stove as it was on the Primus, and tonight, as if on purpose, it seemed to take longer than usual.

"Isn't the beast ever going to boil?" said Peggy at last. "I don't believe it wants to. Let's pump up the Primus and hurry it along."

"Look here, Peggy," said Susan, her mind made up. "It's no good. John and I have just got to go back. We can't leave Titty and Roger alone all night. But you'll be all right, if you want to stay. You can lock yourself in, you know."

This was worse than anything she had expected. Peggy no longer felt at all like Captain Nancy, shivering timbers and afraid of nothing. It was all right with John and Susan, but to sleep alone in the houseboat on the frozen lake was altogether too much of a good thing.

"But that isn't what Nancy wants," she said. "She wants us all to be here, sleeping all round the cabin."

"Well, we can't," said Susan. "John thinks just the same."

Peggy looked at John, but John knew very well that he agreed with Susan, and Peggy could see that he knew it.

"Anyway, you've been here in the dark," said John. "And in the real Arctic it's dark night and day in winter. There's no point in being here at any particular time. And what does it matter where we sleep?"

"Don't let's bother about this wretched cocoa," said Susan. "It's never going to boil tonight. It'll be all right for tomorrow. We'll have it when we come in the morning." She jumped up. "It's a jolly good thing we didn't unpack our blankets and make our beds. Those blankets are an awful job to get into the knapsacks."

It was perfectly clear that John and Susan were bound for Holly Howe. Peggy gave in.

"Nancy'll be pleased about our coming down by moonlight," she said. "But she'll think the *Fram's* wasted all the same."

Susan closed down the draught in the little stove.

"It'll be out by morning," she said, "but it doesn't matter. We've got lots of firewood for starting it again."

John took down the lantern and blew it out. There was no

light in the *Fram* but the moonlight through the windows. A cold breath came in as he opened the door.

"Come on," said Susan.

Peggy locked the door behind them. They dumped the knap-sacks overboard, climbed down by the ladder and pushed it up on deck again. On the ice, in the moonlight, they helped each other on with their burdens, and set off homewards, in a hurry now, and oddly cheerful.

"Hullo!" said John, as they were leaving the *Fram* behind them. "What's that?"

"Where?"

"Moving," said John. "On the ice. Coming this way."

"Oh!" Peggy caught her breath. What was it? There was certainly something moving on the ice, close under the woods that came down to the shores of the bay.

"It isn't," cried Susan. "Yes, it is. It's those two brats. We ought never to have gone out."

*

Roger did not know what waked him. For a moment he lay quiet. Then, suddenly, he felt the emptiness in the room.

"John!" he said.

There was no answer. It was on the other side of the house that the moon was rising; but, even so, because of all the snow on the ground, there was enough light in the room for Roger to see that John's bed looked somehow whiter than usual. In grabbing the blanket, Susan had flung back the patterned quilt and had not put it back.

"John!" called Roger again, and skipped out of bed and ran across the floor. John's bed was empty. But the candlestick was on the table beside it, and the matches too. Roger decided that this was one of the occasions when a rule might properly be broken. He struck a match and lit the candle. Yes, the bed was certainly empty. John was not there, nor were his clothes. Roger opened the door to the landing, stepped out, and listened for a moment. Tick. Tock. Tick. Tock. He could hear the loud slow ticking of the clock in the kitchen, and was startled by the sudden rattle as a chain settled itself on one of the cogwheels. He remembered what that noise was; and, listening again, to make sure that he could hear nothing but the clock, ran across the cold planking to the room that was shared by Susan and Titty. He opened the door and went in, shielding his candle with one hand. What was this? Susan's bed empty too? Titty, in the bed opposite, lifted her head from the pillow and blinked at him sleepily.

"Roger," she said, "what's the matter?"

"Where's the captain and the mate?" asked Roger.

Titty raised herself up on her elbows, flung her hair out of her eyes, and looked at Susan's empty bed.

"Talking to Peggy, I expect," she said.

"But I can't hear anybody at all," said Roger. "Listen!"

Titty hopped out of bed and pushed her feet into her slippers.

"I'm going to see if Peggy's asleep," she said.

Together they tiptoed out on the landing. There was not a sound in the farm except that of the steady old clock downstairs in the kitchen. They opened Peggy's door, quietly, listening for her breathing. There was not a sound. They went in. The light of Roger's candle showed them that Peggy had fairly torn her bed to pieces in getting out the blanket she had wanted. But she was not there.

"They've all gone off to sleep in the *Fram* after all," said Titty.

"The beasts," said Roger.

"Perhaps they made up their minds after we'd gone to sleep," said Titty, "and they thought they'd better not wake us."

"Well, we're awake now, anyhow," said Roger. "Come on. Let's catch them up."

THE *FRAM* IN THE MOONLIGHT

"They may be just lurking in the kitchen," said Titty. "Bring your candle."

Titty first, followed by Roger holding the candlestick, slipped down the dark stairs, to find the lamp low in the kitchen, the fire banked up, and not a sign of the others.

"They can't have gone anywhere else," said Titty. "Bother it all. I wish we hadn't gone to sleep so soon."

"Well, let's go after them," said Roger.

"If Susan's there, it'll be all right," said Titty.

"It won't take two minutes to get dressed," said Roger. "No washing to do. And no teeth."

"Well," said Titty, "don't go and forget your muffler or anything. And give me a light while I get Susan's candle lit."

"Shall we want a lantern?" said Roger.

"We've got torches," said Titty, "and there's lots of moon."

A very few minutes later they blew out the two candles, and left them where they had found them by the beds of the captain and the mate. With the help of their torches they hurried down into the kitchen, found their boots, had the usual struggle with the latch, and opened the farm-house door into the winter night.

The dog, disturbed a second time, came hurrying from the shippen. To be called a good dog by Roger did not satisfy it so well as to be tickled under the chin by John, and it had barked once, shaking them to their very marrows, before Titty quieted its suspicions. Very doubtfully it watched them through the gate, and stayed in the yard while they climbed the track up the snow-covered field. Then, for some queer reason of its own, it turned melancholy, lifted its head, and howled at the moon — long, drawn-out, dismal wails. "Wolves," said Titty; and then, feeling Roger close beside her, she added, "But of course it isn't. We know it's only old Ringman." All the same, whatever doubts they may have felt about the journey before them, that dismal howling in the yard made it easier to go forward than to turn back.

They felt better when they had got into the high road and hurried cheerfully along until they came to the turning down into the wood. The narrow track, white with snow and laced with the blue shadows of the trees, daunted them for a moment. They could see for only such a little way along it.

"What if they aren't there at all?" said Roger.

"But they are," said Titty, "and anyway we've got our torches."

Torches, even on a moonlit night, count for something.

And just then they heard Ringman at Holly Howe, baying at the moon again. Without another word they plunged into the wood. After those awful howls, the cry of an owl, close at hand, though it startled them, was somehow comforting.

"Remember the owl John did at Beckfoot when the Amazons were escaping from the Great-aunt?" said Titty.

"Yes," said Roger, "and Peggy's duck when someone dropped an oar."

At last, through the trees ahead of them, they could see a yellow glimmer; and a moment later, when they came out on the shore, the lit windows of the houseboat told them they had guessed aright.

"They're there all right," said Titty. "I knew they must be. Look out while we're getting on the ice. These stones are most horribly slippery."

"They've gone and put the light out," said Roger.

Dim and dead in the moonlight, the houseboat looked altogether uninhabited. It was hard to believe that only a moment before they had seen those cheerful windows.

"They've probably just this minute settled down to sleep," said Titty.

"We'll wake them up," said Roger. "I say, Titty, we never

brought any blankets. That's what they'd been doing with their beds."

"Botheration!" said Titty. "Never mind. There are lots of sheepskins."

"Let's give them a shout," said Roger.

"A hail," said Titty. "Both together."

"*Fram*, ahoy!"

A faint "Hullo" came back to them.

"There's something coming over the ice," said Roger, stopping suddenly. "Bears!"

Against the dark hull of the houseboat, they had not seen the elders climb down to the ice. A little cloud, for the first time that night, veiled the face of the moon, and, for a moment, they stopped short. Then the moon shone out again, and they knew those dim, shapeless moving things for what they were.

"It's them!" cried Titty, almost thankfully.

"Pretty good bears," said Roger. "Hi! Susan! Hullo!"

"What on earth are you two doing out here?" said Susan. "We left you tucked up in bed."

"We were coming to the *Fram*," said Titty.

"You ought to have stayed in bed," said Susan. "We're on our way home."

"But what did you go there for?" asked Roger.

"We thought you had gone there to sleep," said Titty.

"Quick march!" said Susan. "You ought to be asleep now. You may get no end of a cold coming out of your warm beds like this. Skip along." And, indeed, she set such a pace that everybody was rather short of breath for talking long before they had come up through the wood and out again on the high road.

They were hurrying along the road when they saw two figures black against the snow, going down the field towards the farm.

"It's the Jacksons," said John.

"Hurry up!" said Susan, and the whole party broke into a run.

Ringman's melancholy howling turned suddenly to delighted barking as the Jacksons came to the yard. There he was, leaping round them in the moonlight. The five explorers, very much out of breath, caught them up just as Mr Jackson was closing the yard gate.

"Eh, what's this?" said Mrs Jackson. "And you not in bed. This is no time to go walking, though a grand night it is and no mistake. But what would your mother say to me if she knew?"

"We'll be in bed in two minutes," said Peggy.

She, John and Susan took their chance, and hurried through into the house, to get their knapsacks out of sight and upstairs. Nobody wanted to have to talk about blankets.

"Why did Ringman howl like that?" asked Roger.

"Got a friend in the moon likely," said Mr Jackson.

"Did you have a nice time at the party?" asked Titty.

"Well," said Mrs Jackson, "I never did hear the beat of that. Off to bed with you. But I don't wonder folk can't sleep these nights with all the noise they make with their skating in the bay."

CHAPTER XIX

THE D.'S TAKE CHARGE

In the morning Dick ran up the hill as usual. After all, even if the three elders had slept in the *Fram* at night, they would have gone back to Holly Howe for Titty and Roger, if not for their own breakfasts, and they would be sure to have hung out a signal.

The signal was there. Square over south cone. "Come to the *Fram*." Dorothea was impatient to be off. But their sandwiches were not ready. Mrs Dixon was very busy seeing off Mr Dixon and Silas, who were going to a market town some dozen miles away, and were waiting about in their best clothes. It was no good thinking that they might put in the time by doing some work on the mast for the sledge. So Dick had gone down the field to see what could be done about the reeds in the ice and at the edge of it, that had been a nuisance, always stopping the sledge just when it should have been going its fastest. He cleared a pathway through the reeds, cutting them off close to the ice. By the time he had done that, and gone up to the farm again, he found that Mr Dixon and Silas had already left, and that Dorothea was just packing their dinner into the knapsacks. Mrs Dixon had given them sandwiches, just the same as those she had made for the two men, though, as Dorothea had noticed, she had put no mustard in them. She had also given them a big bottle of milk and two enormous hunks of cake.

"It's going to be much better tobogganing today," said Dick, as he put the sledge in position at the top of the field.

A moment later they were flying down the slope towards the lake.

"More to the left," cried Dick.

Their left heels dug into the snow, and the sledge swerved with a jerk.

"Now then. Hang on. There'll be a bit of a bump."

There was. The sledge shot through the cleared pathway, leapt into the air as it hit the ice, came down on the ice again, and, for the first time not braked by the reeds, went hurtling out over the lake.

"It would have gone farther still if only we hadn't had to put our feet down," said Dick. "Once it's on the ice there's practically no friction at all. That's why those ice-yachts go so fast."

"Yes," said Dorothea, but she was answering only the tone of his voice. If she had been asked what he had said, she would have been puzzled for an answer. There had been the rush of cold air as they flew down the field and out over the ice. There had been the moment when she thought they might be going to turn over. But even in that moment her mind had been elsewhere. Her last thought before she had gone to sleep and her first thought on waking in the morning had been of the *Fram* and Houseboat Bay. She could think of nothing else. Had they slept in the cabin that night? What had it been like? Had they been bothered by strange Eskimos skating late and coming up to see what the light might be behind the cabin windows? Or had they put the light out and slept there in the dark?

She was putting her skates on, and Dick, after one regretful look up the white slope to the farm, did the same. He would have liked to take the sledge back to the farm, to come down again, to make a better shot for the gap in the reeds, and to come flying out even farther over the ice at the end of the run down the field. But, after all, there would be plenty of time for that. Dorothea was in a hurry, and he, too, wanted to get back to the *Fram* and to have another look at those pictures of the sailing sledges.

In a few moments the two of them were ready, and the sledge, jerked into motion, slid over the ice behind them.

H

Away by Long Island there were a lot of people playing hockey on the ice. Here and there, small groups, skating together, moved like black spots over the shining surface. The snow had gone from the trees, melted, perhaps, or shaken down by the wind, and the woods stood out dark against the white hills. Suddenly a white sail shot out between Long Island and the shore.

"There it is again," said Dick. "Just look at it."

"Her," said Dorothea. "They'd never call her 'it'. "

There was very little wind that morning, but the light-built, spidery ice-yacht was flying fast over the smooth ice.

"Ouch!" said Dick. He had stopped skating when he saw the ice-yacht, but Dorothea had not known he was stopping, and the sledge, too, had known nothing about it, and, swinging on its way, had swept his feet from under him.

"It doesn't turn over because its skates are so far apart," said Dick dreamily, "and then it's got a big area for the wind to catch, and very little friction because its skates are short. But I wish I knew how it manages to sail against the wind."

"Ask Captain John."

"They all know," said Dick, "even Roger. Well, anyhow, even they can't sail against the wind in a sledge. Ours'll go all right if we have a wind in the right direction."

"Do get up and come along," said Dorothea. "We haven't got a sail yet."

"We're going to," said Dick. "Mrs Dixon said she'd see what could be done about an old sheet."

The ice-yacht spun round, flew back towards the islands, and disappeared.

Dick turned to practical things once more. He got up, gave the time, "Right. Left. Right. Left." and they struck out again for Houseboat Bay. They rounded the point. There lay the *Fram*, thick smoke pouring from her chimney.

"Susan's just put some more coal on," said Dorothea.

"Say when you're ready."

"Any time now."

"Right. Put the brake on."

They stopped skating, and swerved slightly outwards in opposite directions. The loaded sledge slipped on between them, bothering nobody's heels. They brought it neatly to a standstill, close beside the houseboat.

A moment later Titty and Roger were on deck, looking down at them.

"Where are the others?" asked Dorothea.

"Below," said Titty, "in the cabin."

Dorothea had warned Dick not to say anything to these two about sleeping in the *Fram* at night. She knew that whatever their elders might do, Titty and Roger would have had to spend the night in their beds.

But Roger spoke of it at once.

"We were here in the middle of the night," he said. "Titty and I came by ourselves, and Ringman bayed at the moon."

"Susan didn't let you sleep here?" asked Dorothea.

"No," said Titty. "But we did come down on the ice through the wood long after we'd gone to bed."

The D.'s unfastened their skates, passed them up with their knapsacks to Roger and Titty, and climbed aboard. They went down into the cabin. John, Peggy, and Susan were there, busy with packing-thread and sheepskins.

"Hullo!" said John.

"Hullo!" said the others.

And from the first moment, Dorothea knew that something had gone wrong. Perhaps it was that they had not been able to sleep. Perhaps they had waked up too early. Something was wrong. She had expected a much more cheerful, even a triumphant tone, from explorers who had spent all night in the icebound *Fram*.

"What was it like in the dark?" asked Dick.

"We had to go home to sleep," said Peggy.

"It couldn't be helped," said Susan.

"It was a sort of promise we'd made to mother," said John. "The A.B. and the boy are so beastly young."

"As it was, they were out very late," said Susan.

Dorothea looked from one to another of the three. They couldn't really be making excuses, though it sounded very like it. She went straight to the point that was bothering all of them.

"But what are you going to say to Captain Nancy?" she asked.

"She'll be as sick as anything," said Peggy.

"It can't be helped," said Susan. "Nancy'd understand if she were here."

"She wouldn't," said John. "Not really. But it can't be helped, all the same."

And then, suddenly, Peggy saw a way out.

"Look here," she said. "What about you? You haven't promised anything to anybody. You sleep in her. You're part of the expedition. Nancy said so ages ago. She'll be as pleased as anything."

Dorothea stared. She had never hoped for such an honour for herself and Dick. They had been happy enough at the beginning, just to be allowed to pull the explorers' sledge. Then they had come to have a sledge of their own, though Nancy had never seen it. But this ...

"She didn't mean us when she sent the picture."

"She put in all seven of us," said Titty.

"Of course she meant you too," said Peggy. "She wouldn't have put you in if she hadn't. Shiver my timbers, I mean to say. What does it matter who it is so long as it's someone? She just asked, 'Who?' She wants to know which of us is sleeping here. That's all. Of course, if you'd rather not ... "

"Let's," said Dick. "It would be even better than the

observatory for stars, and we could stay up as long as we liked and make up for it by sleeping in the daytime. Why not?"

"But what about you?" said Dorothea to Peggy.

"I'll sleep here, too, if you will," said Peggy, and then hesitated. She looked doubtfully at Susan and John. If those two hardened sailors, captain and mate of the *Swallow*, had set out to sleep in the *Fram*, and then had changed their minds at the last minute, and gone home again, might not Dorothea and Dick do the same? And that would be much worse. Stay in the *Fram* by herself she would not. But if the D.'s gave up, they would be going off to Dixon's Farm, and she would have to go home by herself the other way. She thought of the wood in the moonlight, and shivered. "Look here," she said, "let her be your ship for one night, just so that we can send an answer to Nancy, and then the next night I'll come too, if you want me."

"We'd simply love to," said Dorothea.

"Good," said Peggy.

"I do wish we could," said John.

"Come on," said Peggy. "Let's do an answer for Nancy right away."

"Semaphore, like hers?" said Dick.

"Of course," said Peggy.

"Just two D.'s," said Titty, "but you needn't draw them both alike."

Peggy sat down to the table at once, borrowed Dick's fountain-pen, and drew her very simple picture. It was as if two of Nancy's crowd of excited Eskimos had wandered away by themselves. She drew her figures rather bigger than Nancy's, and, at Titty's suggestion, gave one of them a pair of spectacles like Dick's, and the other a couple of pigtails. Each held a right arm straight above its head. There could be no mistaking the letters that they stood for.

"Can't we put the houseboat in, too?" said Roger.

"No point in letting every Eskimo know what it's all about."

The moment the drawing was done, Peggy was in a hurry to be off and away, for fear lest the D.'s, like her ancient allies, should have second thoughts and change their minds. She knew too, that there was quite a good chance of catching the doctor on his rounds this side of Rio, and persuading him to get it quickly to Nancy. Once the message was on its way, it would be hard for anybody to draw back.

"Besides," she said, "it's only fair, if they're going to sleep here, that they should have the ship to themselves just for a bit. Come on. Today, they shall have the *Fram*, and we'll go to the igloo."

Dorothea did not try to keep them.

"Look here, Dorothea," said Susan. "But how are you going to manage about the Primus?"

"I can boil water on the stove."

"Ought we to leave them?" said John.

"Nothing can really go wrong," said Susan.

"I know," said John.

"Can't we stop with them?" said Titty.

"No, you can't," said Susan. "It's because of you that we can't either."

"Come on," said Peggy. "We don't want to go and miss the doctor."

The things wanted for an expedition to the igloo were hurriedly collected. The Beckfoot sledge was loaded again, and presently Dorothea and Dick were standing alone on the deck of the *Fram*, waving farewells to a party of explorers who were leaving the ice and disappearing into the trees.

The departing explorers waved back, and were gone.

It was almost like a flight.

★

"Lucky I left my astronomy book here," said Dick, as he and Dorothea went down into their cabin.

Dorothea could not settle down so easily. Somehow or other she had to find a way of making herself feel that she and Dick were not just visitors, but in command of the ship. She knew the inside of the *Fram* as well as anybody, but she went all over it once again. She looked into the fo'c'sle, and at the Primus stoves, though she did not touch them. She looked into the cupboards in which there was now very little left of the generous stores they had found there when first they had come aboard. Seven explorers can get through a lot of provisions in a short time. She made sure that there was a supply of tea, and wondered if Susan had remembered to take some with her up to the igloo. She took her bottle of milk out of her knapsack, and put it in the cupboard with the tea. There was still plenty of sugar in the *Fram*, but that did not matter to her. Mrs Dixon always put a few lumps in a screw of paper for them when they set out in the morning, so that they would have their own share when Susan made the tea. She put her own sugar in the cupboard with the rest. There was no need for all this, but she was trying to get the feel of having the *Fram* all to herself and Dick. In the end she went to the stove and gave the fire a good poking, just to show that she was at home and in charge. "*Two in the Ice.*" Perhaps they had been alone in the ship for six months already. She looked at Dick, who had settled down at the table, and was taking his telescope to pieces, unscrewing the lenses one by one. "*Two in the Ice.*" They might be anywhere. Nansen's *Fram* had gone very near it. This *Fram* might drift across the Pole itself. In a story like that, almost anything might happen.

But from that she came back to reality and Captain Nancy. The answer to Captain Nancy's picture was already on its way. She and Dick had been allowed into the expedition, and now it was they who were to be the first to sleep in the houseboat.

Dorothea did very much indeed want to come up to Nancy's standard of what was fitting in adventures. Sleep in the *Fram* at night, in the dark, with ice all round them? Of course they would. And, in a flash, Dorothea saw herself waking up in the morning, and Dick stirring on his berth and wondering where he was. "Wake up, Professor!" she would say. "Wake up! Another day in the ice." Well, nobody could say her stories never came true. Here they were in the very middle of a story that she herself could hardly have believed was possible three weeks ago, when they had watched that boat rowing down to the island. Here they were in a ship of their own. What would it feel like to come to it over the ice and let themselves in with their own key?

"Come along, Dick," she said. "We've got to get some fresh water."

"Bother," said Dick. "Must we go now?"

"Much better," said Dorothea.

They took the kettle and a jug, and climbed down by the accommodation-ladder. Dorothea pushed the ladder up on deck.

"Why?" said Dick. "We're just coming back."

"Let's come back as if we'd never been here with the others."

Dick said nothing. If Dorothea wanted a thing, he supposed there was some sense in it, though he could not see it at the moment.

Resolutely she walked ashore without looking back. Not until jug and kettle were full and they were on the beach, ready to start back, did she let herself look at the *Fram*.

The old houseboat lay there as she had laid ever since the ice formed about her, but Dorothea saw her differently, and looked at her with an almost choking pride. Her ship and Dick's. The other explorers were up in Greenland, a thousand miles away. She and Dick had the ship to themselves.

She walked back, gloating, and climbed aboard. Dick was in a hurry to get back to his telescope. He never guessed that

Dorothea was tasting the pleasures of discovery, and that she opened the cabin door rather slowly because she had come aboard for the first time, and did not know what she might find there.

But time was going on, and Dorothea had to live up to Susan's standards as well as Nancy's. There was tea to make to drink with their midday dinner. She boiled the kettle on the stove, and when the tea was ready, brought two clean plates out of the fo'c'sle. Sandwiches eaten straight out of a paper packet would have been too much like a picnic. But on plates, cut up with a knife and fork, they were much more like the kind of meal people would have in their own house or ship. There was room for the plates and two mugs on the end of the table, where Dick had pushed back the mess of skins and sewing things so that he could lay his lenses out in a row and look at his star-book while he was polishing them.

"Of course, later on, we'll have to go back to the farm for more milk," she said, when their meal was done, "and to ask Mrs Dixon to let us have something for supper. But we won't go until evening."

"I'll go now and get it over," said Dick, "so as not to waste any of the dark."

"Not until they've done the evening milking," said Dorothea. "I'll go then. There's a lantern in the fo'c'sle that'll do for me to take. There'll be no need for you to come as well."

She washed the plates up with a handful or two of snow. There was really no need for proper washing up, of Susan's kind, after sandwiches which leave plates almost as good as new. She spared a little water to rinse out the mugs. She went down on the ice and put on her skates, but did not like to go far from the ship. She skated round the bay for a time, and then took off her skates and climbed aboard once more. Dick was busy in the cabin with paper and pencil and his star-book. It was no use disturbing him. Even if you got an answer out of him when he was like that, it didn't mean anything. Dorothea did a little hard stitching, trying to carry on the work Susan was doing in making a huge sheepskin rug to go over all the baggage on the top of the Beckfoot sledge. But she knew that nothing would ever make her good at sewing, and presently she gave it up, put on her coat, tied a muffler round her neck, and went on deck, to survey the Arctic scene.

She stood there, well wrapped up and thoroughly warm, watching the distant Eskimos skating on the part of the lake that could be seen from Houseboat Bay. She made up stories about them. There were two big ones and a little one who, if only they had known it, had gone through a lot of adventures before they disappeared. And every one of those distant black figures skimming about over the ice would be going home at night, poor things, while she and Dick ... She let her mind run on. And then, when the afternoon was already closing in, and the red sun dropping low above the western hills, she saw, far away by the end of Long Island, an Eskimo towing a sledge.

Not many of the Eskimos took sledges on the ice, and Dorothea watched him with interest from the first. Just for a moment she had thought he must be an explorer from some rival expedition. But he was too big, and his sledge was too small. He seemed to have come round the end of Long Island, and was skating fast towards Houseboat Bay. As he came nearer, she saw that he was a large fat man in grey clothes. He was towing something on that little sledge of his. A big suitcase with a round parcel tied to the handle. The sight of this large fat man, towing his little sledge, reminded Dorothea of a book she had read about Holland, with pictures of people doing their winter shopping, all with little sledges at their heels to carry their parcels. Yes, he must be a Dutchman, and his suitcase must be full of tulip bulbs. He was coming into Houseboat Bay, straight for the *Fram*. Probably, she thought, he must be aiming for the cart track up through the wood. But he was too good to be wasted and not made into a story.

"The tall Dutchman ... (of course, he ought not to be tall, only broad, but it can't be helped) ... the tall Dutchman bowed low. 'Madam,' he said, 'Your taste in tulips has become proverbial in my country ... (I really do like them) ... and I have come from ... from ... Amsterdam ... to offer you a small collection ...'" *Skates and Tulips* would be the title ... By Dorothea Callum.

But he was coming nearer and nearer. Was he going to say something in real life? Dorothea half turned and thought of going into the cabin. But there was not time.

"Well, I'm jiggered!" said the tall Dutchman.

CHAPTER XX

CAPTAIN NANCY GETS TWO BITS OF NEWS

CAPTAIN NANCY was waiting for the doctor. The worst of getting better was that the doctor came so seldom. And she knew very well that she was going to need him most just when he would stop coming altogether. Three days had passed since she had given him that picture. Perhaps already the *Fram* at night was a floating dormitory, full of explorers, gaily talking from bunk to bunk long after all the Eskimo world was snoring in its stuffy houses. They had only to send the word "All" to her, and she would understand. But no word had come, Perhaps those galoots had failed to read her picture. Or perhaps, they had read it and not seen what a chance was theirs. Susan, she knew, was always a little inclined to take a native view. But surely Peggy could do something with them. If only she had been there herself. All morning, walking solemnly in the garden, she had hardly liked to stir out of sight of the front door. If the doctor brought her a message from the other side of the lake she wanted to be there to take it from him and to see if she could not rope him in and turn him into an ally. Time was going on. Half a dozen things needed doing if the Pole was to be all that she had planned. She was at her wit's end about how to get them done. If Captain Flint had been at home it would have been easy, but with him away she would have to do the best she could with the doctor, and all morning, walking in the garden, she listened eagerly for the sound of his horn at the corners along the road.

The morning passed, and he never came. It was afternoon, and she was back in bed for the day, when she heard him drive up to the door. The bell rang, and a moment later she heard his steps on the stairs. The door opened. There he was, and talking not at all as if he knew she had been waiting for him.

"Well, young woman," he said, "I didn't mean to be seeing you for another two days, but I met the Holly Howe lot in the road, and Peggy made me promise to leave a picture for you. They're poor artists on that side of the lake. Their picture's not a patch on yours. No action. Where is it? I can't have lost the thing."

Nancy sat up furiously, but forced herself to be calm. To make a fuss would give too much away. But it was hard to sit there and keep a polite smile on her face while the doctor dug about, first in one of his pockets and then in another, until, at last, he found the bit of paper he was looking for, slipped into a page of his prescription book.

"I think they might have done better than that," he said, as he handed it over.

One glance at it told Nancy what she wanted to know. A boy and a girl, each with the right arm lifted straight above the head, each signalling the letter D.

"Oh, I don't think it's half bad," said Nancy, looking at it as critically as she could. "Of course, it's a pity they haven't put in a few more."

"Lazy," said the doctor. "That's what they are, and I told them so, sending you nothing but that after the lively affair you drew for them."

"What did they say?" asked Nancy.

"Oh, they said they'd do something different for me, if I wanted a picture to hang up."

Nancy did not laugh, though she very well might have done as she thought of the others being scolded by the doctor for sending her a dull picture. She was just thinking how best to introduce the subject of those odd jobs she wanted done about

To Nancy

PEGGY'S ANSWER

the Pole, when the doctor, with his hand on the door knob, showed that he had not been quite as blind as she had thought him.

"Well, goodbye," he said. "I'm only a messenger today. I haven't come to see you put out your tongue or anything like that. But it looks to me as if in another week you'll be back with your smugglers or pirates or whatever you all are, and I shan't have any more of these pictures and mathematical formulæ to carry about. More in them than meets the eye, to my mind. I'll be glad to be quit of you before you get me into trouble."

Nancy's jaw dropped. No, she thought, this was not the moment to talk to him about the transport of hampers and coal-sacks and getting the people who owned the North Pole to let the expedition have the use of it. Perhaps later in the week he would be in an easier mood. She let him go, and, when the door had safely closed behind him, she looked again at Peggy's picture, and gave herself up to gloating.

The answer to her question was the very last she had expected. Of course, it was a pity that the whole lot of them were not there, but that might have stirred up the Eskimos too much, and sent rumours flying all over the place. She would not have been surprised to hear that the four younger ones were sleeping in their beds, and that John, Peggy, and Susan were in the houseboat. But those two town children from Dixon's Farm, sleeping in the houseboat by themselves. Good for the D.'s. She had not thought they had it in them. Well done, Dick and Dorothea! Sleeping out there in the ice. Wouldn't she like to be with them! Well done! To have explorers actually sleeping in the *Fram* was the best thing that had happened yet. Yes, after all, difficult as it was going to be about the Pole, it was a jolly good thing that Captain Flint was abroad for the winter.

★

The doctor had been gone an hour when Nancy, sitting up

in bed, still chuckling now and then at Peggy's picture, heard another car drive up. It was not the doctor's. She knew that by the note of its horn as it turned in at the gate. There was a colossal peal at the bell, but whoever it was who rang it did not wait for the door to be opened, but charged straight in. She heard luggage thumping down in the hall. She heard a voice, she was almost sure, calling for "Molly". She heard the thrum of the engine (that had been kept running because of the cold) deepen as the driver put it into gear and drove away again. She listened. People were moving about down below. There was laughter. And then, only a very little later, the front door opened and closed once more. She heard her mother running up the stairs.

Mrs Blackett came cheerfully into the room.

"Well," she said, "and who do you think that was?"

"Not Uncle Jim?" said Nancy, hardly able to keep her thoughts out of her voice.

"Yes," said Mrs Blackett. "Just like him. Never a word to say he was coming. He knew nothing whatever about your mumps. I'd written to him, but he never got the letter. He thought you were both back at school."

"Where is he?" said Nancy. "I must see him at once. I must see him before he sees any of the others."

"He's gone. You'll see him in the morning. He'll come and shout at you across the garden. No point in his spreading the mumps round just when you're nearly through it and the others look like escaping altogether."

"But isn't he going to stay here?"

"He's sleeping in the houseboat. He'll be all right there, he says, with that stove of his. He's gone off in a hurry to get everything warmed up before night."

"Golly!" said Nancy. "Giminy! ... Golly ... Golly ... Oh ... Oh well, it's too late to do anything now." She broke off suddenly into fits of horrified laughter.

"But what's the matter?" said Mrs Blackett.

"Nothing really," said Nancy.

"Are you quite sure?" said Mrs Blackett. "You know, I told the doctor this afternoon I thought something must be wrong with you because you're being so good. You know, for you, you really are. All these weeks Ruth has been the right name for you, and not Nancy."

"Nothing's the matter with me," said Nancy.

"Would you like to play a quiet game of dominoes before tea?" said Mrs Blackett.

They played, and went on playing all evening; but, for once, Nancy, who could usually beat her mother easily, lost game after game.

CHAPTER XXI

CAPTAIN FLINT COMES HOME

"Well, I'm jiggered!" said the tall Dutchman.

Dorothea was almost startled to hear him talk English, not Dutch.

He pulled up. His sledge slithered round, and Dorothea saw that the big suitcase had a new, bright label on it, in red, blue, and white, "PASSENGER'S LUGGAGE. WANTED ON THE VOYAGE." That parcel she had seen, swinging from the handle of the suitcase, looked as if it might be a loaf of bread. The tall Dutchman steadied his sledge, sat down on his suitcase, and began taking off his skates.

"Well, I'm jiggered!" he said again. "And, may I ask, who are you?"

"Dorothea Callum," said Dorothea.

"Never heard of her," said the tall Dutchman. "But she seems to be very much at home. Don't you find it rather cold standing about on the deck of a boat when it's freezing as hard as this?"

"Oh no," said Dorothea. "You see, when it begins to feel cold, I go in and get warm by the stove; and then, when it begins to feel too warm inside, why, I just come out again."

"*What?*" said the tall Dutchman, who was becoming less like a Dutchman every minute. "You've got into the cabin? You've lit the stove? I might have noticed that somebody's rigged the chimney. You've got it lit now. And do you mean to say nobody's come to turn you off? I don't know what things are coming to. Why, everybody in the district knows ... Any more of you aboard?"

"Only Dick," said Dorothea.

"And who's Dick?" The tall Dutchman reached up and laid his skates on the deck. He hove up the suitcase and dumped it beside them.

"I don't think we ought to let you come into the houseboat," said Dorothea doubtfully, "not without asking the others."

"Well, I like that!"

He stood on the ice, just ready to climb up, and looked at Dorothea in great astonishment. He was not angry. Nobody ever was angry with Dorothea. But he was very much surprised.

"Who's Dick?" he asked again, "and what others? Not allowed to come aboard! Well, I do like that!"

"Dick's my brother," said Dorothea. "He's busy working in the cabin."

"And the others?"

"Well, the boat doesn't belong to them really," Dorothea explained, "but it belongs to their uncle, and they're taking care of it for him ... Her, I mean ... Her for him."

"I might have guessed it," he laughed. "I suppose I've Peggy to thank for this ... Unless Nancy, mumps and all ... "

He climbed up on deck.

Dorothea put out her hand with a smile. "Perhaps you *are* their uncle," she said. "Of course, that explains everything."

He shook hands with her. "I'm glad it does," he said. "And now, if you don't mind, I'll just take this down below."

"Perhaps I'd better tell Dick," said Dorothea.

"I'll tell him," said Captain Flint. "Hullo, what's this?"

He had just noticed the big label on the key which was in the lock of the cabin door. "So that's what had happened to the spare key. I wondered why I could find only one. But who on earth is F-R-A-M?"

"*Fram*," said Dorothea. "The *Fram*."

Captain Flint looked round over the Arctic scene, the ice,

"TALL DUTCHMAN"

the snow-covered hills. "Captain Nancy thought of that, or I'm a Dutchman," he said. "Just like her. Well, may I go into my own cabin?"

"We'd have got it a bit tidier if we'd known you were coming," said Dorothea. She did not tell him what sort of a Dutchman he had already been.

It would certainly not have been difficult to make the cabin a little tidier than it was. There were bundles of hazel sticks, remains of a rather unsuccessful experiment in making snow-shoes. Then there was a pile of rabbit skins, where a sack of them had been emptied on the floor so that people could pick and choose skins that matched when they were making their fur hats. There were some unfinished mittens. Sheepskins were lying all over the place, and a huge pile of them could be seen through the door into the fo'c'sle. In one corner there was a great pyramid of empty tins. Properly speaking, empty tins should have been thrown overboard, but no one had liked the idea of letting them lie about on the Polar ice. Susan's plan had been to make all the explorers put their waste scraps of fur and other rubbish into the tins and then, on the last day of the pumpkin holiday, to take them ashore and bury them, or, if the ground was still hard, to make a hole in the ice and post them, tin by tin, to the bottom of the Arctic sea. But everybody was always kicking over everybody else's rubbish tin, and in the end the tins had just been piled in a corner, a monument of good food gone the right way. All these signs of the Polar exploration going on at the moment – skins, furs, and empty tins – looked strange under the trophies of very different travels that were hung so neatly on the cabin walls; things from Africa, the Malays, and South America. Most of the cabin table was covered with sewing things and scraps of fur, but the far end of it, by the stove, had been cleared, and here, his spectacles only a few inches from his book, the astronomer was hard at work.

Captain Flint stared at him for a minute or two but did not say a word.

Dick felt the cold draught from the open door, but did not look up.

"Dot," he said. "I've got it right now, I think. About the constellations anyway. Beginning with Orion and the Twins. I'm making a tracing from this map. But I can't make out about the planets. I'll just mark that one I thought I saw, and find out afterwards which it is. Anyway, tonight, there'll be time to have a decent look at them."

"What's this?" said Captain Flint. "Astronomy?"

"Dick," said Dorothea. "It's their uncle. He's come home, and brought his luggage."

Dick looked up with eyes that at first hardly saw. His head was full of his book and the map he was making. Pictures of the constellations swam between him and everything else. He stared at this big clumsy man who, after one gasp at the mess in his cabin, was just standing in the cabin doorway. Suddenly his eyes awoke, as if he had only then for the first time properly seen that anyone was there.

"I say," he said eagerly. "They said you knew all about stars. There's something here I simply can't understand."

He moved the book to the side of the table and swept a sheepskin out of a chair so that there should be room for Captain Flint to sit down.

"He's always like that when he's thinking about something," said Dorothea quickly. "It isn't at all that he means to be rude."

Dick looked at her, but not as if he had heard what she was saying. "It's just this bit," he went on. "If only they'd leave the poetry out it would be so much better. What does he mean just here? I'm awfully glad you've come," he added. "I'd just about given up hope of understanding that particular bit."

"Well," said Captain Flint, who had politely made room for Dorothea to go into the cabin before him, and now closed the door after her, dumping his suitcase on the floor. "I've had a good many queer home-comings, one way and another, but this is the queerest of the lot. I usually do know more or less what to expect. But first of all Nancy with mumps, and being driven out of Beckfoot and told to keep away, and then to come here and find ... well, well! You've got it nice and snug in here, anyhow. Now, what about those stars?" He flung his hat on the top of a pile of sheepskins and went round to the end of the table, where Dick and the book were waiting for him.

In a few moments Dick and he were deep in discussion, and Dorothea was forgotten by both of them.

She found a place for herself, propped her elbows among the skins on the table, and settled down to have a good look at him. It was just as well that she had not got very far with *Frost and Snow*. She would have to begin that story again from the very beginning, and do it differently, so as to be able to work him in. What a good thing it was, too, that he seemed to know all about Dick without having to be told. Not like some people, who never seemed able to understand that Dick was always sure that for them, as for himself, stars, or stones, or birds, or chemical experiments, or whatever at the moment it might be, were more important than anything else in the world. It might have been most awkward if Captain Flint had been like Mr Jenkyns, for example, that day when Dick had succeeded in making sulphuretted hydrogen, and unluckily stumbled by the door and sent his whole apparatus flying into the spare bedroom where Mr Jenkyns was to sleep. Why, about those stars, Captain Flint seemed to be just as bad as Dick. Dorothea watched him and wondered. Had anybody known he was coming home? Perhaps Nancy was his favourite niece, and he had come flying home when he heard of her illness. But no. He had not spoken of Nancy's mumps at all in the way a devoted uncle would speak of the illness of a favourite niece.

For some time the talk at the end of the cabin table was about orbits and eclipses, and how it is that the planets are not to be found on a map of the constellations, and how they have their own time-tables, to be found in the Nautical Almanac, and how it is that the Pole Star keeps over the North Pole in spite of the world's spinning on its axis and flying round the sun at the same time.

"You seem to know quite a lot about it already," said Captain Flint.

"Only what I got out of this book," said Dick, "and the person who wrote it has stuffed in such a lot of Longfellow and Tennyson."

"Probably accustomed to lecture to elegant audiences," said Captain Flint. "Hullo! What's this? 'Log of the *Fram*'?" He shifted some hanks of thread off an exercise book that was lying on the table. "So you've been keeping a log. How long have you been at it?"

"Just since we got the key and moved down from the igloo," said Dick.

"The igloo was the first base of the expedition," said Dorothea, "but the *Fram*'s much better."

"What expedition?" said Captain Flint. "Arctic, I suppose, if this is the *Fram*."

"We got a lot of ideas out of Nansen's book."

"Oh, you found that, did you?" He glanced round at the shelf where, luckily, the two volumes of Nansen were back in their proper places. "Is the log private?"

"Not a bit," said Dorothea. "We've all been putting things in, but mostly John and Titty."

Captain Flint turned from page to page, reading bits aloud.

"Barometer 30.1. Sunshine. Freezing hard ... "

"We ought to have put the temperature properly," said Dick, "but I left my thermometer at home. I didn't think there'd be a chance of using it."

"You see, we would only have been here a week if Captain Nancy hadn't got mumps ... "

"Yes," said Captain Flint. "What's this? 'Open water to west and south-west.' "

"The lake wasn't frozen right across when we came to the *Fram*," said Dick. "Not this part of the lake. Everything in the log is perfectly true."

" 'Seals (perhaps Eskimos),' " read Captain Flint, " 'came and tapped at the cabin windows. We lay low and they went away.' "

"It was Titty's idea to call them seals," said Dorothea.

"I guessed it must have been," said Captain Flint. "Hullo! This looks like Peggy's writing. 'Turned a seal off the deck. He was sitting there with his skates on, and John said he might scratch the deck. So we told him to go away, and he jolly well went.' 'Hm," said Captain Flint. "They always do say that poachers make the best gamekeepers."

He turned a page and read on. "The D.s" ("That's us," said Dorothea) "returned to the ship after a successful expedition to the south-east." ("That's to Mrs Dixon's," said Dorothea. Dick was again wrestling with his astronomy.) "They brought a sledge-load of fine pelts, Polar bear, and Arctic fox. All hands at work making fox-skin hats ... " Captain Flint glanced at the sheepskins and picked up a bit of rabbit fur from the table and a mitten that had never been finished. "Arctic fox, eh?" he said.

"Yes," said Dorothea. "And the others are the bearskins, though they really want a bit of washing to make them properly Polar."

"Look here," said Captain Flint presently. "Isn't it about time for tea? I'd better be slipping round to Holly Howe to get some milk. I forgot to bring any from Beckfoot."

"We've got enough left," said Dorothea. "At least I think it'll be enough. And it is tea-time. I ought to have thought of it. Are you good at Primuses? Because if not we must wait till it boils on the stove."

"I'm good at my own Primuses if Nancy and Peggy haven't been at them."

"Susan did all the primussing," said Dorothea.

"Thank goodness for that," said Captain Flint. "Where have you been getting your water from, with the lake frozen?"

Dick had closed his book. "We melted a lot of snow from the roof the first day," he said, "but it wasn't very good."

"We bring it from the stream – the beck, I mean. Dick and I brought a jugful today as well as filling the kettle."

"That's all right," said Captain Flint. "And now let's see what we can give ourselves for tea. I collared a loaf from Beckfoot, but I've got no butter. We'll have to make do with jam."

"I'm afraid there isn't any jam," said Dorothea.

Captain Flint stared at her, got up, and went to the store cupboard.

"Arctic explorers!" he said, looking from one almost empty shelf to another. "More like locusts, it seems to me."

"Peggy said it was all meant to be eaten," said Dorothea.

"So it was," said Captain Flint. "And so it has been. The young cormorant. She's even scoffed my last tin of biscuits."

"We all had some," said Dorothea. "Would you like some milk chocolate with nuts in it? We've got some fresh from Rio."

It would have been hard to say who was at home and who was the visitor at tea in the cabin of the *Fram*. Captain Flint managed the Primus, and Dorothea swept some more of the skins off the table and spread out the cake they had saved from dinner, and the chocolate from Rio, and the loaf that had come from Beckfoot tied to the handle of Captain Flint's suitcase. There was no butter or jam, but that did not seem to matter. Every now and then Captain Flint could not help noticing the dreadful mess in his cabin, but he said nothing more about it, and it was a very cheerful tea. By the time the last cup had been drunk, and Dorothea was showing Captain Flint how to wash up without using more than a saucerful of water, a method invented by Peggy, there had been enough talk to let him know almost as much about what had been happening as if he had been there himself.

"Nancy's idea, of course," he said. "She'll have to let me in on it, though. I've been to a good many places at one time or another, but I've never been to the North Pole yet."

"Do you know where it is?" asked Dorothea. "We don't. At least not exactly."

"I've a pretty good idea," said Captain Flint, "but I'll have to have a talk with Nancy tomorrow and make sure. It seems to me I've come back just in time."

As he spoke he was turning over the leaves of the log, and suddenly caught sight of the last entry: — "Fine display of Northern lights. 9 p.m. Moon clear and high." "What?" he said. "You haven't been sleeping here at night?"

"Not yet," said Dorothea. "That was last night. They couldn't sleep here because of Titty and Roger. But they saw the lights. Of course they may have been the fireworks in Rio Bay. They were very good. We could see them even from Mrs Dixon's. But nobody's slept here yet. We were going to, tonight; but, of course, we won't now."

"No, you won't," said Captain Flint. "You couldn't expect any Eskimos to approve of that, and it's always well on these expeditions to keep on good terms with the natives."

"It's getting pretty dark already," said Dick. "It doesn't matter a bit where we sleep, but do let's have a look at those stars."

"Come on," said Captain Flint, quite in the tone that Dorothea had grown accustomed to hear from Peggy. "But you'd better put on a bearskin or two."

He and Dick went out of the cabin where, some time before, Captain Flint had lit the lantern. Dick had his telescope, his torch and the sketch map he had copied from his book. Captain Flint had opened his suitcase and pulled out a pair of binoculars. Dorothea put her head out into the light and felt the crisp air on the tip of her nose. She thought of joining the others, but then she thought of something else, went back into the cabin and, by throwing everything off one of the settees on the top of the things that were piled all over the other, made room for a possible bed. She took the red blankets from both settees and spread them on the one she had chosen, turning back the corner of the top blanket as she had seen counterpanes turned back in bedrooms at home. By the time the astronomers came in again to warm themselves by the stove, it really did look as if Captain Flint, in spite of the houseboat having been used for Arctic exploration, was going to have a comfortable night there.

"Hullo!" he said. "Well, I take that very kindly indeed. Returning good for evil. I turn you out and you make my bed. Now then, I'll come along with you to Mrs Dixon's. She'll be surprised to see you."

"She won't really," said Dorothea. "You see we hadn't told her we were going to sleep here. We meant to go and get milk for supper and tell her at the same time."

"Well, perhaps it's lucky you didn't."

Soon after that they were all three on the ice. The moon was rising, so Captain Flint decided not to bother about taking a lantern. Dick and Dorothea, sitting on their sledge, had put their skates on. They waited while Captain Flint was putting on his.

"Ice all clear to Dixon's landing?" he asked.

"It's fine the whole way down the lake," said Dick.

"You know, I was half afraid I'd find a thaw by the time I got back," said Captain Flint.

They were off, towing their sledge, while Captain Flint skated along beside them. Out of Houseboat Bay, where the moon threw their shadows before them, and then round the point and away to the south. At the point, Dorothea looked back at the lighted windows of the *Fram*. They were not to be sleeping there after all. But Captain Flint was. He had come back. What was going to happen now? She was far too much interested to mind that she herself was going to sleep in the farmhouse instead of in a ship, and would wake up in the morning to hear Mrs. Dixon say, "And that's the dozen" just as usual. On they went, she and Dick and that tall Dutchman, whom a few hours before she had not known. On they went down the lake, nearly to Spitzbergen, ghostly in the moonlight, and then in towards the landing where the upturned boat lay, black against the snow. Skates were taken off and packed on the sledge. Captain Flint became a dog like anybody else, helping to pull it up the steep field to the old white farm, where there was a glimmer of light in a window.

They crossed the yard. Captain Flint gave a rat-tat on the door but did not wait and, stamping the snow from his boots outside, walked in with the two of them.

"How do you do, Mrs Dixon," he said. "I've brought you a couple of strays."

"Well, I never, and when did you come back, Mr Turner? We thought you were in foreign parts for the winter."

"And so I was," said Captain Flint, "but when I saw in the papers about the lake freezing, I thought I wouldn't miss it. It's a long time since we've had such a winter as this, and we may not have another for as long again."

"They'd be glad to see you at Beckfoot, I daresay," said Mrs

Dixon. "It's a sad do for Mrs Blackett, with Miss Nancy falling sick and all. A rare upset when they should have been off to school and giving her a bit of peace."

"Glad to see me?" said Captain Flint. "Bundled me out before I'd been in the house two minutes. You might have thought poor Nancy had the plague. It's been a bit of an upset for you, too, hasn't it?" he added, glancing at Dorothea and Dick.

"Nay," said Mrs Dixon. "They give no trouble, don't these."

"No stopping out late at night, for instance?"

"Nay, to-night's first night they've been late. I made sure they'd been kept at Jackson's, but I reckon now it'll be your fault more than theirs."

Captain Flint laughed. "Well," he said, "perhaps it was."

"Will you come in and have a bite of supper, Mr Turner? I'd have it ready for you in two minutes."

"No thank you," said Captain Flint. "I've a lot to do. But I'll tell you what, Mrs Dixon. I was going to ask you if you could let me have a pint of tonight's milk and a dozen of eggs."

Mrs Dixon threw up her hands.

"You'll never be sleeping in the houseboat this weather?"

"And why not?" said Captain Flint. "It's as snug as this kitchen, with the stove burning."

"I could make you up a bed here," said Mrs Dixon.

"I've a bed made up already, thank you all the same," said Captain Flint, and a few minutes later was setting off again with his eggs and his pint of milk.

Dorothea and Dick went out into the yard in the moonlight with him and saw that, instead of taking the gate into the road, he turned down into the field to go back by the way they had come.

"But aren't you going to Holly Howe to see the others?" said Dorothea.

"Not I!" said Captain Flint. "Not tonight. And, by the way,

don't you go along there either. Come straight to the houseboat tomorrow, and not too early. Peggy's given me a bit of a surprise. It'll be her turn for one in the morning."

CHAPTER XXII

NEXT MORNING

At Holly Howe next morning, Peggy was first out of bed. She hurried across the landing to the room that was shared by Susan and Titty, that upper room at the end of the house, from which the signalling to Mars had first been noticed. She banged on the door in a timber-shivering manner, charged in and went straight to the window. Susan and Titty looked sleepily at her from their beds and wondered what was the matter.

"Good," she said. "They slept there all right."

"How do you know?" said Susan. She herself had felt pretty sure that Dick and Dorothea would have changed their minds and gone home. She had even expected them to turn up at the igloo yesterday afternoon. But it certainly did seem that those two were not much worried by the sort of things that so often bothered her and John.

"Yesterday's signal's still on the barn," said Peggy. "They'd have taken it down if they'd been up there. And it was a clear night last night. If they weren't in the *Fram* they'd have gone star-gazing for a certainty and taken the signal down at the same time. Buck up, you two. Let's get breakfast over. I'll just stir up the others."

But the others had been stirred already by her thumps on Susan's door; and they answered at once when Peggy stopped on her way across the landing to thunder at their own.

"All right, we're getting up," said John.

"They did sleep there," said Peggy.

"I wish we could have done," said John.

There was a bubbling noise and then a spluttering shout from Roger. "Could you hear my bubbling? Practising diving. In the basin. Picking up my collar stud under water. In my teeth."

But Peggy was gone and was back in her own room, dealing as fast as she could with the business of washing and dressing. If only she had had a little more faith in them yesterday. If only she could have been sure that the D.'s would really stay in the *Fram*, she could have stayed with them, and added another figure to the picture she had sent in answer to Nancy's, a figure with its left arm straight above its head and its right arm, stiff as a scarecrow's, straight out at the side. And Nancy, seeing that P. beside the two D.'s, would not have felt that her mate was backing out of things. Anyway, she would stay in the *Fram* tonight. Oh, hang that stocking, going on inside out. Off with it and on again. Susan would be bound to notice it. Anyhow, things were beginning to go really well. If she and the D.'s were to sleep in the *Fram* the others would sleep there, too, in the end. Botheration! Why did shoelaces always bust just when people were in most of a hurry? She tied the ends together and worked the knot round till it did not show much and did not hurt unless she pulled the lace too tight. She went downstairs in two jumps, and began bothering Mrs Jackson about the day's provisions. It would all save time later.

By the time the others came down she had a lot of sausages, and some butter to fry them in, ready stowed in her knapsack, and had persuaded Mrs Jackson to give them an extra allowance of milk. "Hurry up, Susan," she said, "and do try to make Roger be quick with his breakfast for once. The crew of the *Fram*'ll be waiting for us, and they won't even have milk for their porridge."

"I don't believe Dorothea'll even *try* porridge," said Susan.

"There's lots of Quaker Oats in the cupboard."

"She doesn't know very much about cooking," said Titty.

I

"Buck up and pitch your food in" said Peggy, "and then we'll go and cook their breakfast for them."

Everybody liked this idea. They had not slept in the *Fram* themselves, but the D.'s had done it for them. They wanted to help in every way they could. And cooking breakfast there would almost seem like having been there all night.

"We could leave room and have another breakfast on board," said Roger.

"No need for you to leave room," said John. "I don't believe you're ever full."

"It depends what with," said Roger.

"Do let's all sleep there tonight," said Titty. "I don't see why we shouldn't if they can."

Even the hungry Roger was quicker than usual. Breakfast was soon over. They were off, down the field, and out of the Holly Howe bay. A relief expedition going to the *Fram*, it was agreed, ought to go over the ice and not down cart tracks in woods.

There was little talking now. They hardly saw the early morning skaters on that great sunlit sheet of ice. The Swallows were wondering what it had been like waking up in the *Fram*. Peggy was full of plans for the evening when she, too, would be staying after dark, ready to sleep out there on the frozen sea, with no more than a plank between her and the Polar ice.

"All the same," said John, "I wouldn't be a bit surprised if they hadn't thought better of it."

"They couldn't think better of it than we do," said Roger.

And just then they passed the northern point of Houseboat Bay. There before them lay the *Fram*, solid in the ice, and from the little stovepipe in the cabin roof a steady stream of blue smoke was pouring up into the winter sky.

"Hurrah!" shouted Peggy. "I knew they were there. Three cheers for the D.'s! Come on!"

★

"Hullo!" said John. "What's that notice?"

A big piece of board had been fixed on the side of the *Fram*, close by the ladder. On it, in big black letters, was printed the word "TRESPASSERS". As the skaters came nearer they were able to read the second line, which was in rather smaller letters, "WILL BE HANGED", and when they were already close to the *Fram* they could read a third line, of letters smaller still, "LIKE THE LAST".

"What cheek!" said Peggy.

"Perhaps some seals have been trying to come aboard again," said Titty.

"Cheek, all the same," said Peggy, "to put up a notice like that. It's all very well Captain Nancy doing things like that. But not the D.'s."

"Well, they're in charge," said John. "I don't see why they shouldn't."

Skates were being unscrewed in a hurry. Several sound slaps had been given to the cold planking of the *Fram*, sparkling all over with a film of frost crystals. But there had been no answer from inside.

There was no shout of welcome. There was no sound at all. There was no sign of anybody aboard when they looked through the windows.

"They'll have got hungry and gone off to Dixon's Farm to get breakfast without waiting for us," said Susan.

"That's why they've left that notice," said Titty. "In case somebody came before they got back."

"It's not half a bad idea really," said John. "But saying 'Hanged' is a bit stiff. And they ought not to have left the ladder down."

Peggy was first on deck. She rattled at the cabin door.

"Bother them!" she cried. "You're right, Susan. They've gone off for the milk and taken the key with them."

"We'll just have to wait for them," said Susan.

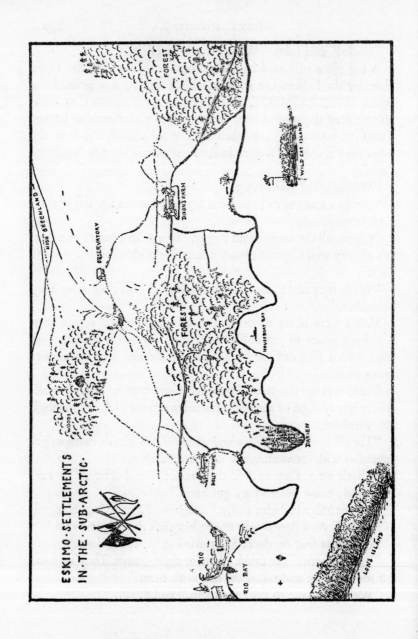

ESKIMO · SETTLEMENTS
IN · THE · SUB · ARCTIC.

In a moment of silence that followed, while some were looking at the place where the cart track came out of the trees on the shore, and some were looking out of the bay, as if they thought the D.'s might appear at any moment, Peggy heard something stirring in the cabin.

"Listen!" she said. "'Sh!"

Everybody heard some small thing drop on the cabin floor.

Peggy rattled the handle of the door and thumped on the panels. "Hi!" she shouted. "Buck up and open! It's us!"

Nothing happened.

"Hurry up," she called again, "or we'll drop some icicles down the chimney and put the stove out! Be quick! Don't be donks. It isn't funny at all."

And just then the door opened.

Peggy started back. Her jaw dropped. She let out a queer little groan of astonishment.

"Hullo!" said Titty cheerfully. "It's Captain Flint!"

"Hullo, Skipper!" said Captain Flint. "Hullo, A.B. And the mate. And the ship's boy!" Then he turned to his niece. "But by jove, Peggy, you're not much of a hand at keeping an eye on things. Talk about burglars. Why, someone's got in here while I was away, and turned the whole place upside down, and eaten all the stores, and piled the place up with dirty sheepskins, and generally played ninepins with everything. And that's not the worst. I caught some of them in the very act. They've been living here. I came back to find a boy and girl, utter strangers of course, camped down here to spend the night in my cabin as calm as you like. Well, it didn't take long to settle *them* ... "

"But look here, Uncle Jim," said Peggy. "It's all of us. At least, it's Nancy and me. We thought you'd be glad to have the house-boat properly aired and all that while she was frozen in. Besides, she would have been simply wasted with the lake frozen and you away and nobody using her at all."

"What?" said Captain Flint. "Do you mean to say it was you who got in here and made such a horrible mess?"

"It wasn't Peggy alone," said John. "It was all of us."

"We were going to make everything perfectly tidy again before we left," said Susan.

Just the beginning of a smile showed round Captain Flint's eyes, but it flickered there only for a moment and then was gone.

"Well," he said, "I suppose I could have trusted Mate Susan to see to that. But I do think that, between the lot of you, you might have seen that the door was properly locked at night, and not left it open, so that I had a couple of burgling scallawags to deal with when I got back. You must have gone away and left the key in the door or they could never have dared to break in. As a matter of fact, I know you did, for I found the key in the door when I came here, and those two ragamuffins making themselves at home. Well they won't go burgling again in a hurry ... I can tell you that."

"But I say," said John, "it was our fault they were here. They never would have come if we hadn't brought them."

Peggy flared up. "Look here, Uncle Jim! They were our friends. We left them here ourselves. What have you done with them?"

"You read the notice, didn't you?" said Captain Flint. "They were the last ... "

"But he can't have hanged them," said Roger. "He's probably got them in the fo'c'sle."

"You ought to let them out at once," said Titty.

"Too late now," said Captain Flint. "There they were in all this mess, treating my boat as if it belonged to them. How could I tell they were friends of yours?"

"And you turned them out," said Peggy. "It's the beastliest thing you've ever done. It wasn't their fault at all. And Dorothea'd never understand *why* you were being beastly ... "

"Where are they?" said John. "We're awfully sorry if we oughtn't to have come into your houseboat, but those two had nothing whatever to do with it. Where are they? We must go and explain it to them right away."

"They aren't in here," said Roger, who had wriggled in past Captain Flint and gone straight through the cabin and opened the door into the fo'c'sle.

"Of course they aren't," said Captain Flint.

"If you've gone and done anything horrid to them we'll never speak to you again," said Peggy. "I don't care a bit about getting into your beastly boat. I'm sorry we didn't make a real mess of it. You don't deserve to have a boat at all if you were nasty to them. You just wait till Nancy hears about it ... " Peggy was so angry that she was on the very edge of weeping in a most unpiratical manner, and not at all like an Arctic explorer either. "Come along, everybody," she said. "Let's leave him. We'll never come back. We ought to go to Dixon's Farm at once."

But at that moment there was a cheerful shout from the ice, and Dick and Dorothea came skating up to the *Fram* towing their sledge behind them.

"Hullo!" Dorothea called out. "Hullo, Susan! Has he already had his breakfast? Mrs Dixon's sent some rashers of bacon in case he's forgotten to get any."

CHAPTER XXIII

THE USES OF AN UNCLE

DOROTHEA never quite got the hang of what had been happening that morning. Everybody was looking in a queer, anxious way at Dick and herself; everybody, that is to say, except Captain Flint, who seemed quite at his ease, smiled in the friendliest manner and thanked her for bringing the bacon from Mrs Dixon. John and Susan seemed to be worried about something. Titty and Roger were staring at her almost as if she were a ghost. And then there was Peggy, to whom Captain Flint really belonged, as he was her uncle, looking almost as if she had been thinking of tears, and as if she was ashamed and indignant at the same time.

"Look here, Dorothea," Peggy said. "Was he beastly? What *did* happen when he turned up?"

Everybody was staring at her. Even Captain Flint. It was as if the whole air was full of question marks. Dorothea tried to remember exactly what had happened after the arrival of the tall Dutchman.

"We had tea," she said, "and afterwards they looked at stars."

"Then why did you pretend you were such a beast?" said Peggy furiously, turning to her uncle.

Dorothea listened with grave interest. This seemed to her a queer way of talking to an uncle, though, as she and Dick had no uncles of their own, she had had no personal experience of dealing with them. However, in a very few minutes, all was peace, and Susan was in the fo'c'sle frying his bacon for him, while everybody else was promising to tidy things up that very morning, and meanwhile sucking the oranges of which he seemed to have a large supply. One thing was clear at once and that was that she had been right not to treat him as a mere Eskimo yesterday afternoon. It would have been impossible, anyhow, when his own ship was being used for the *Fram*, and she had had to explain how it was that his cabin was littered with Arctic equipment. She had been a little troubled, thinking it over afterwards in bed, lest she had let him know too much; but this morning, once hostilities were over, it was clear that all the others were in a hurry to tell him even more.

"Well," he said at last, when he had had his breakfast and smoked a pipe and heard a good deal of what they had to say, "the best thing I can do is to go and have a talk with the chief culprit and find out what she's really up to ... No ... I'll not forget she's had to put up with a face like a water-melon ... beg your pardon, Roger ... pumpkin, if you like it better ... and now will one of you slip away to the shore and bring my sledge. You'll find it just to the right of the old cart track. Yes ... I hid it there last night so as not to give things away too soon this morning. One surprise deserves another, eh, Peggy? ... "

"Where did you find the sledge?" asked Peggy. "Nancy and I hunted all over for it. We could only find the big one."

"Where I put it," said Captain Flint. "The last two years it's been on the beams under the roof of the boathouse, and you're a couple of duffers not to have found it yourselves."

"What do you want it for now?"

"Going shopping," said Captain Flint. "Poor dogs like me must have their bones, even if their cupboards have been eaten bare."

Everybody said they were dreadfully sorry, but he only laughed at them and presently was gone, after telling them they had better stay to cook his dinner for him when he came back.

Susan took complete command the moment he had gone, and the *Fram* was given a regular spring cleaning, middle of winter though it was. A whole sledge-load of Arctic gear, and the rubbish and scraps left over after making it, was taken up to Holly Howe where it was dumped, though not too warmly welcomed. The D.'s' sledge was loaded, too, with things that had to go back to Dixon's Farm, and the Beckfoot sledge was already piled with a second load when Captain Flint came skating back, towing his own small sledge with a cargo of provisions to make up for those the explorers had already eaten.

"Did you see Nancy?" everybody asked him.

"I did," said Captain Flint. "Very disappointing. I seem to have come back too late to see her in bloom. Her face is no bigger than usual."

"Did you talk to her?"

"From one end of the lawn to the other. Semaphore, mostly."

"We're not allowed even to do that," said Peggy.

"I shall have to rub up my signalling," said Captain Flint. "She goes a lot too fast for me."

"We'd been doing signals all these holidays until she got mumps," said Peggy, "and she'd be jolly glad to have someone to practise with."

"I kept on signalling 'Go slow' and 'Repeat' for the first five minutes or so, and in the end I got her down to a reasonable speed."

"Well, well! And what did she say? What's going to happen?"

To that he gave no very definite answer. It seemed that just at first Nancy had been mainly interested to know what had happened the day before when he had found strangers in the houseboat. Then, certainly, there had been talk about the Pole.

"The trouble is," said Captain Flint, "that in these days everything belongs to someone, even the North Pole."

"Polar bears," said Roger.

"Well," said Captain Flint, "I've got to make sure that these particular bears will let us have the key."

"Key?" said Dick – "Key to the North Pole?"

"It's all right," said Peggy. "You wait till you see it and then you'll know."

And what about Nancy herself?" asked John.

"She says the doctor's promised that in another week he'll let her haul down the plague flag and meet the rest of us."

"And we've got another ten days before going back to school," said Titty.

"Unless somebody else goes and starts it," said Susan, "and then there'll be another month."

There was a general opening and shutting of mouths to test the stiffness of jaws.

"The frost won't last all that time," said Captain Flint.

"But will Nancy be able to come to the Pole even if nobody starts mumps?" asked Titty.

"With any luck she will," said Captain Flint. "But it'll be a near thing if a thaw comes. At the first sign of a thaw we shall have to start at once if we're going to do it at all."

Dick and John looked anxiously at the barometer, which at the moment was high and steady, prophesying good weather.

*

There had been fears at first that the return of Captain Flint would mean that the houseboat would no longer be the *Fram*, and that the explorers would have to return to life ashore. But it was not so. Captain Flint had come back for the skating, and to enjoy seeing the lake frozen from end to end as he had seen it when he was a boy. But skating is always better when it has an object; and after that first morning he was invited to join the North Polar Expedition, and at once threw himself into Arctic exploration as keenly as anybody else.

The houseboat was now a much tidier *Fram* than it had been, but it was still the *Fram*. Dinner was eaten there nearly every day. Indeed, the only difference was that, after Captain Flint's return, dinners had rather a tendency to turn into feasts. Also, he got his accordion smuggled out of Beckfoot, where it had been stored for fear of damp; and after that there was sometimes so much noise in the cabin of the *Fram* and such hearty stamping on her deck that the explorers no longer had any right to complain of the rowdiness of the Eskimos dancing in Rio Bay. He was taken up the hillside, and admired the igloo very much, though he said that if they ever built another he would take it kindly if they made a rather larger doorway. One evening, he and Dick took glasses and the telescope up to the observatory and came back late for supper at Dixon's Farm, when Mrs Dixon, who had known Captain Flint when he was a boy, said that growing older and travelling round the world brought no sense to some folk. There was very little wind these days, too little even for the ice yachts, and not enough to move the Beckfoot sledge. But Captain Flint had a good look at it, and showed John a better way of rigging the mast, and told him that for sledge work the nearer he could come to making his sail a square sail the better it would be. And Dick watched and listened, and, when he came home in the evening talked it all over with Mr Dixon.

At the same time everybody knew that Captain Flint was keeping in close touch with Captain Nancy. Every day he skated over to Beckfoot. Mrs Blackett would not let him into the house until the doctor should say that all danger of infection was over. So Nancy and Captain Flint consulted each other through a window pane, or from opposite sides of the garden, noiselessly, by semaphoring or by talking deaf and dumb language with their fingers. Shouting, of course, would have given secrets away. Nancy had been very angry to find herself so weak after being in bed with mumps, which really was nothing of an illness, and now she was fiercely getting herself back into training. In the beginning all she had hoped for was to persuade the doctor to get the North Pole ready for the others. But now, with Captain Flint back and helping, and the doctor promising her freedom in very few more days, it would be horrible if mere weakness prevented her from dashing northwards with the others. Day by day the journey to the Pole was getting nearer. Day by day Nancy was walking up and down the garden path, then to the end of the promontory and back, and latterly was going on the ice each morning and once more growing accustomed to her skates.

Plans for the final journey were growing clearer. It had been all but decided that there should be three separate parties. After all, there were now three sledges and, as Captain Flint pointed out, it was no good thinking of their all starting together, because it would be too much for Nancy to come down the lake to the *Fram* and then, the same day, race for the head of the lake. Not that it was to be a race. Simply, on the day, everybody would set out for the north, the big Beckfoot sledge with its five husky dogs, Dick and Dorothea with their sledge, and Captain Flint and Nancy going together, all to get to the Arctic as fast as they could and to meet at the North Pole.

"But what if we don't know it when we see it?" said Dick.

"Anybody would know it the moment they saw it," said Peggy. "It's right at the head of the lake. The extreme north of the Arctic, and only a few yards off the ice. You can't mistake it."

"And as soon as the first party gets there they hoist a flag," said Titty. "A quarantine flag, because we shall still be lepers till the very day we go back to school."

Peggy alone, of the explorers who met aboard the *Fram*, had actually seen the Pole, but that had been a long time ago, and she really remembered very little about it. Not even she knew what was preparing between Nancy and Captain Flint. One or two odd little things happened that might have been enough to show what they were up to, but, as Peggy said, "It only spoils things to be too beastly clever." So questions were not pushed too hard, and when it was necessary the explorers looked the other way. For example, everybody had known, the day after Captain Flint had had his first talk with Nancy, that he had skated right up to the head of the lake to see those Polar bears of whom he had spoken. But not one single word was said to him about it when he came back. A day or two after that, he disappeared for a long time, and when he came back Roger, after examining his sledge, asked him why it was all black with coal dust. Captain Flint looked at him and shut both eyes, and the others sang out at once that they did not want to know

"If it's anything to do with the Pole, I don't either," said Roger.

"Then everybody'll be content," said Captain Flint.

All the same, as the days went on, everybody knew that the journey to the Pole was coming very near. There was great cleaning of skates and sledge-runners, and a lot of hard work put into the greasing of skating boots. And Dick was getting more and more desperate because, as yet, he had not been able to finish up his mast and make his sail. It was as if the Eskimos at Dixon's Farm hardly realized how urgently needed these things might be.

*

And then one morning, just as Peggy and the Swallows were skating out of Holly Howe Bay after breakfast, on their way to the *Fram*, they saw Captain Flint with his sledge, close to the shore of Long Island and skating towards Rio. They had skated cheerfully in pursuit of him, round the point, past the deserted boatsheds and into the crowded bay of Rio, where they lost him altogether. They looked up the lake towards Beckfoot, and could see no sign of him. They knew he must be somewhere in the bay, which was black with seals and Eskimos. The five of them skated this way and that, looking for him, and in the end skated towards the landing-stages, where newcomers were sitting in rows, putting on their skates.

"Well, he's simply disappeared," said Titty.

"Gone through a hole in the ice," said Roger cheerfully.

But just then they saw him, coming down out of the village, towing his sledge behind him. But the sledge was no longer empty. There was an enormous packing-case on it. They skated round to meet him when he came down on the shore. He sat down on the wooden case to put his skates on, and looked up with surprise when they came crowding round.

"Hullo!" he said. "What are you doing here? You've got that spare key of the cabin, so you can let yourselves in. Be off with you. Don't wait dinner for me. But I'll be wanting tea when I come back."

"What's in that box?" asked Roger.

"It's just about big enough for you, isn't it?" said Captain Flint; and then stood up with his skates on, and a moment later was gliding away from the shore, tugging his loaded sledge behind him.

"Which way are you going?" asked Roger.

"Let's all be dogs and help," said Titty.

"Thanks very much," said Captain Flint, "not this time," and, gathering speed, went on his way into the middle of the crowd of skaters.

"Let's go after him," said Roger.

"Rot!" said Peggy. "Let's go the other way."

John and Susan agreed with Peggy. They skated out from Rio towards Long Island. Just for a moment they caught sight of Captain Flint, with his sledge and the big box on it, going steadily northwards. They turned south, themselves, and reached the *Fram* just in time to stop Dorothea and Dick who, after finding the *Fram* empty and locked up, were setting off towards the shore, thinking that perhaps they had mistaken the signal, and that everybody had gone to the igloo.

"Where's Captain Flint?" Dorothea asked.

"Up in the Arctic somewhere," Peggy replied. "He's coming back after dinner."

"Anybody got any plans?" John asked.

"We've got to get back early," said Dick, who had arranged to spend the afternoon at home with the Eskimos. Mr Dixon had promised to make him a sort of box that was to go near the front of the sledge for the stepping of the mast; and Mrs Dixon, who had been putting it off day after day, had said that if he liked to be at home, to show her just what he wanted, she would get that sail of his finished out of hand.

"Back to Dixon's Farm?" said Peggy. "But why?"

"What for?" said Roger.

Dick looked very bothered. He had set his heart on saying nothing about it to the others until he had made sure his sail would work.

"It's something he's got to do," said Dorothea.

"Secret?" asked Titty.

"It's for the expedition," said Dick.

After that nobody tried to make them stay. After all, in a case like this, the more secrets the better. So the plan for the day was made to include a skating practice, and everybody went at full speed right down the lake, past Spitzbergen, across to Horseshoe Point, where the sharp Pike rock, on which *Swallow* once had been wrecked, was just showing through the ice; back again to Cormorant Island, across to Shark's Bay, and so to the Dixon's Farm landing. Here they parted, and the D.'s went up the field to the farm, while the rest of the explorers went back to the *Fram* for dinner.

In the afternoon, Roger, whose turn it happened to be to keep watch on deck, saw Captain Flint skating wearily home.

"Here he is," he shouted into the cabin. "And that box has gone."

"Don't let's ask him where he's been," said Peggy.

People looked with interest at the empty sledge, and at Captain Flint himself, who was both very hot and very dirty; but the only question that was asked him was asked by Susan, ten minutes later, when they were all sitting round the cabin table, and that was: "How many lumps of sugar would he like to have in his tea?"

"By Jove," said Captain Flint, "I'm so thirsty, I believe I could drink it with forty or with none at all. Make it three for luck."

But today Captain Flint seemed almost to want to be asked questions. He had asked for a little drop of water to wash his hands in, and had held them up, black and sooty, and had said, "Well, how do you think I got them into that sort of mess?" and Susan, after one look at them, had said, "You've been laying a fire."

"Susan," said he, "you'll make a Sherlock Holmes yet. That's exactly what I've been doing. Something else, too. I've been sweeping a chimney that was properly choked with jackdaws' nests."

Everybody stared at him.

"You don't believe me," he said, "but I have. And now I think everything's ready, and I can look forward to a holiday. I little thought when I came back because the lake was frozen, that I was running myself in for such a lot of hard work. Hullo, what's become of the D.'s?"

"Busy at home," said John.

"Up to something," said Peggy.

"Can you make sure of their coming to the *Fram* tomorrow, or must I go up there tonight?"

"They'll be here all right if we put the signal for them."

"Well, you put it," said Captain Flint, and, after his third or fourth mug of tea, had explained why.

"They're going to let Nancy loose on the world tomorrow," he said.

"Three thousand cheers!" shouted John, and the whole lot of them stood up and yelled.

"Wait a minute," said Captain Flint.

"Shut up, everybody," said Peggy. "Don't be a galoot, Roger."

"We don't know yet what time tomorrow. Disinfection, fumigation, and all the rest of it. Not before twelve o'clock at the very earliest, so she says. The doctor's going round there first thing in the morning; and as soon as Nancy knows for certain, she'll hoist a flag on the promontory. If it's white, it means they won't let her come till next day. If it's a red one, it means she's to be allowed to come across here for dinner and to stay the afternoon. We'll have dinner a bit late because she won't anyhow be able to start till twelve or half-past. Then we'll settle everything in full council, and the day after tomorrow, if the weather goes on being decent, we'll liven up the solitary Pole."

*

That was the programme, very neat and tidy. A final council to decide details, and then, the next day, a march to the head of the lake and the discovery of the Pole. If it had only come off, this particular discovery of the North Pole would have been the most orderly bit of Arctic exploration in history. But there had been just a little too much planning. When, next morning, after hoisting the signal, "Come to the *Fram*," Peggy and the Swallows had run up the field above Holly Howe and, through the telescope, had actually seen a big scarlet flag climb the flagstaff on the Beckfoot promontory, they rejoiced that Captain Nancy was free once more, and would that day join them in council. Not one of them knew that nearly a month before, Dick, with Nancy looking over his shoulder, had carefully written in his note-book, "Flag at Beckfoot = Start for Pole."

CHAPTER XXIV

FLAG AT BECKFOOT

BREAKFAST was late that morning, because Mrs Dixon was getting Mr Dixon ready to drive her into Rio in the milk-cart to do her weekly shopping. Mr Dixon had been at work with Silas in the byre, so that, as Mrs Dixon said, he was better fit to scare crows than owt else. Everything was late, and it was long after the usual time when Dick, buttoning his short coat, with his telescope tucked into an inside pocket, set off across the road and up the fell to the old barn.

"I'll be all ready when you come back," Dorothea called after him.

It was cold coming out of the warm kitchen, and Dick took a handful of snow as he climbed the hill, and rubbed his nose with it, just in case of frostbite. It certainly seemed wintry enough, but Dick was not altogether happy about the weather. Last night, when they had been busy with a step for the mast, Mr Dixon had told him he had better use his sledge while he could, for the frost would be coming to an end. This morning, though the big hills in the north were glittering in sunshine, there were clouds away to the south. Dick did not like the look of things, and wondered for the hundredth time how the Dixons could bear not having a barometer. Why, even at school there was a barometer in the hall; and though, at school, he did not keep a record of its readings as he did at home, he usually managed to have a look at it and to know whether it was going up or down. And just now the weather really mattered. It would be dreadful if it turned bad just when most of all they wanted hard frost and a clear sky.

He came up to the barn, and looked down to Holly Howe. There was the signal on the end of the house, square over south cone, the same as yesterday's, "Come to the *Fram*." He looked up at his own signal, hanging on the wall of the barn. There was no need to change it. He had been too busy with mast and sail to come up to the observatory last night, and the square over the south cone that he had hoisted yesterday morning in answer to Holly Howe had hung there ever since.

As usual, just for a moment, he ran up the stone steps to the loft, and looked out through that great window, at the tarn, and then away to the left at the wonderful picture of the big hills at the head of the frozen lake. There were the Rio islands, and beyond them, on the other side of the lake, were the mouth of the Amazon River and Beckfoot, where the heroic Captain Nancy was having her mumps by herself. Suddenly, he stiffened. Where was that little flagstaff she had pointed out to him that day when she had drawn the semaphore signals in his book while the others were skating on the tarn? And what was that dark speck against the snow on the point? Surely he had not seen it there before.

He pulled out his telescope with hands that shook, though not from cold, for he had grown warm climbing the hill. He focussed it on the promontory, and found that speck. Yes, there could be no doubt about it. Far too big for that little flagstaff, a huge scarlet flag flapped in the light wind. Captain Nancy was signalling at last.

He knew at once what her signal meant, but pulled out his pocket-book, to see it in writing. And there it was, at the bottom of a page:

"Flag at Beckfoot = Start for Pole."

"Start for the Pole. Today. Now." Did it mean that Nancy was free and coming too, or did it mean that she thought the weather was changing, and that they ought not to wait another day? Those clouds did look pretty bad. He looked down again at Holly Howe. That signal, "Come to the *Fram*", must, like his own, have been left up since yesterday. They would think nothing else mattered when they saw the flag at Beckfoot. Probably they had started already. Or would they wait? What bad luck it was that today of all days he should be late in going up to the observatory. Thank goodness he was ready. His mast and sail were waiting, and the wind, such as it was, was in the right direction. And now, however careless the others might have been, he would change his signal to show that he had seen and understood. There was no need to look in his book, but he looked all the same, for fear of making any slip. He remembered John saying that a triangle pointing upwards was the north cone storm signal, so that it was right and proper to use it in signalling "North Pole." Yes, there it was, north cone over diamond, "Come to the North Pole." He ran down the steps, hauled down the signal, changed it to north cone over diamond, and hoisted it again. He glanced down at Holly Howe, and saw Titty and Roger racing down the field below the house. Perhaps, after all, it was not too late to catch them up. Once more he looked through the telescope beyond Rio, across the lake, to the Beckfoot promontory. There it was, a flapping scarlet flag. The march to the Pole had begun.

He rammed his telescope into his pocket and ran, as fast as he could without tumbling on the slippery track, down the hill, across the road, and into the farmyard. The milk-cart that had been standing there was gone. Mr and Mrs Dixon were already on their way to Rio. Dorothea had the sledge by the kitchen door. She was just coming out with a knapsack.

"Dot," he cried, "they're off. It's today."

"What?"

"They're starting for the Pole. Come on. Captain Nancy's got a huge flag on the Beckfoot promontory. She said that'd be the signal." He held out his pocket-book, open at the page.

"Today?" said Dorothea.

"The very day we're late," said Dick. "But they've only just started. I saw Titty and Roger going down the field. Quick. You get our bearskins and things. I'll be getting the mast and sail. Oh yes, and we'll want our flag."

Dorothea wasted no time on questions. She bolted into the house, and came out with the sheepskins that were to go on the sledge, and two pairs of rabbit-skin mittens. The explorers were wearing their fur hats already.

Dick charged upstairs for the astronomy book.

"But you don't want that," said Dorothea.

"Of course I do," said Dick. "We may have to come back by starlight. Oh yes, and we must take a lantern, too. Where's Silas?"

"Gone out for something or other."

"Well, he won't mind, anyhow. And I know how to fill it." He took the lantern they used for going up to the observatory in the evenings, unscrewed the little plug at the side, and filled it up from the tap in the big oil drum that stood on trestles in the shed.

"What about food?" he said, as he brought the lantern back.

"It's a beef-roll today, instead of sandwiches."

"Good," said Dick. "We'll manage all right with that. And drink?"

"A bottle of milk. Mrs Dixon thought Susan would be making tea as usual. Perhaps we ought to take a kettle and tea ... "

"Never mind," said Dick. "Every minute matters."

"They'll wait for us," said Dorothea.

"Why should they?" said Dick. "Last time they were talking about it they said we'd be going in separate parties."

"But if we don't find the Pole?" said Dorothea. "The others have got Peggy with them. She knows what to look for. We may miss it altogether if we don't see them."

"Let's hurry up, then," said Dick, busy with ropes, "The quicker we get going the more chance we'll have of catching them."

In a very few minutes the sledge was loaded. The little yellow quarantine flag with its rope and toggle had been tied to a small stick for signal practice. Dick fastened it to the top of the mast, firmly enough but in a manner no sailor would approve. The sheepskins covered the knapsacks and the big coil of clothes-line that Mrs Dixon had given them instead of an Alpine rope. The mast and the sail were roped down on the top of everything else.

"Theirs'll probably be neater," said Dorothea.

"We must tie that lantern on," said Dick.

"Silas'll be back in a minute," said Dorothea. "We'd better wait to say goodbye. Going to the North Pole, you know. It's not like just going to the igloo or the *Fram*."

"We shall miss them altogether if we don't start," said Dick, pulling the sledge out of the yard into the field. "We don't want to meet them coming back and never see the Pole at all."

Dorothea, sitting in front on the loaded sledge, looked over her shoulder in hope that Silas might appear at the last minute. But Dick, saying, "All aboard!" in the nautical manner used when tobogganing by Titty and Roger, gave the sledge a good push, landed sitting on the back of it, and, with the touch of a foot, now on this side, now on that, as it flew down over the snow, steered it for the gap he had cut in the reeds. It flew out on the ice towards the island and, with the extra weight on it, might well have made a record run. But today there were other things to think of.

"Brake! Brake!" cried Dick, sticking both feet firmly down. "No point in going too far."

Dorothea braked too. The sledge came to a standstill. Skates were pulled out from under the sheepskins and, in another minute, Dick and Dorothea, Arctic explorers and their own dog-team, set out with steady strokes for the far north.

"It's no good going too fast," said Dick. "We've got a tremendous way to go. We must just go ahead at the pace we know we can keep up for ever. We'll catch them in the end. They can't go quicker than Roger."

"Are we going to use the sail?"

"Not without some more wind," said Dick, looking over his shoulder at the clouds in the south. "It's the right wind, but there isn't enough of it. It's no better than it was that day it wouldn't move the Beckfoot sledge at all."

"I wish it would blow a bit," said Dorothea. This was not because she looked forward to sailing for its own sake, but because, supposing the others were really well on their way, she was seeing a picture of their arrival in the distant north. There would be the Swallows and Peggy, sailing over the ice on the big Beckfoot sledge, with the flag fluttering at the masthead; and there, a bit late, but coming fast in pursuit of them, would be a little sledge, with its sail made out of an old sheet, it, too, flying its flag. She did want them to see what Dick could do. "What was that, far away over the ice?" That was what they would say. "A sail. A sledge. The D.'s have done it after all." And then the little sledge would stop beside the big one and there would be stamping of cold feet on the ice, and shaking of mittened hands, and they would do the last march to the Pole together. It would be a dreadful pity if the others had got too big a start.

The *Fram*, lying there in the ice, looked deserted when they passed by outside Houseboat Bay. Usually there was at least one sledge lying beside her, and one or two of the explorers would be stamping up and down on the after-deck. Today not a soul was to be seen. There were no sledges. No smoke was climbing from the chimney on the cabin roof, and the ladder was not hanging in its usual place.

"Captain Flint's gone too," said Dorothea. "He's shut up the *Fram* for the day."

"He and Nancy'll be going together," said Dick, "if the doctor's let her out."

In a few minutes they had passed the northern point of the bay, and could see the houseboat no more. They never saw a thick cloud of smoke roll up from the chimney as Susan put fresh coal in the stove which had burned nearly out while Captain Flint had been thinking of other things. They did not know that Captain Flint had, only half an hour earlier, shifted the ladder to the side of the houseboat nearer the shore, so that it should be less inviting to inquisitive seals on the lake. They could not guess that the two sledges had been lying on the ice beside the ladder, hidden from them by the body of the *Fram*.

They skated on, past Darien, with the dark pines on its rocky cliff, and swung eagerly round it into the Holly Howe Bay, more than half hoping that, after all, the Beckfoot sledge and five explorers would be waiting for them. The bay was empty except for two seals in the middle of it, who were cutting figures on the ice as if nothing else mattered in the world.

"They've gone right on," said Dick.

"Let's make quite sure," said Dorothea. "They may be still up at the farm. And even if they've gone, they may have left a message."

"All right," said Dick. "You bring the sledge slowly in, and I'll hare on and run up the field and find out."

He was off, like the wind, so fast that even the figure-skaters turned to watch him, though he never knew it. As hard as he could he skated in to the Holly Howe jetty, got ashore there through the reeds, took his skates off, and ran up the field. It was no good trying to guess from the tracks what the others had been doing, for there were far too many tracks. Very much out of breath he dashed into the farm and opened the kitchen door.

"Nay, you're late for them," said Mrs Jackson. "They were off in a rare hurry today. They went up the field after breakfast and came down talking of Miss Nancy signalling from Beckfoot.

She's got a flag up there, they said. They just packed their things and were off in such a hurry as never was."

"I thought so," panted Dick. "Thank you very much," and he was out of the farm and racing down the field again.

"Mrs Jackson says they started off as soon as they saw the signal," he panted. "Come on, Dot. It doesn't matter. Peggy said we couldn't miss it. And anyway they'll be hoisting a flag as soon as they get there, and we'll see that."

"They can't be so very far ahead," said Dorothea, "if you saw Titty and Roger."

They were off again – left, right, left, right – out of the Holly Howe bay, between Long Island and the mainland, past the boatbuilding sheds, and then across by the steamer buoy and the Hen and Chicken rocks.

Rio Bay was this morning more crowded than ever. It was as if everybody was afraid the weather was going to break, and was taking a last chance on the ice. Half a dozen gramophones were playing at once, and playing different tunes. The D.'s had to slow up for fear of colliding with seals. Two or three times they thought they caught sight of the fur hats of the explorers, and each time something got instantly in the way: a group of hockey-players, or some accidental thickening of the crowd, just where they wanted to be able to see through it.

"Never mind," said Dick. "We know where to go. And we'll be able to see them when we get out of all this."

A man had fixed a sort of coffee-stall on the top of a sledge, and was pushing it about from group to group among the skaters. Dick and Dorothea passed near enough to him to see that he was selling cups of hot coffee and small, steaming pies.

"What about getting some?" said Dick.

"Not coffee," said Dorothea.

"No," said Dick. "It takes too long to drink when it's really hot. And we'd have to wait to give the cups back. But what about those pies? We'd better save our provisions as long as we can."

"I'll get two," said Dorothea. "You take my rope."

After all, it might be a long time before they could stop to have dinner. And they could eat the hot pies without stopping at all. She had a purse in the pocket of her coat with a sixpence in it and a few coppers. She skated off towards the coffee-sledge. "Hot meat pies — twopence each," the man was calling out. She bought two.

"It's the right day, miss, for hot pies," said the man.

"What do you sell on a hot day?" asked Dorothea.

"Ice-creams," said the man.

"Opposites," said Dorothea.

"That's right," said the man, "and lemonade instead of coffee. You'll find my stall in summer by the steamer pier."

Dick had kept moving with the sledge, but Dorothea easily caught him up and took her rope again. They skated on, eating the hot pies.

"Jolly good," said Dick.

"Yes," said Dorothea. She was remembering how Titty, looking at all the busy crowd of skaters, had said, "We can count them seals." Well, you couldn't buy hot meat pies from a seal, and Dorothea liked thinking of the skaters as human beings, crowds and crowds of them, all busy with their own affairs and not suspecting in the least that she and Dick were part of a North Polar expedition, that their sledge was piled with bearskins, and that they had a lantern, an Alpine rope, and a meat-roll and everything else that was necessary. She wondered what they had thought of the main expedition with the five dogs and the big Beckfoot sledge. Almost, indeed, she had thought of asking the man with the coffee sledge if he had seen them go by, but, if the others were counting him a seal, perhaps it would hardly be right to ask him that kind of question.

They were working their way out of the crowds now, and were

close to the little island where they had made a secret cache to mark their "farthest north."

"They'll have left a message in it," said Dorothea, guessing that Dick, too, was thinking of the paper in the ginger-beer bottle as the island came nearer and nearer.

"It won't take a minute to look," said Dick, "and anyway, we ought to put down that we've passed it."

There was a moment's stoppage. They left the sledge on the ice, and, not very easily, because of their skates, they struggled over heather, snow, and rocks to the little pile of stones in which the bottle was hidden. Dick opened the cairn, and pulled it out.

"Lucky the cork's loose," he said, and a moment later was working the paper through the narrow neck. It was a disappointment. "They've forgotten about it," he said. "They must have gone off in a terrific hurry."

"Perhaps there were a lot of Eskimos about, and they didn't want to show them the cache and have them poking into it after they had gone," said Dorothea.

She looked at the paper. Nothing new had been written on it. It was just as they had left it. "Reached this point of northern latitude, 28th January. S., A., and D. North Polar Expedition."

"What shall we write?" she asked.

"Passed Cache Island going north, 10th February," said Dick.

"No message?" said Dorothea regretfully, "in case we never come back."

Dick stared at her. Odd things did come into Dot's head.

"Why," he said, "it's just to show other explorers."

Dorothea pencilled down the short, simple statement of fact, and they each signed it with a D. Dick rolled up the paper, pushed it into the ginger-beer bottle, corked the bottle, and hid it once more in its place among the stones.

"We'll make them look at it on the way home," said Dorothea.

"Let's get going again," said Dick. "We've lost another minute or two."

They scrambled back to the ice, harnessed themselves to the sledge, and were off again – left, right, left, right – as before.

Once clear of the islands, the whole of the frozen Arctic lay before them. There were fewer skaters here, but still too many to let them feel the proper Arctic loneliness. Perhaps, after all, thought Dorothea, Titty was right to count them seals. But where were Titty and the others? The great hills towered above the head of the lake, their rolling sides gleaming bright with blue shadows in the ravines where the sunlight could not reach the snow. Dick and Dorothea stared into the distance, searching this way and that from side to side of the lake and far ahead of them under the hills. They were looking for a sledge with five dogs, or perhaps a sailing sledge with a mast and a yellow flag like their own at the masthead, or perhaps even two sledges together. But, no matter how hard they searched, on all that great sheet of ice no sign of the main body of the expedition was to be seen.

On the Beckfoot promontory away on the farther side of the lake Nancy's red signal was still flapping.

"If only we hadn't been late this morning," said Dick, "and I'd seen it in proper time. They're probably at the head of the lake by now."

"They're bound to get there first, anyhow," said Dorothea, "with Peggy knowing just where it is. I do wonder whether Nancy's coming too. She and Captain Flint may be at the Pole already. But it doesn't really matter, so long as we get there before they start back."

"There's more wind now," said Dick. "What about sailing?"

But Dorothea was not very willing to stop. So long as they kept on skating, no time was being lost, but if they stopped to put up the sail, they might only have to take it down again. She would

have liked Dick to come sailing after the others if the others were
to be there to see. Now, with the others so far ahead, the main
thing was to get on as quickly as possible. But there could be no
doubt about it, there was a little more wind than there had been
for the last few days.

"I'm sure there's enough wind," said Dick, after they had skated
steadily on for some time, and had left Beckfoot far behind them,
and were already on the part of the ice that they had seen only
from High Greenland. "Just look behind us, Dot. There's more
wind coming. I'm sure John would say wind was coming. Just
look at that cloud."

Dorothea looked over her shoulder.

Anybody could see that something was going to happen. A
thick grey cloud hung over the tops of the hills, and from side to
side between them at the southern end of the lake. It was
like looking at a different world, to glance back from the sunlit,
shining slopes of the snow mountains, to that soft grey curtain that seemed to hang across the lake. There were the islands,
and bits of the hills on either side, but beyond that nothing
but grey.

"I believe it's snow," said Dorothea.

"Wind, too," said Dick. "You can feel it. Do let's get the sail
up at once. What's the good of having made the mast and everything? And we'll get along twice as fast. Think of the way their
sledge sailed when there was any wind."

"Well, if there isn't enough wind," said Dorothea, "we mustn't
mind just taking it down again at once, and going on
as dogs."

"All right," said Dick. "Separate and brake."

They stopped skating, and let the sledge slip through between
them. It came to a stop.

"Now then," said Dick, hurriedly unfastening the bundle of
mast and sail. "Lucky we've come so fast and got warm

hands. It'd be awful if they were cold." He slipped off his big fur mittens.

He tried to step the mast, but soon found that he could do nothing with it while he had skates on. At home as he was on the ice, every other second his feet would start off skating when he wanted them to keep still. He sat down on the sledge, and had his skates off in a moment.

"You'll have to put them on again," said Dorothea.

"Not if it really sails," said Dick, "and it ought to."

The wind was coming stronger. With Dorothea kneeling on the sledge to help him, he got the mast up on end and pegged into the place Mr Dixon and Silas had made for its foot. He fastened the shrouds on either side, and then wrestled with the sail, that flapped wildly round him while he tried his best to get it hoisted up the mast.

"You can't say there isn't any wind now," he gasped. "I say, Dot, just sit down now on the top of everything and hang on to that rope."

Dorothea sat down by the mast and hung on to the rope she was given to hold. There was a lucky lull in the wind, and before it was over Dick had the sail hoisted up to the big curtain ring he had fixed at the masthead.

It was easy enough now. The yard, that had been trying to bang him on the head, was still at last, and the sail that had been trying to wind itself round him, hung quiet as could be.

"I say," said Dorothea, "everybody's going off the ice."

But Dick had no eyes for the skaters hurrying towards the shore. What was it to him that with every moment the lake was losing its crowds? He was thinking of nothing but his sail. Now was the chance. He fastened the ropes from the ends of the yard as he had seen them shown in the Nansen pictures. He fastened the ropes from the bottom corners of the sail. Everything was ready. But there was now no wind at all.

He looked back. Had he done it all for nothing?

That grey curtain of cloud was much nearer. The islands off Rio were no longer clear in sunlight, but dim, as if behind a veil.

"It's snow," said Dorothea.

"Here's the wind," cried Dick. "Now!"

He headed the sledge straight up the lake. The wind suddenly filled his sail and blew it out like a balloon. Nothing happened. He gave the sledge a push. The sail flapped again and hung idle. A moment later it filled with a sharp clapping noise. He was just pushing his skates in under the sheepskins, and felt the sledge stir.

"It's moving! It's moving!"

The sledge was pulling away from him. Harder. Harder. The wind freshened with a quick, startling sigh. Dick's feet slid from under him. A mitten rolled off the sledge and was left behind.

"Don't let go! Don't let go!" cried Dorothea.

There was a desperate scramble. Dorothea had him by the shoulder. He pulled himself, chin first, flat on his stomach, over the sheepskins. That mitten was gone. It could not be helped. He made sure of the other. The blue-grey ice was slipping past them faster and faster.

"Hang on, Dot," he said. "We're sailing."

And at that moment the first snowflakes reached them.

Grey, ghostly, tiny figures of skaters making for the shore disappeared. The hills on either side of the lake vanished. The Beckfoot promontory was gone. Far up the lake a patch of sunshine showed on the tops of the snow mountains. A second later even the mountains had disappeared. Dick and Dorothea on their sledge, with the sail bellying out in front of them, and the little yellow quarantine flag flying straight before the masthead, were alone in a thick cloud of driving, hurrying snow. They could see nothing at all but snowflakes and a few yards of ice sliding away

"IT'S MOVING!"

beneath them as the big wind that had come with the snow drove them up the lake like a dead leaf.

"Where are we now?" said Dorothea.

"I knew she would sail if we had a wind," said Dick.

"But where are we?" said Dorothea.

"Hang on," said Dick. "Lie as flat as you can. I don't believe John's sledge ever went faster. Just listen to it."

And the little sledge, roaring as it rushed over the ice, flew northwards in the storm.

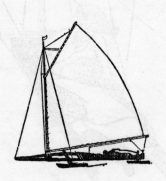

CHAPTER XXV

COUNCIL IN THE *FRAM*

"Bother those D.'s," said Peggy, and then, remembering what
Captain Nancy might have said, she added, "They ought to be
keel-hauled and hung from the yard-arm. Being late for a
council."

"But they don't know it's a council," said Titty.

"Sure you put the right signal up?" said Captain Flint.

"Oh, yes," said John.

"They were busy with something for the expedition," Susan
reminded the others. "Perhaps they didn't get it finished yesterday."

"Somebody'll have to go and stir them up," said Peggy.

"Give them another half-hour," said Captain Flint. "Nancy
won't be here till about one o'clock. She won't be let out of
Beckfoot till after twelve. I gather there's some tremendous
disinfection to be done, and she'll come along smelling like a
chemist's shop."

Roger went out to keep watch for them on deck, but found it
cold, and came back into the cabin, to have another look at the
cabin table and the piles of oranges and chocolates and a huge cake
covered with white icing, a perfect snowfield, on which eight
small Eskimos, with three sledges, were gathered round a tall
candle that served for a North Pole. Captain Flint had planned a
regular banquet to celebrate Nancy's return. Peggy and Titty
were peeling potatoes. Susan had had trouble with a Primus stove,
and Captain Flint was showing her how to unscrew the pump and
put a new washer on the plunger. John was looking into Peary's

North Pole in hope of finding something useful for tomorrow's journey.

The half-hour passed, and another half-hour, and another after that. At first it had not seemed to matter much that the D.'s were a bit late, because, after all, the council would not begin till Nancy arrived. But, as the hands on the cabin clock moved slowly round, the thing became rather more serious.

"Look here, John," said Captain Flint, at last, when he saw the cooks getting ready to put the huge plum-pudding into the biggest of the saucepans. "Look here, John, what about slipping along to Dixon's and routing those two out? Nancy won't be starting just yet, but we don't want to have her here before them. I thought we might go to meet her. Anyhow, she ought to find the lot of us together, ready to give her a cheer."

"I'll have them here in two shakes," said John, grabbed his skates, and was gone.

*

Ten minutes went by, a quarter of an hour, and then Titty, who, after finishing her share of the potatoes, was taking a last look into Nansen's *Farthest North*, found that she could hardly read.

"It's awfully dark," she said.

"Here they are," said Roger, at the same moment, flinging open the cabin door as he heard skates being dumped on deck, and a step on the ladder.

But it was John alone.

"They aren't at the farm," he said, without coming into the cabin. "I say, just look at the sky."

"What is it?" said Peggy.

"Just have a look," said John.

Everybody crowded out of the door. There was something in John's voice that made even Susan leave her cooking for a moment.

"Snow," said Captain Flint, after one look out of the cabin door at the grey cloud that was sweeping over the little bay and darkening the whole sky.

"Look at everybody bolting," said Roger.

The skaters at the end of Long Island, who could be seen from Houseboat Bay, were hurrying away towards Rio. Already the ice was almost clear of them.

"Here it comes," said Captain Flint. "Half a jiffy while I put a cowl on the stovepipe. We don't want the fire put out." He dived down again, went through the cabin, and came up by the fore-hatch with a black metal cowl to keep the snow from coming down into the stove. He fixed it on the pipe, and came aft along the gangway outside.

"It must be coming down pretty hard at the foot of the lake already," he said. "What did you say about those two?"

"They aren't at the farm," said John.

"Well, wherever they are now, I hope they'll stay put," said Captain Flint.

"Hullo, there's a snowflake," cried Roger.

"Lots of them," said Titty.

Captain Flint dodged into the cabin and looked at the clock.

"Well, there's one thing about it," he said. "It's come before Nancy'll have started. It's not twelve o'clock yet, and she's got sense enough not to start with it looking like this. Her mother wouldn't let her, anyway."

The first few flakes seemed harmless enough, but almost before Roger had had time to catch one in his hand, the air was white with them, not just floating down like feathers, but driving sideways in a hard wind. The snow drove along the decks and lodged in every crevice and piled itself against the cabin walls. It drove into Titty's hair and inside Roger's jacket. Peggy shook her head as she felt it melting and trickling down her neck. John had to screw his eyes up tight as he peered into the wind. Nobody could stand without stooping to meet the harder gusts.

"It doesn't look like stopping," said Captain Flint. "We shan't see Nancy today."

"No council!" said Titty.

"No banquet!" said Roger.

"We'll have the banquet all right," said Captain Flint, "and we'll have another for Nancy."

"She'll be most awfully mad if she can't come today," said Peggy.

"Well, just look at it," said Captain Flint.

"Don't bring a lot of snow into the cabin," said Susan. "Come on in, Roger. Shake off as much as you can first."

In those few moments breastplates of driven snow had formed on the fronts of jackets and sweaters. Roger tried to get his off all in one piece.

"You can't see the island," he said.

"You can't even see the shores of the bay," said Titty.

"It's worse than a fog," said Peggy.

"Be quick," said Susan. "Let's get the door shut."

It was midday, but she was lighting the cabin lamp, and was bothered by the wild wind even in the cabin.

"I do hope those two have the sense to keep under cover till this is over," said Captain Flint, stamping his feet, and sweeping the snow off his bald head, as he came in after taking a last look round. "This may last for some time. Nancy'll be all right at Beckfoot. But I'm bothered about those two."

"They're very good at thinking of things," said Titty.

"Well, I hope they think of staying indoors," said Captain Flint. "This is a blizzard, or something very like one, and if it goes on long we'll be having the roads choked and there'll be no moving about to be done without a snow plough. Who was at the farm, John?"

"Mrs Dixon had just come back from Rio, and she said they were getting ready to start just after breakfast. At least, Dorothea was, and Dick had run up to the old barn ... "

Captain Flint slapped his knee.

"Can they see Beckfoot from up there?" he asked. "Could they see Nancy's joy flag?"

"Easily," said John. "Dick always uses a telescope."

"That's what's happened," said Captain Flint. "They've spotted poor old Nancy's signal, and gone straight across there to see what she wanted."

"It's just what they would do," said Titty.

"Your mother wouldn't be too pleased," said Captain Flint to Peggy, "but, after all, she could let them run about the garden or something till the disinfecting was over."

"Nancy'd be bursting to talk to them," said Peggy.

"That's what's happened," said Captain Flint. "They're all right, sitting at Beckfoot with Nancy, trying to get a word in once every ten minutes. We shan't see any of them till this is over, so we'd better be getting on with this banquet. We can't starve, even for their sakes."

"Well, it splits the council in half," said Peggy. "With all of us here, and Nancy talking to the D.'s. She'll tell them everything, so you may as well spit it out, too."

"Let's get at the food," said Captain Flint. He was a good deal happier at the thought that those two unpractical D.'s were not getting into trouble somewhere, but were sitting at Beckfoot having dinner and talking to Nancy.

The snow-covered cake with the eight explorers round the sugar Pole was a melancholy reminder that not all plans work out as they are intended, but Peggy and the four Swallows settled down with Captain Flint to see that the banquet was not wasted altogether. Outside, the blizzard might rage and the whole world be muffled and blinded by flying snow, but in there, in the cabin of the *Fram*, with the stove burning strongly, and cold turkey, and Christmas plum-pudding (that Captain Flint set on fire in the fo'c'sle and brought in triumphantly flaming on its plate), and mugs of hot tea, and oranges, and the fine smell of burnt chestnuts mixing with the smell of the pudding, everybody was snug and comfortable. It was sad that so many of the explorers were not there, but a good thing in a way, because, with those two to keep her company, Nancy would not mind so much having her first afternoon of freedom spoilt by the snowstorm. Anyway, nothing could be done about it. Tomorrow the sledges would be on their way over the trackless ice. Tomorrow, as explorers, they would march steadily towards the Pole. Tomorrow, as dogs, they would strain gallantly at the ropes. Today, in the *Fram*, warm and secure in the midst of the blizzard, they sat and feasted and made plans, or rather heard what Nancy and Captain Flint had planned together. There were no serious disagreements. There would be three sledges: the big Beckfoot sledge in charge of Peggy and the Swallows, the Dixon's farm sledge in charge of the D.'s, and Captain Flint's small sledge with Nancy in command and Captain Flint to help her.

"Nancy's got much the strongest dog," said Roger, between two sucks at an orange, after the bulk of the banquet was done.

"Thank you," said Captain Flint.

"It's only fair," said John. "Think of all the practice we've had."

"And when we get to the Pole?" said Roger.

"See when you get there," said Captain Flint, "if you do get there ... if any of us get there ... We can't go if it's like this," he added, looking out of the cabin windows at the white snow driving by.

All afternoon the blizzard raged outside. It was not until it was already growing dark, and Susan had long been looking anxiously at the clock, that the snow stopped falling and the wind dropped; and Captain Flint, after taking a look round from the deck, said they had better take their chance and get back to Holly Howe.

"The wind's swept the ice for you," he said, "but there'll be deep drifts on shore. I'll come with you, just to see you can get up the field. And then I'm off to Beckfoot to comfort poor old Nancy and bring the D.'s home."

The ice was dark in the twilight, blown clear of snow by the tremendous wind. But the little trees on the northern point of Houseboat Bay looked as if they were wading in snow. There was another big drift against the rocks of Darien, but luckily, the path going up the field from the Holly Howe boathouse was sheltered and clear. Just at the top of the field they had a bit of a scramble through the snow to get to the garden gate, and then there was the great fire in the parlour and the lamp already lit for them, and a kettle boiling, and Mrs Jackson saying what a storm it had been, and what a lucky thing it was they had not been out in the worst of it.

"Those two children from Dixon's Farm haven't looked in, have they?" asked Captain Flint.

"Not since this morning, Mr Turner," said Mrs Jackson. "I've seen never a sign of them since the lad put his nose in and was off again when I told him what a hurry there was here with Miss Nancy signalling to them and all."

"Did you see which way he went?" asked Captain Flint.

"I didn't," said Mrs Jackson. "He just put his head in at my kitchen door and was gone."

"They'll be still at Beckfoot," said Captain Flint. "I'll be off there at once." Nothing would make him stop even for a cup of Mrs Jackson's tea, and without waiting a moment he was away out of the farm-house and hurrying down the field to the lake.

Mrs Jackson had the usual huge tea ready for them, a tea that was a supper as well. Everybody was hungry, in spite of the banquet in the *Fram*, but Roger, Titty, and Peggy did most of the talking. John and Susan had seen that Captain Flint had gone off almost as if he had begun to worry about the D.'s again. What if Dick and Dorothea had not gone to Beckfoot after all?

And then John took the lantern and slipped off into the dark. He told only Susan where he was going.

"You never know with those two," he said. "They may have been in the igloo all the time, and got themselves snowed up or something."

"But you won't be able to get there," said Susan.

"Yes, I will," said John, "keeping to the walls. And I'm taking a long stick to prod into the drifts."

"Why not get Mr Jackson to come too?"

"He's out, already, after his sheep."

"Let me come."

"If you don't stay to keep them quiet, we'll be having Roger and Titty coming after us. Remember that night at the *Fram*."

Susan hesitated. That night was not a comfortable memory. John was gone. She watched the lantern going fast up the field, not along the track, but close along the wall. She watched it swing and lift and vanish as John climbed over into the road. It showed again as he crossed the wall on the other side of the road. It vanished, and then glimmered again, going slowly, slowly up the hillside towards the wood.

Susan sighed. John, she supposed, perhaps knew best. But she did wish those two D.'s had had the sense to obey orders, and to come to the *Fram*. What was the good of signalling if people did not do what they were told? She went back into the farm, and helped Roger and Titty, who were busy greasing their skates and getting their Arctic outfits ready for the morning, while Peggy was making a list of the things that must not be left behind.

It was just about time for the younger explorers to go to bed when there was stamping in the porch, and they heard Captain Flint's voice in the passage.

"Mrs Jackson," he was saying, "can you lend me a lantern?

I've got to get along to the Dixons', and I don't want to go head first into a snowdrift."

"Where are the D.'s?" shouted Peggy and Roger, running out to talk to him.

"He hasn't found them," said Titty.

"They haven't been at Beckfoot," said Captain Flint.

"What about Nancy?" said Peggy.

"She's all right," said Captain Flint. "Making up for being kept at home by burning, destroying, and disinfecting all day. You'd think a gang of pirates had sacked the place, to look at it."

"It's a funny thing," said Mrs Jackson, coming in again. "But I can't find that lantern."

"Oh," said Susan. "John's got it." She stopped, and then, thinking that no harm could be done now, she went on, "He's gone up to the igloo, to see if the D.'s are up there."

"Good lad," said Captain Flint.

"And he never took us," said Roger.

"Traitor!" said Peggy.

"There's another lantern in the byre," said Mrs Jackson. "I'll just give it a wipe over."

"Never mind about that," said Captain Flint. "I expect those two are back at the Dixons', but I want to make sure."

"He's in an awful hurry," said Titty, as they heard the gate clang behind him.

"I do wish John was back," said Susan.

Captain Flint had hardly had time to get well on his way along the road to Dixon's Farm before John came stumbling in, out of breath and covered with snow where he had fallen in the drifts.

"Quick, Susan!" he said. "Quick! There's no time to lose. We've got to start at once. I must put some fresh oil in the lantern."

"What's happened?"

"I got to the igloo all right. Nobody there. And then I thought of their barn. It was a job getting there. There was nobody in the

barn, but I could just see their signal. I hauled it down to make sure.
It must have been up there all day."

"What? What did it say?"

"North Pole," said John. "They've gone there."

"It was *Fram*, this morning," said Titty. "I wonder when they
changed it."

"What's ado?" said Mrs Jackson.

"Dorothea and Dick were out in the blizzard. They've gone
to ... Peggy knows where they've gone. Come on, Peggy. We
must go after them at once. Please, tell Captain Flint, Mr Turner,
I mean. Tell him they started out for the north by themselves,
and we've gone to the rescue. We must have some more oil in
the lantern. It went out as I was coming down the field. Come on,
Peggy. You know the place."

Peggy was already flinging a muffler round her throat and
cramming on her rabbit-skin hat.

"If they got caught in the blizzard," said Susan, "almost
anything may have happened." In spite of herself she glanced at
Titty and Roger, and was thankful that these two, at least, were
safely at home.

Not a second was wasted. John was getting the lantern filled
and explaining to Mrs Jackson. Peggy was loading sheepskins on
the sledge. Who could tell how cold those D.'s might be? Susan
was filling three thermos flasks with hot tea. "They may be
starving," she said, "and it isn't as if Dorothea ever really knew
what to do."

If it had been Mrs Dixon they would probably never have been
allowed to set out. But Mrs Jackson's mind moved more slowly.
"Don't you go too far," she said and, "You won't be long."

"If Uncle Jim comes back here, tell him North Pole," said
Peggy. "He'll understand."

"But what are you going to do?" asked Roger.

"Relief expedition," said John. "We've got to fetch them back.

Hurry up, Susan. We must get down on the ice. The roads are
awful with snow."

They were gone.

"It isn't fair," said Roger.

"Our things are all ready," said Titty.

Mrs Jackson was tidying away the supper things between
parlour and scullery.

"Well," she said presently, "and what about bed for you two?"

There was no answer.

"Funny I never saw them go," she said. "But with Miss Susan
they'll come to no harm."

Captain John and Mates Peggy and Susan took the sledge down
to the lake, slid it out on the ice, put on their skates by the light
of the lantern, and set out.

They had left Holly Howe Bay and were working along near
the shore, past the boatbuilding sheds, when they heard a faint
shout behind them, "Stop! Stop!"

They looked back and saw a spark of light swinging to and fro.

"Bother it!" said Susan. "Roger's torch. I ought to have made
them promise to go to bed and stay there."

There was nothing for it but waiting.

"Do hang on a minute while I get my skate straight," said
Roger, as they came up. "I did it on too quick and Titty didn't
hold the torch still enough."

"What are you doing out here at all?" said Susan. "Go home
at once."

"It isn't fair," said Roger

"Anything may have happened," said Titty. "You said so. You
may want all of us to help."

"Don't let's waste time," said John.

"You may want all the dogs you can get," said Roger.

Susan looked back into the darkness. If she were to send them
back now she would have to go with them, to make sure they

got home. While they were all together there was nothing to worry about. It was bad enough to have the two D.'s lost. But if Titty and Roger were out by themselves as well ... "I don't know what mother would say," she said at last.

"But the D.'s are lost," said Titty. "They've got to be found. You know daddy always says that when it's a case of life and death no rules count."

"Come along," said John. "Peggy's turn with the lantern. The other four of us tow the sledge."

Titty and Roger flung off their knapsacks and strapped them on the sledge, putting a strap from one knapsack under the rope that held the sheepskins down and buckling it to a strap from the other.

They groped for their harness and were ready.

"Don't go too far out, Peggy," said John. "The blizzard may have caught them anywhere, and they're sure to have tried to get into shelter. We'd better keep pretty close along the shore for fear of missing them."

In Rio Bay there were no bonfires, no fireworks, and fewer lights than usual. The blizzard had driven the skaters off the ice and they had given it up for the night. Big drifts had blocked the roads. Here and there along the shore by the steamer pier, cars were being dug out of the snow. On land the snow had lain and drifted deep. Out on the lake it was as if a thousand men with brooms had been at work. On that smooth surface, in that gale of wind, the snow had had no chance of resting. The wind had blown the snow before it and the ice was clear enough for skating. But it was deserted. No one saw the Polar Relief Expedition leave the bay and plunge into the northern night.

*

At Beckfoot it had been very hard on Nancy when, at midday, just as she was making ready to start for the *Fram*, to meet once more the members of the expedition for whom her martyrdom

had won a month of holiday, blowing snow had made it impossible to see more than a yard or two, and Mrs Blackett had
said that she was not to think of going until it cleared. But it had
grown worse and worse, and she had almost forgotten her own
disappointment in her fears that the snow-drifts at the head of the
lake would be so deep that they would have to put off once more
the journey to the Pole that had been planned for tomorrow. She
had got some comfort by throwing herself violently into the
business of disinfecting. It had been already evening before the
wind dropped and the storm was over and then, too late to go to
the council, she had put on the fur hat and mittens that today, at
last, were hers to handle, and had gone out in the garden. She was
wading in the snow there when, as she had hoped he might, her
ally, Captain Flint, came skating into the river.

"Hullo!" she shouted to the dim figure, taking off skates on the
bank. "What did you do about the council? You told them we're
going to do it tomorrow? We will, won't we?"

"Hullo! What have you done with those D.'s?"

"I've never seen them," said Nancy.

"Well, where in the world are they?" said Captain Flint.
"Where's your mother?"

Nancy hurried after him to the house. He ran upstairs, calling
for her mother. She heard quick, bothered words. "Yes. Serious
if they were out in that storm. Is Sammy there? Slip along and tell
him. I must go straight back and see if they've turned up at the
Dixons'."

He came running down again.

"Are the D.'s lost?" she asked.

"For the moment," said Captain Flint, and was gone. Nancy
hurried after him, but he had got his skates on and was off over
the ice by the time she got to the boathouse.

Lost? The D.'s lost? She thought of the way that tremendous
snowstorm had gone on and on sweeping up the lake, while she

and her mother had been busy lighting sulphur candles and pasting paper round the windows and the door of the bedroom that had been a hospital ward. She had imagined them all sitting in the snug cabin of the *Fram* while that wind and snow raged over them. And the D.'s had not been there. Where had they been? At the igloo? Or at the barn and then not able to get home? Slowly, feeling her way, Nancy walked along the shore from the boathouse and out towards the point. It was dark now but for the snow-light from the hills. Cold, too. She had been terribly afraid a thaw would come with the snow. Bother those D.'s being lost, and Captain Flint going off like that without telling her what had happened at the council. Anyhow, everything was ready, if only tomorrow would be a fine day. She stood, looking out into the darkness away to the north. Somewhere, far away up there was the Pole, just as she had planned. Better even than she had hoped to make it, thanks to Captain Flint's return. If only the drifts up there were not too deep. She saw a row of lights twinkling low under the hills, the lights of the village beyond the head of the lake, half a mile or a mile on the other side of the Pole. And then, suddenly, Nancy gasped. What was that? A light lower down, nearer than those distant lights of the village. A light on the shore, at the head of the lake? But there was no house there. The steamer pier was away to the right, and the boat landings. There was nothing there, except ... Nancy gasped again ... Was some native messing round and spoiling all that Captain Flint had made ready? And then the light went out ... flashed ... went out again ... flashed and again went out ... What was happening? Signalling? Nancy watched the flashes. Long. Short. A pause. Short. Long. Long. Short. A pause. And then flashes again, longs and shorts in the same order as before. "Shiver my timbers!" cried Nancy. "Jib-booms and bob-stays! Barbecued billygoats! N.P. ... N.P. ... It's them. Of course it's them. Morse, too. It can't be anybody else. They're at the North Pole. And in all that storm." She ran, helter-skelter, knee-deep, stumbling in the snow, back to the house.

"Hi! Mother! Where's mother?"

"She's gone along to Mrs Lewthwaite's, has your mother," said the old cook.

Mrs Lewthwaite was the mother of Sammy the policeman.

Nancy wasted no time. Her knapsack, too, was ready for next day. She charged into the larder. A cake seemed the handiest thing in the way of food. She pushed it into her knapsack. She grabbed her skates. She scrawled on a bit of paper, "They're at the North Pole. So am I. Tell Uncle Jim. Nancy," and left it for her mother.

"But, Miss Nancy," said cook.

"I've only grabbed a cake," said Nancy, and the door swung to behind her.

"What a donk I was not to bring a torch," she said, as she fastened the straps of her skates by feel. Slowly, carefully, she skated out. The light was still there. But it had stopped flashing. As she watched, it flashed again. "So long as they keep it lit I can't go wrong," said Nancy to herself. "Oh blow it, I do wish the others knew."

And then with steady, even strokes she set out over the silent Arctic, her eyes fixed on the darkness under those dim hills and, in that darkness, on the light, the faint, flickering light, that could be nothing but the Pole itself.

CHAPTER XXVI

THE NORTH POLE

THE little sledge, with Dick and Dorothea clinging to it, as flat as they could lie on the top of their sheepskins and knapsacks, flew on in the snowstorm. The larch-pole mast bent and creaked. The sail, full like a balloon, swayed from side to side and the sledge swayed with it. The ropes thrummed. The iron runners roared over the ice.

"We're going too fast," said Dorothea.

Dick saw her lips move. "What?" he shouted.

"Too fast," she shouted back. "A thousand miles an hour."

"Probably thirty." Thirty was a good wind speed. He knew that, and the sledge would not be going faster than the wind.

He lifted his head and tried to look back into the blizzard. In a moment his glasses were crusted over with driven snow. He tried to wipe them, but the sledge leapt suddenly as a runner struck some small thing, perhaps a bit of loose ice, or a stone, or perhaps just a crack. The sledge leapt and Dick, holding with only one hand, rolled sideways.

"Don't let go!" Dorothea almost screamed.

"All right!" shouted Dick, hanging on firmly with both hands again. His glasses would just have to wait. He could see nothing. But how the little sledge was moving.

Dorothea was not blinded like Dick, but she could see very little more than he could. There was the sail, bellying forward and straining almost as if it would burst or lift the sledge into the air. There was the ice shooting by on either side. Snow was lodged in every fold of coat or sheepskin, and was driven, cold and wet, into her mouth whenever she tried to say anything. But on the ice the snow did not rest but blew along and the little sledge blew with it.

"Where are we going?" she shouted, and Dick lifted his head with its two white eyes, huge as his spectacles, though he could not see her through them.

"Straight up the lake ... Just right."

"How can you tell?"

"Hills on each side," shouted Dick. "The wind can't help blowing straight up. Like blowing through a tube. Peashooter. We're the pea."

Dick clung on, blind but happy. Nobody could say this was not sailing. His mast and the sail they had made with the help of Mrs Dixon had really worked. With every minute the wind lasted they were making up for the time lost through starting late.

"Where are we now?" shouted Dorothea.

"Arctic!" shouted Dick.

And suddenly Dorothea knew that she was afraid. Where were they? She could see nothing before, behind, or on either side of the sledge but driving snow. "Arctic!" was all very well. They might be anywhere. Or nowhere. It was as if they had slipped right out of the world into one in which there was nothing but themselves. And they were going on and on, roaring over the ice in this blinding, racing snow. The sledge was white. Dick lay there clinging to it, white all over. He might be looking at her, but instead of his eyes there were only those round white splashes of snow. His hand, the one that had lost its rabbit-skin mitten, was looking wet and blue about the knuckles. She tried, without moving more than she could help, to shelter it for him with a fold of sheepskin. She, too, began to feel cold. It had been hot enough skating along with the sledge, but now, lying on it, being blown along, she felt that the cold was finding its way through everything that was meant to keep it out. Her mind began to run on ahead, but much less pleasantly than usual ...

Dorothea suddenly shook Dick's shoulder.

"Let's stop!' she cried. "Now! At once!"

Dick scraped at one of his glasses with his bare hand. An eye looked dimly out through the place from which he had smudged the snow away.

"We can't go back," he said. "We can't help coming somewhere if we go on."

Dorothea shook his shoulder almost angrily. How could she know that Dick was trying to calculate how fast they were moving, and wondering how much he ought to allow for friction on the ice, supposing that the speed of the wind was thirty miles an hour. Besides, he was full of delight at having made his sledge go like John's. The very last thing he wanted to do was to stop it. Cold? Yes, it was cold, and he did not know where they were, but they were moving in the right direction. Why couldn't Dorothea lie still? There was nothing to worry about. At least, not yet ... He tried to get some more of the snow off his spectacles.

And then, suddenly, the sledge tilted sharply upwards, flew into the air, touched something hard, leaped ... Prickly snow filled his mouth. His hat was gone. The sledge was gone. There was snow in his sleeves. Right up to his elbows. He was down, down, floundering in snow like a dog struggling in water. Something hurt his ear. His spectacles had been torn off his face but still hung from one ear. It was the other that was hurting. He put up his hand to feel it. It was bleeding a little. Scratched by the spectacles probably. Lucky they had not gone altogether ...

What had happened? Where was the sledge? Where was Dorothea?

"Dot!" he shouted into the driving snow.

"Dick! Dick!"

The answer came from only a few yards away, but he could see nothing but snow, snow driving sideways in the wind, and snow lifted like spray from the crest of a wave and blown onwards and upwards.

"Dot!"

He floundered towards her.

She was standing in the deep snow with her back to the wind.

"Are you all right?" she cried, and almost fell towards him in the snow. "Are you all right?"

She was laughing now, in a shaky kind of way and held firmly to Dick's arm, as if she were afraid it was going to get away from her. Dick peered at her through his spectacles on which the snow was already settling again.

"Dot!" he said in astonishment. "You aren't crying?"

"It's mostly snow," said Dorothea. "But I didn't know what had happened to you when the sledge turned over and the mast broke ... "

"The mast broke?" said Dick. "How do you know?"

"It's here," said Dorothea — "at least it was."

The mast was all but hidden, but there was the sail, already heavy with drift snow, and the little yellow quarantine flag still on its stick, fastened to the masthead.

"The sledge is here, too," said Dick. "Come on, Dot, before we lose it altogether."

The sledge, upside down, was covered with snow, but though several of the ropes had broken when the mast broke, one of the shrouds still held, so that the sledge and the upper part of the mast were anchored to each other. With a good deal of tugging and pushing, while the snow blew down their necks and up their sleeves and blinded Dick again and again by covering his spectacles, they dragged the sledge clear and turned it the right way up. They had lost much less than might have been expected, because of the sheepskins that had been on the top of their baggage. Dick's skates, pushed in underneath, were still there, and the lantern, fortunately, came up out of the snow still tied to the strap of a knapsack.

One of the knapsacks was gone, the one with the food. It must have been quite close to them, but they could not find it, though in feeling for it Dick found his rabbit-skin hat. He shook the snow out of the hat, crammed it down on his head, and turned to go on with the work of squashing the sail into manageable size, and lashing it down with the broken mast on the top of as much of the baggage as was still on the sledge. If that knapsack was lost it was lost. There was no time to waste.

"What are we going to do?" said Dorothea.

"We must be right at the head of the lake," said Dick doubtfully. "The others must be close to us if only we could see. Peggy said the North Pole wasn't very far from the shore."

"I wish Peggy was here," said Dot.

"She wouldn't know any better than us which way to go in this," said Dick.

"We must go somewhere," said Dorothea. "It's getting worse every minute."

Suddenly, in all that flurry of driving snow, while Dorothea was growing colder and colder and hopelessly wishing the snow would stop, if only for a few seconds, long enough to let them see where they were, she felt that something had changed in Dick. He had made up his mind what to do, and was burrowing under the frozen sheepskins at the front end of the sledge.

"What do you want?"

"The Alpine rope," said Dick. He pulled out that great awkward coil of old clothes-line which had seemed so poor a substitute for the real climbing-rope belonging to the rest of the expedition.

"It isn't strong enough," said Dorothea. She was dreadfully disappointed. She had thought at first that he had a real idea, and it seemed he was only thinking of mending the rigging.

"It isn't very strong," said Dick, "but it'll do. Hadn't you

CAPSIZED AND DISMASTED

better get your skates off?" It was not of the rigging that he was thinking.

He unfastened the coil and laid it on the top of the sledge, tying one end of the clothes-line to the broken mast.

"So that we can explore without losing each other," he said. "Come on. You take the other side of the sledge."

"But where are we going?" asked Dorothea.

"North for a bit," said Dick, "the way the snow is driving. And then I'll feel out first on one side and then on the other, at the end of the rope, so that I'll be able to get back to the sledge each time. The others must be somewhere quite near."

"What about shouting?"

"We could try."

They shouted "Hullo!" both together, three or four times and as loud as they could. But it was like shouting in thick cotton-wool. They could not believe anyone could hear them through all that snow. There was no answer at all.

"Let's get it moving," said Dick.

The snow was settling thickly over their sledge. They lugged it forward, foot by foot, steering by the way the snowflakes were blowing.

"Anyhow, if we go far enough we'll come to a road, won't we?" said Dorothea.

Dick said nothing. The first dozen yards of floundering with the sledge through the drifted snow had been enough to show him that they would stand a poor chance if they had to count on reaching that road that ran round the head of the lake on the other side of the Polar region.

They struggled on another dozen yards, another twenty, by which time Dorothea felt that if they had to go far like this there would be nothing for it but abandoning the sledge. That would be failure of the most dreadful kind. Already they had lost their food. Already they had let the main expedition reach the

Pole before them. And now, to have reached the head of the lake, to have crossed the Polar ice, only to struggle to the nearest road without ever seeing the Pole itself, to crawl home without even their sledge ... it was worse than mere failure. And she had been so sure that Dick would somehow manage ... She had so clearly seen the others clapping him on the back, and heard Nancy's loud, cheerful voice telling him he was fit to be a pirate, or something like that ...

But, even if they abandoned the sledge, and, with nothing to carry, forced their way on, could they count on getting through to that road along which they had driven with the doctor when he brought them back from Beckfoot on the day that Nancy had begun her mumps?

Dorothea knew in her heart that they could not.

"You hang on here," said Dick. "I'm going to take the rope and explore as far as it'll let me. I can't get lost."

"Don't let go of it," said Dorothea, who felt that they were lost already.

"You give it a jerk and I'll jerk back," said Dick. "Like divers. But don't jerk too hard. It's not very strong for an Alpine rope."

He took the coil and, trying to shield his spectacles from the snow, floundered off to the right and in a moment was gone, swallowed up in driving snow.

In spite of knowing that he was only a few yards away, Dorothea jerked at the line.

Two jerks came back in answer; and a moment later there was Dick, frantically wiping at his spectacles, struggling back to her out of the storm.

"Oh, I didn't mean to bring you back," said Dorothea.

"I thought perhaps you'd seen something," said Dick.

He set off again, only, instead of going back the way he had come, he bore away to the left. It had felt hopeless and empty away there to the right and, though this was most unscientific, he felt he would like to try the other way first.

He had hardly disappeared in the snowstorm before Dorothea wanted desperately to feel that he was still there at the end of the rope. But she did not let herself give a jerk to it. Two minutes went by. Three. Perhaps more. The rope gave a jerk, seemingly by itself, flicking scraps of frozen snow into the air. Dick was moving slowly round at the end of it. Dorothea put her hand on the rope, just to feel that she was not alone. Suddenly she felt a tug, another, then three or four tugs together. She heard a shout.

Dick struggled back into sight. He had left the rope lying in the snow, to be a guide to them, and was floundering back to the sledge, feeling for the rope where the snow had covered it, but being careful not to pull it with him.

"There's a house," he panted. "I could just see it. Come on."

They set out once more, wading through the snow, dragging the sledge, picking up the rope as they went and using it as a guide.

"Are you sure you saw it?" said Dorothea, as they came to the end of the rope; and Dick stood there, with the end in his hand, looking about him but seeing nothing at all but flying snowflakes.

"I know I saw it," said Dick; and at that moment there was a lull in the wind, the snow fell less thickly and, not a dozen yards away, and a little above them, they both saw the dim grey shape of a small building. They struggled towards it. Each step was now more difficult than the last. The sledge-runners sank deep into the snow, and their own feet went down and down as if there was nothing firm for foot to stand on.

The grey shape of the building disappeared, just for a moment, in a sudden flurry of snow, and then stood out close above them. It was smaller than Dick had thought when first he saw that there was something before him other than the snow. It was queerly shaped and could hardly be described as a house. The end of it that was nearest to them seemed to be nearly all glass, like a bow window, a big bow window, with snow crusted on the panes. It was only one storey high. There was a little chimney at the back. Its roof was thick with snow, and above the roof a tall flagstaff stuck forlornly up into the storm.

A snowdrift was forming round the front of it. The last few yards would have been the worst if the building had not been there to give them fresh hope. Dorothea leant thankfully against the wall under the windows. Dick left her there and forced his way on. It could not be all windows. He found steps and a door. He hammered on it. There was no answer. He turned the handle, the door opened inwards, and he almost fell through it into a small room.

Just over a hundred years ago, the little place had been built as a shelter from which, in all weathers and at all seasons of the year, the old man who had built it could look out on the changing scenery of the lake and its enclosing hills. He could sit there watching the lake in storm and be himself most comfortable behind windows that could be thrown open in the heat of summer, and with a fireplace so that he need fear no cold in winter. For nearly a hundred years he had been dead, but the old view-house, as it was still called, had never been allowed to fall into ruin. This was the building into which Dick had stumbled. He, of course, knew nothing of its history. It was shelter, and that was all he wanted for the moment.

"Dot!" he shouted, and a moment later the two of them were under cover. They closed the door upon the storm, and stood there panting after their struggle.

"But Dick, Dick, look at that!" cried Dorothea.

"Half a minute," said Dick. He was busy wiping his spectacles, which were again covered with snow. He stood blinking, seeing almost nothing. Dorothea was pointing at an enormous box. Dick put on his spectacles and looked.

A queer place it was that they were in. First of all, though there were wooden benches with panelled backs along the walls and round under the windows and on either side of the little fireplace, there was a six-sided seat in the middle of the room, built round the base of the flagstaff they had seen sticking up above the roof, like those seats that are sometimes built round old trees in parks. Then there was a fire already laid, waiting only a match from the box lying handy. There was a small dirty sack that looked as if it must have coal in it. There was a kettle full of water, frozen solid, standing on the hearth. And then, between the flagstaff and the fireplace, there was an enormous box, a great packing-case, roughly roped as if for a journey. On the top of it was written in huge black letters,

"N.P.E."

Dick had no time to wonder what they meant, for he read on the side of the box nearest to the door:

"NORTH POLAR EXPEDITION
S.'s, A.'s, and D.'s"

and then on the end of it by the flagstaff:

";TO BE OPENED BY THE FIRST TO REACH THE POLE."

"The Pole must be somewhere quite close to," said Dorothea. "Captain Flint must have put it here on purpose. But why haven't they opened it?"

"He's left a hammer and a wedge all ready," said Dick.

"But where are the others?" said Dorothea.

"Perhaps we ought to go on," said Dick. "I could try round again with the rope."

"Let's get warm first," said Dorothea.

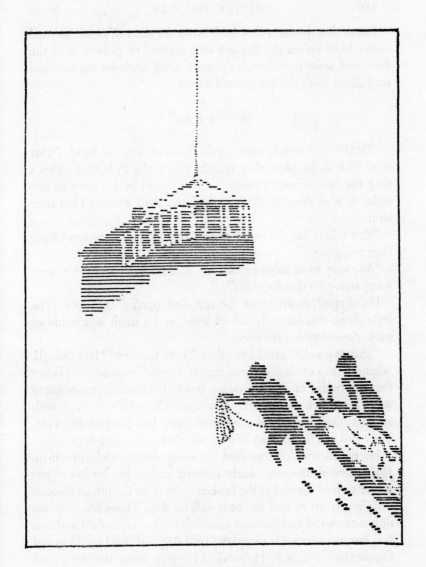

THROUGH THE SNOW

But at that moment they both noticed a sheet of paper fastened rather high up on the flagstaff that seemed to grow out of the floor and went up through the roof. Dick knelt on the seat and read aloud from the big printed letters.

"NORTH POLE."

"Dot!" he shouted, slapping the flagstaff with his hand. "This is it! This is the place they meant. This is the Pole itself. That's why the box is here. I knew the wind must be blowing us just right. We've done it. We've got there. And we aren't last after all ... "

"But where are the others?" said Dorothea. "They can't have been and gone."

"We may have sailed past them," said Dick. "I wonder if there is any string on that flagstaff?"

He slipped down from the seat and opened the door. The little room was instantly full of wind, and a small whirlwind of snow danced round the floor.

"Shut it quick!" cried Dorothea. "Don't go out!" But though, when it was a question of making up stories, Dorothea was better than anybody, in actually doing things Dick often remembered what Dorothea might have forgotten. Once he was busy with an idea, nothing would stop him. They had reached the Pole. They had reached it first. Where was that quarantine flag?

He fell down the steps into the snow, but picked himself up again. The sledge was nearly snowed under, but he knew just where to find the end of the broken mast, with the bits of shrouds dangling from it, and the little yellow flag. Those few minutes out of the wind had brought some life back even to the hand that had lost its mitten. He found the little flag and freed the loop and toggle from the stick. He worked his way along the side of the hut. Better even than he had hoped. There, close by one of the

AT THE POLE

windows, white halyards, new and stiff, came down from the top
of the flagstaff and were fastened loosely round a cleat. Captain
Flint had known that the discovery of the North Pole would be
nothing without the hoisting of a flag. With cold, clumsy fingers,
Dick dusted the snow from the scrap of yellow silk, fastened it to
the halyards, and was just hauling it up when Dorothea, who had
hated even those few minutes of being alone in the hut, came out
into the snow to look for him.

The little yellow flag fluttered as if it would blow to pieces
as it climbed up, up in the snowstorm to the very top of the flagstaff when, with knots that neither Captain Nancy nor Captain
John would have approved, Dick made the halyards fast.

Something trembled in Dorothea's throat as she looked up
and saw that scrap of pale yellow fluttering among the flying
snowflakes. How was it that Dick, who seemed so absent-minded,
could think of things like that?

"Dick, how lovely!" she cried.

"What?" shouted Dick.

"The flag!" she shouted, close to his ear.

Dick scraped almost hopelessly at the snow caked on his
spectacles.

"Of course we had to have it up," he said, and turned to
unload the sledge. "Come on, Dot. We've got here. We'll have
to wait for the others. Let's get the things in."

Between them they carried their gear into the hut, their
sheepskins (shaking off as much snow as they could on the way),
the knapsack that had the star-book in it, their skates, and the
clothes-line that had been so useful. Somewhere in the deep snow
at the edge of the ice they had lost the knapsack with the food.
Dick was without one of his rabbit-skin mittens. The mast was
smashed. There could be no sailing on the return journey even if
the wind were to change. But the main thing was that they had
found shelter and the Pole. Nothing else mattered.

They leaned their sledge upright against the wall, and for the last time floundered up the steps and into the hut. For a moment they had trouble with the door. Snow had blown between the door and the doorpost. In bringing in their gear they had stamped cakes of snow on the floor. More snow kept blowing in nearly as fast as they cleared it out. But they got the door closed in the end, and stood there, smiling at each other from simple pleasure at being out of the wind, at being able to stand upright without having to crouch to lessen the weight of the storm, at being able to look whichever way they wanted without fear of the blinding snow driving cold into their faces.

"I know what's happened," said Dorothea. "You know when all the Eskimos rushed to the shore to get out of the way of the snowstorm? Susan saw it coming, and she wouldn't want Titty and Roger to get caught in it. She probably saw it long before we did, and took shelter in the woods on shore. And we just blew past them when we were sailing and couldn't see anything. They'll be coming along the moment it stops, and we'd better get things ready."

Dick was considering the great, corded packing-case.

"To be opened by the first to reach the Pole," he read aloud. "I wish my fingers weren't so cold." He squeezed them together and blew on them. Rubbing them was much too painful. But something had to be done about those knots. He had known John and Titty long enough to know that it would never do for them to come along and find that a member of a Polar expedition had used a knife to cut good ropes.

"I'm going to light the fire," said Dorothea with decision. "They'll be even colder than we are, waiting about like that."

CHAPTER XXVII

TO THE RESCUE

EVEN though the lights in Rio Bay were fewer than usual, they had been enough to make the night seem black. But once out of the bay, with those lights left behind them, the rescue party soon grew used to the darkness, and found that they could see the dim white shapes of the mountains, the snow-dust on the ice, and the clumps of leafless trees that marked the islands.

John had said they would keep close along the shore, thinking that the blizzard would have driven the D.'s to look for shelter in the woods that here and there came down to the edge of the lake. But the sight of the islands, dim and dark in the faint snow-light, reminded him of something else.

"We'd better just make sure," he said. "Swing left, the dog-team."

"What for?" said Peggy, who was skating ahead with the lantern, keeping a look-out for the places where there was much snow on the ice, and leading the sledge party as well as she could where the wind had swept it clear.

"Cache Island," said John. "They may have left a message there."

"They won't have touched it," said Susan.

"They ought to have left a message there," said Titty, "if they were trying to do things properly."

"But they weren't doing things properly at all," said Peggy. "Going off like that without waiting for anybody else. I don't know what Nancy'll say about it."

"Nancy'd go and look at the cache anyway," said Titty. "Do let's."

"Come on!" said Peggy. The dogs and the sledge had hardly swung left for that dim ghostly little island before Peggy, guide and leader for the moment, was skating ahead of it, her swinging lantern showing the way. Yes, Titty was right. Captain Nancy would never think it waste of time to go and open up the cache when there might be a message in it,

By the time the sledge and its dogs reached the island Peggy was already on her knees in the snow, burrowing under the piled stones of the little cairn.

"Got it," she said. "Here you are, Skipper." It might have been different in daylight, especially as Peggy, unlike the others, knew the northern part of the lake. But at night, John, naturally, was in command. It was for him to see if any message had been left.

"They've been here," he said, the moment he looked at the bottle in the light of the lantern that Peggy held aloft. "Or somebody has. I'm sure I never shoved the cork in like that." The cork was nearly level with the top of the bottle. John got hold of the edge of it with his teeth. That was no good, and his lips nearly froze to the cold glass. The cork had to be slowly worked loose by eager, hurrying fingers. It was out at last. He unfolded the paper. There it was, the announcement of their "Farthest North", just as he had left it. But what was that, below it, in a lighter pencil?

"He can't see to read if you don't keep the lantern steady," said Susan. "Let me help."

"Is there something written?" said Peggy.

"Who's got a torch?"

Two torches flashed at once — Roger's and Titty's.

John read: "Passed Cache Island going north. February 10th, D.D."

"That settles it," said John. "Let's get on."

"Not a word about *why* they started," said Peggy.

"They must have been here before it began to snow," said Susan.

"When we were all sitting in the *Fram* waiting for them," said Titty, "and the sunshine was coming through the windows — before everything went so dark."

"The storm came pretty soon," said John. "They won't have got much farther before it caught them. We may find them any minute. They'll have got off the ice the moment the snow began."

"If only they had any sense," said Susan. "But they haven't got any, not that sort. People oughtn't to be allowed to be brought up in towns."

"Your turn for the lantern, Susan," said Peggy. "Which is your rope?"

"Half a minute," said John. "Oughtn't we to write something?"

"We'll do it properly tomorrow," said Susan. "Do let's go on and find them now."

"In case we miss them," said John; and scribbled hurriedly: "Relief Expedition passed Cache Island, 10th February." "What's the time? I haven't got my watch."

"Horribly late," said Susan.

John wrote, "After nightfall," folded the paper, pushed it back into the bottle, jammed the cork in, scrambled over the rocks, and hid the bottle under the cairn. By the time he was back on the ice the sledge had been turned round, and the other dogs and the lantern-bearer were ready and waiting.

"Work towards the shore, Susan," said John, and they were off once more.

"Hoo!" said Roger, when they were half-way between the island and the shore, "Hoooooooo!" He said no more, and there was no need. Everybody knew what he meant. Cold and loneliness and something more. Out there, on that enormous sheet of ice, with no other living thing in sight, they all understood that owlish cry. The lantern flickered and swung before them, as Susan steadily went on her way. They could see each

MESSAGE AT CACHE ISLAND

other only dimly in the dark, ghosts looking at ghosts. In that tremendous silence there was no noise but that of their own skates and of the sledge runners.

John started giving the time aloud: "One, two, one, two."

"It's much worse for the D.'s," said Titty, "altogether by themselves."

"They may have starved to death," said Roger. "They never remember to have plenty of chocolate."

"What rot!" said Peggy.

"You've had your ration for the day," said John.

"But what about the night?" said Roger.

Everybody laughed, although, inside, not one of them really felt much like laughing. Titty remembered being lost with Roger up on the fells in a summer fog. That had been bad enough. But to be lost in winter and in a snowstorm was much worse.

"They'll know it's us coming to the rescue the moment they see the lantern," she said.

"Unless they're hopeless galoots," said Peggy.

They skated on and on, hoping always to hear a hail out of the darkness.

"When did the blizzard calm down?" said John suddenly.

"Not till it was pretty well dark," said Peggy.

"We could only just see, going up the field," said Titty, "and we started home from the *Fram* almost the moment it stopped."

"Well, they wouldn't try to move once they got ashore," said John. "And by the time it stopped they couldn't get home along the road. They'd simply have to come back over the ice. And they'd keep close to the shore so as not to lose their way. But why on earth didn't they cut straight across to Beckfoot the moment they saw the snow coming?"

"They didn't know Nancy was clear of mumps," said Susan. "We didn't know till yesterday afternoon."

"I say," said Peggy. "Oughtn't we to go and tell Nancy and

get her to come? She'll be awfully sick at not coming when she hears about it."

For a moment John hesitated. Over there, on the other side of the lake, where the great white mass of Kanchenjunga sloped down into the long line of the fells, somewhere over there was the mouth of the Amazon; Beckfoot was there, and Nancy, who had planned everything for the expedition, and was now clear of mumps, and had been done out of the council by the coming of the snowstorm. She was sitting there not knowing that part of the expedition had already started, and was lost, and that a rescue party was racing northwards in the dark. It did seem rather a shame. But, for all he knew, every minute mattered. He thought of Dorothea, a little town girl, not tough like themselves, out all day in that blinding storm. He thought of Dick, who was full of good ideas but was nearly always thinking of the wrong one. They could both skate like anything, but, in weather like today's, could anybody trust them to know what to do? And then he thought again of Captain Nancy, but for whose mumps they would all have been long ago at school.

"Ahoy, Susan!" he called.

"Ahoy!" The lantern stopped, and was moving swiftly back towards them. "What's the matter? Those two getting tired?"

"It's Nancy," said John. "Oughtn't we to go and rope her in?"

"She's probably in bed," said Susan. "They probably send her to bed soon after tea. She's been ill. Nobody would ever let her go out at night."

"I forgot that," said John. Susan was right. It would be a waste of time to go right across the lake to Beckfoot only to find Nancy in bed. And someone would have to stay on this side of the lake in case of missing the D.'s, who might be trying to get home. That would mean splitting up the party, and whenever that happened there were always chances for things to go wrong. It was bad enough to have the D.'s lost without having to bother about what was happening to anybody else.

They wondered if the light they could see over there could be the light in Nancy's window. Peggy thought it probably was. They were very sorry for her, but there was nothing to be done. Presently the light they had seen was gone. They skated on. John took a turn with the lantern, then Peggy again. The elders noticed that Titty and Roger were talking less and less, and began to be afraid that they would be tired out before ever the D.'s had been found. So first Roger and then Titty was made to lie flat on the loaded sledge, and changed from being a dog to being a passenger. But it was far too cold for anybody to be a passenger for very long.

They kept very close to the shore until they were brought up short by running into a snowdrift that had built itself up against a low spit that ran far out into the lake. After that they gave the shore a rather wider berth, but they were never too far away to hear a hail if anybody had been there to shout to them. The blue darkness of each little bay brought them nearer in. And all the time they were watching the white fields that came down to the edge of the ice and the dark fringes of the woods where the trees came down to the beach, hoping every moment to see some sign of Dick and Dorothea.

"It's no good thinking they'd have the sense to light a fire," said Susan, "and they wouldn't know how to do it in a snow-storm. They probably hadn't got any matches, either."

Roger patted his pocket to hear the matches rattle in his box. It was pleasant to feel that he, at least, was properly equipped.

"I don't believe they can have got as far as this," said John. "Not before the snow started."

"They can skate awfully fast," said Titty.

"They can't have been such galoots as to try to go on in the blizzard," said Peggy.

"They couldn't see where they were going," said Roger. "We couldn't even see the shore when we looked out from the *Fram*."

"But what would they do?" said Titty. "They'd have to do something. They may have tried to get back and got lost on the way ... Going in circles, like we did in the fog."

"How far is it to the head of the lake?" asked John.

"Good long way yet," said Peggy.

"Well," said John, "it's no use cutting across now. We'll keep right up this side and then come back down the other if we haven't met them."

On and on they skated. Titty and Roger had long stopped talking. John was counting grimly aloud, "One, two, one, two." Hopes had fallen low. The snow mountains seemed to be closing in on either side. Scattered lights in a line far ahead showed where the village lay close under the fells beyond and above the head of the lake. There were fewer than there had been. Folk were going to bed. Worst of all, the farther north they came the worse was the skating. There was so much snow on the ice that again and again a tired dog was tripped up by it.

"Halt," called John, at last. "It's no good trying to skate here. Better take them off."

That was better. For some time now Titty had been wondering how much longer she could bear the ache down her shins that was almost as bad as it had been in those early days of skating practice on the tarn. Skates were taken off, strapped in pairs, and loaded on the sledge. They trudged on. It was not easy going. The ice was slippery under the snow, but anything was better than skating in the dark and knowing that any minute a little ridge of blown snow might bring one headlong down.

At last, on their right, the wooded shore fell away, and they turned into a deep bay. A light on shore went out.

"It couldn't be them, could it?" said Titty.

"Can't tell," said John.

They trudged steadily round the bay, trying not to lose touch with the shore, in case they might be hailed by desperate, waiting figures. Suddenly, right ahead of them, a high black steamer pier loomed up in the darkness.

"I know where we are now," cried Peggy. "We're close to the head of the lake. They can't have gone much farther. Cheer up, my hearties. If only it was daylight we'd be able to see the Pole itself in a few more minutes."

Titty and Roger blinked hard to keep their eyes from closing altogether. The Pole itself. This was no time to fall asleep. The Pole. In sight. As near as that.

"Nothing for it," said John. "We'll go right round the head of the lake, and then down the other side to Beckfoot."

"We can't possibly have missed them so far," said Susan.

"We must look out for the place where the river comes in at the head of the lake. Right away over the other side," said Peggy. "Captain Flint says it never properly freezes there."

"What?" said John.

"Bad ice," said Peggy. "It isn't safe to go into the mouth of the river."

A dreadful thought struck all of them at once. What if, in the snowstorm, the D.'s had skated blindly on, and, without knowing it, had left the firm ice of the lake ... ?

They left the steamer pier and the little bay that in summer was a harbour. They trudged on, past dim white shores, deep in drifted snow that seemed continually to bear away to the left They were working round the head of the lake.

"Is that a house?" said John suddenly.

They all saw it at once as they passed the promontory that had so far hidden it from them. There it was, a bright light, a lighted window, but a big one, almost like a lighthouse, not far from the edge of the ice, above them in the snow.

"But there are no houses here," said Peggy. "They're all by the pier. There's nothing here except ... Giminy! Come on, you galoots. Come on. It's the Pole itself. It can't be anything else. And there's someone there ... "

Everybody woke up again in a moment. Tiredness was gone. They raced for the shore. Desperately they floundered up off the ice and through the deep snow. The light shone before them.

"Look! Look!" cried Titty.

She was on the left of the sledge, and had seen in the light of the lantern that John was trying to hold above his head something in the snow almost before her. Footprints, deep, clumsy holes in the snow, a single line of them, going towards the light.

"There's only one lot of tracks," said John. "It can't be them."

"We'll know in a minute," said Susan.

"Hang on to the sledge," said John. "The snow's getting deeper and deeper. Stick to it. Only a few more yards. What sort of a place is it?" He lifted the lantern, but his eyes were blinded by its light and the other light that he saw through the window. "Where are those torches?"

"Here."

"Here."

Titty and Roger proudly flashed their torches on the little building now close above them in the snow. The front of it seemed all window. Were those halyards on that cleat? The beams from the torches lifted. A snow-laden roof. Halyards going up above it. A flagstaff and ... what was that pale thing at the masthead?

A sudden joyful shout went up from the whole rescue party. "Hurrah! Hurrah! They're here!"

For a puff of wind had spread for a moment that pale rag hanging up there above the little hut. And everybody, looking up into the darkness, had seen the tiny quarantine flag flap yellow in the white light of the upturned torches.

CHAPTER XXVIII

ARCTIC NIGHT

Hour after hour had gone by. The short winter day was ending. Dorothea and Dick were still alone at the Pole. And still, outside, great gusts of wind filled the air with flying snow. Inside, the little hut looked very different from the bleak place it had been when Dick first stumbled into it. A cheerful fire was blazing in the grate under a simmering kettle. Dick had spent the afternoon in melting snow (dipped from below the window), so that there should be plenty of water when the others should arive. The big saucepan, that had been the first thing taken out of the packing-case, was standing on the hearth, full to the brim. Dorothea had unpacked the case and arranged its contents along one of the benches, food enough to last a dozen people for a whole day: two cold chickens and a Christmas pudding and what not, with plates, knives, forks, spoons, and mugs. She had counted these at once, and found that there were nine of everything. That meant that Nancy was coming too, and Captain Flint, who certainly deserved to, Dorothea thought, after making such careful preparations. The packing-case itself had been turned over to make a table, and one corner of the hut looked almost like a larder. Dorothea thought that even Susan would think that her Polar housekeeping was not half bad.

At first, thinking that the storm would soon be over, when the main body of the expedition would be coming along, she had been very unwilling to break into the stores of food. But Dick had been hungry, and so had she, and in the end, encouraged by what had been written on the outside of the packing-case, they had made themselves some tea, opened a tin of condensed milk and one of meat paste, taken a few biscuits to eat it with, and given themselves an allowance of two Swiss buns apiece (afterwards increased to four).

"It's not snowing like it was," said Dick at last, late in the afternoon, "and not blowing so hard either."

"They'll be coming the moment they can see to move," said Dorothea, "and they may be quite close to us already."

But the last half-hour of daylight passed, and the dark closed down over the little hut. They had lit the lantern some time before.

The noise of the wind had stopped, and Dick opened a window to look out into the darkness.

"They'll be coming soon now," he said. "It's stopped snowing. Let's hang the lantern in a good place."

No one had ever thought of using the viewhouse at night, so there was no place to hang a lantern, but Dick worked one of the nails out of the lid of the packing-case and hammered it into a crack in the Pole as high as he could reach.

"It'll show through all the windows," he said. "They can't miss it, wherever they are."

"Going back in the dark'll be a good deal easier with all of us together," said Dorothea, "but we're going to be dreadfully late."

She came to the open window with him, and looked out at her own shadow and Dick's thrown by the lantern on the snow.

"Good," said Dick suddenly. "Stars. There's Orion."

Away to the south stars showed in a patch of clear sky, and among them were the three bright stars of Orion's Belt. Dick climbed over the window sill and dropped down into the snow.

"Right up to my waist," he said cheerfully.

"Where are you going?"

"Just to look at the Pole Star," he said. "Of course, it won't be really overhead, but still … "

He floundered through the snow round the corner of the hut.
"Come back, Dick," cried Dorothea. "Come back. Do come
back."

"What is it?" He struggled back under the opened window.

"Nothing really," said Dorothea, a little ashamed. "But we
ought to keep the window shut. It's no good getting the hut cold
again. And there isn't an awful lot of coal in that sack."

"You can shut the window," said Dick. "I'm going round to
clear the snow from the door, so that we can open it without
getting another lot inside."

He was gone. She heard him scraping at the door, and presently
he came in after shaking the snow off on the top step.

"It was like swimming just by the door," he said. "Jolly deep,
too. Piled right up. And I couldn't see the Pole Star. All clouds.
But it doesn't matter. Orion's sword showed clear for a moment,
north and south. Anybody could see that the hilt end was pointing straight to us."

Another half-hour went by. Dorothea made some more tea,
and they took two more buns (making six) and some biscuits.
Now, at last, they began to think that something must have gone
seriously wrong. Where could those others be?

"They'd never give it up," said Dick.

"Captain Flint may be with them," said Dorothea. "And
Nancy, too. He may have made them start home when the snow
stopped."

"They wouldn't go," said Dick. "Not without us."

"They started first," said Dorothea, "without waiting for us."

Dick was silent for a minute or two. He had gone to the
window again, and was looking out, where the warmth of the
room had melted the snow on the window-panes, at the faraway
lights on the shores of the lake.

"Perhaps they think we couldn't have got so far," he said.
"They didn't know we had a sail."

"That's just it," said Dorothea. "They wouldn't mind turning back if they thought we were somewhere behind them."

Dick turned suddenly from the windows, and glanced up at the lantern and then at the fire that was sending flickering shadows over the walls.

"We'll show them just where we are," he said. "Let's push the box in front of the fire so that the light from it doesn't show, and then we can signal with the lantern."

"How?"

"Like we did before. Only this time we can send a real signal." He pulled out the little book and turned up the page with the Morse code. "All we've got to do is to signal N-P – North Pole. They'll know at once. A long and a short for N. And P's a short, two longs, and then another short. They'll know at once, and nobody else will."

Hopes rose again. Dorothea remembered that successful signalling to Mars.

In a few minutes the light from the fire was screened by the packing-case, and Dick and Dorothea were busy at the windows, taking turns in showing the lantern and then shielding it with a sheepskin. Long, short ... Short, long, long, short ... Again and again the signal N-P was flashed into the night.

"With all those windows it's as good as a lighthouse," said Dick. "They're bound to see it if they're anywhere about."

Now and then they stopped to see if anywhere in the darkness another lantern was flashing in answer. But there was never a sign that anybody had noticed what they were doing.

At last they tired.

"They must have seen it by now," said Dick, and hung the lantern once more on its nail.

And then, suddenly, Dorothea made up her mind that they must leave the Pole at once. Time was going on and on. What-ever had happened to the others, they themselves must face that struggle through the snow and the long journey home in the darkness. They must not wait another minute.

"Dick," she said, looking at that neat larder, "let's put everything back. We've got to start home."

"But we can't go away now we've signalled," said Dick. "We've told them we're here. They'll be coming, and we'd be sure to miss them in the dark."

This was worse than ever. Dorothea hardly knew what ought to be done. It was not like one of her own stories, in which it was easy to twist things another way or go back a page or two and start again if anything had gone badly. It would not have mattered so much if only they had left a message at Dixon's Farm to say they might be late. She thought of Mrs Dixon, and Mr Dixon and old Silas, with nightfall long past, and empty places at the kitchen table. Dick never thought of things like that. But what could they do? There they were at the North Pole. The others must be somewhere out in the Arctic night. Signals had been made to them. It was too late now to take the signals back. Dick was right. There was nothing to be done but to wait.

She gave in. She was very tired, and so was Dick. They spread their sheepskins on the floor, used the packing-case to lean against, and sat there watching the fire.

★

"Ahoy!"

Dorothea stirred in her sleep. Time to get up? Had Mrs Dixon found a new way of calling them?

"Ahoy!"

There it was again. A long way off.

Dorothea opened her eyes. Where was she? The fire had burnt low, but she saw the red glow of its embers not far from her feet. With a jerk, she pulled her feet away, and then saw that there was no need. She knew where she was now. That hard thing against her back was Captain Flint's packing-case. They were at the North Pole. She looked at Dick, huddled down on the sheepskins, with his chin on his chest. Should she wake him? Or had she dreamed that noise? She must put some more coal on the fire. She stirred and then again, not so far away this time, she heard that call.

"Ahoy!"

The lantern was still burning, hanging from the flagstaff in the middle of the hut. The windows looked black except where the light from inside showed the edging of frozen snow outside the glass. It was black night out there, and the lantern made it seem even blacker than it was.

"Ahoy! Ahoy!"

With a soft plop something hit one of the windows and stuck there, a white splash on the blackness.

"Ahoy! Ahoy, there! North Pole, ahoy!"

"Here they are!" cried Dorothea. "Here they are!" She shook Dick by the shoulder. He woke with a start, rubbed his eyes, and then, as he heard Dorothea crying, "Here they are!" and another lump of snow flattened itself against a window, he jumped to his feet and opened the door. A cold breath of night air came into the hut, and the lantern threw a bar of light sideways across the snow.

"Make straight for the door," Dick shouted. "It was awfully deep, but it's not bad now."

"It's quite deep enough here," said a clear, cheerful voice out of the darkness. "I've been fighting through it for ages. Didn't you hear me yelling?"

Dick and Dorothea stared out into the night, and at last saw a figure struggling in the snow. A moment later Captain Nancy, with her skates hung round her neck, stumbled up the steps at the door.

"Good! Good!" said Dorothea, eagerly dusting the snow off her.

Just for a moment Nancy felt herself dreadfully tired. Even

with all her efforts to get into training she was not yet the sturdy Amazon pirate she had been before she had got the mumps, and had had to spend so long being coddled in a hot bedroom. She sat down on the seat at the foot of the flagstaff.

Dick was still looking out into the night.

"But where are the others?" he said. "They haven't turned back?"

"What others?" said Nancy. "I started the moment I saw your signals. The others are at Holly Howe. But why are you here at all? Everything's fixed now. We're all coming tomorrow."

Dick stared at her.

"But you put up the signal," he said.

"What signal?" said Nancy.

"Flag on the Beckfoot promontory."

"Oh, that! To say I could come to the council in the *Fram*. The blizzard scuppered that. But the others were there all right. Everything's settled. And now you're here already ... "

Dick was digging furiously into his pocket. Out came a lump of tangled string, a handkerchief, an indiarubber, and with them that important pocket-book. He turned hurriedly back, through sketches of the constellations, drawings of the Nansen sledges, the pages on which Nancy herself had drawn the semaphore alphabet for him, and the Morse code, until he came to the page for which he was looking. There, at the bottom of some mixed notes, he found what he wanted, and held it out for her to see.

"Flag on Beckfoot = start for Pole."

"I wrote it down when you told me," he said, "in the top of the observatory the day we were learning the signals."

Nancy's mouth opened. She bit her lower lip. Her indignation was gone.

"Golly," she said. "I remember your doing it. And something happened, and I never told the others. And then came mumps, and I forgot every little bit about it. And then when Captain Flint

NANCY REACHING THE POLE

asked about my getting away soon enough for the council in the
Fram, I said that if I could I'd run up a red flag and the biggest I
could find. And so I did. It was a bedspread."

"I saw it at once," said Dick, "but I was jolly late anyhow, so
I thought the others must have started."

"And you two came by yourselves and got here through all
that blizzard?" said Nancy. "However did you find the Pole?"

"The blizzard helped, really," said Dorothea.

"We were sailing," said Dick.

"Jib-booms and bobstays!" cried Nancy. "Sailing? In that?"

"The wind was just right," said Dick. "It took us straight
here."

"Well," said Nancy, "it's the best thing I ever heard. You
couldn't have made it more real. But what a pity you did it a
day too soon."

"And we've gone and opened the stores," said Dorothea.
"And eaten some of them. You see, we lost our food when the
sledge turned over and the mast broke ... "

"Capsized!" cried Nancy. "Mast gone by the board! Oh, you
lucky, lucky beasts! Of course, you were right to go for the
stores. That's what they were there for."

She looked round at the neat larder, read the writing on the
packing-case, and looked at the label fastened on the flagstaff.

"He's really not done it half badly," she said. "I forgot he'd
have fixed up stores for tomorrow. I swiped a cake, just in case
you might be starving." She pulled it out of her knapsack and
put it on the bench with the rest of the food. "Have you had
supper yet?"

"We haven't properly," said Dorothea.

"You'd much better," said Nancy. "I will, too. How did you
manage about water?"

"There was a kettle full to begin with," said Dick, "and we've
melted a lot of snow."

"Good work," said Nancy. "Let's have supper right away. Anybody'd say we ought to. It's no good thinking of starting back now. I can't, anyway. We'd better not use more coal than we can help."

She broke up the lid of the packing-case, splitting it in pieces with hammer and chisel. The fire blazed up again when fed with the dry wood. The kettle boiled. Tea was made. And all the time Nancy kept asking one question after another. Nearly a month's questions were boiling inside her and waiting to be asked. There was the voyage in the blizzard with the sailing sledge, every detail of which she wanted to know. But there was also that business of the cragfast sheep, of which she had only heard at second-hand, and the story of Captain Flint's finding his houseboat not at all as he had left it.

"Shiver my timbers!" said Captain Nancy, sitting on a sheep-skin in front of the fire with a mug of hot tea in one hand and the leg of a chicken in the other. "Shiver my timbers! The others will be jolly sick at missing this."

"What'll they do?" asked Dorothea.

"Come along tomorrow," said Nancy. "Daylight. Fine weather. Captain Flint to help them. I've left a message to let him know we're here. He'll collect them in the morning and they'll come along as tame as anything ... "

And at that moment there was a chorus of loud "Hurrahs" close outside the hut. At that moment the relief expedition, after struggling up from the shore towards those lighted windows, had noticed the halyards and turned their torches upwards and seen the little yellow quarantine flag that told them their search was ended.

Nancy was up in a flash and had the door open.

The loud "Hurrahs" of the rescuers turned to shouts of astonishment. "It's Nancy!" "Nancy's here, too!" "But Captain Flint said you were at Beckfoot!"

"So I was," said Nancy, "till I saw their flash signals. Proper ones this time. Morse. N-P for North Pole."

"Lantern signals?" said John. "We never saw them."

"But why were they here?" said Susan.

"Why didn't they come to the council?" said Peggy.

Everybody was talking at once. There was Nancy clapping people on the back, shivering timbers, barbecuing billygoats, delighted to be with the others once again. And there were John and Susan, very pleased indeed that the search was over, for they had known that Titty and Roger were too tired to go much farther. And there were Titty and Roger trying to tell the story of their journey. And there were Dick and Dorothea dreadfully anxious to explain that really it had not been their fault that they had started a day too soon. And there was Peggy, tremendously hoping that Captain Nancy would not think she had done so badly, and very pleased indeed that she was back and ready to take command. She herself was quite ready by now to be a mate once more.

Presently Nancy noticed that John, Susan, and Peggy, although they had come to rescue them, had very little to say to the D.'s.

"It's not their fault at all," she said. "It's mine, really." She explained about the signal. "I'd forgotten all about it, with the mumps coming in between."

"That's all right," said John. "I thought all the time they couldn't have done it on purpose."

"Anyway it's a good thing they're found," said Susan. "But I don't know how we're going to get back and rested enough to do it again tomorrow. Titty and Roger are about done."

"So'm I," said Nancy joyously. "So's everybody. That's the best of it. Now you're here there's no need to do it again. We've done it. We've all of us done it. This is miles better than anything we planned ... Sailing to the Pole in a gale of wind and a snow-storm."

"Sailing?" said John.

"Rather," said Nancy. "Sailing ... and then nobody knowing
where anybody was and your tremendous sledge journey in the
Arctic night. Why, tomorrow everything would be easy. A
picnic. Like going for a walk at school. But this was the real
thing. They'd never been farther north than the Amazon and
they found the Pole all by themselves." And then she said things
about the D.'s and their wild sail through the blizzard that made
Dick splutter out that it was only accident, and Dorothea sparkle
with pride in him. First that sheep and then the sailing. They knew
now that he was more than a mere astronomer.

"Everybody's done jolly well," said Nancy.

"Captain Flint, too," said Roger, admiring the larder. And
then, noticing the coal-sack. "That was why his sledge was all
black and sooty."

And then, of course, the relief expedition, although it had set
out after supper, found that after crossing the Arctic to the Pole
it could eat a little more. The big Beckfoot sledge was unpacked.
Sheepskins and knapsacks were brought in.

"It just can't be helped," said Susan. "We've got to spend the
night here now. I'm sure mother wouldn't mind. The main thing
is that we're all here."

CHAPTER XXIX

AND AFTERWARDS

It had been bedtime for Titty and Roger before ever they started on their journey to the North Pole. It had been bedtime for Peggy, John and Susan long before they got there. As for Nancy, she had been going to bed earlier than any of them while she had been recovering from mumps. Dick and Dorothea had had some sleep already, but they were very tired. This late supper at the Pole began most joyfully, but before it was finished eyelids seemed weighted with lead, sentences trailed off into silence, and people found themselves talking without being quite sure what it was they had meant to say. One after another the explorers dropped off to sleep, no matter whether they were sitting on a wooden seat at the foot of the Pole, or on a bench against the wall, or lying about in front of the fire on the sheepskins that had been spread over the floor.

"Eh? What? Sorry," said Nancy, in answer to a question that she thought someone had been asking her. "Look here, we mustn't all go to sleep. Somebody ought to keep watch. We'll take turns."

Susan pointed to Dick, Titty, and Roger, who were asleep already. John was blinking at the fire. Peggy yawned, smiled cheerfully at Nancy, yawned again, and pulled a knapsack into a comfortable position for her head. Susan made up the fire with coal from the nearly empty sack. Dimly, Dorothea saw her cover Titty and Roger with spare sheepskins. Nancy's eyes were closed. Nobody could keep awake. Soon the silence of the Arctic night was broken only by little restless noises from the fire and by the quiet breathing of the eight explorers.

When Dorothea woke it was already far into the night. The lantern (John's lantern[1]) was still burning, but the fire was very low. Dorothea looked at Dick, who was sleeping as easily as if in bed, with his head pillowed on his arm. He was all right. What had there been to disturb her? She looked at Titty, who had turned half over and buried her face in a sheepskin. She looked at Susan, sleeping as she sat in a corner. She looked at John, who had stretched himself along one of the narrow benches. She looked at Nancy, propped up against the packing-case beside her. She looked at Peggy and at Roger, curled up on the floor before the fire, with knapsacks as pillows. No, there was nothing wrong.

She slept again. It was in something very like a dream that she heard a crunching of snow and a faint laugh. She was never quite sure, when they all came to talk about it afterwards, whether she had been dreaming or not when she felt a breath of cold air on her face and knew that the door was open out of the hut into the Arctic night, and that people were moving in the room, Eskimos, friendly Eskimos, who must not be allowed to wake the others. There was a faint noise of the scraping of snow in the doorway, and then the quiet closing of the door.

"'Sh!" said Dorothea, without opening her eyes.

"'Sh!" There was a reassuring answer.

*

It was long hours afterwards, and a new day was beginning when Dorothea woke again, to find Susan looking at her and holding her finger to her lips.

Susan pointed behind her. There, fast asleep, sitting on the bench against the wall opposite the door, was Captain Flint.

[1] Dick's had gone out while they were having their supper. Probably some of its oil had escaped when their sledge had turned over in the snow.

Beside him was his sister, Mrs Blackett, the mother of the Amazons, fast asleep with her head on his shoulder.

"Did you make the fire up?" whispered Susan.

"No," whispered Dorothea.

"They must have done it. However did they get in without waking us? Don't let's wake the others yet if we can help it."

Susan put on a few more bits of coal, filled up the kettle from the saucepan and put it, as quietly as she could, on the fire. But a scrap of coal slipped through the bars and fell on the hearth. Nancy woke up with a start.

"'Sh!" said Dorothea, just as she had in her dream.

"Giminy!" said Nancy, following Susan's pointing finger. "Well done, mother!"

"What's the time?" yawned John.

"Quiet!" whispered Susan, and John sat up and stared at the sleeping Eskimos.

Titty was the next to wake, rolling over and lifting a head as tousled as her sheepskin.

"Susan," she murmured. "Where ... ?"

And there was Susan holding her hand and whispering into her ear.

Peggy and Roger and Dick slept on, while the others watched Susan, busy about fire and larder, as silent as she knew how.

Dorothea crept quietly to the middle window and stood there, trying not to see the lantern's reflection in the glass, while she looked out at the earliest beginnings of the February dawn. White snow everywhere, even on the Arctic ice, and dim dark patches in the distance marking the leafless woods. Immediately below the windows she could see deep footprints and tracks in the snow. No snow had fallen since the rescue parties had arrived, and it was easy to see what a struggle they had had. Faintly, on either side of the frozen lake, she could see the white shapes of the hills. The North Pole? Well, nothing could be more wintry or lonelier than this.

And then she turned round and looked again at the homely, comfortable scene. There was the lantern hanging from the Pole, and the bit of paper labelling the Pole for what it was. There were the sleeping explorers and Captain Flint and Mrs Blackett sleeping too. Titty was dozing again. Steam was drifting from the spout of the kettle. Nancy and Susan were debating in whispers, wanting to break up some more wood for the fire, but afraid of the noise it would make.

"We may as well now," said Susan. "The kettle's very nearly boiling as it is."

"Right," said Nancy. "Here goes." There was a crash and a loud splintering noise, as, with hammer and chisel, she split another plank from the big packing-case. "It's about time people did wake up anyhow."

*

The sleepers woke with a start and looked about them.

"But how did mother get here?" said Peggy, rubbing her eyes.

"Hullo!" said Roger. "Breakfast?"

"Ruth, you dreadful girl," said Mrs Blackett.

"Not Ruth," said Nancy indignantly, but giving her mother a hug.

"Nancy, then, you good-for-nothing, galloping off like that when you ought to have been going to bed. And Peggy, too. And all these years I've been telling people what a lot of sense Susan had ... And I dare say if I knew the truth it would turn out to be your Uncle Jim's fault as much as anybody's ... "

"Oh, look here, Molly," said Captain Flint. "I've been nothing but a beast of burden. And, anyhow, if everything had gone according to programme we should all have come up the lake today, had a feast here, and been carted back by road in the evening. What could have been more harmless than that?"

"Or duller?" said Nancy. "What's happened is a million times better. Why, just think, mother, if it had been like that, you would never have come to the North Pole at all. Anyhow, not charging through the middle of the night. And you wouldn't have missed that for anything!"

"Wouldn't I?" said Mrs Blackett.

"How on earth did you two come to get here yesterday?" said Captain Flint to Dorothea.

Nancy started explaining at once, and poor Dick pulled out his notebook yet again and showed how the signal had been written down there, and told how he had hurried to be off, thinking that the rest of the expedition were far ahead.

"And what about the blizzard?"

"Between you all, you've given a good many people a lively time," said Captain Flint when the explorers paused for breath in their efforts to describe exactly what had happened. "There were the Dixons up half the night, and I'd stirred up the police. And then, just when I had everybody on the go, looking for the D.'s, there was Mrs Jackson like an old hen who'd lost her chickens to say that all her lot had gone out and never come back ... "

"And a note from Nancy saying she was at the North Pole!" said Mrs Blackett. "North Pole, indeed! I didn't know where she was until I'd got over to Holly Howe with Sammy and met your uncle and found Peggy and the others lost too. We'd have been here before, but, of course, he had to race round to stop the search parties ... "

"Search parties?" said Nancy. "Not real ones?"

"Yes," said Captain Flint, "though you wouldn't think it. People who were ready to go looking for a pack of worthless children instead of getting their night's rest."

"And you stopped them all," said Nancy regretfully.

Dorothea's eyes sparkled. It was dreadful, of course, but splendid. She saw group after group of searchers going out into the night with their lanterns. She saw the lost ones struggling through the trackless snow. Days passed. And still the search went on. Digging ... A sheepskin ... An old knapsack ... And then, oh grief! the young explorers frozen where they had fallen and buried deep in snow ... What a story she would be able to write as soon as she had time. And then she looked at Dick pushing his notebook back into his pocket. She came back to reality. Everybody had got to the North Pole after all, and nobody was lost. What was that Mrs Blackett was saying about going back to school?

"Do you take sugar with tea?" said Susan to Mrs Blackett, in so ordinary a tone that Mrs Blackett said, "Please. Two lumps, if I may," more as if she were paying a call than as if she were having breakfast at the North Pole.

Captain Flint laughed aloud.

"Polar hospitality," he said. "Thank you, Susan. Three lumps for me, as usual."

"But it's you we ought to thank," said Dorothea, suddenly remembering. "Dick and I lost all our food in the snowstorm, and we'd have had nothing to eat if you hadn't put all these stores here."

"That's all right," said Captain Flint. "Nancy's idea, the whole thing."

"If only she hadn't been quite so secret about it," said her mother.

"But she had to be secret," said Peggy. "She simply had to be. Shiver my timbers! if we'd all known all about it, it would have been no fun at all."

"What?" said Nancy, very much surprised. "Who taught *you* to shiver timbers?"

"Just while you were away," said Peggy; and Nancy, startled for a moment at hearing Peggy talk in the Nancy manner, remembered that for all these weeks her mate had been the only Amazon in active life.

"That's all right," she said. "Did you use my other words?"

"Some of them," said Peggy.

"Jib-booms and bobstays?"

"Yes."

"Barbecued billygoats?"

"Yes."

"She even called people galoots," said Roger.

"Well," said Nancy, "I bet it all helped."

"Judging from results," said Captain Flint, "I think it did. Look here, Susan, you'd better let me deal with that chicken."